BUTTERFLY LOVE

BOOK Fourteen
of the

SECRET BUTTERFLY SERIES™

A NOVEL BY

Rosemary Lightfoot Ness-Bitner

To order, wherever books are sold:

ISBN 978-1-961850-29-3 for Paperback
ISBN 978-1-961850-30-9 for eBook

A caution and disclaimer

All characters, events, and conversations in this book are fictional, the product of the author's imagination, or used fictitiously. Any resemblance to actual characters, living or dead, events past or present, localities, or conversations, is entirely coincidental.

If you are offended or stressed by characters' offensive behaviors and expressions of strong opinions about controversial subjects, you are advised and cautioned to not purchase this book or listen to this audio book. If you are a child under the age of eighteen, do not purchase this book or listen to this audio book as it contains erotic adult content. Sexual activity may cause diseases. If you engage in sex, please do so responsibly. If you smoke, drink, do drugs, drive a car, raise a child, hunt, fish, brush your teeth, cross the street, cough, sneeze, gamble, or vote, please also do those things responsibly.

THIS BOOK CONTAINS SADISM, MURDER, AND EXPLICIT EROTIC ROMANCE CONTENT. IT IS INTENDED FOR MATURE READERS AND AUDIENCES OVER THE AGE OF EIGHTEEN ONLY. IT MAY BE OFFENSIVE OR STRESSFUL TO SOME READERS. OPINIONS, VIEWS, AND ADVICE GIVEN IN THIS BOOK BY ITS CHARACTERS TO OTHER CHARACTERS, AND BEHAVIORS EXHIBITED AND ADVOCATED BY ITS CHARACTERS DO NOT REFLECT THE OPINIONS, VIEWS, OR ADVICE, OR ADVOCATION OF BEHAVIORS OF, OR BY, THE AUTHOR OR PUBLISHER, OR OF, OR BY, ANY ORGANIZATION OR ENTITY TO WHICH THE AUTHOR OR PUBLISHER ARE AFFILIATED. NEITHER THE AUTHOR, THE PUBLISHER, NOR ANY OTHER PERSONS ASSOCIATED WITH THIS BOOK SHALL BE HELD RESPONSIBLE FOR ANY CONSEQUENCES ARISING FROM THE OPINIONS, VIEWS, ADVICES, BEHAVIORS, OR INTERPRETATIONS EXPRESSED BY THE CHARACTERS IN THIS BOOK; OR, IN ANY OTHER WAY, EXPRESSED IN THIS BOOK, OR BY ITS

This book is dedicated to the quest for love.

The print version layout of BUTTERFLY LOVE was done by Reider Books; print and audio cover design was done by Cheeky Covers; and I'm Minna Morinette, your audio book narrator.

SECRET BUTTERFLY SERIES ™ CHARACTERS INTRODUCED IN "BUTTERFLY LOVE" (MAJOR CHARACTERS ARE BOLDFACED)

Readers reference guide to where a character is introduced. (CHARACTER, DESCRIPTION OF CHARACTER, AND CHAPTER WHERE CHARACTER IS MENTIONED)

LESTER, OBSERVER SPY AT U G G A, BUTTERFLY LOVE (BL) CH,1

CHARLES, LUNCH ROOM SPY AT U G G A, BL, CH1

JUDGE SANDBONE, JUDGE, BL, CH1

SOLOMON, ATTORNEY, BL, CH1

MAC, ATTORNEY, BL, CH1

BEATRICE, CATHOLIC NUN, BL, CH2

MAL GREEN, DEAL MAKER, BL, CH2

JO-JO, BOBBY, PHIL, GUIDO, MUSCLE MEN EMPLOYED BY CHIEF, BL, CH3

LOBO, HALF WOLF, HALF COYOTE, BL, CH10

BEN SLIPPERMAN, ATTORNEY, BL, CH4

CHIEF JUSTICE RENLOW, CHIEF JUSTICE OF THE UNITED STATES SUPREME COURT, BL, CH4

VOICE, MYSTERY CALLER FROM ZURICH, HIRED BY SUSAN, BL, CH5

MARVIN'S GHOST, BL, CH7

HUD, EHUD BURKE, SON OF BOB AND BARBARA, BL, CH12

DEBBIE, OR DEB, DAUGHTER OF BOB AND BARBARA, BL, CH12

RICK, DEB'S HUSBAND, BL, CH12

LITTLE DEER, GRANDDAUGHTER OF BOB AND BAR-BARA, BL, CH12

GRAVE DIGGERS, BUZZY AND WAYNE, BL, CH12

GRAVESTONE BUTTERFLY, SPIRIT OF MARTY, BL, CH14

GRAVEYARD BIRD, SPIRIT OF SUSAN'S SOUL, BL, CH14

GHOST IN CHAINS, THE SPIRIT OF MARVIN'S SOUL, BL, CH14

BIG JIM, RANCHER BIRCH, JACK, JAKE, BUNKHOUSE RANCH HANDS, BL, CH15

SPIRITS OF TESLA, BIG HORSE, LITTLE SPARROW, CHIEF, VISITORS TO HUD'S GOLD CAMP, BL, CH16

Hello, readers and listeners. After BUTTERFLY LOVE, David finds himself matching wits with Barbara. Will Bob escape his clutches? Will David's legal defenses serve him well? Chief reminds Barbara to remember how cornered rats behave. What will David do next? Will Susan make her fateful move? Can lowly ants seek revenge? Can David restart his crumbling empire? Lobo, much larger and stronger than a wolf; wilier and swifter than a coyote, keeps coming.

The beautiful Monarch butterflies are returning from the jungles of Mexico. Their next cycle of life carries their spirits of hope and reincarnation. Like a butterfly's new life, our saga flutters onto a delightful meadow upon brilliantly colored, spring-storied wings. Flutter along with me, Minna Morinette, as I narrate BUTTER-FLY LOVE, the fourteenth book of THE SECRET BUTTERFLY™ SERIES. Enjoy its remarkable fateful twists that bring David to his final understanding of everything.

BUTTERFLY LOVE ©

CHAPTER ONE

The everlasting No. (Thomas Carlyle: Past and Present)
   IL gran rifiuto; the great refusal (Danti Alighieri: Divine Comedy, Inferno)

NO

After a few months, Bob thought less and less about the antelope hunt and The Others' Place episode. Traveling, selling, keeping track of individual salespeople's requests and idiosyncrasies, and making hundreds of flights on time focused his mind on the present. David looked more toward the future. Since the antelope hunt, he'd hired two additional male employees. Their employment duties were more of the same farcical nonsense sorts of jobs that his previous two hires performed.

The first hire, Lester, was a man David found greatly to his liking. The man was malleable, always agreeable to any suggestion David made, had no moral center, and was totally devoid of ethics. He had feminine mannerisms, but not their cleanliness or neatness. His shirt was often unbuttoned by three belly front buttons, his trousers were dirty, his fingernails were grimy, his hair was greasy, his teeth were yellow from smoking, and his halitosis was so vile that the office women often gagged when they conversed with him. He sought the camaraderie of the women in the office, but was shunned. Nevertheless, he often appeared uninvited at their gatherings. Lester's savior for companionship was David, who spent ever increasing after-hours time with Lester and soon gave him a prominent role in the firm. Lester was assigned the role of Office Observer, which was a nice way of describing someone hired to snoop on everyone else. The office women had a code name for Lester. They called him *'Slurp'*

The second hire, Charles, was given the official role of Office Substitute. He was instructed to sit in the lunchroom each day, every day. His job was to eat lunch slowly, extending a normal lunch hour into an eight-hour food fest. He was assigned to always remain in the lunchroom, except for his bathroom breaks, and to report directly to David any conspiratorial conversations that might take place in the lunch room. Officially, Charles was designated on regulatory reports as an assistant employee and carried on the fund's expenses. Although Charles knew absolutely nothing about the company or its various employee duties, or its reporting, and record-keeping requirements, David deemed him intelligent enough to learn the other employees' job functions by simply listening to them talking in the lunchroom.

Charles, or Chas, was the most obese employee U G G A ever hired, perhaps the most obese employee in all of Plaintown. Fat rolled off his face and chin, arms, and legs. His stomach and back-side were so huge he could not fit into a chair—which was a good thing, for if he were to ever sit upon a normal-sized chair with normal-sized legs it was a near certainty his weight would crush the chair and he would likely injure himself. Chas wore specially constructed trousers, made by stitching together two normally double extra large trouser pairs and repositioning the zipper. He had huge lips and an ever-present smile. He was partially bald, although he was only in his late twenties, and combed what little hair he had forward over his dome so it looked as if there was some sort of splattered mural effort glued above his eyes. A special over-sized sofa was constructed for him and placed in the lunchroom.

The office women soon created a nick name for Chas also. They called him 'Sub,' as in subpar. They pitied him for his obesity and openly speculated that his only job skill was giving the other men superlative blow jobs.

Susan's girls, led by Mrs. Rodriguez and Barbara, continued to do the work of the office. The women had plenty of male combinations to quip and laugh about. They devised a man pool, similar to males' football pools. Each woman picked a numbered ticket from a bowl which matched male combination pairings, as well as a jackpot number which represented the total number of verified male pairings that occurred the previous week. Each ticket cost one dollar. There was a winning prize for which number picked the most winning male combinations. There were rules to determine what the males were deemed to be doing based upon who arrived at work with whom, who stayed late with whom, who went to lunch with whom, who was seen behind closed doors with whom, and who brought gifts for whom.

When a male was spotted rubbing his hand over the ass of another male, there was a bonus wild card noted in the female logbook. Those two males, if they appeared on the winning ticket, earned the ticket holder a double bonus, and all other women not holding the ass rub combo ticket had to pony up an additional twenty-five cents each to the winner. Each combination of male incidents had to be verified by two women, and each male combination pairing was given a point ranking for total jackpot points.

Pool ticket pairs included Sub Slurp; Man Muscle; Slurp Man; Muscle Slurp; Sub Man; Muscle Sub; Chas Man; Sub Chas; Slurp Chas; and Muscle Chas. Each ticket had three different pairings. As the weeks rolled by, the log entries lengthened and the pots were paid out. It became obvious that some pairings repeated more often than others. There developed a trading marketplace for certain pairings which sold at a premium. The women developed their own private trading exchange with limits, hours, and floor rules. Suspicions grew amongst the males when one of the ladies would encourage a male to rub the ass of another male in front of two female witnesses, especially when the rubbers were a likely winning pair.

Barbara soon had premium pay offers for certain likely winning pairs. After she had amassed her likely winning tickets, she challenged her pony pairs, as she called them, to rub asses. After a time, the other women lost interest. Barbara won too much of their money. It was good fun while it lasted, except when a shareholder noticed. Watching grown men rubbing asses didn't sit well with the older investors. They pulled their money. David eventually caught on to Barbara's game. He issued an edict forbidding office betting. But no edict forbade ass rubbing.

David's income waxed fat from the Firm's sales growth, despite the added expenses of his two office drones. Money affected his behavior. Although he already had amassed a fortune, his outlook on life was affected by whether his monies were increasing or decreasing. The addition of Bob to the firm had resulted in the quadrupling of firm cash flows, and a ten-fold leap in income. David's ego and sense of self-importance swelled as more riches poured into his fold. He convinced himself he was a business genius and that all his decisions turned into gold. He resented any challenge to his authority. He believed himself invincible.

Bob noticed that the office had become a playpen for homosexual males, and a source of friction for the women relegated to do the work. He told David as much. He made clear his opinion that David's drones were a hindrance to getting work done; that they were an unnecessary, even if affordable, cost which should be eliminated; and that while David always exhorted Bob to do better, it was time for David to look in the mirror. Bob asserted that David needed do better.

David rebuffed Bob. The firm's structure made perfect sense to him. He never sought to be a large investment firm; only a comfortable one. He had a hankering to meddle in the personal lives of others. His bliss was observing their reactions to his meddling. He enjoyed abusing people, much like he abused insects as a child.

After Bob had rejected his amorous advances, David's adoration for his younger partner turned to contempt. David held all straight men, including his late father, in disdain. He longed for a world of homosexual dominance like the one Socrates and the ancient Greeks enjoyed. Until recently, David had disguised his desires well. Since rejection, David harbored new feelings toward Bob. Now he regarded Bob's business acumen with contempt. He reasoned that anyone gullible enough to trust him was merely a fool, ripe for the picking. And any man too rigid to appreciate the beauty of homosexuality was an even bigger fool. As much as he had tried to enlighten Bob about the joys of homosexuality, Bob continued his impossible obstinance. Nothing David did had shaken Bob's adoration of women. Bob's love of femininity and the female vagina continued to exasperate David.

David ascribed Bob's prudish morals to his Christian mother's influence. Estella and David had met when the woman visited Plaintown. David instinctively hated Estella, although he masked his feelings well. He surmised, correctly, that she was a latent Germanic, pro-Nazi antisemite who instinctively hated him as well. Both correctly assessed each other. David reflected:

'I should have listened to Dad. He once said you could take a German out of Germany, but you could not take antisemitism out of a German. But Dad got mixed up with Susan. She's a gentile. But she's Irish blood, not German. And she's female, not male. How did Dad get it so right and I get it so wrong? I caught the signal years ago when Bob said he Jewed someone down over something. I can't remember the particulars; but there it was! Antisemitism! But Bob is

a Jew himself now. He studied for seven years and converted. Did he do all that to deceive me? Ah! Of course! He's not a real Jew! He's one of those reformed Jews where anything goes. He's the deceiver here. My love of men can't be the reason he rejects me. I hid that from him until recently, but that was my business, not his. He needs to respect my choices.'

David chafed at his self-inflicted predicament with Bob. Deeply hurt by Bob's rejections and resentful of his junior's opinions about his office playmates, David's feelings toward Bob turned contemptuous. He tried to disguise the noticeable change in his demeanor toward Bob; but a chill hung in the air between them. It had permanence about it, like a late fall day's penetrating coldness that refused to warm away, even after the sun rose high.

Bob was dismayed over David's decline into squalid behavior. He reasoned perhaps his father figure, this sniveling, sobbing mentor who begged him to become a homosexual lover, had finally found some men who acquiesced to sucking him off, his body odor notwithstanding. Bob had no understanding of male homosexuality and never sought to delve into those behaviors. The notion of a gay father figure was hard for him to stomach at first. His initial feelings were that of revulsion of David and his drones, but then, after it became clear that this was the life David was choosing for himself or the life he was hard wired to live, Bob was able to compartmentalize the older man's personal sex life as a personal dimension to be ignored. And he did his best to ignore it.

But Bob's appeasement with David, who no longer acted like a partner, who had sought to change the fundamental nature of their relationship from business partnership and personal friendship to homosexual lover, was not enough to satisfy David. It's impossible to change the spots on a leopard. Why would the leopard ever want to be without spots, anyway? Spots camouflage and disguise it. It stealthily sneaks about in dark shadows, intent upon ambushing its prey. It always has the upper hand when it strikes. Rarely do prey animals escape a leopard's grip and survive.

But there comes a time when even greatest fraud artists must reveal themselves. Like the leopard must leave the shadows to strike, the fraud must dispense with his part of the bargain which he made with his victim. The essential art of fraud is to cajole, coerce, or falsely promise an action or a deed to be performed later in return for the mark's earlier performance. Frauds range from the simplest, such as promising a child a piece of candy in return for a quarter but then not delivering the candy, to the most heinous, such as telling Jews they are going to a resettlement camp, only to pack them into a gas chamber.

David's fraud was a sordid, disgusting matter which took place over an eleven-year period. It resulted in great diminution of Bob's career potentials and vast unjust enrichment for David. Based upon misplaced trust and false friendship, it was designed from the outset to be a knockoff of the will game that some men play with their mistresses. The woman may perform her favors for years or decades based upon the promise that the man will leave her well provisioned when he dies, only to discover afterward that he leaves her nothing.

While Bob was on the road working his hardest to build long-term relationships for a business he was, by agreement, to inherit, David was secretly on the telephone having conference calls with potential buyers for the Firm business complex. Despite David's dismal, cellar-scraping investment results following the halcyon years enjoyed because of Bob's gold stock picks, Bob's dogged sales efforts resulted in substantial growth of assets under management, and the worth of the operating companies had grown from a quarter-million to over thirty million. David was no longer content with his million-dollar annual compensation. Now a paunchy aging man in his mid-sixties, his libido and interest in playing office games with his staff were both waning. He intended to take the entire worth of the business for himself and leave Bob nothing.

The grip greed held on David's soul was selective and discerning. It was not a universal grip that held any group, tribe, or nation state's membership entirely within its grasp. This greed grip selected its wearer well. Slighted by his circumstances, hated, and reviled by his mother from infancy; shunned and shunted away by his ambitious father; David learned to resent everyone he encountered who was handsome or beautiful; readily accepted, or loved by another soul. The nurturing and bonding which others drew strength from; that love which centered their character, simply wasn't there for David. He learned as a child that he was an object of derision. He felt so rejected that he even learned to loath himself. And he learned to mask his self-loathing extremely well.

He learned to behave as the predictably jovial friend, the shoulder to lean upon for those he recently met or barely knew. Using his bubbly obsequious wife, Eilese, as his welcoming agent, he wormed his way into the homes of the socially prominent. Then, when confidence was gained and the hapless new friend needed a loan to weather a rough spot, David was there with the ready cash; but with the price of a first deed of trust upon the friend's home. *It's just for tax reasons, nothing else,* he always assured his quarry.

Once documents were signed, David surreptitiously moved heaven and earth to create obstacles which made it impossible for his debtor to repay him. If the man was an accountant, he would learn the man's clients and subsidize another accountant to underbid his debtor. Once the debtor's revenue stream was diminished and payment could not be timely met, David pounced. Collateral worth a million on a loan of one hundred thousand was seized. Litigation followed, and either an exorbitant settlement was extracted or the collateral fell into David's hands.

Many employees mortgaged their homes to David, who was very liberal with advances and credit to them against their future salaries. But after he held the first deed on their homes, their employment mysteriously came into jeopardy. They were suddenly no longer performing up to par. Their pay was docked until they fell behind on their payments; then their emotional distress was deemed disruptive to the firm. They were let go with unsatisfactory references. Legal actions followed. These hapless employees lost their homes, unless they agreed to increase their incomes with a side business opportunity financed by David.

One fast friend owned a chain of liquor stores worth three million Dollars. David loaned the man three hundred thousand to help him past a tough divorce. But the man's liquor stores were put up as collateral. Predictably, David took actions to impair his debtor's ability to repay him. Young teens were hired to defile the man's stores with spray paint and throw bricks through his windows. The disruptions mattered. They had their desired effect. David settled for one of the stores. A loan of three hundred thousand returned a million when the store was sold a few months later.

David understood that providing ready liquidity for people in dire straits was a way to make outrageous returns quickly. With the cash flow from the firm servicing his expanded bank credit lines, David became Plaintown's go-to guy for cash. He was the proverbial cash rich, ever liquid, friendly but ugly frog that would throw out his tongue, snap up hapless flies, and swallow them whole. He waxed fat on debtors' miseries, as well as his swelling income from the firm and his illegitimate businesses.

If his father and mother were still alive, David's progression toward greed would not have surprised them. They knew their son. Others who met him after he'd reached adulthood would only see a bizarre jovial sort of fellow, a skilled artisan of financial combat who lurked in waiting for his prey. Compensation for his self-loathing became David's obsession. Projecting his loathing onto others; taking their spirit down to a level as low as his own; destroying his victims financially, became a source of immense joy for him. He saw life and its souls as players in a great game, all arrayed as opponents and victims-to-be. He believed in the adage that all was fair in love and war, especially financial war.

David engaged in financial combat outside the boundaries that other participants in financial squabbles respected. His objectives were to never seek fair resolutions of disputes. Satisfaction for him was only realized by the destruction of the opponent. The feeling he craved was the same feeling of power he'd felt as a child when tearing the wings off flies. David worked as hard out of court as in court in his efforts to ravage his opponents. Wives, children, business associates of the opponent, organizations, charities, and worthy causes supported by his opponent were all fair game in David's quest to demean and destroy. Libel, slander, destruction of property, threats against friends and supporters were all in play.

David defined the rules in the games he played, not society and its norms; and most laughably, not the courts. Those who engaged David in financial combat got to know him well. He was neither the jovial helpful friend he pretended to be, nor the understanding and respected businessman his public relations efforts portrayed him to be; but *rather* a vicious, greed-obsessed, maliciously vindictive malcontent who made his destructive presence felt.

It was to be an eventful Friday afternoon and weekend for Bob. He had plans to go to the mountains, but that was not fated to happen. David called and asked him to come into his office. When he entered, David stood facing him, not at all like the first time they met when David sat in his swivel throne chair with his back turned to his guest. The men were partners now. There was conviviality to this fateful meeting.

David brimmed with charm and cheerfulness as he expressively motioned for Bob to sit in the middle guest chair in the semicircular array of audience chairs. He took a seat next to Bob in an audience chair, something Bob had never seen David do before.

"Here's an agreement I'd like you to sign," David began. *"It's necessary to give us more flexibility in growing the firm. For a time, I'm going to remove you as an officer and director of the operating companies and have you focus on retail sales. I'm giving you a very lucrative contract. It even gives you the entire underwriting concession for your retail sales. If you work hard like you always do, I believe you'll make an even greater income than you're making now, especially since wholesaling is going slowly. You have a chance to make even more money this way, plus you can be home in Plaintown more."*

Bob was shocked. Perhaps Marty had the same sense of shock when David ambushed her with his lethal grip and ether-soaked rag. But Bob had no knowledge of Marty's fateful day in David's barn. He had no inkling that his distressed reaction to David's request shared Marty's commonality of shock and surprise. But in Bob's case, David made a tactical mistake. The leopard within him failed to plan a fatal chloroform ambush for Bob as he had for Marty. Instead, David's arrogance convinced him he could perpetrated his fraud by paper contract.

"Well, let me read through it," Bob said. David pretended to ignore what Bob said and shoved a pen in Bob's face.

"It's just a bunch of legal mumbo jumbo," said David. *"I assure you that nothing in this, changes anything between you and me. It's just lawyer stuff. Go ahead and sign it."*

"Just let me read for a minute." said Bob, ignoring David's urging.

As Bob read the proposed representative's contract, he noted the release language. It stated that there had never been any prior deals or agreements between them, that this agreement was their full and complete understanding.

"Wait a minute," he said. *"There's a release in here. This would release you from our deal, the one I've relied upon to work these past eleven years building the Firm, the deal I took at your urging and the one we made which took me on a whole different career path. By signing this, I'd be saying the sun never rose and the buffalo were never present on the plains. This clause simply is not true. Remember the codicil you showed me in the bank vault? Have you lost your mind?"*

"I haven't lost my mind," David sought to reassure Bob. *"The lawyers just want uniformity for the regulators. We still have our deal. Nothing changes that. Just sign this damn thing and let's get this over with."*

Bob leveled a skeptical gaze at David. *"NO."* he said firmly.

"What do you mean, 'NO'?" David's jaw dropped. For an instant he thought he'd been caught flat-footed once again like when he was caught stealing cookie money from neighborhood housewives.

Bob detected a hint of apoplexy from his mentor and friend. There was before him a petulant child in a man's body, straining at his furthest boundaries of mental projection, insisting his will upon a subordinate junior, and being rebuffed; being told *'no.'* It was simply unfathomable to David that his command to his junior protégé would be refused.

"I want to take it home with me and read it before I sign it, and then I'll get back to you." With that, Bob took the agreement with him and walked toward the door.

"When?" David demanded.

"When I decide to get back to you," Bob shot back. *"That's when."*

During the following week, Bob met with Solomon Slyman, or Sol, an attorney who practiced civil litigation. Thus began a lawsuit that was to become one of America's defining legal cases on the elements of fraud, and in cases involving the use of the Statute of Wills as a defense against claims of fraud in the inducement. It was the beginning of battle royal.

CHAPTER TWO

The first blow is half the battle (Oliver Goldsmith: She stoops to conquer)

For every move, there is a counter move. Never think you've been outplayed. Never stop thinking. There is always a way. Think of it. (Rosemary Ness-Bitner: author)

ASSUMPTIONS AND BARGAINS

Rabbis worth their salt will advise their congregants to: *'Never Assume,'* admonished with an accompanying finger wag in front of the listener's nose. *'Never Assume'* means what it says. Never assume you have all your bases covered in a deal. Never believe you know everything there is to know about something or someone, for to assume based upon what your experience tells you or upon what someone has passed along to you can be your undoing.

Assuming falsely is born of hubris and overconfidence when those two tricksters are paired with underestimation. Never assume you know the outcome of a venture before you embark upon it. Another way of putting it is to say: *'Never underestimate your adversary.'* The military has a succinct way of putting it: *'Every battle plan becomes obsolete as soon as the first shot is fired.'*

From the outset of Bob's Faustian bargain with David, David *always* assumed he would never be held to perform his own part of the deal. The assumptions he relied upon were multifaceted. Most important among all his assumptions was the fact that the maker of a will or a codicil to a will has the freedom to change it. David's confidence in this assumption was ironclad, for he had, independently of Mac, consulted with one of Plaintown's most prestigious law firms. A senior partner, whose practice was Trusts and Estates, assured David that a man had every right to change his will or a codicil to his will at any time and for any reason. Otherwise, he comforted David, testators could be cheated by those whom were promised an inheritance conditioned upon a performance not earned. David, as was his nature, never revealed to this lawyer that he had shown the codicil to Bob to cement their deal, or that he had made an even earlier pledge to his father, Marvin, to leave the businesses, upon his own death, to Israel as the condition for his own inheritance.

David's second assumption was that Bob would never be able to produce a copy of the codicil at trial, should matters ever get that far. In the event the codicil ever ended up as evidence in a courtroom, based upon the Statute of Frauds, the only written evidence of a bargain between the pair would be a standard Registered Representatives contract because Bob did not possess an actual copy of the original codicil. In that eventuality, the dispute forthcoming would devolve into a contest of who said what, and the rep contract would be determinate. No judge could instruct a jury otherwise as a matter of law.

David's third assumption was that Bob would never be able to afford a protracted legal battle and, even if he could, the battle would leave him so depleted he'd have to settle for pennies on the dollar for his claims. David correctly believed the basic axioms of America's legal system. It is set up to ensure the rights of the defendant; the plaintiff has the burden to carry the case forward; and that burden can be made impossibly expensive. David had great faith in the ironclad principle that, in America, rich people crush the financial life out of poor people.

David's fourth assumption was perhaps his most sinister. He counted upon the avarice and low morality of Bob's former secretary, Judith. Should a battle result from his unilaterally breaking his deal with Bob, he believed he could buy Judith's loyalty. By offering her money and introducing her to some unattached wealthy male friends of his, he believed he could bribe Judith, a woman he always regarded as a bitch who would do anything for money, including turning on her former boss. Thus, David could rely on her to fabricate testimony. The possibilities for counterclaims dragging out litigation for years, plus a poisonous witness to rebut Bob's case, assured David it would be a lengthy wrestle in a mud pit. He figured he could break Bob and make him settle cheap.

David held close within his heart his unshakeable fifth assumption that *all* men who strive for betterment of their personal circumstances are likely to suspend their morality until *after* they have seized the fruits of their desire. Judges' decisions, lawyers' commitment to their clients, witnesses who would swear upon a Bible to tell the truth, all who waltzed into and out of courtrooms, and all who met in conferences before and after motions, pleadings, and decisions were mortal men with all their attendant weaknesses and foibles. They could all be bribed and everyone had a price. David looked forward to litigation with confidence.

Bob had three assumptions of his own at the outset of the conflict. His first was that a copy of the codicil he saw in the bank vault would somehow be discovered in the files of the lawyer who drafted it.

The nature of a fraud often goes beyond the simple act of one party lying to another. Fraud can easily don the cloak of conspiracy by drawing in multiple actors at different times along the timeline of the fraud. People necessary to corroborate the fraud can often be bought by the fraud actor to bend the truth, testify falsely, create false records, conceal, or lose important evidence, and so on. And, often enough, parties seemingly unrelated to a fraud conspiracy willfully join it and partake in elements of the fraud in the expectation of personal gain. Bob could only hope that the attorney who drafted the codicil was an honorable man.

Bob recalled a conversation he once had about the topic of legal ethics. The man had explained a lawyer's ethical dilemma by way of personal example. The lawyer's client had taken the lawyer to lunch. The bill was five hundred Dollars because wines were involved. The client pulled out from his wallet five one-hundred-dollar bills for the tab and placed them on the table; then the client pulled out another hundred for a tip and rested that c note, separately on the table. The client left first and the lawyer remained at the table. The lawyer picked up the hundred-dollar bill his client left for the tip, and replaced it with a ten-dollar bill. But only then, the lawyer noticed that the hundred was freshly printed. It was actually two one-hundred-dollar bills stuck together! The lawyer pondered his ethical dilemma, which was not about cheating the waiter out of a ninety-dollar tip, or about calling his client to inform him that he had accidently placed two hundreds on the table; but whether or not he had an ethical duty to tell his partners about the second hundred! Bob shuddered at the thought that David's lawyer might have been a party to the fraud from its outset.

Bob's second assumption was horribly flawed. He believed that David had possibly succumbed to syphilis or some such malady. He could not fathom, despite David's changes in behavior toward him ever since he'd rejected the older man's homosexual advances, that David had befriended him at the outset of their relationship with the full intention of destroying his career and taking from him the fullest measures of his life's work and talents. At the outset of battle, it was inconceivable to Bob that his good best friend, his senior mentor, and self-proclaimed father figure had plotted against him the entire while, over all those years, and was now figuratively thrusting a knife into his back. He actually felt a modicum of pity that his once best friend, David, could have fallen prey to some disease, perhaps of dementia, which was causing his vile conduct.

That empathetic feeling that the one defrauded has for the perpetrator of the fraud is the hallmark of a truly accomplished con artist. It requires a fraudster that shows no empathy for his victim and no remorse for his deed. In fact, the true fraudster feels he's entitled to screw others, as a God-given right!

Perhaps such a character is necessary in the human experience, for God did create Satan as one of his angels. Satan was the one God bantered with; the one he tested Job with; and the one God somehow must believe is necessary to advance the human condition, albeit through endless trials and tribulations with personified evil.

Bob's third assumption was a presumption. Most secretaries stay loyal to their bosses if the relationship is amicable, as Bob's was with Judith. Other themes, however, tend to encroach upon the weak of moral fiber. *Show me the money'* seems to have greater cache than loyalty and honesty in the bosoms of the greedy.

Attorney Solomon's initial complaint included a motion for a restraining order against the disputed companies and against David for the purposes of preserving evidence in discovery. The motion requested that files and records be retained and Bob not be dismissed from the firm. The judge assigned to the case was a bespectacled gray beard with a reputation for harsh maximum punishments when he decided criminal sentencing. A general flavor of disdain for attorneys spiced the judge's utterances, both from his courtroom bench and in his Spartan chambers with its metal folding chairs. He didn't believe lawyers deserved soft chairs.

White-haired, mean-spirited, and impatient, Judge Sandbone sat at his chamber's desk before eleven lawyers, named by defense counsel as all those known to the defendant and the firm's corporate secretary to have performed legal work of any kind for the defendant or the firm during the prior fifteen years. The day before, the judge had issued each of them a summons to appear in person in his chambers at 8:00 a.m. They now all sat before him, mystified and with some trepidation as he took his chair, opened his file, and read from the complaint. Then, looking over his spectacles:

"Any of you gentlemen recall preparing a codicil to a will for a David Sustack, leaving the advisory and underwriting companies of U G G A Universal to a man named Bob, something or other?"

A silence ensued as the lawyers looked around the room at each other. At first it appeared there would be no response. Finally, from the middle of the second row of seats, after assuring himself that no one else would first raise their hand, a lawyer named Mac raised his.

"I believe I prepared such a document, Your Honor," Mac stated.

"Do you, have it? Did you retain a copy?"

"It's been a number of years, Your Honor, but yes, I do believe I retained a copy of that codicil in my files."

"You are hereby ordered to produce that document to me forthwith. Bring it to me in my chambers here no later than one o'clock today. Let no one else see it or touch it before you present it to this court."

"Yes, your Honor," Mac replied.

"But, your Honor, that document, if it's even authentic, hasn't been entered into evidence or attached to any affidavit," responded the attorney for David who was present.

"Never mind formalities. This is this court's pre-discovery evidentiary request from this bench. I want to see what kind of bullshit

I'm going to be dealing with. Do you want me to note any objection to that?" Sandbone's staccato voice was accompanied with a glare and a snarl at his irritator.

"No, sir." David's defense lawyer backed down.

"Do you have any other problems with the way I run my court, counselor?" Judge Sandbone snarled and glared at the David's counsel.

"No, your honor." The reply from David's lawyer was deferential and accompanied with his head shake.

"All right then, gentlemen. The rest of you are dismissed. Let's have you, you, and you back here at one o'clock," he said as he pointed to Solomon, Mac, and the lawyer for David's defense. Bob's complaint survived the opposition's first efforts to kill it in its tracks.

In one respect a lawsuit is somewhat like a track runner at the starting blocks. If the runner stumbles out of the blocks, likely his race will be lost at the outset. But if he has alacrity of mind and foot combined, if he anticipates exactly the instant of the firing of the starting gunshot, then he has the jump on his competitors and great odds to run a good race.

The second chance to kill the complaint came at the one o'clock hearing in chambers. There, Sandbone, after reading the draft of the codicil and noting that it matched identically the language in Bob's complaint, offered the defense a perfect escape hatch. It was their golden opportunity to make their opponent stumble at the start.

"This looks legitimate to me. I'm going to allow discovery to go forward and grant the motion to restrain during discovery, subject to counsel's request for bond."

This seemingly innocuous proposal from the judge was a flubbed opportunity by the defense. Solomon noted the defense counsel was caught flat-footed and had no number in mind, nor had he conferred with his client beforehand should this possibility of discovery and bond arise.

Solomon, ever the fastest afoot, looked at the defense counsel and shrugged as if the request were a mere formality. Then he spoke. *"Sure, Your Honor, we'll give the court a bond. How about fifty bucks?"* He looked at David's lawyer: *"You got any problem with that?"*

David's defense counsel should have rightly said: *"Hell no. Those companies are worth thirty million. I want a bond of ten million."* But he meekly said, *"Okay"* instead, obviously not realizing that the bond could be a barrier to discovery of a multi-million-dollar claim. Solomon was inwardly gleeful, for now he had free run of the books and records of his named defendant and his companies for several months with negligible cost. He quickly fished a Ulysses S. Grant from his wallet and handed it to Judge Sandbone.

"Done," said the judge as he snarled at the defendant's counsel, regarding him an incompetent idiot.

The staff legal team for the defense sat in the second row, sinking back into their chairs as a hush descended upon the judge's chambers. With swift strokes of legal genius, Solomon destroyed any chance the defense had to kill the case in infancy by filing a motion to dismiss, based upon the Statute of Wills, had a substantial bond been demanded. Discovery would have never drawn a breath. Now there would be records and depositions. Two law school students who clerked for the judge sat in the back row of his chambers office. One whispered to the other, *"The plaintiff now has a copy of the codicil! Can you believe what we just saw? Crazy! This case should have died stillborn. Now it's got legs. And it's running!"*

"Amazing how the defense counsel blew it. This is the weirdest case I've seen yet. Could be fascinating." The second law clerk nodded and chuckled. The fight was on!

David's reaction to the production of the codicil was not what his lawyers expected. Far from showing any hint of anger at their bumbling, he was nonplussed and resolute. From the outset, he'd made it clear to his legal team that he viewed this litigation as a great opportunity to totally destroy a man whom he now regarded as a pretender to his throne. His orders were that no legal avenue of counterattack would go unexploited; no method to delay the proceedings and extract their toll on Bob's costs would be bypassed; no motion, no matter how questionable, ridiculous, or unreasonable would be omitted; and every attempt to destroy Bob's relationships would be made.

David ordered that Bob's new upstart investment advisory firm would be attacked. All regulatory contacts that David's law firms had were to be engaged in constantly harassing Bob's new firm. There would be false complaints filed against him at the assorted securities' regulatory bodies. He would be investigated endlessly in an effort to drive him from the securities business, thus proving David's contention that he was not worthy to inherit the companies. David reveled in the anticipation of pitched battle against a weaker, poorly financed foe. He would crush Bob's fledgling business, his reputation, and his morale. It would be like joyfully tearing the wings off a helpless fly.

And so, the battle began. Motions flew. Counterclaims were filed. Expenses mounted. Bob's personal assets dwindled rapidly. His bank account declined to a zero balance in less than two months; his pension plan assets lasted another two. He had two real properties which he sold cheaply for badly needed cash.

All the while, David kept up his off-court pressure. He bribed Judith to sign a false affidavit that Bob was a worthless whoremonger who had boasted to her that he suckered an old man into giving him his companies. She received a free ranch house and season tickets for her favorite professional football team.

She was soon to learn that she'd made her own Faustian bargain. David told her that in order to keep her job she was required to allow a drug dealer from Mexico to move into her home with her and the children. After a short period of time, Judith was sleeping with the criminal who was a permanent fixture in her bed. She was required to make drug drops to local high schools where David's network of distributors supplied Colorado school children their heroin and cocaine. Meanwhile, marijuana plants were grown in her basement. Her marijuana distribution network soon was expanded to cocaine sales smuggled into Colorado from Columbia and Mexico. The proceeds were turned over to David, the drug smugglers' financier.

Things looked dire for Bob. A counterclaim attack was launched against him. Competing mutual fund firms with multiple funds and a dozen or two dozen wholesalers, combined with multimillion-dollar television and print advertising budgets, and with multimillion commission payment kickbacks to broker-dealers for branch office shelf space advertising, raised billions of Dollars compared to Bob's mere hundreds of millions. By the logic of David's counter complaint, Bob should have done as well as any competitor and he should owe David one hundred million in damages and lost profits.

The nefarious counterclaim was eventually dismissed, but it achieved its desired effect. Bob needed to pay legal expenses and experts to continue to bring his case forward and disprove the fallacies of the counterclaims. His resources were rapidly dwindling and he resorted to borrowing on credit cards to pay legal bills, food, and rent. He was beyond broke, reduced to selling personal items to keep himself and his case alive. The stamp collection he'd started as a Boy Scout and his coin collection were both sold. If he were a fly, he would have felt his wings being torn away.

Every day and nights until 9:00 p.m. Bob made cold calls to retail client prospects to try to generate income. His avenues of employment in the traditional brokerage business were shut off. David had filed, as Bob's former employer, reports with the regulatory authorities that he was a dangerous and unstable person who had to be dismissed. Things were looking hopelessly bleak for Bob until, by some miracle, he happened to make a cold call to a former Catholic nun.

As luck, or divine intervention, would have it, this poor nun had a crippling terminal disease and had left her convent to rest at home. A good-hearted soul, she took in men who were afflicted with the AIDS virus as boarders for modest rents. When her phone rang that night, she was in the anguished throes of trying to decide what to do with the ten million Dollars she'd just inherited from her late father. She knew nothing of finances or money management and actually held money in some disdain, but had prayed for guidance from Almighty God to put her inheritance to good use.

It was Bob on the line asking her if she might need investment assistance. A person of faith, Nun Beatrice was certain the call from Bob was divinely inspired. She listened to him for a while and then shouted toward the kitchen ceiling, as if to peer through all man-made structures and call directly to the heavens.

"Thank you, God, for answering my prayers. You have sent this man to me just as I was praying for your guidance." Returning to the phone, she said, *"Young man, you come over here right away."*

And with that, a great relationship was formed. Bob invested Beatrice's monies well. She took in more AIDS sufferers and took out insurance policies on them as well. Beatrice and Bob together combined their wits and wills to postpone death for as many sufferers as possible, for as long as possible.

Nun Beatrice was not a soul who held back. She urged every person known to her, and she knew a great many souls, to come to her home and become acquainted with Bob. She declared that her prayers were answered in her darkest hour. She averred that Bob was sent to her by God and that, as further proof that he was sent as a blessing, Beatrice pointed out how much her cat, loved to rub against Bob.

Knowing that Beatrice's good heart operated from divine guidance, friends of hers were soon calling Bob to help them with their investments as well. She had friends over for coffees to meet him. Beatrice's cat became very attached to him at these get-togethers. Bob was allergic to the cat, but for the goodwill and the good business he overdosed on allergy pills and let the cat rub all over him while he sneezed and snorted into his handkerchief.

Perhaps miracles beget more miracles. There are things that happen in one's life that reach beyond human comprehension. Bob received an anonymous phone call one evening about Judith's new house guest and duty fuck-buddy. He was wanted in Australia on an arrest warrant as an accomplice to a homicide. Bob played sleuth, parking his car several blocks away and watching the house in the evenings. Only two nights into Bob's detective work, the drug dealer pulled his car in front of the garage and stopped briefly while the garage door opened. That was all Bob needed. He casually walked down the street, passing the garage just as the car pulled in and the door was closing. Unseen, Bob got the license plate and went to the police with what he knew. Two days later, a county sheriff came to Judith's, picked up the Columbian, and shipped him off to Australia to serve out a twenty-year prison sentence.

The next miracle came from Judith herself. Completely unexpected, she called Bob the evening before the case went to trial.

"I just called to tell you not to get your hopes up about your trial tomorrow. You are going to lose. The judge has been bought and

paid for. I got that from the chief financial officer at the Firm. He's in on all of it and told me all about it. I can't do anything about what's happened to you in the past except to say I'm sorry. I did what I believed I had to do to survive for me and my kids. I don't expect you to understand and I know we can never be friends again after all that's happened, with the bitterness and all, but I want you to know that I'll try to do what little I can for you when I can. Just don't get upset with your lawyer when you lose tomorrow. You two will have lost before you walk into the courtroom."

Bob related that conversation to Solomon. *"She's crazy,"* Sol declared. *"The judge can't be bribed."*

Bob pondered Sol's reaction. It made him feel uneasy.

The third miracle, or turn of fortune, came in a call from Barbara.

"Bob, I called to talk," she said. *"It's time. The fund is going nowhere without you. The salesmen aren't selling; the assets are dwindling. David is now calling dealers and offering to buy assets to manage temporarily to show that he can grow sales without you, but they aren't real sales. I hear him crowing that he's got you pounded into the ground and nearly destroyed, and it's making me sick to hear it. I just thought I'd call and see if you're ready for some help over there. It must be hard running a one-man band with no money and no help."*

"Well, Barbara, it is hard, and I could use the help, but I can't afford to pay you." Bob's frustration sounded in his voice.

"Never mind that, how much money are you managing, and how much do you need to reach break-even?" Barbara asked.

"I need twelve million to generate fee income sufficient to cover Firm expenses; and I'm about nine million short." Bob explained his situation was dire.

"Okay, so, when do you want me to start?" Barbara was undeterred.

"*Barbara, I just told you I can't afford you.*" Bob thought she hadn't heard him.

"*Yes, you can. I'll bring ten million in new assets with me.*" She replied, matter of factly.

"*Barbara, we can't rip assets out of U G G A. I have a court order prohibiting that. My lawyer and the judge would both kill me. My case would be lost.*" Bob thought she did not understand the tremendous scrutiny he was under.

"*Who said anything about taking client assets from the Fund? I'll bring some of my father's money with me. Chief has controlling interests in six casinos. He also owns three ranches, senior water rights in Montana, Colorado, and California, and overriding royalties on twelve gold mines and three hundred oil wells. I'm one rich Indian princess. I've just been waiting for the right situation to go into business on my own. Chief said I needed to give it time. Well, now it's time, Bob. It's time for us. What do you say we become equal partners?*"

"*You're putting me on.*" Bob couldn't believe his ears.

"*Nope, not putting you on, Big Horse,*" she said. "*I'm Big Chief's only child, and Daddy spoils his Little Sparrow. So, do you want an Injun princess squaw for your very own? She come to you with big heaps of wampum, Big Horse, and she knows the securities business inside and out. And she can do many other things also. She be heaping good trade for you.*"

"*And what's the trade?*" Bob wanted to make sure he was hearing her correctly.

"*I told you. You become an equal partner with this Injun girl. I'll own half, and you'll own half. I'll bring more to the trade too. We'll get an audience with tribal chiefs, some of whom have huge heaps of wampum. Also, this Injun girl knows how to make great whoopee. We'll see about that, but the deal must come first.*"

"*What makes you think I'm interested in whoopee?*" Bob teased her. He loved her. And they both felt it.

"Come on, Horse. All the girls in the office talk, and all office grapevines lead back to me," she answered. *"All girls say white boy Bob looks long and hard at Sparrow's backside when she walks away. You put up many smoke signals, Big Horse. I hear you take deep breaths after you look at my ass. You're not good at concealing your thoughts, white boy."*

"Barbara, I want children and a woman with a home life; not all business."

"That's okay," she assured him. *"I want that too. I have ranches and horses and bows and arrows. Things work themselves out."*

"You make everything sound like it's a business proposition."

"It is. Children will come in time. Big Horse is always in a rush. Chief says to give everything time. He counsels patience. He's very wise. This Injun girl isn't stupid. Sparrow knows what a woman's role is, but this Injun girl also has a master's degree in business administration and all licenses for securities compliance. You could do worse, Horse. Oh, wait! You did do a lot worse, remember? It's time you try thinking with your big head instead of your little head. Deal or no deal, Horse?"

Bob paused for a breath. *"Deal. And from now on, call me Bob."*

"Okay, Bob Big Horse," she teased. *"I'll be at your office tomorrow morning with the paperwork for my stock shares and my license transfers, and some checks to open some accounts."*

"Checks from whom?" he asked.

"From Daddy. I cleared all this with him ahead of time." she answered smugly.

"How did you know I'd go for this?" Bob still couldn't believe how astute she was or how quickly she moved.

"Because I'm Little Sparrow, and I'm a woman. Women know things about men before men can figure out what the woman is even thinking. Trust me and you will never go wrong, Bob. Your decision was never in question; Daddy's was. He thought dealing with a white

boy could end up getting me screwed, but he's okay with you now. I told him that you were my ticket out of David's pederast playpen, and that you were very ethical; not like some white men. I told him I've known you long enough to know you're the guy I want to work with and maybe even marry someday. Anyway, I told him he could trust you. So, now we both trust you, Bob. You and I will need to go meet my father."

"Where and when? Don't tell me he lives in a teepee."

"No, silly, we have a huge ranch in Montana, with a big ranch house. Father does keep a teepee out behind the house. He goes there to think sometimes and to meet with the other chiefs, like the chiefs did in the old days. We're not reservation Indians anymore. We belong to the Cane Breaks Cherokees and the Lakota Sioux tribes. And we are true to our roots and our people."

"How did Cherokees get from Georgia to Montana?"

"It's a story that will make you cry. I'll tell you about it, but this is not the time." she said.

Within an hour, Bob's firm became Bob and Barbara's firm. Its assets instantly quadrupled and Bob went from wondering where he was going to find money for food and rent to being a viable business. He woke that morning a lonely pauper, contemplating the surrender of his licenses and closing his business, possibly even running away to Alaska or South America, and starting life over from scratch. He went to sleep that night with his mind leaping with future possibilities for the firm and anticipation of a shared life with the one woman who took his breath away.

As he fell away into slumber, he visualized her braided hair swinging rhythmically back and forth across her mesmerizing backside while she walked before him that first day he met her. She was mysterious, smart, savvy and had an innocent straight-forward savageness about her. She had more of life's spirit within her than anyone he'd ever known, including Marty. Barbara was an enigma who was slowly absorbing his soul into her own. He felt it happening. He didn't like being apart from her. He began dreaming and wondering what she really thought of him, not as a business partner but as a man.

Barbara made her call to Bob on a Friday and was at his office, unbeknownst to David, on Saturday morning, working on affecting her transfer of licenses and allegiances. Meanwhile, David sat on his veranda that Saturday morning looking at his rose garden. He had had Dolly in his bedroom that morning in her position box. He had the highest regard for Dolly. She never complained nor asked for any payment, and their business matters settled quickly.

He smelled the sweet wafts of rose fragrance and reflected on his genius in pulling off another perfect murder, very pleased at the robust canes his bone-nourished rose plants produced.

David wondered how the authorities could have possibly gotten wind that his Columbian macho man was shacked up with Judith. He decided to cut her loose as soon as his litigation settled. He had all the lawyers and she had none. Still, her kids were just kids, and kids could talk. The more he thought about it, the luckier he felt that they had not been busted selling drugs. It was a stupid idea. Besides, if something happened to Judith or her kids, it could open up the possibility that he'd be linked to Marty's disappearance.

What was he thinking? For the first time in his life David doubted his own judgment. What made him so sure that her kids would actually want to be involved in his drug distribution business? Not all kids were like he was as a child. He remembered how he hated his parents and how he rejoiced when he learned that Marvin was dying.

Judith showed signs of wavering loyalty. Barbara left the Firm to work for Bob. He always suspected that Barbara had designs on his top salesman. Would he now be fighting Barbara, too? As much as he admired Hitler's ruthlessness, when it came to battle tactics, David considered the man an idiot. How smart was any man to get involved in multiple fights at the same time? He reminded himself not to make the same mistake Hitler made. Yet, he was plagued by a nagging feeling that the world closing in on him.

As he sat on his veranda, his thoughts turned to torturing Bob, slowly through the legal processes. And about how that goal could be accomplished at no cost to him. David naturally hated lawyers. He didn't trust any of them, especially the ones who worked for him. He'd reasoned it all out years before. Every lawyer, no matter which side he represented, was really only representing himself. Every law school student, he learned, took a class day where one of the professors, a part-time practicing lawyer, told the students that the legal profession was a business.

The first duty of every lawyer businessman was to make sure they were paid and paid well, regardless of what happened to their client. The client was just a venue for payment and the case was just a piece of business to milk to the maximum. As lawyers, they were not supposed to think about ethics; not about money. The ethics stuff was just for movie and television addicted dummies who believed what they saw on 'Law and Order' shows. Ethics was only a framework that defined limits. So, they mustn't get caught in ethics violations, but they were never to be driven by ethics. If all lawyers were driven by ethics, there would be no compensation incentive to ever become a lawyer in the first place.

With his reasoned understanding of lawyers' motives, David now shaped a plan to take advantage of all the lawyers involved in his litigation. He didn't buy into the lawyers' 'Mano a Mano' mantra. It wasn't about man against man in a pitched court battle; that was lawyer bunk to sell the gullible public on hiring these buzzard bastards in the first place. It was really a matter of 'Mano a Mano' a Mano,' etc., for as many lawyers as there were, with David's Mano being the first and most important Mano against all other Mano lawyer bastards.

As the first step in his diabolical plan, David sought out a lawyer who was an expert at convicting other lawyers of legal malpractice. He retained Mr. Green to advise him how he could set traps for all the lawyers in the case so he could have the greatest chance of either winning the case; or, if he should lose or be forced to settle, make his own lawyers pay for the settlement due to the mistakes they made. Blaming others for his problems was always David's backdoor escape from every jam he'd ever found himself in since he was a little boy.

David was confident. In his world view, he could not possibly lose this fight. A lawyer once told him he could change his will; that settled the matter as far as he was concerned. True to his sociopathic mindset, he believed himself entitled to do anything he wanted in any way he wanted to do it. Anything which caused him to lose or settle could only be due to the malpractice or negligence of his lawyers!

Mal Green kept his practice extremely confidential. David found him through non-legal channels by asking doctors whom they used to defend them in malpractice cases. Then he asked those lawyers whom they used to defend them in malpractice cases, and then he asked those lawyers whom their most feared adversary was in a malpractice case. Eventually, through meticulous searching, the names of the Buzzards that successfully dined upon other Buzzards distilled down to the one Buzzard most feared by all other Buzzards.

By Buzzard shopping, David found a marriage made in heaven. He found Mal Green. Mal advised him to take notes immediately after every meeting he had with his lawyers, and to hold meetings with them in his offices where the room could be bugged whenever possible. The objective of hiring lawyers, Mal explained, was not to win the case, although that would be a nice outcome; but to protract the litigation, make your opponent suffer as much emotional and financial pain as possible, and, regardless of the outcome, make you own lawyers pay for the settlement and forgive their outrageous fees.

Everyone engaged in litigation learned, through depositions, things they never before imagined about other people. In one deposition, when asked why she resigned, a former secretary stated that she liked working late. But people were often running around naked after hours; and their cavorting made it too hard for her to concentrate.

Another revelation was that every other week or so, three armed men with Spanish accents, sunglasses, bald heads, and heavily tattooed arms, necks, and heads arrived shortly after the offices closed. They carried large shopping bags filled with cash. The bags were left in David's office for his vital money laundering role in the Firm's illicit drug trade. After counting the cash, David and the three walked to the elevators together, while smoking large cigars. The men would, all three, kiss David on his cheeks and leave. One man carried a single legal-sized briefcase.

Depositions revealed that several witnesses, supposedly friends who would testify for Bob, were away on extended cruises when their depositions were scheduled. They all had doctors' excuses that they needed to leave the high altitude of Colorado for their health for an extended and indefinite period of time. People Bob thought were reliable, honest friends were easily bought off. He reminded himself that the investment business was, after all, about money.

David's defense team engaged in harassment tactics. They did their level best to prevent Bob's new firm from gaining or retaining clients. They filed motions to discover whether he had stolen clients from David's firm, which necessitated Bob and Barbara's new firm to obtain court issued protective orders so clients' personal files would not be revealed, or that they not be barraged with slanderous or libelous commentary about Bob. The defense attacked Bob's elderly mother, seeking to depose her to determine whether or not he had difficulties getting along with other children when he was a child, as if some comment could possibly be elicited that might tenuously be linked to David's bogus claim that Bob was a dangerous and disruptive force in the office, which necessitated his being let go. That nonsensical avenue of attack was quashed with a protective order.

Barbara also became the object of attacks. Her deposition was taken in an effort to find out whether she and Bob had a romantic relationship which caused them to collude to sabotage David's firm and steal its clients. That fishing expedition went nowhere, as Barbara had no such relationship while at David's firm or at any time up to and including the day of her deposition.

David promised his beloved Dolly that he would destroy 'The Skinny Indian Bitch.' He searched desperately to find whatever dirt there was on his former employee, but he and his private detective service found nothing. All reports that came back to David stated that Barbara was a workaholic; meticulous about details; honest to a fault; an empathetic, kindly human being. Unsatisfied by his third such investigative report, David kicked his dog. He then had Barbara followed by a private detective and her home monitored with a wide antenna listening device.

Yes, he learned, Barbara talked to Bob sometimes in the evenings, but it was always all about business. David's lawyers advised him that harassment charges against a woman in business might give them difficulties to defend, but David persisted. Barbara was tailed by private detectives, around the clock, every day of the week. The private detectives searched again and found nothing; and the surveillance continued.

One evening David's hired surveillance man, sitting in his car across the street from Barbara's home, had an encounter with undocumented aliens. They pulled their car alongside the private eye's. Three men got out. They were armed with baseball bats and hammers. All windows and lights in the surveillance car were smashed, every panel of the car's body was dented, and its four tires were slashed. They dragged David's surveillance man from his car and beat him with their bats until his ribs were broken. Then, just as quickly as they appeared, the illegals drove away. The police interviewed Barbara about the incident, but she genuinely knew nothing about it.

The next day Bob asked Barbara about the dustup.

"Chief has his ways," She answered in non-committal fashion. *"It would be like Father to send somebody and not let me know about it. I never said a word to him about the surveillance guy, but Chief would have known about it anyway. It's strange being his daughter. He is present everywhere; but always unseen, like the Lakota; like the wind. I told you he watches over me. He cannot stand the thought of anyone harming me. He's been like that since I was a little girl. I know this much for sure. If he was behind this, and I'm not saying it was him, the police will never catch him.*

"He's old school, tribal that way; too clever to be caught. He would have used middle men. Those three guys would have been hires from one of Dad's bosses. They will never be found either. Chief is thorough. I think either the surveillance will stop, or David has to pay two guys triple each what he was paying that one guy." Barbara's pride in her father was recognizable in her voice.

"I wonder how David feels getting a taste of his own medicine. Maybe the dirty tricks and harassment he's been putting us through

will stop now. Who were those guys? Do you know them?" Bob was awed by Barbara's father, whom he'd yet to meet.

"I can't know them. You should know that." Barbara tried evasion.

"Indulge me, partner. Take a guess."

"Well, it works like this. Chief gets a cut of the casinos, right off the top. He splits with Jo Jo. Jo Jo's job is to take care of details. Jo-Jo has Bobby, Phil, and Guido. They do groundwork. When Chief needs something, he tells Jo-Jo. When Jo-Jo needs a favor, he asks Dad."

"Wait. Jo-Jo, Bobby, Phil, Guido. Who are these people?"

"They're Dad's 'get it done' guys. Jo-Jo Paulo, Bobby Robbie, Phil Capobianco, and Guido 'Blade' Checini. They are the do things guys. They get things done."

"Your family works with the mob?"

"I never said that. You didn't hear me say that. Dad runs all legitimate businesses. And he prefers to work with people who have good business experience. Now you know all you need to know."

"So where do you and I fit into this?"

"We manage investments, passive investments. Dad happens to be a good client."

"Tell me about the money." Bob probed.

"It's all legitimate," she explained, *"from duly incorporated U.S.-domiciled businesses that pay their taxes, their employees, their license fees, their rents, and utilities. They are totally clean; no criminal complaints; no union problems; and no political problems. Jo-Jo keeps everything clean. Bad actors and bad girls aren't welcome. Legitimate independent operators can do business with Jo-Jo if they're legal and pay rent. Now you know more than you need to know. No more questions, Horse. We are clean. Our firm is clean. We have lawyers who know the securities business. They checked*

you out, checked everything out. We are whistle clean. Sparrow is your good clean partner; best friend you could ever have. No more questions, Big Horse."

Barbara guessed right. David's surveillance did stop. His lawyers told him they'd never get anything from the effort. Besides, he'd look vindictive to a jury if it came out that he was engaging in harassment tactics. He decided to redouble his legal efforts and cease his thug tactics. But for the first time in his life David felt he might be dealing with forces he didn't fully understand.

The legal case morphed into multiple cases against the defendant, David; and against the companies of the codicil; and against the Firm's service company. All actions went the slowest route possible and, all in all, David utilized the services of fifty-four different lawyers to defend himself and the companies. Years passed. Lawyers gave notice of their appearances and later requested permission to withdraw. David found reasons to change law firms several times, causing multiple delays. His strategy of grinding Bob to a pulp wasn't working. And the litigation was costing him a fortune. Bob's attorney, Sol, was on a contingency arrangement. But the long hours and protracted bitter fight also took their toll on Sol.

Finally, after years of delay, David sat at the defendant's table in court listening to Bob testify about their relationship and their agreement to have Bob change careers in exchange for the companies upon David's death. David showed rank audacity to the jurors, the judge, and to Bob and Sol, his attorney.

Through the whole of Bob's testimony, David sat sprawled in his chair, his ass barely resting on the edge of the seat. He obnoxiously chewed gum, smacking it with his mouth open throughout Bob's testimony, and he frequently shoved his hand down into the front of his pants and adjusted his testicles in front of the judge and the entire courtroom. The judge asked David politely, twice, to please sit upright in his chair. He complied for a time, but then reverted to his slouch position. The judge gave up trying to correct him.

When David took the stand, the questioning went along routinely until Sol made him recount his visit to the bank vault with Bob. Then David exploded. He lashed out at Sol from the witness stand.

"Why are you picking on me about this crap?" David bellowed. *"It's my will. It's my fucking will, you fucking son of a bitch!! I can change my will any time I want. That's the fucking law. You're supposed to know that. You're a lawyer. You're just picking on me because I'm a Jew, aren't you? What's the matter with you? You're a Jew yourself, aren't you? Since when does one Jew go out of his way like this to try to fuck over another Jew, huh? Answer me! You say you're a Jew, but no Jew does this to another Jew!* David thought by pointing out that Sol was a Jew that he might bias the jury against Sol. Sol glanced frequently at the jury. Their faces showed interest in the facts. Sol determined that David's tactics were not working. There were no antisemites on the jury.

"Fuck you, and fuck the horse you rode in on! You son of a bitch! You're not going anywhere with this crap. I'll fight you until I'm dead if I have to, you asshole! You and your greedy client are not stealing my companies! You're just a Buzzard; a bastard son of a bitch, trying to steal from a poor old man. You're trying to take away from me what I've worked all my life for; trying to steal everything I have. Fuck you! Fuck you! And Fuck your greedy bastard client, too! You're all just dreck. You're even lower than shit! You're going to end up eating your own shit on this case, buddy. Nobody fucks with me like this and gets away with it." David's face was red. His eyes bulged from his defiant attitude. He screamed like a madman, possessed by demons.

The judge pounded his gavel and shouted for order from the moment he heard David's first sentence. The jurors were appalled.

Men's eyebrows rose to the ceiling. Women held their hands to their mouths and winced. But David could not be stopped. A true sociopath believes that he can do whatever he wishes and nobody has the right to deter him. David relished this moment in the limelight and he wasn't about to let anyone steal it; not even the judge. The judge recessed the court and called both attorneys and David into his chambers. The jurors were filing out when the judge admonished David. He held out his index finger, pointing it as if it were a pistol barrel right between David's eyes, as he peered over its imaginary sights.

"*I'm warning you for the last time,*" the judge admonished David. "*If there's another outburst from you in my courtroom, you will be held in contempt and incarcerated.*"

David shot back at the judge. "*You'd better not try that. You'll regret it.*"

The judge had already agreed to dismiss the case for a payment to his favorite charity. Now he was confronted with outright contempt for his bench. He found himself cornered and stalemated by this devious sociopath. Would David actually go so far as to risk criminal bribery charges just to bring the same charges down upon a sitting judge? Sandbone had already surmised that David was an evil actor. But he had also doubted that David was stupid. But now he realized he might have miscalculated. Lowering himself to this scumbag was exactly what narcissist David wanted. David simply didn't care. He wanted to demonstrate that this whole legal case was just a show which revolved around him, its principal actor. The judge swallowed hard. He changed tactics. He appealed to David's self-interest.

"*Please, Mr. Sustack. Let's all just get through these proceedings here. I'm asking you politely to be reasonable. We must get through these formalities in good order, for the possibility is there that these proceedings will almost certainly be appealed. Do you understand what I'm telling you?"*

David understood the subtle message. The judge was telling him in a nice way that he was actually working for David, trying to earn his bribe, but if David didn't cooperate, the whole matter could be thrown out and David would end up in a different courtroom with a different judge and an uncertain outcome.

CHAPTER THREE

Shall we now contaminate our fingers with base bribes? (Shakespeare: Julius Caesar)

THE URINALS

When the actors had taken their respective positions, Judge Sandbone called the jury back. Bob, the plaintiff, took the stand. He gave testimony about the long-standing relationship he had with David, the money splitting on their handshake, the trips, the gifts, the countless lunches, and dinners. Then Bob related the bank vault scene and described the codicil he was shown by David. His recitation was exactly as he'd stated it in his initial complaint, again in his deposition, and it matched exactly the copy produced by Mac.

David's testimony coincided almost exactly with Bob's. The trial was going smoothly until Bob's lawyer began a line of inquiry that David was not prepared to answer.

"When you inherited the companies from your father, was there any condition attached to your inheritance?"

"What do you mean, condition?" David answered, a little hesitant.

"Let me introduce plaintiff exhibit number forty-six. This is your father's, Mr. Marvin Sustack, last will and testament. I'll read to you the relevant part, David. It says that your father is gifting to you

the ownership of the underwriting and the distribution companies that operate the U G G A Universal Growth Fund, and that as a condition of your inheriting these companies from your father, you pledged to him that upon your own death, you would leave these companies to the State of Israel. Am I reading your father's will correctly, David?"

"Yes, that is a correct reading." David spoke as if the air was deflating from him.

"When you made that promise to your father, was it your intention to honor that promise?" Sol pressed the point.

"Yes." David answered.

"Are you a devoted Jew, David?'

"Yes." David answered.

"Was your father also a devoted Jew?"

"Yes." David answered.

"He certainly was, wasn't he?" Bob's lawyer continued his line of questions. *"In fact, he was a committed Zionist, wasn't he? He helped smuggle Jews out of Nazi Germany, isn't that true? He also gave large donations to Jewish causes throughout his lifetime, didn't he? He was also a major contributor to the American Israeli Political Action Committee, or AIPAC, and a devoted contributor to the Zionist political parties in Israel, isn't that true?"*

"Yes, it's all true, so what? All of it is none of your business. Fuck you and die." David shot back his answer.

"So what? So what? Here's so what!" Bob's lawyer shouted back at David. *"He loved Israel more than he loved you, didn't he? He would never have given you those companies without that pledge you made to him on his deathbed. You needed those companies to make a living so you made that pledge, didn't you?"* When David didn't answer, Sol literally screamed at him: *"DIDN'T YOU??"* The question hung in the courtroom air, awaiting an answer.

"Objection, badgering!" shouted the defense counsel.

"I'll allow it, objection noted!" Sandbone shot back. He'd been bribed to dismiss the case at trial, but he was now so upset with David's conduct he was going to allow the plaintiff every chance to win on appeal.

David glared at Judge Sandbone.

"I'll ask again," Sol said, speaking softly: *"Did you want to keep those companies? Did you intend to keep that pledge to your father?"*

"Yes, I intended to keep the pledge to my father." replied David. An uncertain feeling arose within him.

"Okay," continued Sol, *"So now when it's years later, you have Bob in the bank vault showing him this codicil, promising him you'll leave him the companies if he'll work with you to build the companies. Did you intend to keep the pledge to your father when you showed the codicil to Bob?"*

David refused to answer. He merely shrugged his shoulders as his non-answer.

"Will the court please note the Defendant is non-responsive," asked Sol, facing the judge.

"So noted," responded Judge Sandbone in a tone that sounded like he was bored with the proceedings.

Sol then stepped in front of David's face and roared his next question:

"Did you intend to give the companies to Israel, as you pledged you would do to your father, as a condition of inheriting those companies when you were showing the codicil to Bob?"

"I was just showing it to him." David threw out his fluffy answer.

"That's been established," pressed Sol. *"Listen to my question. My question is, when you were showing Bob the codicil, were you still intending to honor your pledge to your father and the State of Israel? It's a yes or no answer, David. We all know you understand the question. Now we want your answer. Did you intend to honor your pledge to your father while you were showing Bob the codicil?"*

"Yes. I have always tried to be a good son, and I intended to leave the companies to Israel when I died; when I showed Bob the codicil." David's answer relieved the immediate pressure he was feeling from Sol; but it would have consequences later.

"So," Sol's tone became more relaxed now. He knew he had gotten the key piece of testimony he needed. "You were willing to let Bob change his career, work for much less money, make you and the companies worth many millions, and then give millions of Dollars' worth of valuable cash generating companies to Israel and leave Bob with absolutely nothing. Is that what your intentions were?"

"Well, I thought I might give him something later on." replied David as if he was God, rightfully deciding he could do whatever he wanted to do to Bob, including breaking their deal.

"Tell us about that." Sol pushed harder.

"Well, I replaced the codicil with a new one that left him a half million Dollars." David looked smug and his face wore a smirk while he said that.

"When did you do that?" Sol was amazed. This answer indicated David had some guilt about cheating Bob.

"About the same time, when you started this ridiculous lawsuit." David answered with raised eyebrows and an even more disdainful smirk. It appeared as if he was inwardly laughing at Sol.

"I see. When this lawsuit started, the companies were worth about thirty million Dollars. You took away thirty million Dollars from Bob when you removed that codicil and left him that paltry half million. Is that correct?" Sol prodded David for a reaction.

"I can do anything I want with my will, you fucking son of a bitch!" David screamed his answer and snarled and bared his teeth. "You know damn well a man can change his will at any time and for any reason You can just go fuck yourself!" David gave the reaction Sol was seeking.

"My question is, did you ever bother to tell Bob that you replaced the codicil leaving him the companies worth over thirty million dollars with a new codicil that leaves him a half million?" Bob's lawyer continued probing the mind of the sociopath defendant.

"No." stated David flatly.

"Why not?" Bob's lawyer acted surprised.

"What I do with my will is none of his business." David replied smugly.

"Now, is that half-million codicil still in effect?" Bob's lawyer seemed to think this was important.

"No. I destroyed that when he started this lawsuit. He's an ungrateful bastard. I treated him like a son. Now he tries to pull this shit! He deserves nothing!" David's face was beet red. He slobbered spittle from his ugliest, angriest face, yet. His calloused answer caused a juror to gasp and utter a disgusted, deflated: *"Oh."*

"So now Bob gets nothing," summarized Sol. *"The man worked the best years of his life, based upon your promise. He lifts the companies from the financial doldrums and makes them into cash flow powerhouses. And you say you were like a father to him. Really, David? Bob lost his father when he was two. He was a half orphan and you took advantage of him."*

"Objection. He's testifying, your honor." David's attorney stood and raised his hands to Judge Sandbone.

"Sit down and shut up!" barked Judge Sandbone at David's attorney. *"Your objection is overruled. Plaintiff's counsel merely stated facts already in evidence. Proceed."*

Sol took his cue from the judge. He stepped in front of David and put his face mere inches from David's; deliberately invading his personal space, as if daring him to hit him:

"He believed in you based upon the underwriting deals you made with him, splitting four million Dollars on a handshake. He even became a Jew based upon your schtuping—I'm sorry, for those

jurors who are not Jews, based upon your pushings and coaxings— and now he gets nothing? Is that what you're about, David? Ruining a human life to enrich yourself and then giving the money to Israel?"

"Objection, argumentative!" Defense counsel sounded sick and halfhearted this time.

"Sustained," said Sandbone, now also feeling sick to his stomach.

"No! I'll answer this! I want to answer!" David shouted. *"This is all a bunch of fucking bullshit! Fuck all of you! A man can change his will any time he wants to. That's just the law! You're just trying to smear me and the State of Israel! You're all just a bunch of filthy anti-Semites. I don't need to sit here and listen to this shit! And you!"* David, his face beet red, pointed his finger at Sol. *"You need to leave here and go hang yourself. You are a fucking disgrace to your tribe; to Israel; to everything that is Jewish! You represent this filth, this gentile, who pretends to be a Jew. You disgust me. I did nothing wrong. You have no right whatsoever to question what I did with my will, none whatsoever! I have no reason to even be here. Fuck you and the horse you rode in on! Fuck all of you!"*

That last outburst resulted in the courtroom being cleared. Judge Sandbone impaneled the jury while he considered the defense's motion to dismiss the case based upon the Statute of Wills, a codified law adopted into the Uniform Commercial Code as adopted by some thirty-six states. Simply stated, the law provided that the last will and testament was binding upon a deceased's estate, absent a writing presented to the contrary. Based upon the fact that David had not provided Bob with a copy of the codicil when they were in the bank vault, the defense motion argued that Bob could not rely upon the mere showing of it.

After the courtroom cleared, Bob and Sol were standing side-by-side in the men's room before two large five-foot-tall porcelain urinals. Sol was first to speak. *"We're going to get our asses thrown out of here. The judge hates our guts. He may have even taken money from David.”*

“Why do you say he may have taken money?” asked Bob.

“When I went to Sandbone’s chambers for our pretrial conference, David and his lawyer were already there. He clerk told me they were in with the judge a half hour before I got there.”

“Can’t you report the judge for that?”

“It wouldn’t do any good. I can’t prove a thing. Anyway, that doesn’t matter now. Sandbone is going to buy their dismissal argument.”

“After all that? After the way David mouthed off? After you showed his intent was to keep his promise to Marvin?”

“That doesn’t matter. The judge won’t stick his neck out. He won’t buck the statute, regardless of the testimony. He’ll dismiss.”

“Judith told me she heard from the fund’s financial officer that the judge was bribed.”

“You can’t believe what a woman who worked for you says. Can you prove it?’

“Not yet. She said she’d give me the proof when she’s ready to.”

“Okay, I’ll talk to her,” said Sol. “We’ll deal with it later.”

When court reconvened, Judge Sandbone stated that, based on the evidence presented, Bob was an employee of a subsidiary company of a holding company and that the holding company and its owner were not responsible for the acts of an officer of a subsidiary company, even though the persons of the subsidiary and the holding company were the same. Therefore, the case turned on the Statute of Wills. The contract claims fell; thus, the fraud and unjust enrichment claims also fell. The case was dismissed.

Sol and Bob left the courtroom. Sol put his hand upon Bob’s shoulder and said, *“I want you to know that the Jewish people are not at all like David. I see what he did. He showed you a draft codicil or a copy of a draft codicil, all signed and witnessed. Then, later,* when he was alone, he went back to the bank vault, retrieved the codicil draft that he showed you; and then he destroyed it. He's a dirty, filthy cocksucker who gives all of us Jews a bad name. Jews are good, honest people whom you can trust. We've got loving hearts for all humanity. We want to see everyone do better. We're not at all like David."

"I know that from my friends at Temple. All good, warm, honest people."

"Right. That's why I'm so galled over what David did to you. He gives all Jews a bad name. What happened in your case and to your life, and in this jackass judge's ruling, which we got here today, is a moral tragedy. You do not deserve to get fucked like this. I will be appealing this. I'll be filing appeals for the next ten years, but I will stay with you all the way on this. The law is a simple, but elegant concept. In its essence, it's designed to say you can't go around screwing people. You can't get away with this kind of horse shit. That's what we have to have faith in. That's what we must believe. We must believe the law will make this right. And that will be all we need."

"But, Sol, you know I'm totally out of money. I have no assets left to sell. I can't carry your expenses going forward. I'm done. He's broken me."

"Never mind that. I'm in this for a percentage, okay? Don't worry about me. I'll carry expenses from here. I'm like a car that runs best on empty. I'm going to keep going all the way with this. Now, you listen to me. David will throw everything he's got at you. He'll bribe your friends and your relatives to say all kinds of smears against you. He'll claim you rape young kids; steal from your clients; fuck your mother; kick dogs; piss in public places. He'll try to get to you through the regulators and your custodian broker; bribe them to find out who your clients are. Then, if an account declines, he'll finance the disgruntled client to sue you. It's a classic tactic:

'Look! The real problem is over her! It's not me. It's him!'

"It's all designed to deflect attention away from your lawsuit and onto any slightest thing you've ever done wrong. By the way, that woman who works with you. I've seen her in the courtroom. Dark hair. Beauty queen face and body. Magazine cover gorgeous. That was her, right?"

"Yes. That's Barbara."

"What is she? Arab?"

"Her mother was a Lebanese Christian Arab. Her father is a Lakota Indian chief."

"I see. Are you doing her?"

"No."

"She's so hot! How could you not?"

"It's her father. He advises we keep it all business until this litigation is over."

"Smart man. But there was another woman. Named Marty. Right? Also a looker, right? She was the office punch; and you did do her, right?"

"She had emotional issues. Yes. I did her. We loved each other."

"Where is she?"

"I don't know. She's just sort of disappeared."

"He may have murdered her. I wouldn't put it past him."

"You think?"

"Yeah, I think. You're still not getting him, are you?

"What are you getting at, Sol?"

"Look. You're a good-looking guy. He's totally into men and boys. Try seeing him through his eyes, not yours. He sees it that he gave you an opportunity to work with him; and learn from him. He sees it that he gave you a job. Well, in his twisted brain, he believes that makes you, his property. He thinks he owns you; owns all of you; your very life. He thinks he owns all of you from your mouth to your asshole. Are you getting me?"

"Still not sure, Sol."

"Did you ever say 'No' to him?"

"Sure. When he wanted to have me sign that new contract, the one that had the release clause."

"*I don't mean that 'No.' Bob, you need to stop being stupid. I mean a more personal 'No.' Look, did he ever make a play for you? Ask you to blow him? Put his touches on you?*"

"Oh, yes. He did. He wanted me to do gay stuff with him; asked me several times. And I told him 'No.' several times. I told him I'm just not into that stuff; that I like women; really dig women; adore them. Period. He also liked to put his hand on my back. I never responded to that."

"*Well, to him, those 'No's' were your rejection of him as a person. That set him off; set him totally against you. On top of that, you are descended from German ancestry. He may have seen Marty as competition for him. He wanted you; not for love, but to totally dominate you. Getting this?*"

"*I don't know. It all kind of runs together.*"

"*Look, Bob, I'm trying to tell you that David never felt any warm fuzzies for you. It was all an act. He disguised his real feelings about you for eleven years. He's one of those whose mind is all tangled up in the revenge scene. You're dealing with a total psycho. He has a visceral hatred of you. In his mind, there's no such thing as secular law. There's only tribal law. Nation states come and go; but the Tribe is permanent. Are you getting this?*"

"*Sort of. Does he really think like that?*"

"*You bet your ass he does! He holds the grudges of his ancestors. He sees you as his natural, mortal enemy. He believes you are responsible for the sacking of Soloman's temple by the Babylonians; and the sacking of the second temple by the Romans; and the Tsar's Russian pogroms; and Hitler's holocaust. He sat through Torah classes and learned all about all that stuff. But to him, there's no timeline. It's as if all that tragic stuff that happened to Jews all happened yesterday.*

And all that stuff is all your fault! Bob, Shema! Wake up. Hear what I'm telling you. David hates your guts with a passion! He has hated you from the get go. You are not dealing with an ordinary sane secular man. Nothing like that. David wants to destroy you. And he is going to try. He will not fight you by Queensbury rules. The courts and judges rulings mean nothing to him. He simply doesn't give a shit what some court rules. You are locked into tribal warfare with him. It's a fight to annulate you. Anything goes. He is intent upon destroying your life!"

"Fuck. Come on, Sol. He can't be that crazy!"

"He is. I know the type. You need to be wary of him on every level. He sees you as his mortal enemy and he wants a fight to the death. This is not just an ordinary lawsuit. I'm telling you these things so you will understand your enemy. David is from a different world; a different time and place. Expect total barbaric, no holds barred combat. Just be ready for everything. David will make this fight messy. He'll expand the battlefield into all sorts of areas; anything to break you. He'll try to make people believe you were a sex crazed animal and he needed to get rid of you. So, be careful. Expect everything and anything. Do not ever let him break you. Do not give in to him. No matter how badly he hurts you or those closest to you, do not let him get to you. Do not listen to anyone who comes to you and says he can patch things up with David; make all this go away. Do not fall for anything like that. It could come from a rabbi; maybe someone on the Firm's board of directors. But it's a trap to sidetrack you from fighting and buy you away cheap. You're not going away cheap." Sol's face was beet red. Tiny veins showed in his face and on his nose. He was adamant that Bob stay in the fight and not settle cheap. His blood pressure was sky high.

"You need to stay tough; tougher than him. Do not quit this fight. Do not let him make you settle cheap. Understand?" Sol nodded his head.

"Yeah, okay. I understand." Bob reassured Sol. *"I won't give in. I won't settle cheap. I promise. But what about you?"*

"Don't worry about me," assured Sol. Sol's eyes lit up with a faraway twinkle while his face assumed the demeanor of grit and determination. He bared his teeth widely, deliberately showing his canines. For an instant, Bob thought he was seeing the reddened face of an angry Bengel Tiger. Sol's face was the fiercest on a man that Bob had ever seen. David's conduct had triggered Sol and sent him on a mission.

"Look, David's not my kind of Jew. He's really not a Jew. He's a pretender who uses the religion to cover for him. He gives guys like me; all the rest of us, a bad name. He likes to mess up peoples' lives; then when he gets called out on it, he runs to his rabbis for cover. Begs them to interceded for him. He cries like an injured little weenie prick:

Sol whined like a hurt child, pretending to be David: *'Help me, Rabbi. Please help me. They've after me. Make some phone calls. Persuade those who can divert and deflect attentions away from me. Sweep my shit under the rug so no one can see it or smell it. Scream antisemitism for me. Throw some dirt at the other guy.'*

"Well, I'm not having it. I can't stand David or anyone who thinks like he does. I am not a Zionist. I don't believe in protecting David just because he belongs to the Tribe. I believe in the rule of secular laws. That's why I practice law. That's why I took your case. I do not believe that Israel needs to rule the world. I believe in humanity and human goodness. I don't think it's okay to commit genocide against little Palestinian children. There's no way atrocity can be justified. I just want people to get along. I believe in the United Nations, the international rules of law. I think all peoples should just get along. It's hard. It's damn hard; but we must all keep trying. People need to get along. Kapish?"

"Kapish."

"Anyway, you came to me because somewhere deep inside your guts you knew you were headed for a fight. I think you were brought to me for a reason. Maybe God wanted this case for me? I don't know. Maybe I'm being tested, too. Not just you. So, here I am. But don't you worry about me. I love a good fight. I'm a litigator. I love to fight. That's how I'm wired. That's why you came to me in the first place, right?"

"Right."

"Okay. You wanted an attorney who would fight. Well, I do fight. I fight like a son of a bitch. I'm at my best while I'm fighting. David will put me through hell, too. I know that. I expect it. And I'm ready for it." Sol relaxed for a moment. He leaned back and reflected; then let out a chuckle laugh: *"Heh, heh, heh. You're in for a treat, Bob. And you've got the ringside sea! You'll never see a better fight than when two Jews hate each other's guts and they really go at each other. So, watch me! David will attack my reputation in the Jewish community. He'll smear me, like he'll smear you. He'll call me a lunatic. A madman. An obsessed. An enemy of the Tribe. That's okay. I'll deal with it. He can bring it. Fuck him! I live for a good fight. I'll fight David. He's a no-good son of a bitch who's got it coming. I'll fight that son of a bitch in the courts. I'll fight him in the public square. I'll fight him in hell and I'll keep fighting him until hell freezes over."* Sol gritted his teeth and nodded his head. A more serious man, there never was.

"Then what?" asked Bob.

"Then I'll fight him on the ice. But trust me, I'll keep fighting that dirty filthy cocksucker until I sit his slimy ass down in the defense witness chair in front of a jury. I'm going to put him there, no matter what it takes. He's going to answer my questions in front of a jury! I don't care how many lawyers or law firms or how much shit and

money he throws at me. I will show a jury what a pile of shit he is; what a filthy cocksucker he is; that he has no redeeming qualities; none. I will break him. He is the one who is going to break. I swear to you, I am going to break him. You'll see. You'll see a grown man cry. You'll see a dog fight like you've never seen before. And this dog will win that fight!"

Bob leveled a grateful gaze at Sol. *"Thank you, Sol,"* he said.

CHAPTER FOUR

Once to every man and nation, comes the moment to decide, in the strife of truth with falsehood, for the good or evil side. (James Russell Lowell: The Present Crisis)

When life hands you a bag of lemons, make the most of it. Make Lemonade! (Rosemary Ness-Bitner: author)

THE SUPREMES

Bob's case was appealed five times based upon arguments of law as to who was responsible for putting David and Bob together in a bank vault. Was it David, or was it one of the companies? Was Bob really working for David to enrich him and Israel, or was he working only for the companies, just to build the companies and not to inherit them? Were the claims just quantum meruit claims for underpayment for services, brought in another form by a disgruntled employee? Did the Statute of Wills apply here? Did Judge Sandbone err in his ruling to dismiss the case based upon his finding that, by not possessing a writing, Bob had not met the Statute? Could the statute be governing here when it was clearly shown in the evidence that the defendant had no intent to leave the companies to the plaintiff? Back and forth went the appeals, from appeals court to trial court. Years passed. The fight continued. Legal precedents affecting all states that adopted the Statute of Wills as definitive were being decided.

At a second trial, ordered on remand from appeals court where the case was next tried against the companies, that case was also dismissed. David testified that the companies he owned had nothing to do with his personal decisions, and he was not acting as an officer or director of either company when he showed Bob the codicil. After eight years of wrangling in the appeals courts, the cases came down to one man, David, sitting in the witness chair saying in the first case that the companies made the deal with Bob; thus, it was a simple quantum meruit case. But when the companies were tried in the second case, the party responsible for being in the bank vault was David personally; but he had the right to change his will. Sol argued this was a lot of nonsensical Kabuki Theater. It was analogous to watching a clown pointing in opposite directions with his index fingers, shouting: *"He did it!"*

Meanwhile David led the life of luxury. He trotted off to vacation spots all over the world. He had full use of the companies and their enormous cash flows, which Bob had grown by his labors. David continued expanding his growing drug distribution business, poisoning the youth of Colorado and other states, and victimizing others with his loan shark business. Being a sleazy fraud pursed in a legal system that crawled along at a snail's pace, was paying off very well for David.

In a tortured mind, still confused about the true nature of his relationship with David, Bob sometimes allowed himself to believe that his would-be dad was showing him, through cruel example, that many of the things he'd taught him were actually easily born out. Public officials could all be bought off; and that apparently included judges on the Colorado District Court level. Lawyers could be paid to do illegal things for you, such as bribing witnesses and psychologists to give false testimony. Illegal aliens were readily available if one just asked around a bit. They could be employed to damage property and even commit murders for you.

David's personality had always fascinated Bob. Like any Faustian, Bob was entranced by David's bizarre, evil persona. Like many others who succumb to fraud, he actually empathized with the character who was doing him a great wrong. Despite wrongful behavior which Bob had observed David doing to others while they worked together, he deluded himself into believing that somehow, *he* was personally exempt from being on the receiving end of any of David's behaviors. Sol needed several sessions with Bob, during which he told his client that he was just another patsy, just like everybody else who worked with David. Sol eventually got Bob to accept that the only father he ever had, or would ever have, was his dead one. Sol's compassion for Bob went beyond the duties of the lawyer to his client. Like Arlene, the school nurse in Milltown, Sol's deep well of humanity likely saved Bob from living his life in undeserved purgatory.

Then, just when the case appeared to be reaching a final judicial interpretation of the Statute of Wills as related to a defense for fraud, a terrible thing happened. Bob got the shocking news a week before the case was scheduled to be heard in the state supreme court. Sol died of a massive heart attack in the middle of the night. Bob lost his trusted friend. And he needed to obtain new counsel. And that whole process took another three months. Eventually, an attorney with a twenty-percent success rate agreed to represent him, subject to reduced compensation due to Bob's outstanding legal bills owed to Sol's estate. The new lawyer's name was Benjamin Slipperman. His colleagues called him 'Slipup.' Ben was possibly the least imposing personal presence ever seen in a courtroom.

Standing merely five feet tall and weighing over three hundred pounds, Ben carried with him a breast pocket full of cheap cigars and a string of three handkerchiefs, tied together in knots and hanging from his back pocket, dangling halfway to the ground.

It was a bizarre experience to see and hear this living marsh-mallow of a man. One's first impression of Ben was that he was likely a child with a perpetual runny nose, who might still live with his mother. Only a mother could make a grown man carry three knotted handkerchiefs dangling from his back pocket that way. But wait! Ben did live with his mother! He was fifty years old and had always lived with her. He sometimes laughed about his situation, saying that his mother, a New York Jewess, was highly selective about the woman she would allow into Ben's life; and she hadn't yet found any woman as good as herself!

When Ben was before a judge, he often coughed and wheezed due to his chronic bronchitis. Undeterred by the prospect of an early death, he smoked at least three cigars daily. When he spoke, he annoyed every judge who had to endure his orations. His chronic postnasal drip caused a constant stream of snot to flow from his nostrils. And his sentences were interrupted in mid-phrase by the vacuum cleaner-like sound of Ben trying to snort up the snot stream from his dripping roof palate. These snorts were disgustingly followed by a forcible gulp as Ben swallowed his snot harvest. The maneuver caused his Adam's apple to bulge noticeably and his face to redden. Some judges placed their hands over their eyes while this repulsive procedure took place; others looked off to the side. Jurors snickered or lowered their heads into their reading while Ben cleared his nasal passages. In damp winter months, these interruptions took place every two or three minutes.

Ben, his colleagues said, was his own best reason for losing most of his cases. But for all he was lacking physically, he was capable mentally. He was not exceptional, far short of brilliant; but he was capable. His corpulence, his snot problems, and a frequent unlit cigar in his mouth were accented by a pair of glasses with lenses thicker than antique glass soda bottle bottoms. He was the human rendition of a mole; but Ben was a mole that knew how to sniff out money.

As Ben researched cases far into the evenings, he came across an appeals court ruling from Wisconsin with facts involving a Shiksa case, where a woman was denied recovery from an estate even though she had a napkin with a vague written promise of money after death for her lifelong services. He called the plaintiff's counsel.

After discussion and strategizing, the two lawyers petitioned the U.S. Supreme Court to hear Bob's case, represented by Ben, on a writ of certiorari. It was a daring legal maneuver to seek removal to the nation's highest court, especially since no federal court had ever ruled on this issue. It was even outside the Federal Rules of Civil Procedure; yet it did involve a Federal Statute that had been widely adopted as state law. The two lawyers figured their petition for the writ likely only had a one chance in a million of even being heard; but Ben figured it was worth taking the shot. After all, he had nothing to lose. And even if he lost the writ, the move would buy him more time to prepare for his appeals in Colorado. Time went by; first one month; then three months; then six months. Ben told Bob that the justices might be scratching their heads over this one. The joined cases had stirred some national interest because the Statute of Wills was now definitive; governing law in thirty-seven of the fifty states.

One day in late November, just before Thanksgiving, a message courier knocked twice, then opened the door to Ben's office. Behind a pile of files and paper the courier saw a smoking cigar and the dome of a bald, bespectacled head, peering faced down upon a massive oak desk. Its eyes were riveted upon legal papers, three inches below.

"I'm looking for Mr. Benjamin Slipperman, counsel for petitioner Bob Burke?" The courier sounded like Army sergeant material by the way he barked out Ben's name.

"Yes," replied Ben's sleepy voice. Its attached head did not look up.

"Sir, I bear a Writ of Certiorari Order from the United States Supreme Court. It is addressed to you. I require your signature."

Ben hastily opened the packet, and there it was! Just like that! His one-in-a-million shot had been granted! Ben Slipperman, the mamma's boy with the runny nose; the fat kid all the other lawyers laughed at, was getting his shot at making legal history! His petition for writ had been granted! The case that never had a chance to succeed from day one was going to be heard by the United States Supreme Court! Ben's cigar dropped to the floor. He stood to shake the courier's hand.

"Thank you, son," said stunned and humbled Ben. After all his career losses and derisions, Ben's faith in the judicial system was renewed. Tears welled up in his eyes. By all rights and procedures followed in law, the Supreme Court should not have even considered the case. It was like a fantasy come true. But, Ben realized, they were, after all, the Supremes. And, they could do anything they wanted. He felt infused with the same idealism he had when he was a young man on his first day of law school.

On the day of Supreme Court oral arguments, Bob met Ben before the justices took their chairs. Ben showed Bob around the Supreme Court facilities. They were positively luxurious. Large soft leather chairs, a dining room, beautiful offices, thick carpeting, commanding views—the justices had it all.

Ben commented: *"These guys know how to live. I have to believe it would be impossible to bribe any of them. Maybe that's why there are nine of them. If you try for a bribe, you don't know which ones or how many of them will hear your case. And if you do try to bribe one, you could get the wrong one and end up getting thrown in the slammer. It'd be risky, even for David. I don't believe these guys buy into Bullshit for Sale."*

"Then you believe my first judge was bribed?" Bob asked.

"Not saying." Ben coughed. *"Can't say what I can't prove,"* said Ben, but he had a smile that resembled a cat's that had just snagged a canary.

Bob took his seat in the back of the courtroom, joining Barbara. She pointed to David seated in the front row, slouched in his chair. That was his normal signal of contempt for all judges and Justices, and the entire legal process.

During arguments, all nine Justices were present. They wanted to understand why the Statute of Wills did not bar a claim to recovery, since David had not given Bob a copy of the codicil when they were in the bank vault. David's attorney droned on about case precedents. There were no cases on point, ever, anywhere in America's history or in the history of English Common Law, that permitted recovery of any claims of any kind whatsoever without the plaintiff establishing that he had, in possession, a copy of a writing to make a will; or an actual will; or a codicil to an existing will. The statutory law was unambiguous and clear.

Bob's counsel was trying to show what David did was unconscionable conduct, when the chief justice asked his fated question. It was a dagger that touched the very heart of Bob's case. The entire room could feel the Chief Justice was poised to thrust his dagger into Ben's argument.

"Your client had no writing," said the Chief Justice. *"You obtained a copy of the writing through your discovery, but your client never had actual possession of a writing given to him by the defendant. There are numerous cases throughout judicial history where plaintiffs claim that they did thus and such based upon a will promise; but they never prevailed. I think some in some culture even call a will promise, the 'Shiksa game,' but it goes on without any successful challenge. For over four hundred years, the law is clear."*

The chief justice was almost shouting. He was visibly agitated. It was obvious he was angry at what David did, but he could see no way to open the door that was locked shut by the statute. Recovery odds for Bob appeared to be zero.

He continued after a brief pause. *"It's lamentable what happened to your client, Counsel, but that is not a matter of law. Now the English common law has even been chiseled into stone. We now have before this court the Statute of Wills. The law is abundantly clear, Counsel. You have no writing! How can you expect this court to render a decision other than one that is consistent with the statute?"*

A long hush descended over the courtroom and the visitors' gallery. Ben took off his glasses and set down his briefing book upon his lectern. He stepped away and stood directly below Chief Justice Renlow, who was poised upon the forward half of his chair staring down, fiercely, at Ben. A certain charge of electricity flew between the two men. The small fat man had to tilt his head far back to look skyward at the Chief Justice, seated high above him.

Chief Justice Renlow wanted so much to not have this case before him, yet he could see the injustice being done. He was clearly frustrated that he couldn't quite point his finger in the direction of a path to relief. All routes were blocked by the statute. He could see how a man's life and career had been screwed. That wasn't supposed to happen in America. The chief justice knew that. That basic rooted belief that you can't use the law to screw people was his main sustaining force for his entire life. He was beside himself with the conundrum posed by this case; and had even told his fellow Justices so. They'd reluctantly agreed to grant the writ request by a five-to-four majority.

The most conservative justices wanted nothing to do with the case. Their position was to let the state legislatures deal with the issue; but they were outvoted. The idea of just letting people get screwed by the Statute of Wills defense until some legislatures decided to do something was a terrible injustice to those persons who were out there, the next ones to be screwed by this misuse of the law. But a majority of the Justices just couldn't stand the status quo. Now they were tasked with figuring out what was wrong with a law of the land that could be used as a shield for wrongdoing.

The Chief Justice had a dilemma. The idea of ruling to deny remand and upholding this sham misuse of the law to shield a fraud sickened him. He was all ears, waiting and wanting to be unburdened; but at the same time, he was extremely skeptical. There stood before and below him a man who was so short, he could barely even be seen from the bench.

Ben was clearly not a skilled orator; David's lawyer was. He'd just summed up a very convincing argument that this matter must be left to the states and their legislatures to remedy, if they even decided remedy was desired. It was a balance between rights of decedents giving upon death versus those who could be harmed by a wrongful predator. The chief justice hoped this coughing, wheezing, cigar stench-soaked man could somehow make an argument, if he didn't keel over from anxiety first.

Ben's attention wandered when he heard the question from the Chief Justice. It appeared to everyone that the nervous little man was afraid to speak. There passed a fearful moment where all present thought the fat little lawyer might faint. Gently, Chief Justice Renlow repeated the question; his arms extended with his hands palms up.

"How can you expect us to render a decision that is inconsistent with the statute when your client had no writing?" He widely spread his fingers and raised his eyebrows as if he were a wide receiver waiting to receive a football pass. This was to be the defining moment. The whole case would fall or go forward based upon Ben's response.

There were about one hundred people in the gallery that day, including the press corps that followed Supreme Court cases. They all stopped taking notes and looked down from the gallery. All eyes focused on the perspiring, snorting, little fat man. He needed to make his case at that moment, or pack his bags and return to flyover country.

Ben spoke in what would be his finest performance, ever. *"I agree with everything my eloquent opponent says and every point you make, Your Honor. We have no writing, and based upon that simple fact our appeal must be denied."* The Justices and the spectators held their collective breaths.

Ben continued:

"Except for one significant thing, Your Honor. And this is why you cannot rule to deny! When David was in the bank vault, it is his testimony, by his own unrecanted words, that he intended, at all times, that he would keep his pledge to his father, to leave the companies to Israel upon his own death; while at the same time he was showing the codicil to Bob. Therefore, his true intent could never have been to leave the companies to Bob. David concealed the truth of his actual intent from Bob. His true intention was in fact to defraud Bob, defraud him into giving up his career, his life, essentially, for a false promise in the inducement to gain his performance for all those years. David's intent could not have been anything other than to defraud. This court cannot find that the statute shields such unconscionable conduct! It simply cannot be a shield for fraud! The court must remand our cause with instructions; with instructions directing the trial court to order a trial by a jury. No other ruling could be just."

Ben wiped his eyes, choking back his emotions as he uttered his final soft-spoken words: *"Petitioner rests."* The phrase hung silently in the air, as if its absent echo continued resounding from the walls of the courtroom. The gallery spectators knew a magnificent oratorical performance when they heard one.

With his eloquent delivery, Ben Slipperman made legal history. The Chief Justice knew it when he heard it. His head went back. His eyes closed. His mouth gaped open. He slumped back in his chair. A second Justice reacted as well, lifting up his hands above the bench as if to reflect he was having a 'eureka' moment. The Chief Justice now had his chance to render an opinion that would be cited in cases of fraud and fraudulent intent. His ruling would set a judicial precedent that would be carried down through the ages. He had just heard a precedent-setting case, a case that pushed aside the notion that the Statute of Wills was inviolate; that will makers could use that statute to defraud innocents by falsely promising an inheritance in the face of clear credible testimony that there was no such intent. He recognized he'd been given the means to rule such conduct could not be so.

Ben had laid out the groundwork of the matter clearly before his court. Of course! It was now all clear to the court. The truth burst through decisively and suddenly, like it was wont to do in matters of convoluted logic that must become untangled. The Chief Justice knew from his old days as a judge's clerk that one always had to look to the testimony and the conduct of the parties. His frustration with this case was lifted from his shoulders. He'd opened his eyes, literally. Ben had removed the legal scales from them just seconds before. He appreciated legal genius. He knew he'd just heard it from the little fat man who hardly ever won a case.

Rarely did Chief Justice Renlow shown any hint of his leanings. Lawyers who came before him referred to him as 'Old Poker Face.' Today was different.

"Thank you for that eloquent elucidation, Counsel, and thank you for highlighting that item of testimony taken at trial. In matters of law, this court ordinarily does not seek to rule based upon interpretation of testimony, but in this case the testimony divides the

proofs of the claims of contract and contract to make a will shielded by the Statute and the claim of fraud, and the requirements of The Statute of Frauds. Thus, this court shall consider it. We Justices will retire to our chambers now. You will have your opinion after we finish our deliberations."

There was a twinkle in Chief Justice Renlow's eye as he gave a wan smile toward Ben. Petitioner's counsel had awakened one of his fondest memories from his first year of law school. His old professor was a retired Federal Judge who had a passion for the rule of law. His esteemed teacher had often said that the law is the only thing that separates us from the animals. Another thing his professor often said was: *"Look always to the testimony of the parties and the conduct of the parties; and therein lies Truth. Discover her! Cling fast to her! And respect her. And love her! The wrongdoer will deny her and abuse her; the miscreant will disdain and mock her; the fool will ignore her at his peril. But in your final analysis you will discover that Truth, alone, survives all attacks on her. She stands there, tall, and proud, waiting for you to know her. Run to Truth. Embrace her and love her with your whole heart. She alone is pure and precious and beautiful. Honor her and she will never disappoint you."* Those clairvoyant words echoed through Chief Justice Renlow's mind as he arose from the bench to return to his chambers.

Bob was in shock. He knew something significant had just happened, but he wasn't sure he understood it. Tears streamed down his cheeks. A twelve-year legal ordeal had just passed a crucial turning point. The justices were going to consider his case, based upon testimony, something they always left to lower courts. But, then again, as Ben had told him, they were the Supremes, and the Supremes could do anything they wanted. He turned his head from side to side and looked far away, seeing his life telescoped before him into a moment he could only pray went well.

Barbara was more attuned to administrative and procedural matters than Bob. She took his hand and squeezed it. *"You just won your case, Big Horse"*

Ben was more cautious and reserved, telling Bob later that he thought they did all right.

On his way out of the courtroom, David passed by Barbara and put his face up close to hers. Then he hissed and stuck out his tongue at her as if he were some sort of reptile. She later recounted the incident to Bob. *"I thought for a minute there I was looking into the eyes of an evil snake."*

"You were." Bob said. He no longer felt sympathy for David, or his pitiful childhood stories about the mastoids in his ears; his body odor problems; his sexual hang-ups about women; his ungainly appearance; his homosexual needs; his tortured and distorted views about the inferiorities of women and other cultures; his lack of respect for authority and social rules; any and all of it. He was finally free of the monstrous sociopath, his endless manipulations, and his barf bag filled with self-pity.

The oral argument that Ben made awakened Bob from a long nightmare. The real David was just a sleazy scumbag and closet criminal; a pustule on the ass of social normalcy; a disgrace to his Levite namesake ancestral king. He was just a pathetic sham of a man who played his 'I'm just a poor persecuted Jew' card whenever it suited him to gain sympathy. He was quick to allege that his actions were being challenged because he was discriminated against. He blamed his religion, when in fact his religion had nothing whatsoever to do with the charges brought against him. He was just a low life dirt bag crook. Bob was free of David at last.

"Why do you think David did what he did?" Barbara wanted to understand what happened through Bob's eyes.

Bob started to explain his understanding of the factor that drove David to behave the way he did, as best he could. *"Well,* there is a certain subset of the tribe, those Jews who God created as an ingenious social invention. God saw the need for the Goyim to be deceived into taking actions they otherwise would not take. So, in my case, he sent David as his agent to deceive me into building a firm that otherwise would never have been built. On a larger scale, he set up central banking to induce spending through the government to advance society faster than it otherwise would advance. You see, the Goyim tend to take the bait of instant gratification. God knows that, so he sends his agents, the Lucifers, to issue the temptations to the Goyim. The deal the Lucifers have with God is that they will tempt and promise and deceive; and God is okay with that because he wants to see if there will ever come a time when the human condition advances past the hatreds of the tribe against the Goyim and the Goyim against the tribe.

"Meanwhile, there are sordid interplays of false promises, reactions, and hatred, and the tribe turning inward in reaction to when those hatreds play out, like the Holocaust; and the reaction to it, which was the founding of Israel. It's a cycle that is not unlike holding out candy to a child and then taking it away. The child and the Goyim both react and throw their temper tantrums, or a holocaust or a pogrom, as the case may be. The parent, the tribe, hardens against the behavior it receives. The reaction of the tribe knits it closer together; and there are factions within the tribe that derive their power base by constantly reminding the tribe's members of their woes and grievances. The Goyim constantly hold suspicions about the tribe. There are some within each faction of tribe and Goyim who seek to extract vengeance against the other. They are championed by their hard-core base factions. So, the cycle goes on."

"But why do you believe God would create such a vicious dynamic?" Barbara sought a deeper understanding.

"To move humanity forward, I suppose," answered Bob. "And also, to see if humanity will ever become secular and rise above the cycle. It's not new. It's an interplay you can pick up by reading ancient scriptures, like in the Book of Judges. The tribe goes astray from God; gets its ass kicked in battle; rallies and fights off a potential destroyer with God's help; and then goes back to God."

"But wouldn't rising above that dynamic eliminate the need for God?" questioned Barbara. "Could there be another reason?"

"Yes, possibly," reflected Bob. "I think the ultimate reason for it all is God creates the interplay for God's amusement. It makes for great human drama. Almost everybody loves amusement, even God."

"Almost everyone?"

"Well, yes, except the liberal Democrats. They believe they know better and more than everyone else. They always tell everyone what everyone else should do. They don't know how to laugh. Unfortunately, they take themselves too seriously."

"Funny! But the advance and retreat cycle, the aggress and repent cycle? Everyone has a choice to sign on to this cycle or not, right?" Barbara sought to understand Bob's mind.

"Yes. Everyone has free will. Everyone may make their own choice. But people do not like to think independently. They are like herd animals. They herd. They tend to follow their crowd; and crowds tend to respond to those who shout the loudest." Bob answered her.

CHAPTER FIVE

Between the idea and the reality, between the motion and the act falls the shadow (Thomas Stearns Eliot: The Hollow Men)

MISSING SHEEP

Mothers like to believe their daughters will turn out well and have good lives. No mother gives birth to a daughter and wishes upon her child that she'll grow up to become a hard-core porn slut or an amoral nymphomaniac fuck-bunny. But that is what happened to Susan's little Marty. Between the time when she was Joseph's little girl, bouncing on his knee, laughing, running about in the yard with her pinwheels, bubble-blowing soaps, little dolls, and her little pets; and between the time when she suddenly disappeared into a time warp and later returned to Plaintown, something went terribly wrong with Marty.

Susan sat alone with her thoughts this late afternoon, after the office staff had long gone home. '*What went wrong with my daughter? Why did Marty turn out to be the adult she turned out to be? How did I contribute to Marty's life choices, and what's to be done about it now?*'

Susan reminisced over her countless days and nights with Marvin, how she immersed herself in his world while relegating Marty to second place for her attentions. She had told herself, unconvincingly; that she was doing the best she could to raise her daughter. Marty always had the best of everything through those years; the best clothes, the best schools, nice cars, plenty of money. But Susan was frustrated during those years. She knew that money wasn't a substitute for parental love. She lived with an uneasy guilt about how she treated her daughter. She never did anything with her daughter. Her and Marty's lives would have been so perfectly wonderful if only she could have had Marty with her in a family life that included Marvin; but try as she might, she could not pry Marvin away from his wife.

Eloweiss would have none of Susan's dream scheme. She would rather ruin the business and her husband's life just to spite the two of them, if that's what it took to prevent Marvin from leaving her for Susan. A bitter stalemate took hold between the two women. Marvin's life was caught between them. He lived in a female no-man's land. He was tugged and pulled and fought over. His time spent and affections given to one was carefully monitored by the other. This stalemate developed its own unspoken rules. Susan could have lunches and dinners with him. She could bed him, fuck him in the office and the rental house; and in Susan's house; and on their trips away. But Susan could *not* have relations with Marvin in Eloweiss's house, or on Friday nights; nor could Susan see him on Saturday Bar Mitzvah days, or during Jewish High Holy Days.

Now, years later while sitting in her office, Susan thought:

'Maybe I should have just broken it off with Marvin. Maybe all my money wasn't worth what I put myself and my daughter through.'

Susan hadn't birthed those thoughts while Marvin lived, but now that he was gone the remorse of losing Marty had her second-guessing her life's choices. Guilt haunted her and gave her no peace. Today, she allowed her mind to relax. Her thoughts drifted while she wondered.

Susan gazed at her suit jacket hanging behind her office door. Her gaze narrowed to a stare. It fixated upon the Monarch butterfly pin that Marty gave her on her fiftieth birthday. As a proud mother, Susan always wore the pin now, regardless of the garment she wore. It was a striking piece of jewelry with golden orange mother of pearl wings, a line of deep red rubies making up the body of the pin, and ten white diamonds bordering the edges of each wingtip. The black veins of its wings were delicately hand-painted. The artist who fashioned it was very clever. He created the illusion of a woman's eyes behind the translucent wings and inviting red lips peering out from the bottom of the butterfly's body. When Marty first gifted her the pin, Susan's reaction was to gasp. With the mother of pearl, rubies, and diamonds, the piece had surely cost her daughter a small fortune. It was a large pin, a good four inches across; and clearly custom-made.

At first, Susan merely thought of the pin as a unique piece of spectacular jewelry, but the more she wore it, the more she wondered about her relationship with her daughter. With her gift, had Marty intended to make a subtle statement from daughter to mother? Was Marty trying to declare, in her muted painful way, that she also earned big money by prostituting herself, just like her mother had done?

Susan thought back to the time when she'd visited Marty during her last year of boarding school. As Marty was getting dressed, Susan was shocked to notice Marty's tattoos. Marty sported a red and blue butterfly tattoo low over her backside; and there was another noticeable orange-winged Monarch butterfly on the inside of her uppermost thighs. Although Susan only had a fleeting look at the tattoo that surrounded Marty's vagina, she instantly understood it represented her daughter's declaration of uninhibited sexuality. Perhaps Marty's pin gift to her mother messaged that Marty was as accomplished in her whore craft as Susan was. Perhaps the butterfly pin was intended to be a constant reminder to Mother that Daughter had also mastered the erotic artistry of carnal leg-spreading.

Susan could now only wonder about Marty's true feelings toward her. She pondered those thoughts in her heart. Regardless of Marty's intentions, Susan wore the butterfly with deep maternal love for her daughter. She loved her adult daughter unconditionally. While staring at the pin this afternoon, she felt Marty's soul reaching out to her, through the pin.

She recalled that day when she visited Marty. Her daughter told her in no uncertain terms that she intended to go through life putting her carnal pleasures first. Perhaps she should have slapped her daughter then. Perhaps she should have upbraided her, yanked her out of WEX School, and immediately taken her home to Colorado. That's what a good, righteous mother would have done. But how could *she* do that? Susan knew she had no moral authority. How could she lecture Marty about morality when she had put her own desires first, throughout her entire life?

'Later, when Marty worked as a prostitute out of the Firm's offices, why didn't I try to stop her?' Susan wondered:

'Could I have had any influence on my grown daughter at that point?' Probably not, Susan had reasoned at the time. Now she realized how true that was. Marty would have just worked her tricks out of some other business. Only a loving mother could wonder these thoughts about her daughter's life, second guessing herself in such ways.

At least with Marty at the Firm, Susan could know whom she was seeing, based on the expense and sales reports. When Carl's wife made the news with her suicide, it saddened Susan; but it didn't surprise her. Marty was capable of wreaking havoc in others' marriages, and her daughter never shied from confrontations with hostile wives. Susan only hoped some crazed wife wouldn't kill Marty or hire someone to do it. She told Marty to try to keep things on the light side and not to try to separate women from their husbands. She, herself, was never as brazen as her daughter in her own efforts to subvert Eloweiss. Caution was the only advice she had the moral authority to give Marty during her years at the Firm, but Marty paid no heed to Susan.

'Maybe Marty felt she needed to one-up me,' thought Susan. *Maybe that's what sent her into the dark region of malicious intent and her quest to wreck others' marriages. Maybe she saw the same things in me. Maybe she figured out that it was my behavior that drove Joseph to suicide. Maybe she was trying to prove to me that she could get some man's spouse to commit suicide also.'*

Those maddening thoughts resounded through Susan's mind again and again, until she became obsessed with them. Nothing she could do now could bring Marty back. But perhaps she could finally be an honorable mother to her now presumed-dead daughter. She could find out what happened to Marty and have some sense of honor and decency befitting her little girl, whom she had loved so dearly and now missed so terribly.

'What happened to my little Marty?' That question dogged Susan every day and sleepless night for the past year and a half. Even with their relationship strains, Marty always called Susan on her birthday and on Mother's Day. She always sent a Christmas card; always called the week before the Mass of Saint Cecilia, to see whether they could attend together. Susan knew her daughter loved her deeply despite her shortcomings as a mother. Marty always wanted to have a closer relationship than Susan would permit. These thoughts left her heartbroken now. Susan convinced herself that Marty had been taken to some faraway place by her Savior. She believed her child finally found peace with God. She intuited that Marty had not run away on some fling, as David wanted everyone to believe.

Susan took to prayers in these dark times, something she had not done in years. She often sat in her office and prayed her Rosary.

This day she prayed fervently. Her prayers were now deeply felt and sincerely spoken. They held a conviction that they would be heard now; faith that the rote prayers she recited as a child never had. But then, she reflected:

'*What can children know about life? How can a child or young woman know the pitfalls, the trials, the sufferings, and the pains of life?*' She prayed that Marty, in her final moments, had found some measure of peace. Marty was gone for good. Likely, she was dead. Deeply within her gut, Susan believed that with certainty.

Now she patiently waited for the silent blinking light under her desk, indicating an incoming call on her private line; the line that no one, not even David or Barbara, knew she had. David was gone from the office. He had left about an hour after the markets closed. John, her dutiful friend, and trusted lover, told her the laboratory would call her after five. They knew they were making a delicate and confidential inquiry. Susan paid extra for the secrecy. When the light blinked, she lifted the receiver from under her desk. "*This is she.*"

"*This is your report,*" said the caller.

"*And where are you calling from?*" asked Susan.

"*It's a local landline call, from the Cow and Steer Hotel's Travel Agency.*" answered the caller.

"*Verify the work order, please.*" commanded Susan.

"*It's from Lab Termanspeil, Neumuehlequai, Zurich, 8006. Order 3PLR34.*" responded the caller.

"*Take it to the UPS box in the basement of the Western Bank building,*" ordered Susan. "*At exactly six o'clock, drop the envelope with the report inside it on the floor in front of the box and leave the building without looking back.*"

"*Understood.*" said the caller.

At the appointed time, Susan waited inconspicuously around the corner of the bank's basement corridor. She heard the drop and waited until the messenger entered the elevator and she heard the elevator doors close behind him. Picking up the report, she went straight home. She sat on her reading chair and held the envelope for a long moment before she opened it. Hopefully her suspicions would be proven wrong. The report looked very thorough, very official in appearance. It was the sort of report one would expect a top Interpol crime lab to create for a homicide detective.

Her lips quivered as she read the analysis aloud:

"Both of the hair samples were reviewed by microscopic spectrometry, which indicated they were from the same species: Human, Caucasian. The DNA comparison of the two samples revealed a match correlation of 99.9999 percent. Based upon microscopic spectrometry and DNA analysis, the two samples are from the identical source with probable certainty of 99.9999 percent."

Susan now knew what she'd dreaded acknowledging. The hair from the fox picture in Bob's office and Marty's hair sample she'd supplied to the lab from the cutting she kept in a locket with Marty's childhood picture, were identical hair. That meant Marty had to have been in David's barn sometime between the time Bob last saw her and when he found the scalp cut with her hair attached. Susan's focus narrowed. How could Marty's scalp and hair have gotten into David's barn?

Susan was no fool. She was David's babysitter for years. She remembered him as a precocious child. She knew he was capable of wrongdoings to animals, especially insects, but was it a logical extension to believe he could have harmed Marty? She wondered:

'Did David figure out that Marty was his half sister? Would that have mattered to David if he had figured that out? Would he have been that vindictive toward me and Marvin that he would have taken Marty's life?'

Susan suspected that David was capable of committing murder. He was a devious monster; always conniving; always slipping away; always hiding from the truth; always doing bad things for no other discernable reason, other than because he could get away with doing them. He always tried to get people to pity him. And he then used their pity as a ruse to gain their confidence and take advantage of them. That was his predictable pattern. She remembered thinking when he was a child that he would be a strong competitor for Hitler, if David ever managed to get an army behind him. Fortunately, he could only wreak his havoc in the corporate dictatorship that Marvin had set up for him. Susan now had a firm foundation upon which to base her suspicions. She knew she was likely dealing with a murderer. She also knew that David was both secretive and ruthless. She proceeded with caution.

Susan thought hard to recall those times she'd been at David's. She tried to remember everything she could about each visit. Details suddenly mattered:

'What was there to focus on? Where the cars were parked? How many people were at the parties? What did Marty do at the parties? Whom did Marty talk to? What food was served?'

It was all a blur. Susan needed to focus, but focus on what, exactly? She made herself a Gibson, sipped it slowly and tried to relax. She believed she was on the right track, but she needed to be certain. Heading to bed, she lay there, looking at the ceiling. Nothing came to her. Life was like that for her, night after night, for the next vexatious week:

'How was it that only Marty's streak of red hair ended up in David's barn? Why not any of her black hair?'

The mind can be a peculiar companion. When it's given a problem that has it stymied, it places that problem into a kind of storage. It seals it up in a figurative mouse jar, of sorts, until it's prompted to recall the problem and resume its deliberations. It was ten days since Susan first pondered the question of how

Marty's red hair scalp had found its way into the corner of David's barn. Foul play could not be ruled out or in, without a theory.

Susan's mind was in this mental straight-jacket, when John, now her weekly dinner date, suggested they dine at the Ritz Chateau that Saturday evening. His wife had passed since the days when he controlled the union pension plan. His dinner dates with Susan were the high point of his week. He showed his appreciation by always taking her to the finest dining rooms in the city. They'd finished cocktails, discussed the play, and ordered wine. Susan ordered flounder for her entrée. John often ordered whatever she ordered; but this evening he chose lamb chops. As he closed his menu book, he remarked that the way they prepared lamb chops at the Chateau made for the best meal in Plaintown. When the entrées arrived, Susan had order envy. John's chops looked absolutely succulent.

"Maybe I should have ordered the lamb chops as well! They look delicious."

Susan's mental mouse jar flew open, Her mental mouse scrambled out. Susan first stared at John's chops.

'*Yes, they Do mean something!*' Her mind raced. She knew she was on to something. Then she stared at John's tie.

'*No, it's not the tie. It's not John. It's not anything about John!*' Her mind assured her that this was the right track to follow. She stared back at the chops.

'*It's the lamb chops! Yes! The lamb chops are the key to all of it!*' Her mind flooded with its revelation.

Then Susan looked up. She stared, dumbstruck, into her dinner partner's eyes.

"*John, give me a moment, won't you, dear? I need to think. Something just came to me.*"

John, affable as always, replied, "*Sure, babe. Take your time.*"

He looked away at the tables around him and sipped his cabernet. All the while, Susan's mind raced over observations she had made in years past. At David's parties, he sometimes served lamb chops or leg of mutton to his guests! She recalled one particular occasion, about three years past, when she had dropped off some filings that needed David's signature. He was going on one of his 'hunts,' but the government filing deadline was that afternoon.

After she got David's signatures, she paused for a moment on the driveway next to the barnyard to count the sheep. She had no reason to do that, other than idle curiosity, before she drove downtown. There was the omnipresent black sheep. Dolly. There were also seven white ewes and one white ram. It was in the fall; she was sure of it. Her filing deadline was September 30th. David was going to Texas on one of his luxury hunts for an Ibex.

The following spring, at David's Memorial Day office party, lamb chops and leg of mutton were served. Staring at John's lamb chops she now recalled that there were fewer sheep in the barnyard on Memorial Day than the prior fall. Instead of the seven ewes she counted in the fall, there were then only four ewes and the ram—and of course Dolly, the black sheep.

David received many compliments about the meat selection that spring day. But no one, including Susan, asked where the meat came from. She was the only staffer who made occasional trips to the house; at least that's what she believed back then. Thus, no other employee would have noticed that three ewes were missing. At the time of the Memorial Day party, Susan assumed that David had sent the three off, to be sold. Now a nagging doubt overshadowed her prior assumption.

"You're off to a faraway place, and very deep in thought, sweetheart." John gently brought Susan back to the dinner they were sharing.

"Sorry, dear. It's just one of those moments where I thought I forgot to do something important at the office."

But her thoughts were indeed off in faraway places and times. She could tell white lies to John. He knew she did it, often. He really didn't care. He had become like an old faithful dog, always there for her; always eager to please her. That night while she bedded him in her comfortable maiden position, she looked up at the ceiling, and back into her past. Then, next to John, she fell asleep.

The next afternoon, she was again sitting in her office. Her thoughts raced through time; through all the actors she knew on a time-traveled stage. Before her mind passed Marvin, her beloved; Joseph, her betrothed; Marty, her great failure and heartache; and David with his boy-toy harem playmates she'd been tolerating these last few years. She was smoking an occasional panatela cigar, while alternately staring at the portrait of Marvin and the butterfly pin which Marty had given her, wondering how life passes one by, so quickly.

CHAPTER SIX

Its horror and its beauty are divine (Mary Wollstonecraft Shelly: The Medusa of Leonardo Da Vinci)

You have no idea what you just have unleashed (words spoken by Ericka Kirk after the murder of her husband, Charles Kirk)

CHAIN FALL

Susan came to the office the following Monday with a sense of purpose she hadn't felt in years. The firm had been drifting listlessly for months. David was embroiled in litigation, often away in conferences with his lawyers. Barbara had run off to join forces with Bob. The departure of those two had taken the wind from everyone's sails. Bob and Barbara were the energy of the place. Everyone liked them. But David now told everyone they needed to hate them. *"They are the enemy,"* he announced. *"They are traitors to the Firm, to me; and to all you other employees,"* he proclaimed. Susan chuckled silently to herself when she found out that Bob had won the U.S. Supreme Court decision.

David knew he'd lost that day, long before the decision was handed down. He was in his office that afternoon, screaming at Susan's staff girls for failing to keep his desk cleaned off and his papers properly filed. He always had some difficulty with the men's bathroom door. It had become warped from age and humidity. For decades David, and all other men who used the facility, simply gave the door a slight increase in force to open it, but not this day.

David kicked at the door and continued kicking it. After repeated kicking, David finally succeeded in destroying the beautiful fruitwood-paneled door. He went to Mrs. Rodriguez and ordered her to call building maintenance and have the door properly repaired so it no longer stuck. He chastised her for not calling them years before.

"Make sure you tell them to shave that door down so it no longer warps in its frame. And tell them to search for identical replacement paneling," he barked.

Susan noted that David was still the little boy she used to babysit. He was still behaving the same ways; only now he wasn't tearing wings from helpless flies; or tearing legs from ants. He was bullying poor Mrs. Rodriguez, a woman with leg burns injuries and a handicapped husband. David was always eager to inflict his miseries upon the most helpless beings of this world. Some things and some people, Susan reflected, never change.

But this latest adult version of David was more dangerous to people than the David she knew as a little boy. Marvin must have seen that evil quality in his son. That explained why Marvin created an unofficial unaffiliated advisory board to continue watching over the firm, and David, after Marvin's death. Marvin structured the firm's service contracts to leave Susan to watch out for David, putting her in the position to try, always, to make sure the businesses continued to obey all the regulations and laws after Marvin died. Marvin also deeded the mineral rights in all his properties to Susan's wholly owned service company. He took great pains to have the duck ponds dug on the ranch house property. He had six-foot-deep casements excavated below the bottoms of the ponds. He placed the jewels, and their twelve notebooks of ownership histories into sealed, steel boxes and covered the boxes with fill dirt. He had a protective rubber covering placed over the fill dirt.

Then he opened the water well and filled the ponds. He deeded the property's surface rights to David.

This structure tied Susan to David. She knew all about the jewels, but she could not get them without disclosing to David that she needed to drain the duck ponds. David had some knowledge of the jewels; but he had no idea of the extent of Marvin's holdings. He only knew of the small ten percent portion of them that Marvin had given to Eloweiss. Susan understood why Marvin made her a lifetime fixture at the Firm and why she had control over the mineral rights where the jewels were safely stored.

After Marvin's death, he wanted to be certain David would stay on track with the law and the regulators. He wanted Susan tied to David through his scheme to store the jewels. He knew that Susan would need to make a deal with David to get them. Likely, that would come late in her life, She'd want them for her estate and would likely leave them in place until near her death, unless David predeceased her. Marvin controlled both Susan and David from his grave.

Susan fully understood Marvin's wishes now. She would always be true and obedient to Marvin, even after his death. Susan owed the love of her life that much and she forgave Marvin for making her carry her unsavory burden. But today she wanted to understand the depths of David's treachery.

Muscle Boy was the likely suspect for Susan's inquiry, but she needed to be discreet about confirming her suspicions. He was seated at his office drawing board. His woefully small intellect was now in its third year of trying to create a new Firm logo design, when Susan walked into his office unannounced. When Susan saw his latest logo rendition, which looked like a flying saucer being struck by lightning, both from above and below, she could barely keep a straight face.

"Good morning, Muscles," Susan began cheerfully, trying to dispel the natural antagonism Muscles felt toward all women. *"I'm in a bit of a jam and I don't know where else I could turn to for help. I'm going to be hosting a party for my women's executive club ladies and I wanted to serve a sumptuous dinner of lamb chops and leg of lamb. I remember that party at David's a few years back, when lamb was served. I didn't want to trouble him with this, but maybe you could be kind enough to tell me which butcher shop supplied the meat?"*

Susan had the most imploring look of sincerity Muscle Boy had ever seen on a woman's face. Ordinarily he would have told Susan to stop bothering him because he was concentrating on getting his logo's lightning bolts properly angled, but seeing her sincerity, he allowed the female organization to pierce his male force shield just this one time.

"Why, Ms. Mallory, David didn't use a butcher for that. I did it," he said proudly.

"You, did it? What did you do, Muscles? Did you go fetch the meat?" Susan's query was most sincere.

"No!" Muscle Boy was getting ruffled. *"I butchered the sheep for the dinner."* His reply intoned a measure of self-importance.

"Really!" Susan put her hand over her heart in amazement. *"I had no idea you were such a tremendous talent, Muscles. I should have made good friends with you long ago! Tell me, where did you do the butchering?"* Her eyes widened. She was on the trail of her missing daughter. She could sense it.

"Why, I butchered three of David's sheep in the barn at David's farm." Muscle Boy was suddenly friendlier. Rarely did anyone ever pay him a compliment. David never did.

"Good heavens! How did you do that?" Susan feigned disbelief. *"I've heard they're pretty strong animals. How did you hold them down while you cut them up? How did you get them to stand still for*

that?" Susan was wily. She projected honest curiosity about Muscle Boy's talents.

"Oh no, Ms. Mallory, I strung them up and killed them kosher style," he beamed. *"David showed me how the rabbis kill kosher. He uses me to do it because he doesn't like paying a rabbi to do it. I didn't do any blessings on them though. I just cut their throats and let them bleed out before I cut the guts out of them."*

"Well, you must be very strong to do that. Did you hold them up with one hand while you slit their throats? You do amaze me, Muscles." Susan looked as if she was in awe of the cretin, but she was only playacting.

"No, ma'am. You don't understand. I grab their back legs and tie them up first. Then I lift them up with the chain fall." Muscle Boy was eager to tell all.

"Really?" Susan was fascinated. *"What's a chain fall?"*

"It's a long chain on a block of double pulleys, ma'am," he explained proudly. *"David keeps it in the barn, in his tool shed in the back corner. I hook it up to the big hook on the top rafter of the barn and hook the bottom hook to the rope that ties the sheep's back legs together. When I pull on the chain, it's easy to lift a sheep up in the air."*

"Oh, I bet you're just saying that. You're very strong, aren't you?" teased Susan.

"Yes, I am very strong. But no, ma'am," Muscle Boy shook his head. *"I'm not just saying that. Using that pulley, even a weak man like David, or even a child, could easily hoist up a fully grown Angus bull."*

"You don't say. Have you ever seen David hoist anything with it?" Susan continued to probe.

"Oh yes, ma'am. He's hoisted up a big sheep. It was a three-hundred-pound ram. He hoisted it up so I could sheer it for its wool. He hoisted that big one up before I got there."

"Well, I guess I won't be getting my chops at David's," said Susan. *"I wouldn't want one of his sheep to die for my sake. I think I'll just go to a butcher shop. Thank you, Muscles."* As she started to leave, Susan turned back to her new information source. *"Tell me. What on earth do you do with the parts of the sheep that can't be eaten after you butcher one of them?"* Susan posed her afterthought as a mere natural curiosity.

"Well, first we sheer the sheep while she's hanging upside down," answered Muscle Boy. *"That way David doesn't waste any wool. He sells the wool to some lady who comes around every year. She exchanges knitted socks and scarves for the wool. But the gut piles David feeds to his pigs and the bones and skulls go through his wood chipper several times until they're just fine bone chips. He uses those to fertilize his vegetable garden and rose beds. He turns the chips into the ground, mixed in with his compost from his compost pile."*

"I see. Well, I'll run along now, Muscles," said Susan while trying to mask her horror. *"Thank you for all that. Now I know I'll go to a butcher for my meat. I couldn't bear the thought of hurting one of those darling ewes. They are all so, so cute."* Susan acted the part of a squeamish little girl and turned away.

Muscle Boy returned to his logo quest, thinking that Susan was kind of okay for a woman; but that she acted overly girly.

Susan left Muscle Boy to his drawing board and walked slowly back to her own office, trying hard not to throw up. The thought of her beloved child, Marty, being butchered by David, flooded her constitution with revulsion, remorse, and despondency:

'What did my poor darling child feel while hanging there, upside down?'What thoughts, what terrible turmoil did my poor, innocent child suffer? What did she do to deserve such a horrible end?' Susan felt agony.

Susan knew Marty busted up some marriages, but marriages that were too fragile to withstand a little whoring weren't worth being marriages in the first place, she silently opined. In her mind Marty was always honest innocence and virginal purity. Her adorable daughter was as uncontaminated by immorality as freshly driven snow. All the men who whored with her daughter did so with their eyes wide open. They were at least equal in fault.

'And David! What about him? Why would he do such a thing? Had he discovered Marty was his half-sister? What were the chances of that? Surely, Marvin never told him. I know I certainly didn't. Marty never knew who her real father was. I never told her. Maybe David had a different reason for murdering her. Did he murder her as a favor to some broker's estranged wife? What on Earth was David's reason?' She was completely in the dark about David's motive for murder.

When it rains, it pours! Connections in Susan's mind now came together rapidly. The answers began coming like pitter-patter rain drops; a few at first, then more connections, coming faster and faster. She finally saw it!

'David wanted Bob for his lover! In David's mind Bob was David's property. He saw Bob as his boy toy! He didn't want anyone else to play with him. That stupid, arrogant little bastard! Bob was totally straight. He did not have a homosexual bone in his body. He could never be made into a gay person. Bob loved women. He loved my Marty. Marty got in David's way. She had to be murdered so David could have his chance with Bob. That explained the fishing trips, the antelope hunt, and it explained the destroyed Jeep! Bob must have rejected David! He refused to become one of David's pathetic fuck-buddies.'

Gay men are no different than straight men when dealing with rejection. Some handle it well, some not very well at all. Rejected in love, David took out his frustration, first on the Jeep; then on Marty. David acted out behaviors like a child in a sandbox who can't have his way. He took his toys away. He systematically took away everything and everyone he had given Bob. He took away Barbara when he saw that Bob and Barbara could strike out on their own. He took away Marty when he saw Bob falling in love with her. Out of rejection anger, he took away the Jeep by destroying it; and he took away the good portfolio performance that enabled sales to build the Firm. He took away all those things to capture or punish Bob. Finally, he decided to take away their deal and the Firm, with all is assets, and keep everything for himself.

'*That devious little prick probably showed Bob the codicil I witnessed; then destroyed it afterwards,*' reflected Susan during one of her insightful moments.

David's behavior fit! Marty's death was a revenge play to destroy Bob's life. If he couldn't have Bob, then Bob couldn't have a life without him. That had to be the operative theory. Everything suddenly made sense! Susan noticed that David had stopped spending time with Bob. He only played with his gay employees now. Their commonality was that they were all women-hating creeps. David had picked them up off the streets, gay clubs, or bathhouses. He was a vengeful, lonely man who'd scraped the barrel bottom of male partnership choices. And he still lived his childhood play times with Hirsh.

Yes! Now Susan understood why Barbara left after the lawsuit commenced. It started out as business for her, but became much more. Barbara saw that, with Marty gone and Bob on his own, she finally had her chance to become Bob's partner on her own terms. Susan knew people well. She felt distinct vibrations from Barbara whenever Bob was around. But Barbara was always discreet. The Indian Princess was very careful to hide her feelings. Susan suspected, but she could never be certain.

If Marty had lived, Bob would still be at the Firm. Barbara would still be her assistant. Susan's life and chore load would be much easier than it was presently. But David's jealousy had caused him to do terrible things, including murder. Now Barbara was gone, too. Susan had long ago thought of Barbara as her second daughter. She was brilliant, diligent, ethical, honest, wise, and dependable. Susan missed her terribly. She decided she needed to let Barbara know that she fully supported her decision to join forces with Bob.

Susan gazed at her blazer hanging on the back of her door. Marty's beautiful butterfly pin over its right pocket seemed to come alive and flutter. It symbolized so many things now. And it connected her to many memories.

CHAPTER SEVEN

This country exists as the fulfillment of a promise made by God himself. It would be ridiculous to ask it to account for its legitimacy (Golda Meir)

ISRAEL'S SIDE

David sat in a conference room chair in his lawyer's office. He was absorbed in his thoughts; reflecting, strategizing, contemplating the antics of his antagonist; planning and mentally rehearsing his own responses. Long gone were the years before when the litigation first commenced. Then, he was flush with confidence that he would crush Bob and Sol. He'd hired the most reputable and most expensive law firms in the city. He'd trusted their advice. They had the plush offices, the deep blue and red carpeting, and the chrome and brass railings on their opulent staircases. They showed off their impressive quarters, their panoramic views from the Rockies, all the way around to the east, seeing as far as Kansas. Their trappings gave David confidence. He had assured himself:

'These high-powered firms know how to fuck over pathetic little people.'

And, why shouldn't he have believed them? There was the Statute of Wills. He had the right to change his will. Repeatedly, they all had assured him that he was in the right:

'Money-thieving bastards! They said it was just a simple quantum meruit case, payment owed for work done. They assured me

that the case wasn't about the deal I made. It was about the comparable cost to get a salesman to do the same work that Bob did. They said they were ninety nine percent certain of their position. They'd looked at hundreds of precedent cases and they charged him plenty for all that research work. Fucking pricks! Cocksuckers! They advised me to never settle at the outset; never told me to write Bob a check and part as amicable as possible.'

But they frequently reminded him, he had told them he wanted the most aggressive defense they could possibly mount. He told them that settlement before discovery was completed was not an option. He had demanded a ferocious counterattack, complete with sketchy counterclaims. He looked back on all of it now. He was losing. He lost in the Supreme Court. He felt more like a jilted lover than a businessman.

The lawyers he hired had played off court as he'd instructed them. To buy time and delay, they moved move the goal posts on Bob so he couldn't get closer to relief. David changed his major law firm in charge of the case, not once or twice, but now for the fourth time. Each change bought him a good three months' time, or more. But the cost to destroy Bob was now running over three million Dollars; and he had not yet achieved the younger man's destruction. Success eluded him. Bob did not break.

Try as he might, David was unable to crack the key to the success of Bob's firm. How could a no-name upstart, without clients, staffed by a man embroiled in litigation, with no money and a quiet, skinny Native American girl as partner and secretary, possibly survive in the competitive investment business? David tried twice to use a trumped-up excuse to get a court order that would allow him to see Bob's books and records. Unfortunately, he couldn't prove that he had a silent enemy hiding in the weeds, backing Bob's litigation. He had no evidence of that, but he suspected it. But twice Barbara had filed for protective orders to block his demands for discovery and twice the courts granted her order. He was furious. The skinny little Indian bitch was outsmarting him. He was unable to find any dirt on Bob, or Barbara, or their business. He was getting nowhere with his secret enemy idea.

David kicked one of his dogs the night his lawyer told him he needed to drop the idea of harassing Bob's firm. He was told Bob or Barbara could file harassment charges if he persisted. David hated feeling stymied. He tried to find out more about Barbara; her parentage; her family's wealth and connections. He learned she was the daughter of some Indian chief. But that fact had no significance to David. Susan told him she didn't know anything about her. That surprised David. Ordinarily Susan could rattle off all sorts of information about any of her staff employees, but she was strangely silent about Barbara. All he could pry out of Susan was that Barbara was extremely bright and very competent, a very diligent worker who never talked about herself or her background. She didn't smoke or drink. That made sense for an Indian, he figured. She knew all the Firm's corporate evolutions, understood the Investment Advisor's Act, the Investment Company Act, the Securities Act, the Securities Distribution act, and all the pertinent rules that were promulgated by all regulatory agencies under those acts. She was diligent at keeping up with changing regulations, and she was so savvy at reading the government agencies' requests for comments that she could actually anticipate regulatory changes before they were promulgated. That skill was a tremendous advantage for any firm to have. Now Bob had her skills. And he didn't.

He knew she was a trusted resource that Susan sorely missed, but why in the world had she left his firm to join Bob? She was paid well enough to have a modest living and she was given time off whenever she needed it. David couldn't imagine that Barbara saw Bob's firm as her once-in-a-lifetime opportunity. He had no idea that her family had money, political power, and staying power. All he knew was that her father lived on some Indian reservation, but that meant nothing to David. He imagined her father fishing and hunting, chanting, and dancing while pounding on a drum, and weaving baskets or making silver jewelry; nothing more. As far as David was concerned, Indians were total losers; a defeated people, doomed to poverty and misery.

For David, business boiled down to the personal. Either Barbara was holding a grudge against him for the time he shoved his hands down her blouse and squeezed her breasts, or else Bob had been secretly fucking her all the time she was working at David's firm. But that would be impossible because Marty was fucking Bob practically every night, non-stop; and Marty drew so much energy from a man he couldn't possibly have strength enough left to fuck a second woman. David wondered if Barbara was fucking Bob, now that she'd left the firm. He reasoned those probabilities unlikely because she was always very reserved and businesslike; and Bob was always selling. Besides, Barbara was an Indian. Daviid reasoned that Indians tended to stick to their own kind.

The question that vexed David remained. Why did Barbara leave his firm? His paranoia landed on anti-Semitism:

'It has to be either that Barbara secretly hates me because of my playful tit-squeezing incident, or because she simply hates Jews.'

David whittled his reasoning down to his belief that Barbara hated all Jews:

'The way I see it, all women secretly love having their tits squeezed and having their pussies grabbed. They only pretend that they didn't like it, but in fact, they actually love the attention. That's how they know that men are interested in them. So, it has to be the Jewish thing. But then again, it is remotely possible that the prim, studious Indian girl has wanted to get Bob into her teepee, all along.'

David couldn't quite put all the pieces together and eventually gave up trying, chalking up Barbara's decision to just another case of a stupid woman thinking with her vagina instead of with her brains. Nothing else made sense to David. He couldn't comprehend that anyone would be repulsed by his unethical personal conduct.

Bob lived in David's head. The very thought of Bob made David scream out loud. Occasionally he just erupted in screams when he sat alone in his office. He forbade any of the office staff from speaking Bob's name. All letterhead with Bob's name on it was destroyed. If anyone on staff heard Bob's name spoken, the speaker was to be reported immediately to David and that offense was grounds for dismissal. David personally destroyed all the furniture in Bob's office. He smashed it with a hatchet; had it broken up and sawed into pieces, taken to his barnyard, doused in gasoline, and burned. David had paid handsomely to obtain that furniture from the finest furniture store in Plaintown. Didn't matter now. It was contaminated.

Bob's former office was locked. Yellow crime scene tape was strung in dramatic fashion across the door in a forbidden, oversized X. To propagandize his position, David instructed that all visitors be told Bob's former office was still an active crime scene, although the space had long been stripped of its contents and his dispute with Bob was strictly a civil; not a criminal matter. These theatrics were David's way of rewriting history; to generate false rumors by lying to hapless visitors. He demanded that his staff, if not the courts and the real world beyond the Firm, see the world the same way he saw it.

David was still haunted by thoughts of Bob:

'Why has Bob rejected me, after all I've done for him? What could he possibly get from a woman that I couldn't provide? If Bob had to have a woman, why couldn't he also allow me into his love

life as a male companion? I've offered Bob friendship, love, wealth, status, and all the benefits of my priceless wisdom; yet Bob still rejected me!'

David's heart ached from his alienation from Bob. He worked to replace the ache with relentless fury and his quest for vengeance. Bob was now a man who knew Judaism, its rituals, and holidays, even much better than David knew Judaism. He even spoke and read Hebrew, something David had never troubled to master. After his Bar Mitzvah, David had quickly forgotten what little Hebrew he had absorbed in religious school.

'Bob was, in many respects, a perfect son. I coached him to always see a fight through to the end; to think the way the enemy thinks; to take over companies; wage proxy fights; gain control of corporate boards; all of it. Now Bob is fighting me to the death. He and his lawyer, Sol, are fighting me like the Jews of Masada fought the Romans to the bitter end.'

Through all the legal pounding and harassment David threw at him, Bob was not giving up. It really had become a fight to the death; or at least a fight to the demise of one or the other's corporations.

David remembered telling Bob that every good Jew loved a good fight, especially when it was against another Jew. Now his protégé was taking David's lessons literally. Ben had told David that Bob would fight him until hell froze over; and then he would fight him on the ice, rather than settle with him. These were the same determined words David's lawyers told him that Sol had said when the idea of a settlement had been broached. Ben told David's lawyers that Bob no longer regarded David as a father figure; but as a no-good son of a bitch. Ben had passed along that tidbit in no uncertain terms. Ben told David's attorneys that there was no way Bob was going to pass this off as a simple misunderstanding. David was appalled. Bob had taken on the same tenacious determination that David had taught him; and that David saw in his own father, Marvin.

This past night, David had a terrible dream. The image of his father, Marvin, had appeared to him. David dreamed he was sitting on the edge of his bed, like he did when he was a child and when his father came into his room to talk with him before he went to sleep. In the dream, Marvin was sitting in the bedroom chair. The chair itself held great significance. It was the inanimate repository of generations of family tribulations and history. Marvin brought it with him to Plaintown from Chicago. It was the only piece of furniture Marvin took with him when he pulled up roots and traveled west. The chair had been Marvin's father's chair. Many days Marvin learned wisdom at the hand of his own father, who sat in that very chair in their Chicago home's family study.

The chair was the only piece of furniture that Marvin's great, great grandfather's father brought with him to America when he escaped the pogrom of his village in Russia. The Old Russian was the rabbi of their village. In the Tsar's spiteful holocaust, seven members of his dependable minyan followers were murdered, along with many others in the village. Days later, the three survivors found each other in the forest. They wailed and lamented their losses. They agreed they should wait until the Tzar's troops left. Then they would scatter. Each man should find his own way out of Russia. At nightfall, days after the Tsar's soldiers departed, they decided it was safe to return to the rubble of their burned village and scavenge what possessions they could before they departed their homes forever. The old rabbi had lost his wife, his brothers and sisters, his home, and his oldest son. When he returned to the charred ruins of his former home, he discovered his youngest son, Marvin's fifth generation ancestor. The lad had miraculously survived. Amidst the rubble he discovered his favorite sitting chair was still usable. It had some fire chars on one of its legs, but its frame, seat and cloth covering were unscathed.

As chairs go there was nothing remarkable about it, except it had rising side posts that bordered the padded headrest, and its backrest leaned back slightly at an angle that made it perfect and comfortable for the old man when he sat in it. Then, to the old rabbi's great joy, he discovered the family's parchment torah scrolls, untouched by the fire, in their metal cabinet.

'*The heathen have no use for God, or for wisdom,*' thought the old man to himself.

The old man scavenged a few leather straps from the rubble of a neighbor's home, and then fastened his torah case with its precious scrolls to his chair. He secured his few personal belongings to the chair, strapped the chair to his son's back, and told the boy he needed to leave Russia. The old rabbi died a few days later. His son, Marvin's ancestor, walked seven hundred eighty-nine miles out of Russia, to freedom in Austria.

David knew the story of the old rabbi and his son well. Every generation of Sustack passed the story down faithfully to the children of the next generation to follow; and with each telling of the story, the old rabbi's son's journey became ten or twenty miles longer than it was for the generation before. Marvin kept the chair at his rental property for many years. Sometimes he sat in the chair and contemplated his family heritage and the wisdom that his ancestors had dispensed to family members while sitting in the chair. Marvin loved that chair. He treasured it for its symbolism of integrity, family loyalty, and unshakable faith in God. But then, Marvin fell in love with Susan.

For months Marvin and Susan made love in his rental home, in his bedroom, right there in front of the family chair. After each time he made love with Susan, Marvin looked at the chair. The chair made Marvin feel guilty. Never before, to the best of his knowledge, had any of his ancestors made love outside of their marriage to a woman who was not a Jewess. Oh, there were plenty of tales about affairs that went on among members of the faith; but none that he knew about had ever happened with a woman who was not a member of the tribe. Adulterous love making session followed adulterous love making session before that wise old chair, and after each session Marvin's guilt grew stronger. He could almost imagine the words of his ancestral rabbi admonishing him not to commit adultery. He was vexed by his dilemma. Finally, one evening, after he had made love with Susan and driven her to her home, Marvin returned to his rental home and sat on the bed where he had just committed adultery. For hours he sat and stared at the chair, seeking its wisdom and some resolution to his moral conundrum.

"What must I do?" Marvin asked the chair, as if it could give him an answer. *"I can not be honorable in your eyes and also make love with her, here before your eyes. You haunt my thoughts with guilt. I drown in Jewish guilt because you serve as a constant reminder to me of who I am and where I came from; and of all the anguish we have suffered as a people. My loyalty to the tribe is without question. I am a pillar of our community now, just like the old rabbi was a pillar of his community. I know I should give her up and return all my love and affections to Eloweiss. But, dear old chair, dear source of all my guilt, I can not do that. I can not love Eloweiss as a woman, but only as a good and loyal friend. She has born me a son after her great suffering to deliver him. She's done more than our families ever agreed she would do to seal our marriage bargain. So, my guilt is heavy. I do not know honest love for her; but I have searched my heart, dear chair, and I know I will never love Eloweiss.*

"But I know that I can only love Susan. Oh, my dear God and my dear family chair, please try to understand. I must have Susan. I must hold her in my arms as she holds me in her arms and I must

love her. I would descend into madness if I could not have her and love her. She is a most glorious, marvelous whore. I know she is a whore. I have made her into one. But I adore her. I love her as a woman and as a whore; a most glorious unrepentant whore. My soul knows rapture when I am with her. I cannot help myself. I have built my world around her. I love her more than mere carnal love. I even love her thoughts and her questions. I love the way she's able to raise herself above her religion and all her own moral teachings to love me in return.

"We are as husband and wife in our own conceptual way, old chair. I have pimped Susan to our largest client prospects and she has complied with my request. Are we not like Abram and Sarai, when he asked her to pretend to be only his sister and not disclose that she was also his wife; and cause her to go and make love with Pharaoh in order that Abram might survive and prosper? Perhaps we are much the same, old chair. Consider that we may be the start of something, like Abram and Sarai once were.

"I love that Susan is willing to joyfully prostitute herself in order to do what needs to be done in order for our business to thrive and prosper. Yes, our business, old chair. I have effectively given her half of everything. By becoming my willing and loving whore, she has drawn our loves even closer together. We are as inseparable as Abram and Sarai were and as committed to our cause as they were to the cause of the Tribe of Israel. You must understand me, dear chair. I adore Susan. She is woman; all woman. I adore her immoral ways. I adore the ground she walks over, and the air she breathes. I adore the scent of her, the divine tastes of her sex, and the touching of her. I love to lie naked beside her with my head upon her breast and her head upon mine. We are as one, dear old chair. I love her body, her mind, and her soul, and I will love her forever. If I was forced to choose, I would gladly give up my life for her. I love her unconditionally.

"And so, dear family chair and source of my feelings of guilt for loving what is so beautiful and natural, I have decided a decision that you may not like; but I have made it. You must go away from my presence, dear chair. No longer will I hear you heralding to me, from your voiceless hardened woods, your admonitions of faith and loyalty to the tribe. No more, chair, no more! Did not Abram himself have ancestors and traditions? Did he not do what he had to do? Am I less a man than any other man, patriarch or not?"

A feeling of unease and anger welled up within Marvin. Dare he condemn the chair and all the traditions it represented? Dare he turn his back on his ancestors? Would any of his paternal lineages have married a Shiksa, even as an office wife, and placed their love of such a woman above their love of wife and son? Never! No, they would only sneak away and see their Shiksas in the dark of night; give them little token gifts. But they would never openly cavort with them, flaunt them to all their friends in their daily lives. No, they would not soil their wives and marriages with such wanton displays. Conflict within Marvin made him tremble as he stared at the chair. Where would he place his loyalty? What was loyalty anyway? He wrestled with these questions until he came to the realization that there was a force at work within him that was stronger than any other. It was love! Love was in his blood. It was a stronger force than any he had ever known. He could fight against it; but he could not win. Love was much stronger than his traditions. Love would win.

"I am a man! Damn you, old chair!" Marvin confronted the chair and shouted at it. *"I will not feel one shred of guilt while I make the sweetest love with the only woman I can love. Have you ever been in love, old chair? Have you ever tasted its wonders? Has your heart ever opened with joy at the sight of your lover? No, of course it hasn't! You are only a piece of wood! You don't know the delicious joy of her sex over your mouth, opened for your tongue, do*

you? Of course, you don't! You can only dream of such a deliriously, mind-altering delight. I feel sorry for you, old chair. You can never know nirvana. How is it for you to sit and wonder about such things and yet criticize those who live them? How can you criticize what you can not know, you old fool?

"How hypocritically must you be to judge me? Was not the Patriarch of our tribe a shameless pimp? Did he not connive to share his wife to get established in Egypt? Was not our Matriarch a whore? Was she not a willing participant in Abram's scheme? Do you think for a moment that she did not enjoy those evenings that she bedded Pharaoh? She stayed with him many years, old chair. Pharaoh must have enjoyed Sarai's love making, don't you think? Do you think that he did not penetrate her, or that he did not taste her? Perhaps she bore his child? Perhaps his name was Moses? Our tribe never wrote about that. Have you considered that possibility as you sit there and pass judgment on everyone?

"Did Abram and Sarai not do what they had to do for their love to survive? Did they not lie and cheat their way into favor with Pharaoh? And did not Abram love Sarai even more; much, much more; because she willingly became a whore? Do we not sing their praises now? Yes, we do! We love our whores! How dare you hold up the adultery commandment before me and tell me I am a wrong-doer when you would have me sing praises to Abraham and Sarah? Your foundation is rickety and weak, old chair. You rest on sand, not rock. Perhaps the Christians' Jesus had a firmer understanding of this conundrum, old chair. When asked what to do with an adulter-ess he chided the Sanhedrin members to have any one of them who was guiltless of the same crime to cast the first stone. Ah Ha! No one dared pick up a stone! All the priests of the tribe whored! So, by what authority do you now cause me to wrestle with guilt, old chair?

"How is your prohibition against adultery any different from a prohibition against eating or sleeping? What you fail to see is that *sex and love are as necessary as eating and sleeping. Life ends without sex and love. So, you see, you are at odds with life itself, old chair. Your logic wrestles nature's. And it must lose! You have pitted yourself against the force of love. You sit there with your certain cold authority while Susan calls to me with her warmth and love. I need her. She restores my soul every day I am with her. She warms my heart and gives my life joy and meaning.*

"Not so with my son. I have failed with him. I know I have failed. I have tried with David to the limits of my wit and will and time and love; and I can go no further with him. I can not pound my head upon a solid door that will not yield to me. I must stop giving myself a headache. And I can not allow you to make me feel your guilt with my decision any longer.

"No, I will not feel your guilt when you think of me or my decisions; or when you look at me; not for one day longer! I will not have you watching me. I am too much in love and too happy with my love of Susan to allow your presence to place your thoughts of guilt in me. Neither do you hold any power over Susan, old chair. Did not God bless Sarah with a child of Abraham's, after she had whored? Why would not God also bless Susan with my child, after she has whored? Ha! You have no answer for me, old chair. Know that I would love such a child of Susan's and give it every advantage. And there is such a child. I know her. Her name is Marty. She is a girl. I pray that she learns the fine arts of love from her mother; and, yes, I pray that she becomes a glorious porn star whore, who knows the finest arts of love making, since that path appears to be her choice. Yes, I will love my daughter all the more should she continue that pursuit.

"The end does indeed justify the means when love is the means and the end, old chair. Perhaps God loves his whores, just as he loves all of us? Perhaps God loves his whores more than he loves those women who do not whore? And why would he not? Do whores not open wide their gates of love? Are they not God's agents of truth and change? Are not truth and change and love the very facilitators of life? Have you considered that, old chair? And have you considered, old chair, that people enjoy making love because God wants people to enjoy making love, and, yes, even making love with different partners when the feeling of love commands them?

"God loves Susan, old chair. How could he not love a woman so beautiful and perfect and loving? I know with certainty that I am correct, old chair. I love Susan and God loves Susan, so who are you to say our love is wrong, old chair? Yes, old chair, God loves my beautiful, wanton whore, Susan. She has conquered God's heart and mine. My love of her has no limits and her love joined with mine is all pervasive. Love, her love, has even joined with and conquered the mind of God. And love has conquered you, old chair. Love has conquered your guilt. You and your guilt have ridden upon the back of every generation of my ancestors since the Russian pogrom. You have embedded your guilt into our family psyche. You embedded your gnarled, creaking, heartless wisdom into our family fiber. I'm sorry that your original master lost his wife and almost everything he had, dear old chair; but by being rid of you, I will gain my true love, my freedom from guilt and I will finally have everything I want. You are our family's anchor to Jewish guilt; but now it is time for me to wash my hands of you and the feelings you draw out of me.

"Old chair, I want you to know that I will love Susan all the days of my life and forever after my life, and even into my spirit life I will love only Susan, and all of her and everything about her, and our child for whom we are so blessed. So, that is my final pledge to you. Yes, I am obsessed with Susan. And my obsession pleases me. It has freed me from my obsession with guilt and it has freed me from you! I will not be chained to Jewish guilt any longer.

"And, so, dear chair, I thank you for your service. I have decided it is time for me to pass our family's custody of you to David, my son.

Perhaps you can work your guilt on him. He needs correction in the ways he lives his life and there is only so much I can do for him. Now, perhaps, you and your presence in his home will influence David to live a more moral life; but, as for me, I am from this moment onward, finished with you."

That very evening, Marvin took the chair to David's home and left it with David.

Now, years later, David recalled hearing Marvin tell him of the times Marvin, Marvin's father, and Marvin's father's father, and the fathers before them had all sat before the man in the chair and listened, as the family patriarch dispensed his wisdom. Over the generations, the chair had acquired a mystique about it. Family members revered it for the travels it had made and for the words and thoughts it had heard. The old chair had become the symbol of the family's survival and the repository of its wisdom and inspiration; and Jewish guilt.

Then the night came of David's fateful dream. In his dream, David saw the apparition of Marvin sitting in the ancient chair across from David's bed. David had awakened from a horrible nightmare. In his dream he'd heard how much Bob now hated him. Now his dream continued. In his dream he saw Marvin sitting in the family chair. Before Marvin, sitting on the floor, as David himself had done as a little boy, sat Bob. Marvin and Bob were talking. His dead father, whom Bob had never met, and Bob, David's protégé, were talking about David, as their common enemy,

"He's always been a sissy," said Marvin to Bob. *"I did what I could for him. But now, here you are. You're more like a son to me than he ever was."*

Bob said to Marvin, *"I always had to look through him to see you. All this time I knew him I secretly laughed at him. He had no character or integrity; no honor, no dignity; no pride except false pride; and he had no ethics or morals. He was never the man you were.*" The two men who haunted David's nightmares stood and embraced, as a father and a son might embrace. They then closed a door on David who was sitting in a chair in an adjoining room, watching them.

It was a horrible dream. David sat upright in his sleep. In his cold sweat in the dark, he cried out. He wept to the ghost of his father who was now, once again, seated in the chair.

"*DAD? DAD!*" *Father, are you there? Can you hear me, Father? Why is this happening to me, Father? Why didn't you love me, Father? Why didn't Mother love me? Why doesn't anyone love me? What should I do, Father? Whose side are you on, Father? Whose side are you on?*"

Then David had a vision of Marvin rising from the chair and floating in the air. Now he stood in the air. He was wearing his tallit that he wore at temple. His father was joyfully singing the '*Shema.*' Marvin's voice was speaking for the hearts of the People of the Book. Then Bob appeared again, standing next to Marvin. Bob also wore his tallit. Marvin put his arm around Bob's shoulders and spoke to Bob. And David overheard his father say to Bob:

"*Israel is all you'll ever need to know and trust and believe in. I and the good souls of Israel will deal with this wrongdoing that my son has done to you, wherever it goes. I will always stay in touch with you. I will always guide your way upon the path you must travel. You will never be alone. You and Barbara have my love and my blessing. Go on building your business and enjoy your lives.*"

David sweated profusely. His pajamas were soaked. He was shaken by what he had dreamed. His body chilled and shivered. He had heard Marvin's voice leap out from the family Torah Scrolls. The voice roared at him with a frightening, booming thunder. It was louder than the sounds of an avalanche knocking down trees. The voice then grabbed David and pushed him to the ground. It held him down by his throat. David wrestled with the voice and tried to shake free of it; but his father's voice would not leave him. It refused to relax its grip on his throat:

'*You will know my wrath. You will also know the wrath of my father and his father and his father before him. Mark this day on your soul and bind it to your forehead and hold my words in your heart. By all that is holy before God, I will not forget nor will I ever forgive what you have done. All your life I have lifted you up before God as my son. But no more! What becomes of you and your soul is now in God's hands. May you know his punishment. I will never again intercede for you*'

Then David awakened. He was horrified. He screamed and trembled. He was terrified for his life and soul as the dawn broke. He had betrayed Father and Israel, and he had been caught! Father had always told him to earn money legally and to send money to Israel. David had disgraced his father and Israel by making money illegally and keeping it all for himself. Marvin's ghost had found him out. It had grabbed David by his throat and shaken him to his core. "*Ahhh, Ahhh,*" David screamed.

David's wife, Eilese, ran into his bedroom and asked if he was ill. He sent her back to her room. Then he lay there for hours, terrified by his dream. He wondered whose side Marvin's ghost was taking in his fight with Bob. He stared at the ceiling. What was happening to him? Then David heard his father's voice boom again. He screamed again:

"*Ahhh, Ahhh, Ahhh.*"

His wife returned again to David's room. This time, she also heard Marvin's voice. It was condemning David for murdering Marty and for all his other evil deeds. Eilese also began screaming:

'*Ahhh, Ahhh, Ahhh, Ahhh.*'

Her voice was not a normal woman's voice. It was more like a chorus of thousands of wailing Jewish voices. It was coming through her mouth from Marvin's grave! It was the voice of three hundred generations, screaming and echoing through the ages into David's ears and into Eilese's ears. It echoed and reechoed the anguish of three hundred generations of Jewish persecution. It was terrifying. And, it was real! Eilese looked at David and asked:

"What is happening, David? What is happening? I am possessed by the spirits. These voices that come from my mouth are not mine!"

But David's tongue could not speak. Instead, the chair turned toward Eilese, as if a person were sitting in the chair and had moved it to face her. She thought it was some sort of trick:

"David, stop this!" she commanded, thinking the chair had moved by David's doing.

But then a loud, commanding voice came to her. It resembled Marvin's voice, but it resonated and echoed as it spoke. It spoke as if it came from a spirit that was seated in the chair:

"Eilese, hear me! I am your God. I am the God of Abraham and the God of your father and all the fathers before him. I am the beginning and the end. Leave us now."

"I don't understand," stammered Eilese. *"What is happening? Why must I go? What have I done?"*

A few seconds of silence passed. Then the voice from the chair bellowed its command in a voice so loud that it shook the entire room and the entire house:

"LEAVE US!"

It became suddenly clear to Eilese that the voice chose not to answer her questions; and that it demanded to be obeyed. She was terrified by the commanding voice. Shaken, she ran to her bedroom, screaming: *"Ahhhh!"* and put on her coat. It was a blustery night. Dark clouds swirled ominously. Amidst the rumblings of distant thunder, she ran to the garage, got into her car, and left the house. Eliese drove to her synagogue. She slipped inside before the custodian locked the doors for the evening. Now, alone with her God, Eilese knelt before the holy of holies. Still terrified, she trembled while whispering her devout prayers; often jumbling together her Hebrew words from different prayer chants and mumbling incoherently. She did not have her prayer books and there were no other congregants there, beside her, chanting prayers with her, giving support to her and reinforcing her memories of the words. As lightning flashed and thunder claps rattled the windows of the synagogue, Eilese begged God to forgive all her sins and look favorably upon her in the Book of Life:

'I had nothing to do with David's crimes or his immorality. We never even consummated our marriage. I have always lived apart from him. He is the wrongdoer; not me. I have been a good woman. Please, dear, sweet Adonai, have mercy upon me. Please do not enter a bad mark against me in the Book of Life. I promise to always be a good woman from now on. I promise you; I will stop my affairs with my lesbian friends. I will live a clean and pure life from now on.'

She prayed devoutly this way, sniveling and whimpering like a hurt child; all the while shuddering in fright from the lightning and thunder claps, until she passed out. She was finally at peace with her atonement, sound asleep before the altar.

David, meanwhile, stared at the chair. He held his hands to his ears and screamed in hopes he would no longer hear the voice, *"Ahhhh!"* but his hands only made the voice grow even louder. Now it roared at him in its deafening shout. It became louder than the loudest thunder. *"AHHHHH!"* It went into David's ears and into his mind. It's loud, deep, booming voice shook all of David's senses, as if it rode upon a bolt of lightning's thunderclap, shot from a clear blue sky. David heard the deep, booming voice of God:

"YOU ARE A DISGRACE TO ME AND A DISGRACE TO ALL ISRAEL! YOU HAVE BETRAYED ALL YOUR FATHERS AND YOU HAVE BETRAYED ME! I DO NOT KNOW YOU! YOU HAVE EARNED THE ENTIRE WRATH THAT WILL NOW BEFALL YOU!"

It was suddenly clear to David: Marvin was on the side of Israel! Marvin's friends and family ties would not stand by him or forgive his transgression. They, too, were on the side of Israel.

"Israel! Oh, Israel," cried David. *"Your wrath is now upon me! I can not hide from you. I am doomed!"* David cried and trembled from concern that a harsh judgment would be rendered against him at the end of his life. He was terrified that he would be recorded badly in the Book of Life. He closed his eyes and held his hands over his eyes. Now he saw the image of Marvin. He was in his tallit, his back turned away from him. His father was walking away from him, and disappearing. David got out of bed and sat naked in the family chair, shaking in fear, crying, and shivering. He screamed out:

"NO, NO, OH GOD, NO! FATHER, COME BACK TO ME. FATHER! FATHER! SPARE MY SOUL!"

But Marvin's image did not return to him. David was now shunned. He was an outcast. Marvin's tormented angry voice had cried out and rendered its final verdict. The voice had spoken. It was the voice of good. It was the voice of God. It had spoken for the People of the Book.

CHAPTER EIGHT

And in trust I have found treason (Queen Elizabeth 1: Speach to Parliament, 1586)

Men never do evil so completely and cheerfully as when they do it with religious conviction (Blaise Pascal)

Unless we love the truth, we cannot know it (Blaise Pascal)

Fight. Fight until hell freezes over, then fight on the ice; but never stop fighting and never give up. Keep fighting until the other side gives up (Rosemary Ness-Bitner: author)

PARTNERS

As David looked out the window of his newest lawyer's office, he watched two birds chirping and splashing in a fountain birdbath. What carefree fun they had in their fluttered duet!

'Silly birds,' thought David, '*they have no idea about life's struggles. Their happiness is an illusion that lets their guard down and prevents them from seeing life as it is. No wonder cats catch them and eat them.*'

Long passed were the glory days of David's case. Gone were his grandiose meetings with five or six lawyers and their secretaries, all seated at a big conference table looking out over the city to the Rockies, strategizing on how to destroy Bob's case and Bob's life; with David paying them a collective ten thousand Dollars per hour to do little more than chew the fat. Everything they said seemed so important then; so fascinating and intriguing. But it had all come to naught. Bob had moved on from David. He had started another firm. And David still faced the daunting prospect of going to trial. Those lawyers had made a fortune off him. Now they sought to pluck him further. Filthy pricks!

All that seemed important now was to get this messy affair finished and behind him so he could relax and play a little, enjoying his twilight years like the two happy birds in the fountain. But his struggle wasn't finished. David reminded himself that he needed to be tough. He dared not show the slightest sign of weakness. Like the biblical period of the Judges, he needed to be the personification of Israel's strength renewed. He needed to sweep the Golan, the Gaza, and Samaria; and he needed to retake Jericho, engage, and destroy the Canaanites, Sidonians, Hivites; all the evil worshipers of Baal; all the evil forces that were encroaching upon the sacred land given to his people by God. David promised himself he would atone for letting his guard down, for failing to be as strong in his generation as Marvin had been strong in his time. He would fight his way back into the good graces of the tribe. He was older now. And wiser; beaten in the courts, but defiant and unbowed.

Mal Green, David's most trusted lawyer and his secret weapon against the entire filthy legal community, had dutifully tracked the practices of all the lawyers involved in the case. He had meticulously observed all the proceedings, recorded them secretly, and made notes of who was in the courtrooms at each appearance before a judge. He had gathered enough malpractice dirt on two of the firms to make a valid case that they had harmed David to the tune of several million Dollars. Even though David had been the instigator of the law firms' dirty tricks strategies; and even though he had paid them double their customary fees to execute his bribes to judges, Mal had made sure that David was buffered by one or two intermediaries in each instance; so, he could be exonerated of any criminal wrongdoing. Mal made certain that David was in the clear and that his former attorneys were on the hook.

Mal also ran exhaustive checks on Ben. He knew every person operating in opposition to every other person or team of lawyers had to have a weakness. David reasoned if neither Bob nor Barbara was the chink in his determined plaintiff's armor, then perhaps the weak link would be Bob's attorney, Ben. Mal's reports convinced David that his hunch was on target. Ben had no money. His mother was ailing; Ben himself was ailing; and Ben had a sister of no means, whom Ben also supported. Diabetes ran wild in Ben's family. They had no insurance, but all three needed regular dialysis treatments. Ben owed money to Sol's estate for Sol's hours of prior case work. That debt made it imperative that Ben not lose at trial. Trial was a risk Ben couldn't take any more than David could take. Ben had to know that David could possibly find a way to bribe a judge or a couple of jurors, again; and that, even with the U.S. Supreme Court behind him, Ben realistically could still lose. David reasoned there had to be a settlement deal that would separate Ben's interests from his client's interests.

After cordialities, the lawyers got down to talking about money. Ben made his first mistake by speaking first. That indicated that he wanted to settle the matter in the first place. David noted that weakness. He felt confident of Mal's assessment. Ben threw out the first offer.

David scoffed, *"Your case is still a quantum meruit case. I could have easily hired a man to do what Bob did for one-tenth of what you're asking, and I'm sure a jury will see it that way."*

"Not true," Ben fired back. *"You and I both know you acquired Bob's services by fraud. Even the Supreme Court saw it that way. Read the remand instructions back from the Court of Appeals."*

"I don't give a shit what the Supreme Court says," scoffed David.

"Listen, David. I will tell you this," spoke Ben softly but firmly, as if bringing a man into reality. *"The longer this matter drags out, the more valuable the case becomes. You can hire new counsel all you want, but the clock is running against you, not us. Damages are compounding. You have other exposures also. No one in the world would want to invest with you, after knowing what they're going to find out about you when this goes to trial. Your assets will flee.*

"Israel also has some exposure here. Did you ever think of that? What were you thinking when you took him into the bank vault? You were just going to take advantage of a half orphan, screw his life and career to the wall and run away with everything, weren't you? Israel wasn't going to get a dime either. Isn't that true? You were just going to have a big playtime with all the money, weren't you? You were trying to sell the companies while Bob was out there working his ass off. How do you like what I'm saying? How do you think a jury will like it?"

"You assume too much, sir. You could lose. I have a witness who says Bob had a plot to take over the companies."

"You're talking about your blubbering idiot cousin Judith, the one you and your lawyer bribed for a condo and a pickup truck to commit perjury. Go ahead and put her on the stand in district court. Put her up where I can get some decent cross on her instead of your cheap-shot 'I feel threatened' horse shit restraining order. A jury will see right through that. She cried her eyes out under a gentle soft cross, and she made a record that proved she had no idea what she was talking about. She'll come off like a bought-and-paid-for nincompoop, and you know it. I can't wait to tear into her with a hard cross. I'll end up nailing you for witness tampering and perjury.

"Why did she call Bob asking for some money before she agreed to commit perjury for you? Two weeks before! She's the one who called Bob! How do you explain the interval? She was never afraid of Bob! She called me after the stunt, called me eight times bawling

her eyes out. 'Tell Bob I'm sorry,' she said to me, all eight times. You put her up to that horseshit, David. Put her on the stand and you'll be getting perjury and libel on top of everything else. All you'll end up with is nothing. Put her up. I dare you. All you're going to prove is that you are a dirty off-court player and a bribing bastard.

"He had a plot to take over your companies, you say. Hah! You mean the companies that you already gave him in the bank vault. Don't be ridiculous. He can't take away from you something you already gave him. You're being fucking ridiculous. You're through, David.

"You want to throw mud in the puddle, David? Okay, Bob had an all-expenses paid love affair with the company whore. Big whoop! And now he's stolen away your prized Indian girl administrator. Well, whoop, whoop! Remember the deposition testimony of the woman who closed the office that night, instead of Judith? Will a jury believe you have any credibility after I put her on the stand? She's going to say you were hopping down the hall naked, wearing rabbit ears with a golf ball stuck in your ass; being chased by your lover boys dressed up as hound dogs. Oh, don't forget, David. She's certain it was you. She can identify the black birthmark on your tuchus! You want muddy, David? I'll give you muddy! Those jurors will hear about your fuck the bunny act. They'll fall out of their chairs and roll on the floor laughing their asses off. I dare you to go muddy, David. You'll never recover credibility after that!"

"Gentlemen, lets back up a minute. We're not here to try the case. We're here to see if there's some way that we can both put this tedious nightmare behind us," said Mal, David's mouthpiece.

"Frankly, Ben," David chimed in as if on cue, beginning his well-rehearsed lines, "I've heard great things about your work over the years." Actually, the opposite was true. He knew that Ben usually lost cases. "You were absolutely brilliant when you were in front of the Supreme Court." Flattery always opened a door. David needed to make a friend of this newcomer lawyer and enlist him in a common cause.

"*You know, if I'd had decent lawyers to start with, the case would never have gone this far. The advice I kept getting from them was to fight Bob every step of the way, fight him with everything I had. They should have advised me to settle at the outset, but they didn't.*" David proffered a half-truth. He had wanted to destroy Bob. His attorneys had consistently advised him to settle. They only told him they could provide a vigorous defense. "*Anyway, I apologize. Things got completely out of hand. Tell me something that I don't understand, though. Why on earth did you agree to take on this gentile goy in a fight against Israel?*" David reflected upon his tilt toward graciousness:

'*Flattery from a fox will get a crow to drop his meal from his high branch into the mouth of the cunning fox.*' It was an old European fable. David understood its meaning and he worked it well.

"*You know, Ben, I'm so impressed with your work, I'd like you to do some legal work for me after we settle this mess.*"

David was on a roll. He was playing his '*do for me now and I'll do for you later*' song.

"*The way I see it is like this. Here you are, risking your practice and reputation in the Jewish community by helping this gentile. Why not take a sure settlement, get paid for all you've done and all Sol did; and then I'll let you have some easy work and I'll pay you some more. Doesn't that make more sense than rolling the dice?*"

"*David,*" said Ben, "*it's not about fighting against Israel. Do you see Israel named as a defendant? It's a fight of Bob against you, David, against the wrong you've caused my client, the wrong to his career, to his new business, all your harassments, all your vindictiveness. Whatever made you decide to take off on Bob like you did?*"

"*Well, I just didn't want to see him stealing something that was going to belong to Israel,*" David made up his stock answer. "*You

"Bob's a Jew as well, David," Ben wasn't about to let David play the persecuted Jew card, unopposed. *"You even witnessed his conversion. Let's just keep money as the issue here."* Ben stated his response firmly.

"He's not a Jew!" exploded David in mock rage, *"He's just a Reformed, a wannabe Jew. Reformed Jews aren't real Jews! They are just idiotic fuckups! I offered to help him get an Orthodox rabbi and he didn't want to take me up on it. He didn't want to become a real Jew!"*

"What if he had, David?" Ben responded calmly. He didn't want to get drawn into David's emotional cauldron. *"Would you then have pushed him to become a Hasidic Jew? Where would it all stop, David? You just wanted to make him into your boy-toy, didn't you? You wanted another fuck-buddy, something besides that black sheep of yours, didn't you? What's the matter? The sheep won't talk to you? Not intimate enough? And Bob rejected you, didn't he? That's really what this is all about, isn't it?"*

"He's not a Jew!" David shouted strenuously. *"Reformed Jews aren't real Jews!"*

"Oh, they're not? Thank you for telling me that, David," Ben drew his head back. His eyebrows raised. His mouth became pursed. *"If they are not Jews, then what are they?"*

"They're dog shit, that's all. They're some bastardized religion that started out as Jews, but got eaten by the assimilation craze, like good food gets eaten by a dog and the dog turns the food into shit. Secular society broke off a part of Judaism and ate it, like a dog eats its dog food, and digested it; made it into something unrecognizable with its relaxed practices and its permissible marriages to gentiles.

"And now it's like dog shit. It's useless to God or anyone who believes. And they take in people like Bob and allow conversions to kind of spread their shit around. I fed Bob a great idea; told him how wonderful it was to be a Jew, better than any country club; like I was

Jew from the steak he ate. He became a Reformed Jew. He turned my good steak into shit! He's not a pure Jew. I might have kept my deal with him had he become a pure Jew; but he refused to go any further with his conversion. He wanted to stay with the Reformed Jews. He wanted to live in shit."

Ben shook his head and exhaled, holding back his tears. He was appalled that David could be so deranged:

"This is supremacy talk, David. It has no place. Bob is a Jew. That's the truth. You instigated his conversion. Accept that truth also."

"Horseshit," screamed David. His face was beet red. He was furious. *"It's more than talk. It's fact. The Reformed aren't real Jews. They are inferior. Bob is not a real Jew. He did not come all the way with me. He did not become Orthodox. He played a joke. Now he's getting his joke back. He is only dog shit. I stepped in it. I stepped in his dog shit. And now I'm getting it off my shoe, that's all!"*

"David, he's as much a Jew as you or me or any other Jew. Stop with your fucking nonsense talk. Stop with your fake indignation. He knows Torah, Tanakh, the services rituals, the Holidays, the mitzvahs, Talmud, all of it. He knows it all, as well as you and me; probably even more so. We're here to talk money, David. I can't bring him back to you. Bob doesn't love you, David. He's not like you that way. He could never be your lover, or your son. It's over, David. Whatever fantasies you had about him; they are over. Everything is just about money now."

Five thousand years before men penned the Declaration of Independence, which gave birth to a republic founded upon secular principles, God's words were forever etched into the minds of Jews: *'I am the Lord, your God; I shall have no other God's before me.'* God's words as spoken to Moses were decidedly non-secular and excluded those who were not of blood issue.

"It can't be just about money," David glared at Ben as he spoke. *"It's also about Judaism."* David tried a new tact. *"If Bob is really a*

Jew, he should know I could never leave him Dad's companies. They are my companies, Israel's companies."

"How can you say that?" Ben shrugged off David's protest. "When you made your deal with him, it was before he converted. He was still a gentile. You concealed from him your pledge to Marvin that you would leave the companies to Israel upon your death. Then, after you took away the codicil that you showed him in the bank vault, you were telling salesmen in Bob's presence that Bob would inherit the companies. You knew that wasn't true, but you repeated it to several different salesmen at different times, so they'd keep selling fund shares. Your Firm was built on a lie. Your whole life is built on a lie. You've got fraud written all over you, plus violations of the Securities Distribution Act. How could Bob know any of this?"

"Well, none of those things matter. He knows now; yet he keeps after me in court," said David, playing the part of an indignant offended man. "And he became a Jew; so, he says; so, you also say; so, some stupid Reformed rabbis say. Well then, he should know the meaning of the story of Abraham!"

"Excuse me," snorted Ben. "I must be missing something. The deal you made was made under twentieth-century secular laws. It was not made under Torah laws from five thousand years ago."

"He testified he's a Jew! He isn't stupid," David elevated his voice for effect. "He knows when God and Abraham made their berit, their covenant between the cut-up animals, that God told Abraham that Abraham's own issue shall be his heir."

"That was about Ishmael and Isaac. They were both Abraham's issue." corrected Ben. "Abraham and Sarah had Isaac. Sarah and Isaac pushed out Hagar and Ishmael because their blood wasn't Hebrew. Stop trying to rationalize what you did to my client by playing the Jew card. That's never going to fly, David. You made a secular deal. You made a covenant deal, one man to another man; and you made it under secular law; and you broke your deal, David!

It's clear. You live in the United States of America, not in the land of Ur or the land of Canaan.

"Besides, Abraham pimped out his wife, Sarah, to the Pharaoh for his fucking food stamps; so maybe Moses' bloodlines didn't even have pure Hebrew blood in the first place. I don't think you're using the greatest example to invoke sanctimonious purity and integrity in your dealings. If anybody should be trusted to give those companies to Israel, it should be Bob. Your intent was to sell them and go spend the money. You have no honor, David."

"I made a deal under our tribal laws!" Daid sputtered spital from his drool. He sometimes did that when he got upset. *"Can't you see? Bob doesn't count! What I did to him doesn't matter! Why can't you see that?"*

"Listen to me, David," Ben was earnest as he leveled a sincere gaze at David, *"we are no longer living in the world of 2500 before the Common Era. We have moved on from tribal law to secular law. We no longer slaughter red heifers on the tribal altar. We no longer slit their jugulars to bleed them. We no longer gut them and remove their entrails and eat their warm livers and still beating hearts. We go to grocery stores now, like everyone else. Our meats are kosher killed and packaged for us. We have moved on, David. You must move on."*

But David wasn't moving on. Ben's words had triggered him. He returned Ben's erstwhile gaze with a vacant stare. His mind was away from the conversation. It had retreated back to the safety of his barn. He was in the barn with his good friend, Don. And they had just murdered Marty and removed her fetus. His thoughts were spinning wildly:

'Why did Ben bring up the red heifer sacrifice? Does he know what I did to Marty? Did I leave the barn door open while I sacrificed her? Did someone see me? Did they tell Ben? Did they see me rip out her heart? Could they tell how confused I was in that

moment? Did Don tell Ben? Did Don see inside my mind? Could Don tell how I got confused over Marty's bloodline? Her mother was Goyim and Dad was a Jew. So, what was I to do? If I ate her heart, would I be taking her Jewishness inside me; or would I be defiling myself by taking in her Goyim? Would I be making myself stronger, like Father; or would I be making myself into an immoral whore like her mother? Does Ben know I did a halfway measure by only eating a small bite of her heart and leaving the rest of it for the pigs? What does he know? Why that red heifer comment? Is he telling me he's got Don on his side?'

"*David! Hello David! This is Planet Earth calling you.*" Ben mocked his adversary. He could tell something he had said to David had struck a nerve. "*Would you care to join us, David? Would you care to return to the twenty first century? Can we dispense with your phony tribal schtick and get back to business, David?*"

But David wasn't ready to return to present day reality. Like a stubborn mule, he dug his feet into the ground and refused to surrender his position:

"*God also told Abraham that his descendants would people many lands and inherit great wealth,*" persisted David. "*Your client is not a descendent of Abraham. I did not cut a covenant deal with Bob. We did not cut the animals and agree over their bodies and their blood. A deal that is not a covenant deal is no deal at all. You should know that, Ben. Shame on you for betraying our ways. What I did with Bob was enhance the gift my father left me to give to Israel. That was the only agreement that mattered. You know that. Goyim think their laws matter. But their laws do not matter. Goyim only believe their laws mater because they are stupid. And that's not my problem. Only a covenant, a bris, matters. When we were in the bank vault, Bob was a gentile. Your own words acknowledge that. That makes his deal a secular Goy's deal, not a covenant deal. I merely made use of a fool, but I made no deal.*"

"Cut out the bullshit, David." Ben wasn't buying into five-thousand-year-old reasoning. *"Wahhabis use that same thinking to justify taking from those who are outside of Islam. You're spewing tribal thinking; but we now live in a secular world. God said a lot of stuff to a lot of people and you can use scripture to rationalize anything; but we live under secular laws. Law matters. Learn the story of Ruth."*

"I know it." said David.

"Well, Bob fits that scripture story." said Ben.

"That Ruth story is fucking horseshit." David rejected Ben's attempt at reasoning that Ruth's story meant that conversions to become a member of the Tribe of Israel were acceptable. *"Reformed rabbis use it to justify conversions. They're just desperate for members and cash flow."* David wasn't about to let Ben make him feel empathy for Bob.

"Don't get righteous with me, David," admonished Ben. *"First you said he's a Jew; but now you say he's not a Jew. You're such an easy take down, David. Your own roots are Khazarian, not Ashkenazi. Your tribe was forced to choose a religion so they'd stop thieving or the Turks were going to kill every one of you assholes. You're not from the blood of Abraham, either. Your blood is no better than Bob's."* Ben liked to keep topics in sharp focus. He wasn't about to let David mix logic.

"My parents and their parents before them belonged to a temple. Bob's mother is not a Jewess," David blurted out his latest attempt at misplaced logic, like a hurt child sometimes does. He scrambled to change the reference frame of his argument from where he'd started to one which had a timeline that more suited his rebuttal.

"Let's quit fucking around and get down to business," said an exasperated Ben. *"The time for bullshitting about three-thousand-year-old Tanakh passages is over. Do we deal or do we go to trial? I assure you, every day that passes this case becomes more valuable,*

not less. It's just about money, David. We're done with religious philosophy."

"No! It's not just about money!" David was still shouting. His face strained to beet red. "It's about my father, Marvin, and the promise I made to him," he insisted. "Marvin was a Zionist. You surely know that."

"Yes, I know that. Everybody knows that. And what about you, David? Are you a Zionist, like Marvin was?" Ben's voice was calm.

"Not like Marvin was. With Marvin it was Israel this and Israel that; everything for Israel. He believed America should be Israel's bitch; her vassal state; give Israel all the money, the weapons, the foreign aid, the tourism, everything she wants and needs to survive so there would never be another Shoah. He loved Israel. He loved that bitch whore Susan; but he never loved me! He never had time for me!"

"Maybe he felt you didn't take your faith seriously, David." Ben dropped his adversarial attack and tried to be human to human with David; tried to open David to self-reflection.

"I tried to get into the Zionist thing; but I couldn't get to where Dad was with it. I couldn't be obsessed with Israel like he was. But I'm a Zionist too," pleaded David. "I just had a weak moment, that's all. I made a mistake when I made my deal with Bob. Can't a man make a mistake just once in his life? Can't you see your way to help me get past a simple mistake? I'm an old man. I shouldn't have to suffer so much. My heart isn't good. My kidneys aren't right. I have gout. My prostate needs to come out. All this is stressful and it's hurting my health. It's not human to put me through this. Let's say we work something out where this all didn't happen and nobody knows about it. We should be able to come up with something workable. You and Mal are smart lawyers. Come up with something reasonable."

"Let's be clear, David. This is not my doing. You put yourself through this. And, reasonable to you means the Jewish community can't know about your deal, is that right? Am I hearing you correctly, now?" asked Ben.

"Yes. You know these companies must go to Israel, especially now. We can't screw Israel! Why did Sol and you ever even take this case? No one needed to know what happened here. The secular laws of the United States are irrelevant in this matter! When it comes to Israel, it's the laws of Torah that matter, nothing else. The mitzvah's matter, nothing else. There are no other laws; only God's laws. Nowhere in the mitzvahs does it say that you must honor your promises to a gentile. Goyim are beneath us! Fuck them; use them; piss on their pathetic lives. It doesn't matter what we do to them. They don't matter. Their laws don't matter. Their wretched lives don't matter. Their fucking American country doesn't matter. God is all that matters."

Ben didn't buy into David's rationalizations. "David, you need a reality check. You are about to face a jury of your peers and they happen to believe that their laws do matter. They will relish the chance to skewer a fat lying Jew who broke a deal. You are fucked, David. And if you persist in going forward and not settling this, when we get to trial, I will fuck you up way your ass. I promise you. So, stop kidding yourself. This isn't about God or mitzvahs. It isn't even about you giving the companies to Israel. You broke that deal. You might as well go piss on Marvin's grave. You've made an inconceivable mess, David. Money is the only thing that can fix this now. It's only about money, David. You fucked up, fella."

"All right, since it's about money, what about you, Ben? What about your money? I can't believe your practice is going gangbusters," snarled David. "Be honest."

"It's not about me, David," reproached Ben. "It's about my client and, by the way, he's pushing me to get a trial date set. Once I do that, there will be no settlement. And I WILL start fucking you!" Ben's voice was heated. He was losing patience with David.

"Listen, both of you. We're all trying to get to the same place here," said softly spoken Mal. *"We all want out of this terrible mess, this case. You want your money, Ben. You need the money, and you want to move on."*

Ben was suddenly paying attention. Mal had struck a nerve. By the hourly rate Sol put into the case, Ben was out a fortune in fees he owed Sol's estate and he couldn't pay Sol's estate unless he won or settled. He looked his steady gaze at David, but said nothing.

David sensed he and Mal had finally driven a wedge into Ben's wall of solid bluff. Now he needed to take control of the meeting. *"Look, I don't begrudge you making a good living, Ben,"* said David. *"But I don't want to enrich a man for more than he was worth to me. I'm willing to put some serious money on the table for you; but you need to be a reasonable man. And we can't be putting a stain on Israel."*

"Tell me what you're offering." Ben's voice had softened.

"It's like this. I can sell my old lawyers up the river and deliver them to you on a silver platter. They did malpractice. And I can prove it. Mal here can show you the stuff I have on them. I hired him to check over everything they did. There are many millions there for you. You agree to settle this case for what I'm offering; nothing more, and I'll let you represent me afterwards against my former lawyers; or you can just blackmail them and pocket the money yourself. Bob can have his costs back, nothing more. You'll make more money than your cut of a win at trial would get you; and you'll be taking no risk."

"That's unethical. I can't do that." Ben bristled at the thought of betraying his client.

David shouted, spittle flying, *"What do you mean, unethical? Don't give me that shit! You're a fucking lawyer! All you cocksuckers are unethical. Look at it this way, Ben. If you don't take my deal and you go forward, you could win; but then, you'll still lose. I already have all my assets in offshore trusts and you'll never find a dime of any of it. I'll have my money moved to new jurisdictions every six months. I don't care what it costs. Also, I've bribed a judge and witnesses before; and nobody stopped me. I'll just do it again! I can't believe you've been a lawyer all these years and still haven't figured out that the legal system is not about making things right. The legal system is only about helping rich guys fuck over little guys while you lawyers and judges get paid to make the whole crooked farce look honest. Bob is never going to see one dime above what I'm offering. I understand you need to get him some money to walk a smelly deal past a judge. He can have that much, but that's all he's going to get."*

"You can't do this," protested Ben. *"What you're offering for stealing a man's life's work is too little."*

"Too little, you say. I've spent three and a half million and burned through fifty-four lawyers fighting you and Sol, you fucking idiotic morons. You are broke, Ben. Sol died fucking broke. Everything he made as a lawyer he lost in the markets. He was a fucking idiot as a stock player. You want to help somebody, Ben? Go help Sol's pathetic widow. She's a fucking charity case. She could use some gleanings from the corners of the field. You aren't worth much, yourself, either, Ben. I've checked. You and your wife are down to your last two hundred thousand. You haven't taken home any real money for years. I bet your wife loves being broke, doesn't she?" David snarled.

"Let me tell you about too little." David lifted his face to show his chin and nose nostrils in tried-and-true intimidation to Ben. David knew money was trump in these negotiations; and he held all the cards. *"If you go forward to trial, I'll gladly spend another three million objecting, appealing, switching lawyers, filing frivolous motions you'll need to respond to. I'll run you into the ground. I'll bankrupt you, Ben. I drive you into the dirt like the slimy cocksucker you are. I know your legal games even better than you do. The big guy keeps spending the little guy into the ground until the little guy*

drops fucking dead. The more I play this game, the more I like it. It reminds me of when I was a kid. I stepped on caterpillars and watched their guts squirt out. Then I scraped my shoes on the side-walk and smeared their guts all over the place. I felt great when I was fucking over those little caterpillars. That's what I'll do to you and Bob, if you two idiots go forward. I'll squash the two of you like little caterpillars. You will lose, big time. I will destroy both of you; and you will get nothing."

David had made it clear to Ben that the nuanced factor in making his offer was the amount of money he needed to pay out of pocket to get a sham settlement past a judge. Anything above that he simply would not pay. He'd fight. He'd rather resort to a scorched-earth strategy, where Ben would get nothing; even though David's business would be tarred and possibly ruined. But David would keep most of the monies he had amassed through his nefarious dealings over the years.

"*Stop it, David,*" commanded Ben sharply. "*Bob's a human being. He has lost his career and half his professional life because of you. For the sake of decency, think about what you've done.*"

"*I don't give a fucking shit about what I've done. Fuck him!*" David sneered as he slammed that door shut. "*Morality has no bank account. Morality can't pay bills.*"

Ben tried a different approach to soften David's resolve. "*Let me ask you something, David. Why weren't you honest with Bob from the start? Why didn't you just say: 'I made this promise to my father to leave these companies to Israel and I intend to keep it, so after ten years of great experience you'll have to go somewhere else'? Why couldn't you just make an up-front deal?*"

"*My testimony and his testimony covered that,*" replied David. "*He was going to leave me to go to Texas. He was going to take that fucking idiot Indian bitch with him. He was going to abandon me, after all I did for him. How else could I keep him?*"

"David, that's just business," Ben shook his head. "People move around all the time. You don't own people."

"It was more than business," glared David. "He was like a son to me. I loved him. I treated him well. He was just going to take the Indian bitch with him and leave me. What would you expect me to do? I gave him a terrific opportunity to make good money."

"He made less than he was making before your phony deal, but let's not belabor that," rejoined Ben. "We have experts for that. What I want to know is why you didn't settle this, right away, when your codicil was discovered. Why did you fight through five appeals courts? Surely you had to know you'd eventually lose. And why did you put crime scene tape over Bob's office door after his case discovery was completed? You've made yourself look like a crazed maniac. Why did you personally destroy his desk with a hatchet after he left? What possessed you to do that? And why did you forbid the employees from ever speaking his name? I guess he got to you, huh? I mean, if you were honestly going to give the companies to Israel, why would you care so much about this and why would you destroy your own company's property? Why did you take this so hard? Bob lives in your head, doesn't he? You've allowed yourself to become a psychological mess over this."

"I didn't like feeling betrayed, that's all. He upset me." David looked away. He did that sometimes when he was caught off guard by someone who touched his feelings.

"Betrayed? How? In what way did Bob betray you, David?" Ben's jaw went slack. He couldn't believe betrayer David felt that he was the one betrayed.

"Well. I gave hm things. I set him up to live the life of a top executive. Cars, trips, the office, perks."

"Perks? Like what, David?"

"Well, I set him up with Marty, that sales gal I had. I paid for him to fuck her all over the country."

"Why would you do that, David? She had a reputation for being a fast woman. Why would you want your number two man to consort with her?"

"He was naive. He needed to learn the darker sides of life. I wanted him to understand evil and immorality. I figured by knowing Marty, he'd learn a lot. And to be a successful executive, one must understand those things."

"I see. That's a strange way to develop an executive. And Marty, didn't she go missing?"

"Yeah, she just disappeared. Noone has heard from her."

"Why do you think she disappeared, David?" Ben's natural tendency to discover facts was taking him away from the settlement discussion, but he couldn't help himself.

"Who Knows? She's a woman; a fucking dumb cunt. Noone can understand them."

"Oh, thank you for that, David. I can assure you that I'll get seven women on your jury. And when I get you under oath saying women are dumb cunts, I can assure you they will cut your nuts off. Can you see what an easy take down you are?"

"Fuck you, Ben. This is about Israel and keeping this out of the public's eye."

"I don't believe you, David. It's not about Israel. It's about you. If you cared about Israel, you would have prevented all this adverse publicity. What you did reflects terribly on all Jews, everywhere. You can't sugarcoat what you did. People who find out about this will assume we all do business this way. No, David, I believe you were taking calls from business brokers because you never had any intention of keeping your pledge to your father. You didn't have any intention of leaving these companies to Israel. You acted more like a jilted lover and a thief. And you got emotional over Bob, didn't you?

"You wanted to sell the companies. You wanted to steal from Marvin, steal from Bob, and steal from Israel, didn't you? All your

father's friends who put money into the Firm, thinking they were helping Israel, were also going to be betrayed, weren't they? You betrayed everyone, didn't you? You're no different from some little kid, stealing cookies from a cookie jar. Isn't that true David?"

"I own those companies," David said with a raised threatening voice. "What I do with them is MY business!" David became animated and began shouting again. *"Fuck Bob, and fuck his Indian girlfriend. And fuck Marvin! And fuck Israel too!"* David now lowered his voice, like he often did when he sought sympathy:

"All my life, all I heard was: 'Marvin this, Marvin that. Look how handsome Marvin is. Isn't Marvin so smart? Doesn't Marvin do so much for the community? If you have a problem, see Marvin! Marvin! Marvin!' How much of Marvin's shit is his son supposed to swallow, huh? Everything Dad did was for his Shiksha and for Israel! Am I'm supposed to choke that down and give my business to a fucking Goy? What about ME? Was I too ugly to be loved? Fuck all of you. I don't give a shit what the community thinks of me. Fuck them, too; and their money! I made all of them money! They've got no damages. They can't sue me. Those companies are mine. They are mine!"

David was shaking. He leaned forward into Ben's face. *"The companies are not going to Israel. I don't give a flying shit about Israel! All my life, everything Dad did was for Israel. Well, I don't even give a shit if the German army overruns Israel. I have no heirs. I don't need a place to escape to. I don't need Israel. I've never even been there. What happens to Israel is no skin off my nose!"*

"So, you lied in your testimony that you intended to keep your promise to your father!" Ben sat back and responded calmly. *"You never actually intended to leave the companies to Israel. See what I can do to you on the witness stand, David? Even if we had an all-Jew jury, they'd all side with Bob after hearing what you just said. By*

the way, David, World War Two has been over for a long time. The Germans aren't about to overrun Israel." He stared at David, as if he were seeing the defendant for the first time. Never before had he heard a Jew say that he didn't care about Israel. Never before had he met a man who didn't care about his own soul.

"Fuck off!" David shot back; but this time his voice was sharp and biting, like a cornered rat's. It carried a threat with its tone. *"If you go to trial with this, you could ruin me with the community, but I will ruin you, too. The difference us, Ben, is, I don't give a shit."* David glared at Ben. He glared like a trapped, angry rat that had nowhere to go. And he was willing to bite.

"Side deals give us all a bad name. This flies in the face of assimilation. Think about the consequences of what you've proposed." Ben sounded the trumpet of reason. *"This is how anti-Semitism gets its credibility. This is shame."* Ben's eyes were heavy. He was sad that this choice was being forced upon him. *"I'm making a last-ditch appeal to your loyalty to the community; to the tribe."*

"Fuck the tribe and fuck shame. I don't give a shit about shame. I don't understand the feeling." David remembered all the angst he'd suffered as a child because his mother never loved him. *"Where was Mother's shame for the way she shunned me? Where was Dad's shame when he wouldn't see me for months at a time? Dad never spent time with me. Where was his shame when he was away all those times whoring with Susan? Where's the shame in that? I feel no guilt. I owe no feelings of shame to anyone,"* David said matter-of-factly. His emotions were back under control.

"You need help," spoke Ben, as if speaking to a friend. *"Your mind is off, thinking this way. Everybody needs somebody. A moment ago, you were pleading for me to help you out of your mistake, save face. Now you say you don't care about anybody or Israel. Which is it? Who are you, David? Who am I talking to?"* Ben tried to pry a crowbar into David's inconsistency.

"Cut the crap," snorted David. "You're talking like a fucking lunatic." David was a big donor to many Jewish causes and no lawyer was going to threaten his standing in the community. "You hear me now!" he shouted into Ben's face. "This is only business and money we're talking about. If you go forward, I'll let the American Israeli Political Action Committee, all the synagogues, and every Jewish charity know that you're the one who is fucking over Israel. I'll take out full-page ads in the Jerusalem Post. I'll piss all over you. Every rabbi within a hundred miles of here will get a letter from me. You'll never get one more fucking dime of business. You'll never see another client in Plaintown. You'll be hurt so badly you'll wish you'd had a fence post driving machine pounding sand up your ass, instead of what I'm going to do to you. You'll see what happens when you turn your back on one of your own. You'll be known all over the country as the lawyer who gave Israel a bad rap. That Goy may have what I'm offering and not one more dime for him. You may have a fabulous extra compensation for yourself as my collection agent for my injuries from legal malpractice; you can run lifetime blackmails on those filthy lawyer cocksuckers; or you can go to trial and I'll ruin your life. It's your choice."

"Your malpractice money, do you mean the malpractice that you directed and paid for, that malpractice?" Ben wasn't about to let David's slight of tongue slip by him just because it was blended with threats and insults.

"Don't get your back up. They were all Goy firms. They were all stupid. They all deserve the fucking you're going to give them. You can keep all of the malpractice money. I wash my hands of it. It comes to more than you'd likely win for your share of a contingency at trial, which you'd never collect from me, anyway. I'll show you our proof against our other lawyers; our billing records; my agreements with them to bribe the judge; the payments to the judge's wife's charity; the canceled checks from the witness bribes; all of it, everything *we have. They'll all be easy takedowns for you. They're all slimy cocksuckers. I'll draw a memo of understanding between us, and you can have all the collection money, all of it. They are easy proofs and the Goy firms will want to settle with you. I'm giving you easy money, right now! Bob can make it up later. He's younger than we are. This way, we both keep our good standing with the tribe, and you don't screw Israel. That's my final offer, Ben."*

Ben just stared at David. He felt like throwing up his lunch. Finally, he spoke:

"It's not enough money."

Mal spoke up after Ben's remark threatened to collapse the negotiations:

"Gentlemen, gentlemen, let's not lose our focus here. We're getting close. I've listened to you both. Mir kenntn a tsores mochen! I can seal a deal between you two. I can find a way out of this stain on our lives for everybody. David, you want to have and enjoy the companies. You don't want to lose your standing in the community. You don't want to bring shame to Israel. We all agree to that. Ben, you need money. Bob needs money. Israel needs to stay unblemished from this shameful fiasco. We all agree to those principles. Here's the solution. David and Ben draw up an agreement giving Bob his costs back plus something for his borrowings to stay alive while he fought this battle. Not much money, David, just enough to walk it past a judge who will hold her nose so she can't smell how unfair this deal is to Bob.

"Ben, you force the pittance settlement on Bob. Shove it down his throat. Threaten to quit, threaten to put a lien on the case files, tell him you'll sue him for nonpayment of fees. Do whatever you need to do to get rid of the case.

"David, you pay the settlement you offered Bob. Give Ben the dirt on the firms so he can fuck them, but you also make a new will. In your new will, you leave the companies and all your personal

wealth, except enough to provide for your wife, to Ben. After you die, Ben inherits your assets. The assets stay with the tribe.

"You give a copy of this new will to Ben so no one needs to go through this litigation again, after you die, David. Ben, you now have a huge incentive to get yourself healthy and stop smoking those stinking cigars so you can outlive David who is twenty years older than you. I'll put a borrow provision in the will. You can borrow money on a will instrument like that. Ben, you, your mother, and your sister can stop living on your starvation diets. Then you can join a gym. Spend time there and take off seventy pounds, so you can fuck your wife again. Think about living again, Ben.

"Bob continues in business with his Indian lover, but like you, yourself, said, Ben, he still has half his life. So, you can stop feeling sorry for him. We leave Bob and the Indian Princess alone. All the fighting stops. This will be our secret Khazarian side deal, a very beautiful side deal to end all side deals. And it will be our only real deal. Secular law can just go fuck itself. We'll abide by our covenant deal here. There's Abraham, there's God, and there's us. That's it! Goyim secular law is cut out; fuck all of them! No one knows about our side deal, outside of us three.

"Ben, you make a writing to David that, upon your death, these companies go to Israel. David, you give Ben's writing to your rabbi for safekeeping. Ben, you cannot sell the companies when they are yours; nor can you will them to any other person or entity. After David dies you can take profit distributions from them, until you die. This way, David's pledge to Marvin is kept whole. Marvin's pledges to give the companies to Israel is kept whole. David can be buried in Mount of Olives, when he dies. Israel gets everything that Marvin Sustack promised her; only she gets it a little later. And Israel lives on. Israel stays whole!"

"So, the only one who gets screwed is the guy who built up the business. This is terrible shame." Ben had to poke Mal and David with one last insult.

"Shut up, Ben. That is our deal." Mal placed his hands, fists closed, in front of his face; and then he opened his fists and held his palms together. Then, he cut his hands away as if he were Abraham cutting the bris animals in half, in Abraham's covenant with God; or like Moses parting away the Red Sea. The gesture signified the end of one thing and the beginning of another. Mal stared at Ben with a matter-of-fact, clenched jaw look that said he knew that they both knew that there was no other way. Then Mal gave the same stare to David. He intended his words and his gesture to be the final say about this matter.

Ben thought for a long moment:

'I am selling my soul and my honor, but I have my mother and sister to care for; and I am not well, myself. It's getting harder to hide that fact. The old saying that a bird in hand is worth more than two in a bush is finding resonance in my mind. David does have a valid point. I do need ongoing business from my community. How far has this profession come from the English solicitors who were not allowed to sue clients who would not pay? The legal community was once about service to the people and civic harmony, back then. Oh God, why do I feel so dirty? Some things will never change. The tribe of Israel will last into perpetuity. The sun will rise and it will set. The oceans will rise and they will fall with the pulls of the moon, and life will go on. And everyone who became involved in this sordid mess will carry their filthy deeds with them into the Book of Life. May God hold his nose when he reads about our deeds here today.'

"Have your counsel Mal draw the memorandum of agreement," said Ben softly. *"Also give me copies of all your evidences of malpractice. I may decide to pursue those lawyers separately, after all this is settled. I can threaten them with exposure for payment. After all, they were Goy firms, so who gives a shit about them. I'll sign for your evidence under confidence to you, of course."* Ben felt he'd done all he could.

"Of course," said David, smiling like the happy frog that had just swallowed a fly as he extended his hand to Ben; thinking at the same time that nothing solved a sticky problem better and faster than a bribe to a lawyer, who was willing to commit legal malpractice.

Ben took David's hand, thinking at the same time that he was sealing a deal with the scum of the earth; but it was a highly profitable deal. Mal placed his hands above and below the two adversaries' clasped hands.

David and Ben and Mal all spoke the tribe's covenantal promise words. *"Mazul um Bruchah."* Their word was now their bond. Mal was their deal broker and witness. Their side deal, the real deal, had now been officially sealed by the rules of the tribe. And thus, it was as it should be; and as it needed to be; and as it had to be. And all three of these men knew it had to come to this, a sacred, covenantal handshake. How else could the tribe survive and wander across nations, nations' laws, and the passages of time? How else could continuity of its religion and its cult mystique prevail over kings, queens, and presidents; over congressional oversights, court decisions, legislative deliberations, administrative bodies' rules, and punishments? How else; what of this entire secular clap trap world could one believe in, if there were no core principles to bind God's eternal, chosen tribe together? Nothing else could be trusted! None of the world's secular ways were dependable. Those ways were too fickle; subject to the whims of a hostile throne, or an anti-Semitic judge or jury. Those risks must never be taken; those uncertain outcomes can never be allowed.

The tribe was birthed by the covenantal bargain between Father Abraham and God, a verbal deal between man and man's most high and holy god; and the tribe evolved from that day forward with its squabbles amongst its members decided by negotiations and bargains struck; and handshakes to seal those bargains trusted. Could the word of a fellow tribesman and his handshake on their bargain ever be subjugated to secular law? No, of course not! That would be heresy of the first order; one could be cast out and shunned by the tribe if that were to happen.

And, so it was. The deal, the real deal, the complete deal that included the side deal; the concealed deal that meant something, but was not the deal that was written into the secular court record, was the deal that was struck this day. It was the deal that two tribal members had shaken hands on, and had been witnessed and blessed by their third member. Secular rule of law would be smoothed over to suit the real deal; and Mal would work with Ben to provide the legal asphalt and paving equipment to bury the real deal beneath the form of the written settlement agreement; placed into smoothed words to pass by a beleaguered, overworked judge, who would hold her nose, look the other way, ask no questions; and stamp it done! And feel good to finally get this messy business off her desk and out of her court.

Ben, now David's partner, would go on to force a shabby settlement down client Bob's throat. He lied to Bob, telling him this was only a necessary step toward getting a larger settlement from David's earlier law firm, a much bigger settlement for bribery of a listed witness, libel, ex-parte communications with a judge, and bribery of a judge. He also promised Bob that there would come a reopening of the case they were about to settle once the wrongdoing was exposed, after David died. None of that was true, of course, but Ben reasoned that, with time, witnesses would die, or move away from Plaintown; the time barrier of latches would bar a reopening of this historic case based upon legal malpractice; and quite possibly he himself would also be dead and the companies would be safely in the hands of Israel. And Israel would give thanks to God for her gift.

Ben threatened to resign as Bob's attorney unless he settled, and to place a lien on the case for all his and Sol's hours of work, and said he would refuse to release Bob's case files to another attorney. Bob's funds to put experts on the stand again were another consideration for his case, and Ben shut that down by stating he'd not allow third-party lenders to become involved in his case files. He'd not allow Bob to get help from Barbara, Bob's new partner in business. He'd go to the judge and request to withdraw from representation, stating that Bob refused to cooperate. Ben told Bob he was not allowed to make any inquiries to sell off a portion of the case, or to seek financing for another round of expert testimony before a jury. By these unethical tactics and a false promise of future litigation once Ben uncovered the wrongdoings of David's previous lawyers, which he had no intention of pursuing, Ben forced Bob to settle.

Ben concealed the true terms of the settlement from the court. He omitted the side deal he'd made with David and then submitted the false settlement terms to the court. The judge ordered the case closed and Ben became a wealthy man at the expense of betraying his client:

'*David had a point,*' thought Ben. '*Mitzvahs matter. Countries and their laws and legal systems will come and go, but the tribe will endure, as it always has. Secular law doesn't really matter, even though I make my living practicing it. It's all just a game anyway. Let the Goyim believe in it. Let them believe in Lady Justice and her stupid blindfold. It's all just bullshit to preserve social order and to make a good living representing the fools who are stupid enough to sue each other. And maybe I was wrong about the Reformed Jews. Maybe they really aren't very much different than gentiles.*'

That last thought was too philosophical, too theological for Ben to contemplate. He didn't dwell on it. '*Anyway, having a lot of money in my own pocket is a good thing. Yes, having money in this narcissistic dishonest world is a very good thing.'*

It was perhaps too much to expect a man to go beyond his moral limitations, especially if that man was a lawyer. For years after the case settled, Ben would visit Bob, pretending to be a trusted friend; continuing to mislead him to believe that, upon David's death, there would be evidence brought forward that would open a fresh case against David's previous law firms, when in fact Ben himself had long since personally collected on that opportunity. Ben mentally calculated that his malpractice potentially exposed him to sixty to a hundred and twenty million Dollars of liability, but he figured the millions he got up front were worth taking the risk.

Being the deceitful scumbag that he'd become, Ben made sure that any wrongdoing he committed; any breach of professional ethics; would likely not survive a latches defense. Thus, Bob could be time barred if he figured out what happened and tried to bring a case. People did die; witnesses did move away; the truth did get shoved under the rug; and Israel prospered. The pathetic human Goy beast continued its toiling, blindfolded to the ways of the world, unjustly enriching the more powerful and corrupt among the populace. Life went on. The only risk to Israel and the community was that, somehow, word would get out about what had actually happened. Public sympathy for Israel would suffer; but the sympathetic media, the rabbis, and the political machinery would easily bury this sordid episode. Anyway, it would be someone else's worry, not Ben's.

Besides, Ben rationalized; the case in chief was so voluminous, so complex and intertwined, that even a determined ethical lawyer would blanch at the idea of taking on a malpractice case against him, especially if the lawyer was from Plaintown, where every lawyer knew every other. Gentlemen of the bar didn't normally sue each other out of professional courtesy. Ben stayed friendly with his client long after he'd screwed him.

Ben hoped no evidence would ever turn up to trip him up, and the statute of limitations on malpractice would run out before Bob became the wiser. Ben reasoned it was unlikely there would ever be charges brought against him or David's earlier lawyers for suborning perjury, malpractice, the ongoing bribes paid to conceal perjury, or the circumvention of justice, whatever that was. Ben stopped smoking cigars and got himself healthy.

Ben and Bob saw each other every quarter for twenty years under Ben's guise that, when David died, they'd come into possession of bribery evidence that would allow a reopening of the case. Ben promised Bob the case would be worth sixty to one hundred million Dollars with the libel component.

At long last, after David's death, Bob asked when they'd have the evidence to proceed against David's former attorneys. It was the moment of truth. Ben confessed that he'd worked for David years before, collecting a handsome sum of millions on a side deal concealed from Bob and that he'd *"cleaned up some loose ends for David."*

"Forget about suing his old lawyers," Ben said. *"People have died and moved away. Too much time has gone by. Forget about suing me too. All the money I got from David; I lost in the stock market. I am without much means."*

Bob asked but one question of his shadow friend and betrayer. *"When you had the settlement discussions with David and Mal, why wasn't I included?"*

"You are a Reformed Jew. David and Mal and I are Conservative Jews, closer to the ways of the Orthodox traditions. David and Mal would not allow your attendance. It was two against one."

"You mean three against one, so you could work your side deal to screw me, don't you?" Bob's question was met by Ben's stare into the floor. Ben could not hold Bob's eyes.

"Get away from me. Shame on you! You are without ethics or morals. You are a disgusting scumbag. Never call me again, said Bob."

As Ben left the table, Bob was alone with his thoughts:

'*Those who rail most against anti-Semitic sentiment are Semites who refuse to assimilate into a secular society, try as they might or pretend to believe that they can. When all cards are laid bare, it is the law of the tribe that prevails. That's why the Tribe survives nation states; why it will endure forever. Until there is no theology, no religion, and until secular notions of inclusive society are believed by all, those who believe in universal honorable conduct amongst fellow humans are delusional fools. It is a noble goal but an unobtainable one.*

'*It is a blood thing at its core. It's the blood of the Hebrew tribe, the tribe of Terah, Abram and Sara against the many other tribes that would destroy them. Blood trusts only like blood. If I had married a Hebrew woman, she would likely be trusted; I likely would still not be trusted. Only our child, with its mother's bloodline, would be trusted because mothers impresses their beliefs upon their children. The rabbis know this and keep the axiom: Only if your mother is a Jew, can you be a Jew. My mother was a Gentile; nevertheless, I tried to bridge the bloodline gap. I wonder, had I gone further and become Orthodox, would that have mattered? Probably not. Would I have also had to become a homosexual? Probably; but it likely would not have mattered. Perhaps embrace bestiality? Who knows? Would I have needed to join David in threesomes with Dolly, his favorite sheep? Unthinkable. Regardless, nothing would have mattered. Only the bloodline matters.*

'And what about his wife, his corporate board members, his friends in the tribe? They knew what he was doing. I'm sure, they did. They certainly could not pretend ignorance once my lawsuit was filed. Should I be surprised that none of them came forward? No, of course I shouldn't be surprised. After all, their strength, their very survival, depends upon their loyalty to the tribe. They closed ranks; stayed silent; individually, they did nothing. Of course they did nothing! Had any of them crossed the tribal boundary and testified on behalf of a Reformed Jew, they would be seen as traitors to the Tribe. I can't blame them. They were just being human; playing it safe; thinking about their own hides.

'Be realistic. Staying with the Tribe; staying loyal to the Tribe, and not to secular society, is what works and endures. It has worked to keep the tribal wealth intact since Sara prostituted herself to separate ancient Egypt from half its massive wealth. Money is the blood of commerce. The unspoken tribal mantra is: Keep the money in the tribe. It uniquely combines bloodline loyalty with loyalty to its wealth. The Tribe fights hard over money; making it and keeping it. Money and wealth are key to the tribe's survival. Without its wealth, what political influence would it have? What start-up ideas would get funded? So, the wealth is used wisely. It gains favored treatment in legislation. It gains the insider, plum position in start up investments. Money multiplies money.

'So, now that I have had this rare experience, what do I take away from it? Wisdom? Maybe a little? Maybe an understanding that there are people who have bad intentions; and one must be very circumspect in one's dealings? Absolutely. Understanding? Perhaps. Realize that change does not happen when the psychology is tribal. When preservation depends upon blood loyalty, nothing will change until the preservation psychology changes. And the preservation psychology will never change. There will always be the fear of them against us. There will always be the threat of another Babylonian *conquest; Roman conquest; or another Hitler. The People of the Book will never change because their psychology can never risk change. Well, maybe I played a very small part in changing it. Maybe in another six thousand years Jews will be more inclusive? Maybe then, there will be less animus towards Jews? Maybe humanity will be living on many different planets and moons; and all my thoughts will be moot. I hope so. I do not wish my experience upon anyone.*

'The Torah asks whether God should spare a sinful city to save the life of one righteous person. It should be spared. The converse might be, 'Should an entire religious tribe be blamed for the misdeeds of one unethical dirt bag? No. It should not be blamed. What happened to me is not the Tribe's fault. It is not my fault. It is not my mother's fault for not being a Jewess. There is only one person at fault, here; and that is David. Ben got dragged along; but that is understandable; even somewhat excusable. But David cannot be excused. He is not like other Jews. He does not have a heart that loves humanity. He is evil. He must be fewer than one Jew in a million. He has no soul. Likely, insanity snatched his soul from him; or he hated himself so much that he wanted to lose his soul so he could depart from it; separate himself from everyone and the world; perhaps, psychologically, become an insect? I think so. I think by mentally transforming himself into an insect, David believed he was no longer a human; no longer needing to have ethics or morality. He often spoke of insects. Insects fascinated him. What else explains why he betrayed his father, the Tribe, and the Zionist faction of the Tribe? It had to be a greater motive than money. It had to be his desire to escape the culpabilities that humans have for their decisions and actions. David had plenty of money without the companies. Yet, he betrayed his religion! He betrayed Israel! That's inconceivable. Even I, a non-Zionist Reformed Jew, cannot contemplate betraying Israel. David had to be truly evil in his heart of hearts to do that. And he did it willfully. He had to have great self-loathing to do that.'

Bob contemplated over a second iced tea before he left the lunch table:

'If goodwill amongst people is nurtured by thousands of good deeds, then this fragile tower of goodwill must be cherished; for there is great goodness in it, despite my individual pain. It is a cut into the soul of goodness, yes; but it is not a fatal cut. I must learn from this and move on with my life. I must not succumb to clichés such as 'do not trust a person from such or such a tribe or profession.'

'I must accept that wrongs often go unaddressed, like Aaron, brother of Moses, needed to accept that he was told his sons were somehow killed by a holy flame and God never allowed him to know why. Accept that God has a purpose for each of us; for all persons on Earth; and we are not allowed to know God's reasoning. Let those who choose to live like immoral unethical scums live that way. But continue to love God with all your heart and move on. And that assumes there is a God. Who knows? Spinosa wrestled with that question and concluded that God exists and is everywhere in all our thoughts and deeds. But is the great Spinosa is wrong; if there is no God, then love goodness with all your heart and be an ethical human being. Do the best you can. Be thankful for your blessings and be a good partner for Barbara. She is a good woman for you; and she loves you; and she needs you. Be strong for her; give her children; and be her good Big Horse.'

CHAPTER NINE

Whom the Gods would destroy they first make mad (Henry Wadsworth Longfellow: The Masque of Pandora)

MADNESS

After his side deal with Ben, David felt the need to share his hard learned lessons with his new protégé. He locked up the barn and went into the main house; then, to his secret green room to spend time with Andy. He had a problem in the arena with his champion tarantula. In the battle with the scorpion, the giant spider had lost three of its legs. It was useless as a combatant for future fights and it needed to be disposed of. David took Andy down from his shelf and positioned the fetus so its head was turned toward the arena case. He flipped a switch on the wall behind him. A low-frequency humming sound filled the room.

Once situated, Andy and David watched the disposal crew do their work. David opened some glass dividers that linked connecting corridors of red army ants to the gladiator case. It didn't take long for the hungry ants to get the scent of the injured spider. Soon, a few advance scout ants entered the case. They attacked immediately, biting the tarantula's remaining legs. When the ants bit into the hairy legs, the humming sound intensified in volume. The gladiatorial chamber's sound system was uniquely adapted to receive frequency vibrations from the spider and the various insects that were engaged in mortal combat.

While the scout ants carried a prized leg back to their colony, they were passed by swarms of their pheromone-sensing comrades headed toward the feast. The doomed spider was soon covered with ants. It writhed in agony. The humming sound's pitch increased noticeably. David quietly watched the animal begin its death throes while sipping whiskey on ice. Andy sat silently during his mentoring lesson.

David's Firm had been reduced to shambles. The stresses of litigation had aged him terribly. His reasoning powers were failing. He was on the borderline of permanent dementia. His abnormal sociopathy spiraled further downward into full blown psychopathy. He was reduced to coaching and mentoring a dead fetus that floated in a formaldehyde-filled jar.

From his dementia wracked mind and hatred devoured heart, David attempted to dutifully pass along his accumulated wisdom to a protégé, like his father, Marvin, had tried to do with him. Facts no longer mattered to David. He imagined he was grooming a viable successor to a vast business kingdom. The fetus was, of course, still as a stone and deaf as a stump. And yet, in David's mental state, this lifeless pulp seemed the ideal repository for absorbing ageless wisdom. David finally enjoyed an advantage with the fetus that he never had with Bob. Comforted that the dead fetus couldn't question or interrupt him, as Bob had so often, hurtfully, rudely done, David earnestly imparted his wisdom spew.

"Andy," David spoke authoritatively to his fetus protégé: *"Today I concluded some messy business. I want it to be a lesson to you. Lawyers can't be trusted. When I first went to see a law firm about defending myself against Bob, I asked them what the entire process would cost. They told me there wouldn't be a process. They told me this whole mess would die on preliminary motions. It will go away in three months, six months tops, they said. As for the money, they told me it wouldn't cost much. Their best guess was it would only take ten*

or twenty grand; thirty grand tops. Well, here we are Andy. It's been a twelve-year fight! It cost me over six million Dollars. And after all, all that fighting I still had to write big checks to Bob. This is the lesson you need to understand, Andy. Lawyers exist for one reason only. They are a pack of wolves in a sheep pen. The lawyers' mission is to destroy the lives of everyone who is not a lawyer. It's that simple. There's no such thing as a good lawyer or a lawyer you can trust. They are all blood-sucking, blood-thirsty animals. Avoid them.

"Bob was your father, Andy. I loved him, but he betrayed me. After all I did for him; the status, the office, the secretaries, the cars. I even set him up to fuck your mother, Andy. She was the best whore in the entire firm. All I ever asked in return was that he love me and become an Orthodox Jew. But he wouldn't suck me off; or even let me suck him off. He refused to compromise. He was not a good friend. Don't make the same mistake I made. Surround yourself with honest, honorable people, like me. Get good treatment before you give good treatment. The same goes for lawyers. Make them show you up front what they can do for you, before you give those pricks a dime.

"Lawyers are deceitful, Andy. That's their true nature. They work together to suck you into their process. They con you into believing it will be quick, and dirty, and over; but in truth the whole time they are supposedly working with you, they're actually working with the other side's lawyers to keep you locked into the process; to drag it out; prolong it; milk it for all the money they can. The truth is, Andy, lawyers don't give a flying fuck about their clients. That's their public image bullshit. Their only concern in every case is where the money is. Then, both sides conspire to carve up the money, like it's their Thanksgiving feast.

"Andy, here's my advice: Never sue and never get sued. Always make a deal without getting lawyers involved. That way you save time and expense. If I'd paid Bob a million or two right off, I'd have been better off. Instead, I paid far more than what we could have

worked out. I can't get back the money from the five appeals court decisions. That research and those bribes cost me millions, Andy. I paid hundreds of thousands for each appeal so these idiots could waste more of my money yammering at each other. I paid thousands just to have those pricks read e-mails they sent to each other. What were those e-mails about? Where's the best whorehouse? Which whores fuck best? What? What? I'm not allowed to see those emails. Those are privileged between lawyers. What a racket! Dirt bags! I'll show you the bills, Andy. You won't believe the charges!

"They charged for research hours! How do I know if they researched for five hundred hours or one-half hour? How can you know if they already knew the things they were supposedly research-ing? They spent hours conferring with opposing counsel, but they don't say what they talked about. I bet they talked about weather, sports, and the best places to get pussy; and then they charged me for it. All lawyers must be communists, Andy. They belong to a private communist organization. They design laws to get everybody to sue everyone else; and make cocksucker lawyers rich. They're parasites; like the lice and silverfish in our cleanup crews. They pick the bones clean from their litigation victims.

"Make your law firm give you an audited financial statement before you ever hire them, Andy. If they are overextended with their bank lines, they'll run fees on you like crazy. You can't trust them. Pay attention when I give you great advice, Andy. Look at their ref-erences; their revenues; and the kinds of cases they worked. Get a list of their last twenty clients and see for yourself if they had a conflict. I'm telling you, Andy, do not trust them.

"Someday I'll get control of the American government, Andy. When I grow our money big enough, I'll do that. I'll do it for you, Andy. The whole American government is for sale. When I buy it, the first thing I'm going to do is replace all the lawyers with baboons that sit in the chambers of Congress and throw paper and banana *peelings at each other. Things couldn't be worse than they are now."* David took another sip of whiskey and turned his attention from his protégé back to the glass arena.

"Look, Andy! The ants are tearing another leg off the spider! Can you hear the spider screaming?" The pitch in the humming sound increased. The speakers of David's ultrasensitive sound system gave out a strange hissing sound with intermittent spikes or screeches, much like a chalk scratch upon a blackboard.

"This is great fun, isn't it? Just stick with me, Andy. You are the perfect friend I've always wanted. We'll go far together.

"Now understand this, Andy. I enjoy a good fight, so I'd do it all over again. It was worth all that money just to torture Bob. I thought I got him close to suicide a couple of times; but he didn't do it. Damn it! So, Andy, here's a case of do as I say but not as I do. Take this lesson to heart and don't forget it. You'll be a fine executive someday, Andy. All you need to do is remember everything I've told you." David sipped more whiskey.

"Women are the cause of all the problems in the world, Andy. You need to understand this. That bitch, Susan woman got to Dad; and her daughter bitch, Marty, got to Bob. That spoiled my chances to make him my lover. Now that damn Indian bitch, Barbara, has gotten to Bob. He's gone forever.

'But I've got the best of Bob right here, Andy; in you! Back in the good old days, women never had the kind of power they have today. Back in good old ancient Greece, every man was a homosexual. That proves a man can become gay if he works at it. The Greeks kept women in their proper place. They only used them for housework and breeding. Then something went horribly wrong with the world and gay men like me became the bad guys.

"Women caused that change, Andy. They are dangerous. They lay traps of inducements to draw you in close. Once you become vulnerable, they spring their trap. They make you think you love them,

instead of loving a man. It all started when they figured out how to make their pussies smell better. A pussy has a natural advantage over a mouth, Andy. If you can get past the pussy's smell it slides smoothly over your shaft. But don't mistake that good feeling for love, Andy. Only men know what love is. No one deeply loves you like I do, Andy.

"I did my best to even the score. I wish I could have taken you from your mother's womb before I gutted her. You would have been right there beside me watching my good deeds. Booboo, one of my goats, put his hoofs on Marty's body. He was trying to eat her blood-soaked hair. I had to push him away. Then I took revenge for all sons who had mothers that rejected them. I struck a courageous blow against their wretched hateful sex, Andy. I wanted to do it all that afternoon, while I looked at it; but I held back and let Marty reveal all her wicked ways. Finally, I had the courage to do what I almost succeeded to do to little Betty Trout. I bit Marty's pussy! I finally did it! And do you know what? It didn't taste that great. I don't know why some men get so excited about kissing a pussy. I don't understand it.

"Just know this, Andy. You can trust me. I have your best interests at heart. My genius knows how the world works. I also have years of experience dealing with all sorts of filthy creeps. With your good looks and your youth, Andy, together we'll build a huge organization. I'll think the great thoughts. I'll come up with lots of brilliant ideas. You'll do the leg work and fly all over the country to carry out my ideas. You'll meet top salesmen, top businessmen, wealthy movie stars, pension plan executives, you name it. People will love you, Andy. You'll have the finest suits, the best shoes, and cars. People will hang on your every word. We'll go far together. We'll conquer the entire world!"

Andy, the fetus in the formaldehyde jar, sat silent and motionless facing the glass gladiator arena. The ants carried off another whole leg of the tarantula. Others began to dig the meat out of its abdomen. David continued with Andy's lesson:

"Oh Andy, look at those ants! They are working! I love it when they tear apart a spider. It's thrilling! Can you see the agony of the spider? See it moving its remaining legs wildly about? It's helpless to combat the ants that are eating its flesh. Hear how tormented it is! Can you hear its screams? Imagine the pain it's in! I love that sound, Andy. It's the sound of helplessness and pain. The spider is out-of-its-mind crazy with agonizing pain. It's a beautiful sound. Very few people know the thrill of meeting out pain to another animal. I made Bob feel pain, Andy. I couldn't hurt him physically, but I made his mind suffer; like that spider is suffering now.

"I kept Bob from getting to a jury trial, twice. Yes, I did! The first time I bribed the judge to dismiss the case. I also had a couple witnesses I bribed to make up lies about Bob, in case I needed them for trial. I was going to make him out to be a nut case that I had to fire, even though he built the company. You always need a backup plan, Andy; or, as I prefer to call it, a back door out of the problem. You need to see problems before they crop up, Andy. You need to anticipate what your enemy will do. And you need to have your moves in place, ahead of time.

"The second time I kept Bob from getting to a jury was when I bribed his lawyer. That was easy. I, my lawyer, and Bob's lawyer were all Conservatives. All I needed to do was persuade Bob's lawyer that it was okay to screw his client because Bob wasn't really a Jew. He was only Reformed, whatever they are. Imagine the torment Bob felt when his lawyer sold him up the river! After all his appeals wins, I still screwed him, Hahahaha!" David laughed uncontrollably.

"Just like the spider is writhing with the insanity of approaching death that he can do nothing about, I'm sure Bob went out of his mind with agony. I'm sure discovering that his own lawyer lied to him was painful. Ha!"

David regained his composure and spoke in a low, serious voice to his protégé. *"You need to be unmerciful and cruel in combat. We are rich, Andy. Bob is poor. I used my money to screw him; and win. That's the beauty of being rich, Andy. We can use our money to bait little people. Then, we screw them later, when it suits us. In court fights, the guy with the most money, who uses it to bribe the judges and lawyers, wins!"*

David poured a fresh glass of whiskey as he launched into the conclusion of Andy's lesson. *"The legal system is a farce, Andy. Little people believe there is justice that makes things right. Understand it like I do, Andy. The legal system is made up of people. They are morally weak, like all humans. We bribe judges and lawyers to get whatever we want. You must use money as a combat weapon, Andy. It's like hitting a little guy by dropping a bomb on him from ten miles above his head; when all he has to fight with is a knife.*

"Politicians are another farce, Andy. They are useless whores who do the bidding of the Federal Reserve and the bankers. They are merely accomplished in the same sense that female whores, like Susan and Marty, became accomplished. A great female whore learns that success in business doesn't come by catering to the whims and jealousies of other women. The whore knows it matters not who goes to whose parties; who gossips about whom; which woman wears what; whether her own selfish needs are being bested by her girlfriends' selfish needs. No, the successful whore knows that what she needs to do to get ahead is fuck and suck the right men; and get them to do her bidding.

"Politicians are exactly like whores, Andy. Harness politicians to benefit the firm. Use them like Dad used Susan and like I used Marty and Bob. Let them fuck the other guy for you. Pay them to pass the legislation or the rule-making you need, and they will gladly fuck for you. Unfortunately, their primary clients are the Fed and the bankers. Politicians will always fuck the public and pass laws

to squeeze the blood from the public for their masters. But you can still find occasional opportunities for bribing politicians, if you stay alert. Listen for those who are open to 'fresh ideas,' or for finding a new way to 'compromise.'

"Chat them up at a gathering. Tell them you need a private moment to discuss something of great importance. Slip a thousand or two in their pocket while you're talking to them. That's you, letting them know that you're willing to pay to play. They'll give you an audience. They like untraceable cash, even if they're rich. That way they can buy whores and cheat on their wives. They'll appreciate you. America is rapidly sliding into the sewer, Andy. In this environment, you have to think and live like a sewer rat to prosper. Remember that. Just think the way I do. Together, we'll go far."

After another whisky sip, David turned to Andy to give his protégé instructions about how to see the broader world:

"Andy, think of yourself as one of those ants. Like the ant takes his little bite out of the spider, our business takes a little bite out of America. See, Andy, we're no different; no better or worse than a corrupt government official who regulates big banks or commodity markets or anything else; and then takes a job with the law firm that represents the clients he regulated. He's just taking his bite out of the carcass.

"America will fall to a fascist or a communist dictator, Andy. Things can't go on the way they are. The country can not remain a democracy. The country is failing because of that son of a bitch Woodrow Wilson putting in the Fed and the IRS. He stole the country from the people. He fucked over the concepts of our founding fathers, Ben Franklin, Bob Hope, Abraham Lincoln, Johnnie Carson, Bob Hope, John Wayne, Mel Gibson, Lucile Ball, Jack Benny, Bob Hope, Winston Churchill; and Generals Douglas MacArthur, Bob Hope, and George Patton.

"Watch out for the Bilderbunkers, the Bank for Internal Settlements and the Diablos crowd, Andy. Those fuckers' days of power are numbered and the world's banking system will be turned on its head. They sowed the seeds of their own destruction with fractional banking. Their fiat money attempts to suffocate freedom and enslave humanity are ending. You need to be vigilant, Andy. I can't tell you how their power will end, but likely it will either be Arabs that want honest money for their oil; or the Chinese and the Russians will take them head-on in a war; or the mob will get wise to them and overrun their barricaded homes and meeting places with pitchforks.

"War is coming, Andy. It's like the old 'King of the Hill' game. There are all sorts of elements seeking to throw the established powers off the hill. I don't think it will come through the vote. These communist democrat party pricks rig the votes. Votes don't matter anymore, Andy. Only honest money can save the country, Andy. With honest money, all the tensions that divide the people will end. It's so simple to see, but first the people need to take the scales from their eyes. Just never get into a car with anyone named Teddy, Andy. He'll drive you off a bridge and drown you like he did that girl, especially when he's drunk. He's a no-good hypocrite son of a bitch the way he struts like a pompous-ass peacock, pretending to give a shit about women. Also, beware of any women named Hillary, who wear pastel pantsuits and screech like angry reptiles. Don't try to do dishonest business with them. They are stupid and careless. Only do business with smart crooks. Avoid them.

"America is dying the same way as that spider. We just need to bite off our piece of the carcass and gobble up all we can. Buy all the gold and silver you can get your hands on, Andy. We've got to be ready. When the end comes, there will be all sorts of destruction. Remember when the Chinese conquered Alexandria and burned that library and replaced all that knowledge with the Little Red Book of Bullshit from Mao? Mao was just a fat nut who loved to fuck *whores, Andy. Remember when the Nazis took over Cambodia and killed all the Jews? Or when Hitler invaded Tunisia in the Punic Wars and killed all the Carthaginians and the school teachers and burned their books? The Aztecs were the same way, Andy. When they overran France in the First World War, they raped women and cut their heads off. The present tide of socialism-communism has run its course, Andy. Change is coming!"* The people are getting smart and they are going to fight back. David was drunk; and he never let facts disrupt his train of thought. He took another swig of whiskey.

"The Buildyourbunkers Better Boys and the central bankers they control have gained control of the world, Andy." David slurred his words now. The alcohol fogged his mind and weighed upon his tongue. Nevertheless, he continued to mentor Andy. *"These top bankers meet on the eightieth floor of the Big Stick Tower in Basel, Cuba, or maybe it's in Portugal or Ireland, one of those communist countries,"* Andy. *"It doesn't matter where it is, because they have telephones. Telephones are a big deal, Andy. I use them myself. Anyway, Andy, what you need to appreciate is these banker scammers are trying to control the world for their own personal benefit. They want to use fiat money issued by their controlled governments through their debt-based banking systems so they can suck off the interest from the world's labor and goods production. They want to avoid using honest weights and measures as prescribed in the Torah mitzvahs, so they're doomed to failure. They're jerking off the world.*

"In the end, all banks will screw their depositors. Most will fail. It's not a maybe, Andy. It's a for sure, for sure. The Todly Frankie Bullshit Law puts the derivative holders of bad holding company trades first in F D I C liquidation. There's quadrillions of Dollars of banker bets and quant software programs that have no idea what values are. It's a hugely leveraged, levitated, roll of the dice, shit show. The wealth of the world will implode and impoverish

everybody who doesn't get it. People who have assets in brokerage and trust accounts in bank holding companies will lose everything. Poof! After the financial crisis of 2008, these clever deviants reorganized themselves into bank holding companies so they could be bank regulated instead of S E C regulated. Now they can reach into client accounts and invoke their bank account hypothecation clauses and steal everything. Hypothecation means they can use your money to gamble and when they lose, they can screw you. But you can't screw them, unless you get smart. Like me.

"This is a worldwide theft scheme, Andy. It bypasses and circumvents F D I C and S I P I C protections and lets the banks take everything everybody has. The little sticker on the bank window is for confidence purposes only. There's only one drop-of-piss fiat money in the ten-gallon fiat money piss bucket for every dollar that sticker guarantees. It doesn't mean shit. There's nothing behind the sticker! They are set up to steal your money, Andy. Do not trust their shit show.

"The morons who are bank officers and directors will get screwed along with everyone else, Andy. They get held personally liable for derivative counterparty losses of the holding companies. So do not be stupid Andy. Do not go on any bank boards. The bank fraudsters are running scared, Andy. That's why they passed even more legislation after their Toddy Frankie Law. They can't go back to the public taxpayer for another bailout like T A R P. They are like the ants, Andy. They kept ripping meat off the carcass until there was nothing left. Next time the credit cycle goes down, it stays down.

"Global bank failures on a colossal scale are coming at the bankers at light speed. They are shitting their pants. Their game is over, Andy. They have no gold or silver; and no street credibility. Just be ready for when fiat money becomes worthless. It's coming at you fast, Andy. Buy lots of good toilet paper while you can still get it. Dollars don't wipe well. They smear your ass.

"We need to watch the next election carefully, Andy. Both candidates have flaws and vocal detractors, but remember this, Andy. You are an American, and you must give your heart and soul and affections to whichever candidate wins. You must believe that, whatever the flaws, the winner will rule with goodness and benevolence toward all Americans and with malice toward none. Even if a female reptile wins, Andy, we must support her for the common good. We know in our heart of hearts, Andy, that women are smarter than we are. Just never let them hear that. What goes on in this room stays in this room. If you ever tell anyone that women are smart, I'll take you out of your jar and spank you.

"Now, Andy, pay attention! This is important! If America doesn't soon choose honest money over Bilderbunker Builders' fiat communism, we'll need to run away before the country descends into a police state. It's going to happen fast." As the alcohol took its effect, David slurred his words together and drooled streams of saliva. His vision went into and out of focus and his mind became tipsy as he blabbered incoherently to his imaginary protégé.

"Everything will blow apart at once. Pay attention, Andy. This is important! The hundreds of trillions of undisclosed unaudited Federal Reserve swap lines of Dollars for Pounds, Euros, Yen, Loonies, Aussies, Pesos, Kiwis, Francs, Pesetas, Yuan, Won, Dong, Rupees, Escudos, Lira, Drachma, and other currencies will all want gold at once. And with Federal Reserve bank and member bank balance sheets chock-a-block full of no income, no job loans to illegal immigrants who buy cars and disappear; and chop up the collateral cars for dope money, everything will fly into chaos. These insane derivative positions, holding up phony bank loans are going to blow apart and the leveraged credit implosion of the banking abortion will fall like the Eiffel Tower standing upside down on its head on a pinpoint; collapsing thousands of trillions in derivatives and collar trades to worthlessness when the debt shit show tips over. All this magical

financial engineering, the interest rate swaps, currency collars, insur-ance-guaranteed portfolios, hedges on bonds and bank stocks will all crash and burn. Poof! Whoosh! Gone! Blown away! AHHH! When it all blows apart, we'll watch it together on TV Andy. It will be wonderful!" David drank some more whiskey. He was slobbering all over his shirt and getting drunk. And he blathered on:

"The least disturbance; a butterfly flapping its wings; a Parisian whore, spreading her legs too quickly, will set off a breeze that will take the tower of financial babble out of perfect normal and bring the whole façade crashing down. It'll be a bigger crash than the Tower of Babble coming down. The hubris of the banking elite will take a huge drubbing and it won't recover until new gold and silver backed honest money returns. That's called a reset of the bank credit proxy, Andy.

"See, banks can't make new loans until they have a fresh base of honest money which enables them to renew their currency debasing cycle. It's a process they must go through. It's a lot like jerking off. They have to do it every once in a while. The hubris of man against God and nature will end. Then, another John Law, John Maynard Keynes, Alan Greenspan, Mario Draghi, or Robert Rubin will come along. He'll start playing his Pied Piper's meat whistle; his sweet siren sound of debt creation and money debase-ment. It's not voodoo rocket science, Andy. It's the bankers' con game. Dark pools and high frequency trades will blow the markets apart; fuck the little people and their pensions and kids' college funds. Then, the gamers will even fuck each other. Don't get upset, Andy. It's all normal. It happens every hundred or so years. People without ethics or conscience are attracted to power. And greed is natural to the human species. Screwing the little people with dis-honest money is perfectly normal.

"Vote-switching software in crooked voting machines won't stop peoples' cry for freedom when it comes, Andy. People will rise up

against their communist oppressors and make sure only honest votes are counted. Voting machines will get tossed into lakes in favor of honest paper hand counts with voter Identification required before anyone can vote. Thugs breaking the law by blocking votes at polling stations with their baseball bats will be met by honest people with guns. Honest voters will not be denied by commie bully thugs. Dead people and illegal immigrants will no longer get to vote a hundred times each. People will put a stop to the communists' vote-rigging scam tactics. People have had enough of phony communist, bullshit rigged elections.

"The establishment banking order is going to end in complete destruction. Players of the game don't understand it; neither do the agencies that pretend to regulate it. Only those who own gold and silver will survive. People will eat their pets and mothers-in-law to stay alive, Andy. No, it will be worse than that! There won't be any TV! There will be no money for extras. Hollywood will lose its moviegoers. People will read books; talk to each other; and go to church again.

"I'm serious, Andy. So far, the game has held together because the governments went all-in, supplying gold and silver inventory to the market; keeping metal prices down and their scam going. Now, they are down to stealing gold from allocated accounts, raiding gold exchange traded funds, begging gold, and silver from the Vatican, and conning dummy Americans into sell their heirloom gold and silver coins for worthless paper cash. The Pope is in the tank for the banks, Andy. He's a closet communist. But even he is getting upset with the commies. It's not smart to get the Pope upset. He wants secularism to end. He wants old-fashioned religion. That's how his bread gets buttered. He will get his way. The Imams, Chinese and Buddhists all want gold and silver money, too. The Pope and the rest of the world want to go back to gold because they have gold. But the American people don't have gold. Fort Knox gold hasn't been

audited for over sixty years. That indicates there is very little gold there; just show gold and gold held for others; maybe some leased gold. But we don't know the truth. That indicates we are screwed, Andy. Deep pocket players will soon upset America's money game. Dad told me this day was coming.

"Commie Marxists who want a single world order will have their nuts cut off, Andy. Banks will fail, countries will fail, but you and I will keep our nuts on because we're smarter than the other nuts. Don't let women handle your nuts, Andy. Don't make the same mistake our fathers made.

"But there may be hope, Andy. There are three wise men, Carlson, Hannity, and Levin. They seek to discover the truth; kind of like the three guys who rode their camels looking for Jesus Christ. Find them, Andy. Tell them the country must return to honest money. Explain the way forward to them. They will listen to you. They will guide the people to the right path. Andy, you will save the world!

"If everything fails, you and I will pick up and move to another country before the roof caves in. We'll find a place where there is real money and an honest society. I might have to take you out of your jar and carry you in my pocket to get you through Homeland Security, Andy, but don't worry. I don't leave a man behind. I don't cut and run. I'm not Joe Biden. I'm like the United States Marine Corps, Andy. We'll just wash off your formaldehyde smells. We can do this. Depend on me. Believe everything I tell you. I've got your back. I'll take good care of you."

David's demented mind, polluted with alcohol, wandered. He skipped from one random subject to another, spewing advice to his imaginary student:

"To become a complete executive, Andy, you need to understand Europe. I can give you great advice on Europe because I went there once when I was a kid. I became an expert on Europe. Dad took me there on a five-day trip. Dad wanted to stay longer, but we had *to come home because I kept throwing up; because Europe smells funny because the people eat fish all the time. What I learned about Europe is that you should never bother going there. It's too far north. It's next to the North Pole, so you're always cold there. It rains all the time in Europe. The people are always coughing because they are always cold and they all smoke five packs of cigarettes a day. It takes forever to get there, even by plane. You also risk some terrorist blowing your plane up coming and going; so you worry constantly about surviving the trip.*

"When you eventually, finally, get to Europe after five exhausting days on an airplane, you'll find that nobody speaks English except for a couple of people in a couple of countries, like England, so it's impossible to make sense out of anything anybody says. But even in England, the people don't speak proper English. They speak with golf balls stuck up their noses and they use the wrong words for things, like calling a sweater a 'jersey' or a 'pullover.' The entire place is a jumbled mess of people who don't know what anyone is saying. You always have to be careful because they try to steal your money. When it rains, you go to museums and look at worthless old junk.

"The whole country of Europe is a continuous museum. When you go into museums, you stand in front of glass cases where they show you the clubs guys used a thousand years ago to clobber the crap out of other guys. They had torture racks on display. Those are really exciting; but other than that, nothing else in Europe is interesting. After all, who gives a shit about how one guy killed another guy a thousand years ago? The most insulting thing about those museums, Andy, is they make you pay to enter so you can be bored out of your mind, looking at old junk.

"If you grow up liking women, Andy, you especially don't want to go to Europe. The women over there all look undernourished compared to American girls. The women in Europe are hairy, smelly,

and skinny; and their tits sag. My executive advice to you, Andy, is save your money. Stay in America.

"Every now and then you'll encounter a person called a liberal, Andy. They can't help the way they are or that they can't think logically. They think they know what's best for you. Never listen to them. I know what's best for you. Don't get upset with them, Andy. We need more of them, because they never know what's going on. They are useful idiots. When we dump a stock position, we need dummies to buy from us. We need stupid people who believe what they hear on TV.

"There's another really big secret I need to tell you about, Andy. It's about warts. It'll be important to you when you get older. See, there's this special subset of doctor quacks called dermatologists. These guys make a fortune going around with little nitrogen spray cans, zapping warts. They charge fifty to a hundred Dollars a wart. Now, if you're like me, with dozens of warts, that adds up to real money. You need to be really smart when it comes to money, Andy. Warts are a perfect example.

"I discovered that I can get rid of them just as easily by biting them off and then digging out the residual wart residue with my fingernails. But, when your warts are on your chest, your back, your feet, or your ass, you need a wart removal buddy who will take your warts off in exchange for you taking his warts off, like I do with my lifelong friend, Hirsh. Hirsh and I have saved thousands of Dollars by removing each other's warts. All you need is a simple pocket knife. It's important to think about these things, Andy, because with all the money you save by cutting off your own warts you can buy stocks, instead of throwing it away on some quack doctor.

"I want to be totally honest with you Andy. You know I'd never advise you to do anything that would hurt you. A lot of times when I have Hirsh bite a wart off, later I get two new warts at just about the same place. In fact, my back looks kind of like a wart field. And

getting those damn things off is painful. But I'm okay with pain, Andy. I associate life with pain. Life is a never-ending pain in the ass that gets more and more unbearable, the older you get. Sometimes I wish I was never born in the first place, in the same way Mother wished I'd never been born. She hated me, Andy. And now I even hate myself. Life makes me cry, Andy. It will make you cry too. It's painful to go through life, but you have to keep fighting life and never give up that fight, Andy. After you've fought life as long and hard as I have, someday you will wish you'd never been born, too."

Andy sat there in his jar of formaldehyde with his tiny head facing the carnage taking place in the glass arena. The ants were massing. Their red bodies were a living ball of destruction that engulfed the spider. The tearing and ripping away of spider flesh was in full force. The grand finale of arachnid agony approached.

"Andy, there's news!" David screamed breathlessly. *"I just heard on the radio that conservatives won the election! That means the liberals likely won't get to use the Doddly Frankie law to seize everybody's assets. The world will spend its way into hell and oblivion instead, and the currency will get monetized by the Fed buying up all the government debt. That means our money will become worthless even faster than before, Andy. You need to get your hands on as much gold and silver as you can afford to buy. Stick with me, Andy. You'll be wealthy beyond your wildest dreams!*

"I just had a brilliant thought, Andy! The more I drink the smarter I get. The President wants to build a wall and have Mexico pay for it. He'll do it, all right; by putting silver back into U. S. coinage and getting rid of the Federal Reserve. That's it, Andy! I've figured it out! Mexico will make a fortune on rising silver prices, and part of that price rise the Mexicans will remit back to the U. S. to pay for that border wall. Mexicans will do great because their peso currency will rise. Mexicans might even want to stay in Mexico! Americans will do great because they'll have an honest weights

and measures country and an honest government again. The government will shrink in size! The economy will soar!

"Andy, I've decided to take you with me to an executive meeting. We're going to China to make a proposal to Xi Ding a Ling. He's a good man to do business with, Andy. He's one of those intelligent people who can see change coming and who positions to take advantage of it. Lots of successful companies, like Nike, Apple, Coke a Cola, and the big banks do business with him. The human rights people say you should not do business with him because he tramples human rights. They point out that his troops invade Muslim homes. They take away the children, make slaves of the men, and turn the women into prostitutes. They say this is terrible. You'd expect them to say that, but it's just the way of the world, Andy.

"It's actually wonderful to have more prostitutes in the world, Andy. You'll appreciate that when you get older. Things change and attitudes change. From what I hear, after those women had their children and husbands taken away from them, and after they'd been repeatedly raped by dozens of Chinese soldiers, they enjoyed it; and craved more of it. Many enthusiastically become whores.

"Xi reoriented their concepts of morality. He changed their belief system. He's a genius! Now, these women love having men touching and feeling them constantly. They love having fine clothes and flaunting their pussies; and they especially love being fucked several times a day by different men. They don't want their old lives back. Even when they are offered their old lives back, most of them choose to continue being whores. They love the lifestyle and the pleasures. That proves the human rights people don't understand human nature. It's not clear to me that old ways are the best ways, Andy. Many of the old ways are confining and restrictive. They hold back human progress. So, Andy, instead of listening to the human rights people, you need to make your business decisions based on what makes the most money.

"Xi sees trends and makes money on opportunities. I'm sure he can see, like I can, that America's morality standards are deteriorating. Your mother helped me see that, Andy. More and more, Americans love and adore their favorite porn star whores. Well, we'll go to China and offer Xe a 25% interest in our whorehouse, child trafficking, drug distribution, and money laundering operations for a modest Ten Billion Dollar investment. We have the know-how to take our operation into all fifty states. We know how to get the houses sited in residential zoned neighborhoods. We know who to work with to staff our houses and run them properly. We know how to make the right political, police and justice system contacts and how to bribe the right people.

"Xi should go for our proposal. I think he will. He sees change and opportunity. He doesn't let vague, nonsense concepts like morality get in the way of progress. Let's face facts, Andy. The facts regarding Epstein and Maxwell's operation prove that grown men love fucking underaged girls. That's a huge market, Andy; and we are in an ideal position to supply it. We'll reap a fortune!

"I believe most young girls will love the opportunity we'll give them, and the money they'll make. They'll be thrilled to become whores who can fuck twenty to thirty times a day, making terrific money while doing it. Remember, Andy, you must turn a blind eye to morality. People who oppose a trend like this will just see their power eroded. They make lots of noise, but they can't stop the trend. Remember, Andy, the trend is your friend!

"I believe millions of American women secretly wish they could become porn stars. But they are just too timid, or too hung up over what someone might think of them. hey are too shy to make that first porn film and getting their careers rolling. But I think more and more women will come around to doing prostitution and making porn as a fabulous career choice. After all, fucking hundreds of men because it's enjoyable is a better proposition than fucking one *man because he brings home a paycheck. It makes perfect sense for a woman to get into porn. That seems to be the national trend, Andy. Who knows what morality is, anyway? America is not about morality. It's about money."*

Andy sat inside his formaldehyde jar, still facing the carnage taking place inside the glass gladiator cage. David changed topics from his executive lessons to events in the combat arena. As the ants tore away another leg from the spider, he whispered breathlessly to his student fetus:

"Look how wonderful this is, Andy!" David's head swiveled in circles from his inebriation, while he spoke:

"Can you see the beauty of this? Look at that spider shaking. He's well into his death throes! He deserves to die. He's a loser!! Hear those sounds? I'll turn up the volume on the sound translation system. Can you hear him screeching and screaming? It's a unique sound, Andy. It's the sound of pain! His body is being ripped apart and he can't stop it from happening! You won't hear that sound anywhere else in the world, Andy. That's the sound of unrelenting agony."

David's head laid back upon his shoulders. He rolled it from shoulder to shoulder, drinking in the sounds of the spider's pain. He relished the horrifying sounds of mutilating dismemberment more than seasoned opera goers savor their Arias.

"It's so beautiful to hear his pain, Andy. He's in horrible, unbearable pain. Can you hear it? He can't escape from it! It's fascinating to watch him tremble and quiver in pain, Andy. I love this part so much! Listen to him suffer! He's pleading for mercy, for the pain to stop. He wants to die so his pain and torture will end. But the ants can't give him mercy. They don't know how to do that. They have no feelings, themselves; and they have no empathy for the spyder. They just keep tearing his flesh away and eating more of him. He only gets to die when his body is eaten away so badly that his body can no longer live. This is how life really is, Andy. People

They keep hurting you until you die inside. Like Mom and Dad hurt me. Remember that.

"Someday the little people are going to hurt the banks, Andy. There will come a time when little guys get even, just like those ants ganging up on that spider. The ants are like the little people who are killing the big evil banks by buying gold and silver, Andy. When they buy the metals, it is their way of taking their small tiny bites out of the big banks! I wanted you to see this. This is your lesson in class warfare. It's happening just like Dad said it would. Dad said the little people would win in the end. As you can see, Andy, the little people are winning. This is a special lesson for you to watch and hear. It's a wonderful lesson, Andy. I love it so much, and I love you too, Andy. This is better than watching reality TV, don't you think? Here, Andy, have a drink with me."

David poured a shot of whiskey over the top of Andy's jar. Then, David took another healthy gulp of whiskey, leaned over, and kissed the top of Andy's formaldehyde jar. He then put down his glass of whiskey. He drew his pants zipper down and reached for his penis with his free hand. His experienced fingers began their familiar work. They stroked and coaxed David's truest and most trusted longtime friend until its little head ejaculated. David's limbic zone was aroused by the excitement and tortured sounds of arachnid carnage. His mind was long gone. Inebriated, David experienced nirvana.

Andy was David's perfect protégé. The spider twisted and screeched in spasmodic twitches of agony. The ants were executing David's sadistic death sentence. Andy looked on as the ever loyal, unquestioning observer. Safe in his formaldehyde jar, he showed no signs of letting his emotions cloud his judgment. He would never get distracted by the silly needs of women. He never talked back to David, nor did he ever question David's wisdom, behaviors, or entertainment preferences. Andy had a promising

CHAPTER TEN

There is no passion in the mind of man so weak, but it mates and masters the fear of death...Revenge triumphs over death: love slights it; honor aspires to it; grief flies to it (Francis Bacon: Of Death)

ANTS

Travelers to Rocky Mountain National Park, Yellowstone, or the Tetons will notice little signs along the roadsides of the surrounding towns and in the parks themselves; signs that caution the unwary. The signs say: *'Caution! Bears are active in this area. Avoid all bears!'* Those who live near these parks heed these warnings. Especially to be avoided are female bears' cubs. Getting near a cub, playing with it, touching it, getting between it and its mother is not merely a bad idea. It's a terrible idea.

Something instinctual happens when a mother senses that her cub is threatened. It matters not what the cub did or whether the cub first approached the human. The mother bear has no human capacity to rationalize, and no ability to tell a good person from a bad one. All momma bears feel is their primordial drive. That drive tells them they must kill the intruder; rescue their cubs from any dangers, real or perceived. All ursine, feline, canine, and most human mothers share this protective instinct. And woe to those who trigger it.

Whatever composure Susan normally maintained was overwhelmed by the gnawing realization that her precious darling

Marty had likely been murdered by David. She visualized her daughter being hoisted into the air by David, using his block and tackle apparatus; then being taunted while suspended in midair, like a helpless sheep; then slaughtered like a hapless animal. Did David taunt her before she died? Did he sneer at her while he butchered her? Did he dismember her; feed her guts to his pigs; shove her bones into his wood chipper? Did he mulch her bone chips with his composter? Were her teeth smashed and scattered for the Guinea hens to use in their crops? Were Marty's remains giving sustenance to David's roses?

'*What have you done to my daughter, you sick son of a bitch?*' Susan's motherly instincts cried out for an answer.

Susan was sickened and enraged by the revelations of Muscle Man. Remorse dogged Susan. It was too late to save Marty, but not to avenge her. David was the child nemeses that Susan never liked. He got in the way of her love for Marvin. He disgusted her. His thievery, lack of ethics and morals, and his impish pranks nauseated her. She had tolerated him for these many years, leaving Mrs. Rodriguez and Barbara to bear the brunt of his petty annoyances. Marvin had provided extremely well for Susan. But at what horrific cost to her daughter? He had vastly enriched her and ensconced her securely in the firm. But now this! Murder! Horror of horrors! Her world was thrown into turmoil. '*You little bastard!*' Incensed, Susan seethed with rage.

She was enraged by David's audacity. As his lifetime sitter, she saw him do many deplorable acts. And she tolerated those acts. But not this! He was not going to kill her precious flesh and blood! He was not going to get away with it! He must not! Going to the authorities was out of the question. He would simply lawyer up and bribe a judge or a juror. She could visualize David laughing at her as he walked out of a hung jury courtroom and a declared mistrial dismissal.

Susan knew that justice for David could not be trusted to normal bureaucratic channels. The criminal justice system would be too good for him, even if it convicted him and sentenced him to life in prison. She recognized that this was a matter that needed to be settled in a biblical way; by an eye for an eye and a tooth for a tooth. Revenge through personal vendetta has a finality about it. Punishment meted out by a jury can't approach it. When murder becomes personal, the system can serve its justice; but only blood adequately answers for blood. And Susan's rage boiled her blood.

There was no body, no witness, to Marty's murder; just that one piece of circumstantial evidence; that scalped shock of Marty's hair. The thought occurred to Susan that the perpetrator could possibly be someone other than David. She doubted that, but her administrator's sense of getting things one hundred percent right told her she needed to take steps to be certain.

David was in his office, feeling jovial. He'd just settled his litigation with Bob and was now contemplating a long trip to the Caribbean to relax. There were brochures of vacation spots on his desk when Susan walked in. She sensed that she had caught him off guard.

"David, I'm trying to create an abstract painting of Marty and I need some help to make her image realistic. Do you remember seeing her in blue shorts or do you remember seeing her in red shorts?" The request seemed perfectly straightforward and with no hidden purpose. Susan could have been an actress.

"Blue shorts. I don't recall her wearing red shorts," David said without thinking, before returning to his brochures.

That clinched it for Susan. Marty *never* wore shorts to the office. She always wore business suits or skirts to the office and to company functions. The only way David could have seen Marty in shorts was if he'd been to her home; or if she had gone to David's for some nefarious purpose, without mentioning it to her. Marty wore shorts on summer weekends. She went missing over a weekend. Probably she was with David while wearing shorts. The reason she was with David didn't matter.

It didn't take long for Susan to get her first bit of proof that David was the culprit. After about five minutes, he gave her door his gentle knock before he entered. She was ready for him, working on an acrylic painting of Marty, right there in her office. Her inquiry had seemed perfectly plausible. Still, David now blundered further into her trap:

"You know, Susan, come to think of it, I don't think I ever saw Marty in a pair of shorts. I only ever saw her in skirts. I must have been remembering her wearing a blue skirt. I hope that helps you some." David turned and left. Susan watched his movement closely. He walked more deliberately than usual; like he was still a child trying to sneak away from his theft of a cookie from a cookie jar, before he broke into a full run.

Susan's confirmation came from David's well-thought-out denial. It was much more deliberate than his spontaneous comment, when she'd caught him distracted and off guard. She knew David by his behaviors from childhood. He hadn't changed. He still sneaked away from his bad deeds; hoping to not be noticed; hoping to not get caught. Susan had her confirmation.

David sought to slip away from Susan's trap. He pretended there was no reason to suspect him. He hoped Susan wouldn't notice that he was rattled by his own blunder. But Susan had watched him carefully; noticed how he tiptoed from her office, like a little boy, trying to sneak away. But cowardly little boy David hadn't fooled sitter Susan for a second. Instead, he reinforced her maternal instincts. They now brought David sharply into focus. Susan planned her next move carefully.

Days elapsed after Susan's inquiry about Marty's shorts. David assumed the incident was all about nothing; but it nagged his conscience that he could be so forgetful and glib. Susan wasn't stupid; but she *was* getting older. He rationalized that Susan had no reason to suspect anything. He assured himself he was in the clear. He had avenged Bob's rejection by screwing him out of the companies. He had avenged his miserable childhood by murdering his half-sister, Marty. He believed he had gotten away with everything. He thought all was well in his world.

It was getting on toward dusk. It was late summer. A circus show was moving into town. There was going to be a parade with horses and clowns moving through the main downtown street. Downtown would soon become a bedlam of traffic if he stayed much longer. He went to get his car from the garage. It was his oldest Cadillac, the beat-up car from hell that he used to intimidate other drivers. As he approached his favorite car, he saw the strangest thing. Someone had attached a chain fall to the steel beam above the vehicle. A chain hung from a block pulley suspended from the beam. There was a stepladder off to the side of his car. David stood there for a moment, dumbfounded. He couldn't imagine why someone from the garage was working on something so late in the day; nor could he imagine what it was. He stood behind his car and gazed at the chain fall. As he began to gain a dim awareness that something was amiss, he received a conk on the back of his head from a pipe wrench. He fell to the ground, unconscious.

Susan remembered everything that Muscle had told her; that even a child could lift a mature bull with the chain fall apparatus. She was about to find out. She removed David's car keys from his pocket and opened the car's trunk. She wrapped a rope around David's waist several times; knotted it; attached the hook at the chain's end to her makeshift rope belt; then, pulling on the chain, hoisted David into the trunk of his car. That was easily done! Pleased, she climbed on her stepladder; removed the block pulley and chain; tossed the chain fall apparatus and the stepladder into the trunk, onto unconscious David; then she drove away.

She drove two hours south of Plaintown to the Shadow Mountain range. It was late. The dirt bikers who rode these foothills trails had gone, probably to see the circus show. A logging road she'd scouted days before took her to an isolated clearing. It was crossed with game trails, but no bike trails. She stopped on a high bluff above a tributary to the Platte River. There, she stood beside a nearby tree and listened. She heard no motorbike noises. The only sound was from the peaceful water ripples of the stream coursing its way over the gentle, shallow rapids far below. Susan's mood was in tune with the soothing sounds that stream made that warm late summer evening. She breathed a sigh of relief while working with a calm deliberation, using the full moon's natural light. She'd brought a flashlight, but she hesitated to use it. Being seen by campers on the other side of the stream, or by ranch hands from the bunkhouse cabin far below, was not something she wanted.

She used a convenient tree to rig her chain fall. Then, she swung David out of the car trunk. He was a little groggy. She conked him on his head again. He was safely knocked out a second time. After Susan finished arranging his body, she took her chain fall down and returned it, along with her stepladder, to the car's trunk. When she had everything prepared for David, she poured water on his face. He revived to discover his mouth was taped shut with duct tape. He was naked. His arms and legs were spread out and staked down tightly against the ground. He couldn't move an inch. Susan had placed large rocks upon and around his torso. All he could do was breathe. His legs and arms were tautly tied to the nearby trees. Even if, by some miracle, he could work loose one leg or one arm from a staked-down fastener, he wouldn't be able to use his free limb to reach any other limb. Susan had thought of everything. She always was a thorough and competent administrator. Her work was finished.

Susan stood over David. She looked down at him for the last time. So many thoughts and decisions, over so many years, had brought everything to this. If only Marvin had let his heart rule him. If only Eloweiss had summoned the courage to ask for a divorce. If only David had been a more normal child; one she could at least be friends with. If only she had left the Firm when she knew she could have no family with Marvin. She asked herself:

'What kept me there? Was it love? The security? The sex? The jewels? If only I had kept Marty in Plaintown and not blocked my child out of my life. What was my own role in all of what brought me to this? Yes, I am committing a murder, of a sort. But it is well planned. I will not be caught. I am not the one doing the dirty work of this murder. Those actors deserve a measure of revenge, too. Well, enough of my maudlin thoughts. Enough of thinking that I can rewrite history. What has transpired has come and gone. This is all there is left to do. I am here now. David is here now. He is awake again. Likely his head hurts from the bumps I gave him. But I don't care how he feels anymore. He can't cry with his mouth taped shut. I'll never hear him cry again. His eyes are open. It is time to say my good-byes.'

"I've placed you near an ant hill, David," she spoke to him now, matter of factly, as if she was going over a regulatory report. *"It's home to those big red ones that you loved to torture as a child. Also, I've selected a spot above a stream for you. You have some good neighbors here. There's a yellow jacket nest under a nearby log. From this high vantage point, Crows, Clark's Jays, and Ravens often sit to watch the river far below. See, look up into the high branches, David. That's where they'll sit and watch you before they drop down to peck out your eyes. Daybreak will come in about seven hours, David. I've made sure you'll have some visitors. I've poured some honey on your*

penis. *You always like having your little pee-pee played with, don't you? I've also dabbed some honey in your hair. That's to remind you of Marty's hair. I'm sure you remember the patch of her hair you cut from her scalp, don't you?"*

David shook his head slightly. He was determined to lie to the end.

"That doesn't cut it, David. There's only one way out of this for you. If you admit you killed her, I'll get you out of this and I'll take you to the police. Okay?"

David nodded. Susan opened the duct tape for him to speak, telling him that if he screamed, she'd bash in his face with the pipe wrench. He didn't scream. He was terrified.

"Answer me, David. How did you kill her?'

"I drugged her," David spoke in hurried frightened speech. He was a little boy again, confessing to his baby sitter; believing Susan; believing his confession would save him. *"Then I hoisted her in my barn and I sacrificed her to God. She was a sinner, Susan. You know that. Let me go. I'll give you all my money, my share of father's diamonds. You can have all my businesses; everything. Just name your price."* His eyebrows raised in hopes he could talk his way out of his terrible predicament.

"Thank you for that, David, I needed to be sure. You under-stand, it's the administrator in me." Susan reapplied the duct tape to cover his mouth. She now knew for certain she was not making a mistake. David whined and grunted. He knew he was in dire mortal straits. Susan spoke to him in a compassionate voice, as she would to a baby she was about to put to sleep for the last time.

"Your father, your mother, and I all tried very hard to bring you up properly, but you failed all of us. You've failed your god as well as all of his creatures. I've watched you from the time you were a little boy pulling wings from butterflies, pulling legs from ants. How do you think those insects felt? How do you think Bob felt when you

took his career from him? How do you think Marty felt when you hung her up and butchered her?"

David puffed his chest out, attempting to push off the pile of rocks. But they were big flat rocks. And very heavy. He had no success. He twisted his torso as best he could; but there was nothing gained from that effort either. He glowered at Susan with his beady, reddish, hate-filled eyes. Susan noticed the true David. She shook her head at the devil in his eyes.

"You've never considered anyone's feelings your entire life," continued Susan. *"You didn't learn all your behaviors, David. I suppose they were just traits you were born with. But you're not like your father, David. You could never be like him. Marvin was a good man at heart. He was just trapped by his religion in a marriage to a woman he never loved. He never sought to hurt others or be evil for his enjoyment like you did. Now you're going to learn how other people felt when you hurt them without caring. When these ants begin eating your balls, and when they start digging into your scalp and your eyes, you'll know how it feels to be hurt by someone who simply doesn't care. There's no other way to teach you this lesson, David. And this is your last lesson. I'm resigning as your babysitter."* Susan ignored David's insistent grunts. She was not going to let him have his way this night.

"When the sun comes up, the hornets will smell the honey. They'll come to visit you, David. You better stay motionless while they walk on your skin. They might sting you. Remember how boo boos make you cry?" continued Susan, mocking him. She was speaking as a calm murderess now. *"The crows and the Jays may eat your eyes. You probably didn't know they did that, did you? I think your eyes will be the first things you'll lose. You'll have to live for a while without seeing. That's too bad.*

"You're not answering me, David. Oh, that's right, I almost forgot. You can't cry or complain or scream with your mouth taped

shut. I see you are shaking your head. That's not going to cut it, David. Trust me. Your baby sitter is doing what's best for you. Good-bye David. We have nothing more to discuss. Be a good little boy tonight. Remember to say your prayers. Pray to God that he takes you into his bosom. Pray that you've made some good marks in your Book of Life. Good night, baby David. Sleep well."

Having said her final good-bye to her lover's son and her one-time charge, Susan spit on David's face. She did that to make sure he understood that she meant him disrespect. Then she drove back to Plaintown. She'd finally realized one of her long-sought dreams. Her life was finally free of David. She had atoned to Marty as best she could for her failings as a mother. Perhaps Marty's spirit was watching David's demise from afar. She hoped so. Hopefully it would know, somehow, that her gruesome murder had finally been avenged. Susan said a silent, tearful prayer to her daughter's spirit as she drove away from David. It was her prayer for forgiveness.

On her drive back to Plaintown Susan noticed a Monarch butterfly had gotten inside the car. It sat on the seat next to her. *"Well, hello there, little one,"* she said with some cheer in her voice, *"did you flutter in here through an open window? I must have left a window open."*

The Monarch opened its wings and then closed them again. *"Did you understand what I said?"* Susan glanced down at her riding companion.

The Monarch again opened and closed its wings. *"You must be here from Mexico. You're coming here to lay your eggs, aren't you?"*

Again, the Monarch fluttered open and closed. *"Did you see what I did back there?"*

The Monarch responded by opening and closing its wings twice. *"Do you know how bad he was and what he did to my daughter?"*

Again, the Monarch opened and closed its wings. *"Are you just doing that because I'm speaking; or do you understand something?"*

This time the Monarch sat still with its wings upright and closed. *"I've always wondered, do you butterflies understand things in a spiritual sort of way; and by your migration cycles, do you know about things your parents and grandparents saw?"*

This time the butterfly opened and closed its wings twice; then repeated its opening and closing twice, as if it was saying yes to both Susan's questions. *"Then, do you think I did a good thing back there?"*

The butterfly opened its wings and held them open for a prolonged time before it closed them. *"Well, I'm glad you feel that way. Then would you like me to stop the car and open the window, so you can fly away?"*

Again, the Monarch opened its wings. Susan stopped the car and opened the passenger window. The Monarch fluttered up to the open car window and sat on the top of the window. It turned completely around and stared at Susan for a long while. Then it opened its wings and held its open stance for another long moment as if it wasn't quite ready to leave. It was waiting for something. *"Goodbye, little friend,"* said Susan.

Then the butterfly lifted off the open car window and fluttered away.

Driving back to Plaintown, Susan's mind reflected upon her life and the choices she made. Her heart was heavy. She knew she had just concluded something; had just closed an important chapter of her life. But she felt hollow inside; incomplete. She needed to address something. Marty. She needed to explain herself to Marty; to atone to her daughter, dead now; but perhaps present in spirit. Yes, perhaps if she explained herself, Marty's spirit would understand her; possibly forgive her. Maybe? She could only hope. She was not a religious person. She gave that up long ago in her teen years. But she was not without a soul, either. She could confess her soul's shortcomings and misgivings and sins to Marty's spirit, couldn't she? Why not? Why not here, on the road back to Plain-town? It wasn't a confessional booth, but it was private, wasn't it? Just her spirit and her daughter's spirit. Finally, long overdue, honesty. Susan began speaking to Marty's spirit:

'Marty, dearest, there are things I need to say to you. I need to tell you how sorry I am for the way our lives have turned out. It's all my fault, my grievous fault. And I need you to know how profoundly sorry and regretful I am for the things I have done. I do not expect you to ever forgive me. I only want to tell you that none of this would have happened if I had been a decent mother.

'I can only imagine how hurt you must have been when Joseph, your daddy, left you by committing suicide. You need to know that he didn't want to leave you. I drove him to commit his suicide. I wanted him dead so I could have more time with Marvin; so, I could be free to spend long hours in the office with Marvin. I'm sure you felt a kind of rejection and separation when Joseph left you; but your daddy never rejected you, Marty. He loved you very much. I'm certain his dying thoughts were about how much he loved you. I used to watch the two of you playing together. It was beautiful to see how happy you both were. Joseph was like a child, himself. He could relate to you on a child's level; something I could never do.

'But you see, Marty, I wanted Marvin. I saw how he lived; how much wealth and power he had; how much wisdom he had; how well he understood people and cultures; how he spotted a weakness in someone and used it to his advantage. And I wanted all of that for myself. I wanted to become his wife. That's why I drove your dad to suicide. I wanted to make my pathway to Marvin clear; so, I pushed your father out of your life and out of his life, also. I wanted *what Eloweiss had. I tried to take her place as Marvin's wife. I did a horrible thing to you in order to get what I wanted, for me. I sent you far away, to the WEX boarding school for girls. I'm sure that made you feel rejected by me. Your feelings were right. I did reject you. I rejected you for a lifestyle that gave me money and power and seemingly endless sexual pleasures.*

'I became Marvin's whore. Office wife, we both called me; but in truth, I became the company whore. I did think of you during those years. I thought about the hurt I must have been causing you; but I rationalized. I told myself that I'd make it all up to you, someday. I guess I even convinced myself that I was being honest. But in truth, I knew I didn't know whether what I was telling myself was true or even possible. I was delusional. I believed I could have my cake; and eat it, too. But that can't be, not for anyone. Life's about choices; one or the other; and the consequences of our choices.

'I tricked my mind into believing that I could someday make everything up to you and everything would be all right between us. That's why I told you about the jewels and why I willed them to you. Now that you are dead, I'll will them to Barbara. She's become close to me and she's a good person. I think, if you had gotten to know her, you would agree that she should have them. Of all of us in this sordidly evil company, she's the only one who would actually use them to create good in the world. She wants the buffalo to return. Well, that's crazy; but, why not? Maybe she and her foundation will make it happen.

'Then, there you were at WEX. You tried to reach out to me; tried to explain how those righteous Christian girls were rejecting you. More rejection. My poor baby! I can understand how you coped by pretending that stones loved you. Maybe they did. Maybe you got more love from stones than you did from me or anyone else before you met Maria and Bob. Those two friends and lovers became your salvation, didn't they? They were your link to life and happiness,

weren't they? I am so sorry I couldn't be a part of your life. I see that now. I see all my shortcomings. I was a lousy mother.

'That's why I tried to change you when you came to the Firm, after your affair with that bank president. I thought I could keep you from becoming the same kind of company whore that I was. But I underestimated you. I can't blame you for becoming a porn star. In fact, I was proud of you when you became ranked as the world's number one porn star. Yes, Marty, I was proud. In a world ruled by men and religions, you showed all of us that you could be your own person; you could take control and you didn't give a damn who didn't approve, because you didn't need approval. You showed me something then. You made me proud to be your mother. I got there, to that place of pride, in a very round about way; but I got there. I am very proud of you, baby.

'I just want you to know that I love you very much. I would live my life very differently if I could live it all over again. I don't know about the church scene. Grandmother Mallory laid that on very thick, I'm sure you remember. She's the driver that drove me away from her and religion and into the arms of Marvin. So, I wouldn't do things her way if I could do them over again. Maybe more like a little bit of your way, and with a man like Bob, who loves a woman for who she is; not for what he can change her into, like Marvin did to me.

'I'm glad I had this chance to talk with you, dearest daughter. I think we'll have many more talks like this in the future. For the first time in many years, I feel good about myself. I'm glad I've murdered David. I'm sure you're okay with that, too, aren't you? Doesn't it feel wonderful to get that son of a bitch, that sicko psycho, out of our lives? Sure, it does! And, Mommy promises, if we do get next lives; next time, Mommy will be a very good Mommy to you. Mommy loves you very, very much.'

Susan's good-bye was the last human sound David heard. Two Clark's Jays perched in the branches above him studiously took in the pre-dawn scene, making sure they had a safe chance for a meal. They were positioned to take David's eyes before the crows discovered him. As David lay there, he already felt little bites pinching flesh away from his testicle sac. The ants weren't waiting for daybreak.

Before the Jays could summon their courage to swoop down and peck his eyes out, David heard an animal skid to a sudden stop on the loose gravel near his body. He smelled its hot breath and heard its low-pitched growl, while it sniffed him.

Minna: Pause briefly here, please try your best here to make a snarling growling sound from deep in your throat like a wolf that's about to bite, like: GRRRR, GRRRR.GRRRR (Or have an audio from an animal, dog, coyote or wolf, growling.)

Hoping it was a friendly dog with its owner nearby, David turned his head to look. Eyeing the Lobo shocked David. This was not someone's friendly household pet. It was not even a coyote or a wolf. It was much larger than a wolf. It had glowing yellow eyes. Curled lips bared its huge canine teeth. It drooled on David. Its throat rumbled with a low steady growl. A sudden fear swept David. It was a fear unlike anything he'd never known before. He did not have this fear when he shot his game farmed lion at long distance, or when his corralled moose faced him in the instant before he fired his fatal shot. He was in control then. Those animals had no chance. This was different. This beast had all the power; he had none. For the first time in his life, David knew a deep, primal terror.

He grasped a horrible reality. This half-wolf, half-coyote beast was half-starved and hungry. It was clear to David. The beast was going to eat him alive! David lost control of his bowels and evacuated. Adrenalin surged through David's body producing a burst of superhuman strength. He needed to fight for his life. With a mighty yank, he freed one hand from its binding. He removed the duct tape from his mouth and screamed in terror, hoping that would bring someone to his rescue. But no one heard his screams. And no one came. He flailed at the Lobo with his free hand as he struggled vainly, trying to free himself from his other bindings.

The Lobo brooked none of David's feeble resistance. The beast sized up his prey as a ridiculously bloated creature. The man on the ground thrashed harmlessly with his freed limb, much like jack rabbits kick helplessly while the Lobo holds them captured in his massive jaws. The man screamed like a rabbits screamed. This annoyed the Lobo. He didn't like being annoyed while going about his work. He became furious.

Minna, pause briefly here try to make the sounds of a furious wolf, like: ARRRR, GRRRRR, ARRRR, ARRRR from deep in your throat. Here the Lobo's anger is rising and the volume of his throat sounds has increased. He's just about to bite.

The Lobo's massive head suddenly lunged into David's face. He savagely bit David's mouth and facial cheeks. Using his powerful neck muscles, the Lobo shook David's face violently. He tore away a huge chunk of David's cheeks and lips. The Lobo hadn't eaten for three days. Having food in his mouth was a pleasurable sensation. He gulped down the cheeks and lips from whence the man's sounds had come. But the man still made annoying shouting sounds from his throat.

The continuing sounds enraged the Lobo. Fury swept through the body of the beast, heightening its senses. It puzzled the defiance it received from the man and tried to understand why it made the sounds it did.

'*How dare this helpless creature defy me while I seek to eat peacefully? Why does it not lie silently like a wounded antelope does while I partake of my fill from its flesh? What purpose does its screaming serve? It screams like a rabbit or prairie dog or squirrel. It does not lie silent like an antelope or deer or elk. It has no dignity. I must silence it.*'

To silence David's shouting sounds the Lobo clamped down upon David's throat with his mighty jaws and again fiercely shook its head. He ripped away David's voice box along with considerable tissue and blood veins. He chewed the voice box and gulped the crunchy cartilage tissue down his gullet. Now he could dine peacefully upon the still living man.

The beast ignored David's flailing arm and its feeble hits on his body. They could do him no harm. With his throat ripped open, he knew the man's flailing would stop soon enough. He wanted meat. Eating was his sole priority now. He chomped down upon David's thighs, shook his massive head, and tore out huge chunks of David's flesh. He devoured huge chunks of meat. The empty hunger pangs in his stomach finally eased. He was a ravenous eater; easily able to devour fifty pounds of meat at one sitting. As he gulped down David's flesh, he reckoned this carcass would feed him for three or four days.

David's moans and grunt-like sounds were now silenced, but he was still alive, still breathing. He lay there helpless, not unlike the many insects that he had once torn limbs from when he was a child. His thoughts during this state of semi-consciousness were not on remorse for all the misery he had inflicted upon others throughout his life. His dying thoughts were of his childhood:

'*Why was I cursed with the parents I had? Why didn't anyone love me? Maybe this big dog will make a mistake. Maybe it will lie on my face. I still have my teeth. I could bite the son of a bitch back. Fuck this animal. Fuck him.'*

But the Lobo didn't lie upon David's face. He was too experienced with kills and too intelligent to make a mistake like that. Instead, the Lobo sought to satisfy his taste buds with the best choices of meats the carcass offered him. With his sharp claws the Lobo ripped David's stomach open. He thrust his muzzle upward into David's chest cavity. He scoured David's insides. He quickly found David's liver, effortlessly ripped it away from its attaching membranes. He sat there above the still living body and gulped down its liver.

David knew he was doomed. When the Lobo ripped out his liver, his last thoughts were that he wished he could have been born to parents who loved him as a child and where people believed it was okay to love men and not women. His final thoughts flickered about all the pain he'd caused others. That was his last fleeting sense of satisfaction.

'They all deserved everything they got' he thought. David had no remorse.

After David's liver was securely down the Lobo's gullet, filling his empty stomach, he again thrust his muzzle into the chest cavity and found David's faintly beating heart. He ripped out the heart and ate that too. His prey lay still. Its breathing stopped. David was dead.

The Lobo feasted leisurely upon David's carcass for three days, staying close to it; guarding his kill. He allowed the jays and crows to eat the eyes and portions of entrails. Those were items that the Lobo didn't want. He liked having jays and crows nearby. They would shriek and caw their warnings if an intruder approached. None did. After he picked the carcass clean of meat the Lobo mouthed David's leg and arm bones. His mighty jaws exerted a bite force greater than a wolf's.

After cracking open the bones the Lobo stripped out David's bone marrow. He was an efficient predator, leaving little waste. He chewed and ate some bone before he left the carcass. He spent his time, when not feasting, looking over the valley below. He noticed a small cabin set back about a hundred yards from the stream. Twice during the late afternoons, Mule Deer does and their fawns came about a hundred yards upstream from the cabin to drink. He decided to leave his kill, cross the stream below, and stealthily work his way closer to the game trail used by the deer. Rodent squirrels and mice could gnaw upon the remnant bones of his kill. He was finished with it.

David's car was found in the parking garage in the exact same spot where he'd parked it. There were no fingerprints on the car, no chain fall, no stepladder, and no sign of foul play. Susan, always the meticulous administrator, had been thorough. Seven weeks later, David's bone remnants were discovered by a forest ranger on horseback. The horse was standing a way off from the edge of the scattered remains when it stopped to evacuate itself; otherwise, the ranger might have ridden past the site without noticing anything.

As he took in the widely scattered bone fragments, the ranger realized they were possibly human. There was a lone field mouse gnawing upon one of the bones, drawing its ration of calcium. The site had no other sign of life. David's carcass had been picked clean of all flesh and tissue; it appeared that coyotes or possibly bears and mountain lions had scattered the bones. Most were cracked open and their marrow removed. The ranger's report stated that coyotes and other animals had likely gleaned the carcass.

There were ropes tied to the trees surrounding the site. Ground stakes indicated this was a homicide and a terribly agonizing death for the victim. How David's body ended up on that bluff above the tributary baffled the authorities. The case remains unsolved to this day. Susan dutifully made her calls to David's home that next day when he didn't arrive at the office. A few days later, she helped his wife file a missing person report. Some teeth from a jaw fragment sufficed to identify David's body. What bones could be gathered were placed into a wooden box and given to David's widow. She took them for burial in Israel. No obituary of David's death was ever published.

CHAPTER ELEVEN

Wherever you tread the blushing flowers shall rise, and all things flourish where you turn your eyes (Alexander Pope: Pastorals, Summer)

SIGNS

Bob and Barbara took a trip back to Milltown to visit Bob's mother. Estella was old now. She walked with a cane and her eyesight had dimmed, but her feisty nature and her combativeness never yielded to the march of time. Her eyes beamed at seeing Bob with Barbara. She greeted the happy couple with forceful, lingering hugs. When Estella saw Barbara, she knew Bob and this woman would soon marry. Mothers have a way of knowing such things. She was happy for her son and bluntly told him so.

"I'm glad you got your life straightened out," she remarked to her son, as if everything adverse that ever happened in Bob's life was his fault alone. After lunch, she got down to mother's business. There were questions she had to ask:

"You don't look like an Indian," she said addressing Barbara. *"Bob said you were an Indian. Is that true? You're an awfully pretty woman, Barbara. She's one of the prettiest women I've ever seen, Bob. Lordy! Lordy!"*

"Yes, Estella, I am an Indian," smiled Barbara proudly. *"I know the Indian ways and I believe I am one of the Great Spirit's creations*

and a child of Mother Earth. My father is a Lakota tribal chief. My mother was a Lebanese Christian woman. She was a small-boned Arab. I believe it was the will of the Great Spirit that they met, and by his will he brought me into this world, through them."

"How on Earth did an American Indian get himself married to a Lebanese? Your mother was part Arab, you said?" Estella needed to categorize Barbara's lineage.

"Dad was a United States Marine, ma'am," explained Barbara. "He was stationed in Lebanon for a while. They fell in love. I am part of them both. Mother died seven years ago, from cancer. Mother was all Arab; not part Arab."

"That's why you look more like an Arab. Well, you are very beautiful. Bob tells me you are also very smart. That's a lovely pin you're wearing, Barbara. Where on Earth did you find that?" The butterfly pin Barbara wore was a natural conversation piece.

"Oh, thank you, Estella," replied Barbara. "That's my butterfly pin. It's a fond reminder of a woman I used to work for before Bob and I went into business together. Her name was Susan. She had a daughter who died. It was originally a gift from her daughter to her. A week before Susan passed away, she gave this pin to me. She told me I was like a second daughter to her and she wanted me to wear it in memory of her and her real daughter."

"Oh, so you knew Susan and her daughter too, did you? They must have been very nice people." Estella knew of whom Barbara spoke. Bob had told her of his intentions toward Marty, years before; but Estella pretended that Bob never mentioned that he wanted to marry Marty.

"Yes. For a while at the Firm, all three of us worked together." Barbara nodded.

"I see. Well, that gift was very thoughtful of her. And now you two will be getting married?" Estella nodded.

"Yes; soon." Barbara confirmed what Estella suspected.

"And I take it that you love my son and you will be a good woman to him. You're not one to run around with other men or drink and gamble or smoke. You're not one of those kinds of girls, are you?"

"Yes and no, ma'am." answered Barbara.

"Well, which is it?" Estella looked confused.

"Yes, Estella. I love Bob. I love him deeply. I promise you I will be good to him. And no, Estella, I'm not a bad woman. I'm a good one. Bob is getting a good woman."

"I see. And the children, if you have them? How will you raise them?"

"We'll raise them as Reformed Jews with Christian and Indian Spirits all blended in, ma'am. You see, we don't actually believe God would choose one people over another, not the God we embrace. We think that's a false message used to help exclusive cliques exclude others. We think it limits those who take the message too literally; and it prevents them from open friendships and honest understandings of others; kind of like eating the same bowl of mush day in and day out."

"But without religious groupings amongst peoples, you'll have anarchy!" Estella objected.

"Or acceptance that we are all God's children; all of us equal in God's eyes." Barbara was quick of mind and tongue. *"The priests and rabbis and Imams will just have to catch up with us, Estella. The world is always changing, and peoples' understandings are changing with it."*

Estella smiled. Barbara had a ring of truth and confidence about her. Estella liked that this woman stood her ground. She felt good for her son. She had felt the same inner happiness when she was with Paul for their last time together, when they created Bob, before Paul left to die on the Russian front.

"Well, you're both old enough to do whatever you want, with or without my blessings, but you certainly have my blessings; my love

and my best wishes for you both. I am very happy for both of you. I am a happy old woman."

After visiting Estella, Bob and Barbara walked the old path down to the dam on Cedar Creek. They sat together on the cement abutment that adjoined the spillway. It was a perfect day for an afternoon outdoors. They looked out over the dam. Two wood ducks dived upside down in the water; their tail feathers and wings splashing to cleanse their down of fleas and lice. Their antics made Barbara laugh. Her laugh was mirthful, and pleasing to Bob. *"Silly ducks,"* she said. They sat looking out over the waters and up into the far reaches of the creek, where it disappeared from view under the overhang of pines at its upstream bend. A pair of coupled dragonflies appeared in front of them, as if by magic. They paused in midair. The giant insects hovered suspended, three feet before their eyes. They were absorbed in their serious business of mating.

Barbara looked at Bob and smiled: *"Those dragonflies are telling us something."* She leaned against him, then placed a soft, loving kiss on his lips.

"Is your Great Spirit speaking to us through his messengers?" Big Horse teased Little Sparrow.

"It must be so." Little Sparrow nodded and smiled. She looked deeply into Bob's eyes. They knew their futures belonged together.

"Then let's follow their example. Let's go to the special place where I went as a young boy." Bob stood and took her hand.

"Take me. I want to see it with you. I want it to be special. I want it to be special for both of us. I love you. Take me with you to your secret place," she giggled in anticipation.

They waded across Cedar Creek downstream from the dam. Anticipation moistened Barbara. As cool fresh water coursed over her legs, she noticed her inside wetness as well.

Bob led her up a long fold in the mountain, and up further to a glen where the mountain briefly leveled off. She felt the exertions from the climb and was glad for a rest. *"So, this is where you came as a little boy?"* She smiled, looking at Bob. She was seeing the boy in her man. She loved his happiness at being where they were, together. *"Are we almost there?"*

"Almost," answered Bob. *"It's a bit farther, but it's worth it, I promise."* Bob's eagerness came through in his voice. *"The view is spectacular,"* he assured her. *"We'll climb this little draw to a spring that gushes out of the mountain about fifty yards from the top. Deer come there to drink."*

"Oh, I'd love to see it gushing!" Barbara giggled her suggestive thought for Bob as if he didn't already have the same idea. They resumed their climb to the spring. *"It will always gush and gush, won't it?"* she teased her inuendo again. They fell to their knees and drank the cool water.

After they drank, Bob led her about ten yards farther upslope, where they came to a game trail. *"This is Deer Freeway. We follow it west for a while."*

Barbara looked at the rutted path. The deer used this trail when coming down from the pines near the mountaintop. It seemed to disappear into nowhere. They followed it for a couple hundred yards into a deep, dark pine forest. The tree trunks had grown closely together here. The trail grew more narrow and less certain. The thickened pines blocked out the sunlight. Deer and man needed to crawl under low pine boughs to move forward.

As they progressed, the ground became less competent. The soft earth of the trail yielded to loose shale. When it seemed the crawl through the pine thicket would never end, they came upon a boulder-strewn clearing. Above them was a sheer granite cliff wall, created by geologic forces millions of years before. Near the top of the rock formation, caves' dark entrance holes appeared. Hidden from the valley floor by pines and the fold in the mountain, this amazing feature remained undiscovered, except by Bob and the Indians that had come here, many years before. Seeing it for the first time, Barbara stood speechless. *"You found this place as a boy? You came to these cliffs as a child? Weren't you afraid to come this far? Weren't you afraid to climb them?"* She found it hard to imagine a child of four or five would attempt such an adventure.

"When I was a boy, I needed a special place to go; a place where no one could find me or follow me," said Bob. He shrugged, hands in his pockets.

"You could have fallen off those cliffs and died here. No one would have ever found you."

"I know that now; but when I was a boy, I never thought about risks. Are you afraid? Are you up for this?"

"I've been up for this all my life." She held Bob close and kissed him full on his mouth. *"Let's climb. Lead the way, Big Horse."*

They climbed upward through the rock crevices to a near-level transom trail that appeared from nowhere and ended abruptly at the entrance of the Indian Caves. When their eyes became accustomed to the dimmed light, they made their way about ten yards into the largest cave. The cave walls were damp. Ground water trickled down the wall on Barbara's left. It was a tiny rivulet of glistening clear fluid against the black surface. She became aroused. That curious trickle of life coursing over the black granite rock wall made her heart flutter. She held Bob's face in her hands:

'I've come back to this place. My spirit was here before. I feel it. I have made love here, many times. This place sheltered my ancestors from storms and predators thousands of years ago. Big Horse's spirit was with me then as he is with me now. We are living in our spirits. I am SO READY.'

"Look, etched in the stone," she exclaimed when she discovered the same markings Bob first saw when he was a boy. *"There's an arrow mark pointed up and there's the mark of the 'V' beside it."*

"Yeah, I saw those when I was a kid. I wondered what they meant, and I'd forgotten about them. They look very old. Do you know what they mean?"

"*I do!*" exclaimed Barbara. "*Follow me!*" She entered her very own magical moment. She led Bob out of the cave. They climbed in earnest, going higher. As she placed one hand above the other, gripping the indented rock holds, Barbara throbbed inside. This was the perfect time; the perfect place; with her perfect man. She climbed toward the top of the cliffs with her man and her dreams. She knew her life would be with him. She felt their spirits coming together. She yearned to consummate their beginning.

She climbed higher up the rock face, never looking down; always looking forward, never back. She rose steadily, until she reached the protruding ledge that jutted over the top of the cave. There it was! She recognized it by how Bob had described it. This was the very spot that Bob visited as a boy. Here is where he looked out over his hometown; sitting and wondering about the world beyond it. She intuited that his spirit had come here, searching for her spirit, from the time he was a boy! He could not have known it then; but her spirit had also searched for his, from the time she was a child living alone with her father. She often wondered then: '*Who will be with me when Father leaves me? What spirit will have Father's strength and love? What future awaits me, beyond Father's home and my tribe? What will become of me?*'

Barbara was as nimble as a mountain goat. She had five minutes alone on the rock ledge before Bob caught up with her. She squeezed her legs together, realizing all her dreams were about to come true; all her desires fulfilled. Bob was a handsome, well-muscled pillar of a man. She yearned to have him. '*Hurry, hurry. Come to me,*' she whispered to herself, as if that might help him climb faster.

When Bob's eyes reached above the level of the ledge, they beheld Barbara. She stood naked on the very spot where he contemplated the world as a boy. He climbed the final few feet, then joined her on the precipice. She smiled and opened her arms to him. He went to her. And they held each other in their arms.

All Bob's childhood wonders about what mysteries lay beyond the town were mysteries no more. All the truths, lies, hopes, and betrayals were out there, where he had come from. He had run the gauntlet of betrayals. And he survived them! As a boy, he had often thought of jumping off this cliff. But he never did. He had defeated his once-dark thoughts of suicide. He had endured the crushing loss of his father; his beatings from his mother; and the betrayals of his former partner and second lawyer. Those things were behind him now. He'd consorted with the immoral siren Marty; partaken of her sweet lips and nectars; joined his spirit to hers. He had loved her deeply; but fate took his life in a different direction. Murder swallowed Marty, and the life he might have had with her. He was discovering, with Barbara, that his life's spirit was destined to be shared with two women's spirits. Barbara's spirit was finally being revealed to him. It was goodness, strength, and sweetness. It flooded into his spirit, coursing through his soul and entwining itself there, forever binding its love with his love. They were becoming one. Bob's memories of Marty began drifting away. They were leaving him in an understanding, quiet way, like gently flowing Cedar Creek, far below.

Bob had wrestled with many forms of evil. Now, he was finally free. Life had found its way. It offered its loving hand to him. Like a little boy, who had dreamed that God would magically place a beautiful goddess woman in his bed, Bob silently thanked the Almighty for hearing his pleas. Silent seconds of appreciation and reverence passed. He held the heaven-sent goddess beside him.

From the first moment he first saw Barbara, there was something about her that kept drawing him toward her. He'd often wondered if she had feelings for him; even while he was with Marty. In the deepest recesses of his mind, in a place he never mentioned, he had often wondered if he might somehow, someday, know Barbara intimately; whether a magical moment like this could ever happen?

Her friendship felt much like his childhood friendship with Pam, but Pam wished to take him away from his career interest. She became drawn to another man. She spoke excitedly about plowing fields and milking cows with him. Barbara was different. She only sought to enhance his career interests and never spoke to him about thoughts of another man. Life unfolded much as Arlene, the nurse who first took an interest in him when he was a toddler, had prophesized. She had related to Bob the same wisdom her rabbi had told her. The right woman would find him; she had assured him. And, the right woman did. There was Rosie, Marty, and some others. He had desired all of them at one time or another; but life had raised its barriers; and prevented them from being with him. He tried to make sense of it all:

'Life sorts through questions of relationships. It's a good thing, too, because relationships are too complicated for men to sort through. Barbara was always off-limits, but now she is with me. She is Little Sparrow, the mysterious silent woman. She is like the enchanted nature of this forest I once knew as a boy. I will explore her forever and learn her ways. I will love her forever. I yearn to be one with her. Now it is our time. She exudes sex so much! I have always craved having her. She's different from Marty and Rosie. She never puts it out there for gawkers. She is always discreet, as if she protects a precious jewel. I will defend her from any harm or untoward advances from other men. They will not dare to belittle her ethnicity or her family; soon to be my family. I will always uphold her

dignity and honor. If I am challenged to fight for her, I will; just as I fought and bloodied ignorant boys in my school years. I will never tolerate any person who makes her cry or tries to embarrass her. I love her completely and will always give her the fullest measure of my devotion. I will devote my life to her and her causes. She is a special, glorious woman. And she will be my wife. Yes, finally, I will marry. And Barbara shall be my wife.'

Bob always suspected Sparrow knew more than she ever revealed. He sensed she would never want a man who tried to force a relationship, so he left her alone during their intriguing years. Besides, she'd told him early on that they needed to wait. His heart now pounded with desires to hold her and embrace life with her. An upwelling of joy overwhelmed him. His eyes filled with happiness that gushed up from his soul.

Barbara knew this was the moment that culminated the vision she'd had for Bob the first day she saw him when he stepped off the elevator and into her life. Bob was her destiny; her life mate. Soon, so soon, everything would come together for both of them.

'I look into his eyes and I see happiness. I know he wants me. What will it be like this first time? Will he be gentle? Will I please him?'

She would soon lie with him on the moss-covered outcrop, would soon feel him entering her. She was ready now, ready to go forward forever with Bob and never look back; never regret her choice.

As she smiled at the love of her life, a kaleidoscope of white Pieridae butterflies fluttered between them, attracted to the shimmering ultraviolet radiance of Barbara's lustrous dark hair. One briefly lighted upon her hair, as if to give its blessings for what was soon to come. Then it fluttered away to rejoin the others. *"So, what do those ancient markings mean?"* Bob asked, his eyes beholding hers.

"They mean this is a wonderful place for lovers to make love," Barbara replied softly as she embraced Bob closely, collapsing the distance between them. The daylight between them disappeared. So did their years of abuse in the insane asylum that was the Firm. Barbara held Bob in her arms; her body heat melted away all cares from their past. They held each other in a close embrace. Happiness, appreciation, and love bonded them with a unity that would last and sustain them for the rest of their lives.

And, so it was. On the secret mountain ledge, high above a cliff face, while the soft voice of Spirits whispered through the fragrant pine forest, Barbara discovered Bob's full measure as a wonderful, unselfish lover. The two lovers lay down together on the moss-covered outcrop. Their lips met in a long passionate kiss. After moments of touching tenderness and eager, loving mouth kisses, Bob lightly touched her inner thighs. Barbara opened her sex to receive his kisses. She said a silent prayer: *'Great Spirit of all Living Things, bless this day and always. Thank you for showing us the way. Our love is good. And this will be our first good day.'*

They began their lovemaking slowly. Bob, ever mindful of his mitzvah, began kissing Barbara's sex. He was painstakingly deliberate and gentle. When he coaxed her clitoris to arousal, he began gently massaging and caressing it with the underside of his tongue. She felt a sensation that she had never imagined existed. As she ran her fingers through the shock of wavy blond hair positioned between her legs, she resonated with Bob's loving tongue. She felt her body tremble and quiver as his tongue stroked her clitoris.

'I did not know this feeling existed. This is intimacy of the most endearing kind. He is mine now. He is everything I ever wanted in a man. I feel like I am floating on a cloud with happiness flowing out of my sex. I feel wonderful; and I know I am so deeply loved. I wish this feeling would never end. I am blessed to have my Big Horse. He is sufficient in his own wealth; he earns his own income, and he

loves me without selfishness or inhibition. He is a one-woman man, and he will never have eyes for another. I will give all of myself to him, always.'

She relaxed and released a full orgasm into Bob's mouth while he continued working the magic of his loving tongue upon her throbbing clitoris. *"Big Horse, tell me, my lover, what made you want to do what you just did?"* she asked in her pleased wonder.

"It's mitzvah, a requirement that a man should wet his woman to prepare her for lovemaking. I've thought about kissing you there for a long time. I couldn't hold back. I love you so much. When I kiss you there, I don't ever want to stop. I feel good inside, knowing you feel my love for you. I wanted to do it to let you know how wonderful and special you are. I can't get enough of you."

"Well, Big Horse, I need to tell you something as a woman to a man."

"Yes, Sparrow?"

"You are welcome to mitzvah with me whenever you wish. I liked doing mitzvah very much." She giggled.

Bob clasped her buttocks firmly and lifted her toward his waiting penis. Her orgasmic secretions increased and coaxed Bob's thrusts to increase their tempo. She was one with him. She could feel his penis throb with her delightful pulsing passions as it stretched her and plunged deeper and deeper, yearning to have more and more of her. All her other thoughts vanished from this spiritual moment. She spoke softly to her future husband: *"Big Horse, now that I have given myself to you, you may have no others. You will be my husband. Our marriage will last forever and I will never share you."*

"I will be your husband, Little Sparrow. I want for no other woman and will never have another. Our marriage will last forever, and I also will never share you with anyone. We will always be as one."

Barbara's inner spirit assured her that Big Horse would be faithful to her. They had spoken vows to each other from their hearts. She knew he was a man of honor. She finally had all she wanted in a husband and a father for her children. She silently thanked the Great Spirit for the wisdom he bestowed upon Chief, and she thanked Chief for counseling her to be patient. Now she could give herself freely, and often, to this man. Big Horse was now hers; only hers. All hers.

Just as Barbara was beginning to feel the onset of her second release, Bob rolled her over on her side while maintaining their connection. She was daunted at first, thinking that perhaps she would lose the sensation she was feeling, but that momentary uncertainty was suddenly swept away.

Bob grabbed her buttocks with his large strong hands and easily lifted Barbara on top of him. The outcrop had a slight down slope, and Bob lay with his head somewhat lower than his legs. The effect of this new position was wildly sensuous for Barbara. His penis, now rock-hard and fully swollen, had an uphill-angled position which placed it firmly against her clitoris. When Bob thrusted upward into the deepest part of her sex, his penis made its presence known.

Never had Barbara experienced a swollen penis pressed firmly against her clitoris that way; and with such strength and endurance! She loved the wild sensations she felt and wanted more and more. She straddled him. He was hers; all of him; only hers. Her knees welcomed the coolness of the thick bed of soft damp moss as she looked out from their mountain perch to the valley floor below. Barbara's arousal was complete. Her thoughts were with Bob in their new intimate world:

'I belong with him and he belongs with me'

An ecstasy of pent-up joys she'd saved for years was about to release. It was unlike any feeling she'd ever known before. As their rhythm quickened, Barbara was transported to another time and place.

In her euphoric state, she gazed down upon the land below. Her mind time traveled to another place and time. She had a vision of the valley below as it was before the Whites came; the land as her people knew it. There was the river, its gleaming white ripples over blue water coursing south where Cedar Creek flowed into it. Both waters teemed with fish. Two braves were putting out seine nets along the near shore. The land was no longer a town with streets, squares, houses, schools, and churches. It was a wide, vast plateau; rising abruptly above the bluff that footed the river and the creek.

Below her spread vast forests of chestnut, hickory, oak, walnut, birch, and maple. She saw men in hunting parties, scouting for deer and elk with bow and arrow. And there, near the clearing where the tribe camped, a boy was putting out his snares for rabbits. In the camp clearing, she saw teepees and a few women tending a fire. Others were bringing wood to fuel it. Still others were gathering nuts from the forest floor. One woman was scraping an elk hide to prepare it for curing. It would help keep her family warm during the cold, damp winter ahead. She heard the dull chanting melodies of the tribal shaman and the laughter of children. And there! She could see a woman with a papoose wrap and a bundled baby on her back. This land was her land by heritage. It was the land of the Munsee, the Unalachtigo, the Algonquin, and the Delaware.

This was the land of the people, the land upon which the great chief Seneca once walked. These simple people loved this place, this land. And then, the white men came. The whites were hungry for land. They had to 'own' land, a concept the People never understood. The land was, for the People, part of the gift to everyone from the Great Spirit and the ancestors.

But the White men coveted the land that was the Great Spirit's. The White men cleared the mighty trees. They killed the animals, then put the land under the plow. They would, if left unchecked, defile all the Great Spirit's land. So, the People fought the White men. The land below her became drenched in the blood of both the People and the Whites.

And in the end, the People lost many great battles with the Whites; lost their historic usage of these lands. They moved west to the Ohio Valley. There, they fought the Whites again and again; and they lost again and again. The People became sickened by the White man's diseases and the White man's greed. They moved far to the west. They became absorbed by larger tribes. And eventually, centuries later, even the larger tribes were conquered by the palefaces.

The People were gone from here now, but their love of this place never left it. The valley below was tranquil again. The town's houses thinned away to rich rolling farmlands. But it was now her place, too. In the grand scheme of life, her presence here was symbolic of the permanence of the spirit of the People; her People. Barbara felt their presence now while making passionate love with a descendent of her People's conquerors.

But her lovemaking and her life with Bob would not be a contest of conquests. Their life together would be a wondrous unison of past cultures and traditions with modernity. It would always bask in the glory of their love. She would be a good woman for this man. She knew he would be a good and wonderful man for her. On this mountain ledge, on this day, Barbara became larger than her own life.

'Today, I surrender myself to the Great Spirit of All Living Things. This day I fulfill his will. I will be Earth Goddess of all my people. I will triumph with the will of the Spirit. My soul sings with joy. I am serene and joyous. This is my Spirit moment. I will conceive our first

child this day. I release myself to the wonders of my man and the Spirits within us.'

Barbara's second orgasm began with a low moaning sound that rose from deep inside her. She felt her dam of juices about to burst in an even more powerful release. She moaned louder now, uninhibited, alone with Bob in the wilds on their mountain. Her body trembled uncontrollably, and then: Barbara bloomed!

Her swollen vagina could no longer hold back her bursting flood. Her deep moaning changed to a low-pitched *"Ohhhhhh"* when her release commenced. It was a small release at first, but then she gained her full voice. She howled out, unrestrained as her flower fully opened. Her joy resounded over the mountainside and her sounds reached the creek below as she entered the throes of her massive orgasm. She threw her head back and looked skyward, her body trembled violently as she slammed her eager pelvis hard against Bob. It was the most wondrous moment of her life. She was alive as never before. She was creating life.

She shouted out in a full voice for the world to hear, *"YES! YES! YES!! Oh! YESSSS! Don't stop! Don't stop!"*

Barbara cried, *"More, MORE! That's IT, my Big Horse. KEEP GOING! DON'T STOP! OHHH! THAT FEELS SOOO GOOD! I LOVE YOU SOOO MUCH! Oh, how I love you. OH, WOW, hold me CLOSE. Hold me VERY CLOSE!"* She kissed him wildly on his lips and all over his face. She was out of her mind with love.

On the banks of the Cedar, far below the lovers' ledge, a lone female coyote worked the marsh grasses searching for rodents. She stopped and stood silent. She cocked her head to better hear the sounds coming from the mountain high above her. She sat on her haunches. She understood that life was being formed. She gave three soft yip barks, *'yip; yip; yip'*, voicing her approval of what she heard. Then she resumed her hunting.

Bob's penis throbbed as his thrusts quickened. The stream of semen released was strong and full, pulsing and shooting forcefully. As his sperm frantically searched for Barbara's ovulated egg, her stomach and chest heaved with desire. Her thoughts lifted into rapture:

'This is so wonderful! With each kiss he's telling me that he'll never have enough of me. No woman was ever treasured more. If I could imagine creating the perfect man from Earth's clays with my own hands, he could not be as wonderful as this man who holds me now.'

Barbara closed her eyes in her delirious state of ecstasy. She had a vision and said to the spirit, *'With this man I will help the people of the world put aside their divisions and hatreds. They will know the wonders of nature and peace as did my forbearers. They will feel the harmony of the Great Spirit of All Living Things.'*

Multiple visions flashed through her mind. She imagined her future with Big Horse: *'I am naked, riding a big sorrel mustang stallion. We are racing across the prairie, scouting a herd of buffalo. I dismount and open myself to him. With each forward thrust of his mighty haunches, Big Horse's huge member thrusts deeply into me. He strains to please me and he goes faster and faster; always faster, until he is finally one with me.'*

'There's a teepee on the plains overlooking a long valley. The flap is open and I look out. The Rosebud River courses by below me. A pale, full orange moon begins to lift in the sky as the sunset glows behind a bluff. I am faced outward. I am looking at all the creation works of the Great Spirit of All Living Things. I see a flock of Canadian geese flying across the face of the moon.

'Big Horse lies under me; and I straddle him. His hands cup my breasts; his fingers tease my nipples. I tremble in anticipation. I touch his huge member, feeling it grow larger and harder as he raises his head and kisses my back in many places. Tingles of desire shoot

through my entire body. I will have Big Horse this night and we will make love for hours until the moon rises high and bright in the night sky. I am crazy with passions for what we are about to do.

'He places his big hands around my slender waist. Now he lifts me up and guides my love place over his gigantic member. Lovingly, he holds me perfectly in place before guiding me down over it. I am hot and wet inside and I want him inside me; the two of us moving faster and faster. I am so ready for this. I have been ready for two full years. My vagina is like a juicy, fully ripened peach. I want his member to probe all of me; and deeply know me, until I become delirious with my joys of being his woman.

'We make love this way for hours. I come together with him many times. Cool prairie breezes flow over me. I know I am one with nature and my man. I am complete now. I am happy. I collapse onto him and sleep the whole night in his arms. I have endless nights like this with my Big Horse. I am with spirit and nature. He and I have become one. I am woman. I know love.'

'I stand on the porch of our log ranch house, looking across the prairie toward the hills. Two little children, a boy, and a girl, are racing each other and laughing in the tall grass. The children fall and get up, laughing. And then they race some more. Big Horse stands beside me and wraps his huge arms around me. He holds me tightly to him and kisses my neck. He cups my breasts. He pushes his pelvis against me. I know he wants me.

'It's time to take him inside, to our bedroom; time to push him down on our king-sized bed. He lies there while I slowly undress before him. His huge member stands upright. It wants me. It waits hungrily, for me. This is so wonderful and good. I tease him by slowly taking off each piece of my clothing. I cup my breasts and smile to him. My eyes tell him I love him. My smile promises him he will know my love this night. I stoke his appetite for me. I face him on my knees and hover over him, rubbing his member against my mound.

He can feel that I am slippery wet and ready. Now our moment is right. His massive hands come to my waist. And he lifts me up, gently, effortlessly, before slowly lowering me onto his mighty column.'

'I am back in the present now. I am making love with Big Horse on a ledge on a mountainside. We are surrounded by a fragrant pine forest. I hear Cedar Creek moving far below us. The soft winds ripple its waters. They lap softly against its banks. I hear the soft yips of a female coyote searching the marsh bank for her meal. Her female spirit must know we are making love, high above her on our mountain. She must be telling us that our love making is good. Yes, surely, she is telling us that. I know I have found love forever. I know that I want this Big Horse inside me many, many times. I do love him so much.'

When Barbara opened her eyes the white Pieridae kaleidoscope returned. They fluttered all around her head. They lingered, suspended in the mountain sky, as if to fix Barbara's pheromones and the ultraviolet radiance from her hair in their collective memory, as only butterflies can do. Then they fluttered away, descending through the forest below, making their way to the creek.

'I am eternally satisfied. This is love. This is the love Chief promised I would discover, if I was patient. This is the love my man needs from me.'

Barbara and Bob were married that fall at the Pepke Park Gazebo in Aspen, Colorado. It was a traditional Indian ceremony, with six little girls from the tribe acting as flower bearers. It was also a Jewish wedding ceremony with elements of a Catholic ceremony. Barbara wore an elegant white gown with raised-embossed, red-throated sparrows, hand-sewn in their natural colors around its fringe. Her hair was done up in plaits, wrapped high upon her head, and stayed with silver ribbons. She held her head high throughout the ceremony. She appeared as a beautiful princess goddess. She was noble. She was royalty. And, she was lovely.

Bob wore a black tuxedo with tails. A judge showed up with the marriage license from the Pitkin County Courthouse, understandably late. He wore his fly-fishing hip waders. He'd been fishing a good hatch on Frying Pan Creek. Chief counseled the waiting guests to be patient for the judge because it was right and good to wait for any man who was having a good day fishing.

The guests included many of Chief's friends, including the Italians from the casino businesses; the *get things done* guys. They came to express their support. Chief gave Little Sparrow away to Big Horse by joining their hands; then squeezing them together in his big, strong arms, clasped within his giant paws, before the judge.

Chief and his entourage wore their buckskins, jeweled finery, and best headdresses. The Jews wore colorful yarmulkes. They voiced their support and good wishes; and brought gifts of silver and gold. The Catholics, mostly Italian-Americans, brought flowers and many cases of wine. Everyone danced together in a big circle. It was the original combination dance, a blend of the Jewish wedding dance and the Indian spirit dance. It was the first time this unique, uplifting dance was ever performed. And, it was beautiful. The smiles and laughter from all the guests were captured brilliantly in the wedding photos.

Pictures of Barbara's wedding were preserved in perpetuity in two photo albums. Barbara kept one copy under her bed; the other was stored in the vault of one of Aspen's favorite old hotels. Aspen Mountain stood tall in the background, making for splendid, inspiring photos. A light early fall snow graced the revelers, Many of the photos showed sparkling snow spots. After the judge pronounced the couple married, Chief gave Bob a crushing bear hug. The huge man had tears in his eyes. He spoke only one word:

"*Good.*"

The men took turns kissing the bride. Some became overly enthusiastic about this kissing; and they had to be pried away from Barbara by Chief.

Then Chief lit himself a fine Cuban cigar and passed out cigars to each male, ordering:

"You smoke." And every man smoked his cigar in honor of the new couple.

Barbara made a wish. Then, she threw her wedding bouquet high into the air. It was caught by a snow squall and lifted skyward over Aspen Mountain. It floated on the wind until it landed upon the antlers of an eight-point bull elk. The elk ran swiftly into the forest with the bouquet stuck upon his massive antler rack. He disappeared into the deep timber. To this very day, would-be brides go searching for Little Sparrow's bridal bouquet on Aspen Mountain. Legend has it that whoever finds Barbara's flowers will have a long, happy marriage and be blessed with many children.

In the many years they shared, Barbara and Bob used a secret code. Whenever they were at a social function and Barbara grew tired of the pleasantries; or when they were at home alone, or somewhere away, she knew how to tell him she wanted him. She would turn to him and whisper: *"It is a good time, Big Horse."*

"For what, sweetheart?" Bob would ask.

"For When the Butterflies Come." She would whisper in his ear.

CHAPTER TWELVE

Ah the souls of those that die are but sunbeams lifted higher (Henry Wadsworth Longfellow: The Golden Legend)

BONES

After murdering David, Susan wrote two letters to Mount of Olives Cemetery in Jerusalem, seeking permission to be buried as near as possible to Marvin and Eloweiss. Both her requests were refused. Susan then became religious for the first time in her life. She attended Catholic Mass every single day until she became elderly and infirm. She prayed her Rosary twice daily. After she was diagnosed with emphysema, she gave up smoking her demitasse cigars.

Eloweiss was the first of the Sustacks to die. Marvin followed her in death; David's gruesome murder happened years later. Marvin's last will and testament contained contingency provisions. Everything that was Marvin's estate and trusts, held in David's custody or beneficial interest, other than the companies, which were to go to Israel, upon his death, was to go to Susan. Nothing was to go to David's wife, unless David created a company of his own, with his own earned monies and efforts, and made it into a worthwhile asset.

David failed to accomplish that. Everything he did was illegal. He invested his illegal monies in his mother's trust, with himself as the beneficiary. As fate would have it, by the terms of Marvin's will and the contingent beneficiary clause in Marvin's Eloweiss trust, Susan became its beneficiary upon David's death. Susan also owned the service company with its mineral rights. Upon David's death the operating companies went to Ben Slipperman, the attorney. Upon Ben's death, the companies went to Israel.

Susan had a dilemma. With Marty dead, and no grandchildren, she had no natural heirs. Upon reflection and counsel, she bequeathed everything she owned to Barbara, as She and Barbara had become close friends. She told Barbara about the jewels; and a storage locker where the personal items of Eloweiss had been kept since her death.

"Susan, shouldn't these jewels be given to Israel?" Barbara was overcome with amazement at the scope of wealth contained in the jewels.

"No, Barbara. I know you and I trust you. You are a good woman with a good heart. You put them to good use. Use them to help all people, as you deem fit."

"Susan, please tell me about Marvin." Barbara sought to understand the Firm's founder, as she had known intimacy with his spirit soul.

"He was a wonderful, caring man," replied Susan, wistfully. Her voice revealed her love for Marvin and her deep sadness for his absence. It was clear to Barbara that Susan wished she and Marvin could still be together.

"Marvin was the love of my life. I started falling in love with him when I was just a young servant girl for Eloweiss. When I came of age, I let Marvin know of my interest. I seduced him. We had our love. It was a wonderful love. He taught me so many things. We did everything together. We traveled. We loved.

"We had a child, Marty. Sadly, there was no room for her in our lives until she was finished with WEX School. We had another child,

the business. Honestly, we loved the business more than anything or anyone else; even more than Marty. Marvin worked tirelessly to build it. I whored to enlarge it and nurture it. We were devoted to it. Now it's gone. As fate has it, I inherited everything, except the operating companies which went to Israel, because David and Marty and Eloweiss are all gone now. And, of course, I inherited the jewels."

Susan smiled a wistful smile. Here, near the end of her life, it was clear that she loved her life and the way she lived it. The way she treated Marty was her one great regret. She would carry that pain to her grave. Her eyes told Barbara that she suffered her regret. But by taking Barbara into her confidence and giving her the jewels, she tried, in the only way she could, to atone for the way she treated Marty.

"What are all those jewels worth, Susan?"

"Marvin kept detailed records of the origin of each jewel and what he paid for it. Today, they are worth one hundred billion dollars, easily."

"But, wholesale? Are they worth ten billion dollars?"

"No, Barbara. The hundred billion is wholesale. Likely they are worth two hundred to five hundred billion, retail. Marvin only paid wholesale prices to acquire them. He told me that was the going price, the best price; and he would not pay more."

"But these were given in return for life."

"Yes, I know; but to Marvin it was all business. He repaid Eloweiss's family the money he used to initially fund his rescue operation. The jewels I am giving you are his profit. Wholesale prices were the going price for a Jews life in Hitler's Germany. It was a desperate time. Life for German's Jews was so precarious. Desperation to live drove the price of life. And that desperation is reflected in the value of Marvin's jewels. That enormous wealth is the testament to the cruelty of Hitler and his Nazi regime; their heartlessness. That cruelty and heartlessness drove the market price for life.

"And, as you can see, that price was limitless. And Marvin understood he was the only buyer in a uniquely priced market. Marvin would not pay more than he could get if he needed to sell them. Marvin was also shrewd. He knew his market. He knew he could charge the most extreme monopoly price; essentially, Marvin charged the refugee Jew all the wealth he or she had plus all they could beg and borrow."

"Sounds cruel, Susan. I didn't know that about Marvin."

"Yes, when it came to a business deal, Marvin could be ruthless. He always got as much as he could from any deal he made. I saw that trait in him. Marvin was always all about business. I suppose I was his only distraction from business. I loved him. I knew him better than anyone, even his wife. But Marvin was not like David. Marvin loved all the peoples of the world. He looked to know a person's heart. I know that about him. If he had known you, I'm sure he would have loved your heart, Barbara. He would be happy for you to have the jewels. I know that is true. So, take them, my loving child that I did not have but wished I had had. Take them and use them wisely."

"I will use them wisely, Susan. I promise you. Thank you and bless you."

Barbara had the jewels removed from David's former property and sent to her father's reservation. There, the jewels remain to this day. They are kept in a huge safe in the basement of the log ranch house that Chief used for his living quarters until he passed. And Barbara and Bob lived there after Chief died.

Barbara went to Susan's storage unit to search through Eloweiss's possessions. There, among the furniture from her house, was a large storage trunk. She opened it. It contained all of Eloweiss's most personal things; her Torahs, including her five-volume Rashi Torah set; her High Holy Days Prayer Books; her Siddur; her menorahs, candelabras, and personal jewelry; her cosmetics and unused medications; and packets of letters written to her by her family and friends. Curiously, there was also a large manila envelope with the word Marvin written on it in bold red lipstick. Barbara opened the envelope. It contained six glossy print photos and a letter. Barbara gasped.

There were six pictures of Susan when she was younger. They would have been taken about the time when she was still married to Joseph Maloney. She was naked in all the photos; and in every photo she was posed in very provocative sensual positions upon a white lynx fur, or on white pillows, and surrounded by diamonds and rubies. She wore a diamond neckless with a diamond pendant that held an outsized ruby. Her red hair flowed beautifully over her shoulders and lay tantalizingly upon her breasts in some of the photos.

The photos were taken in natural daylight. The sunshine over her shoulders caused her red hair to assume a tint of gold. She held her sex open in another photo. It captured her evocative, come hither and make love with me, smile. Her green chromed nails accented the near fiendish glow in her eyes. The photo all but spoke to the viewer saying:

'Yes, see, I've just made love; but I'm not finished. I need more. I want you to pleasure me more.'

But it was one photo in particular that made Barbara gasp. Who could have taken it? Surely, Marvin had taken the others; but how could he have taken this photo, featuring his own hand? And how had Eloweiss come to possess the photos?

There, propped up, nearly vertically upright, upon a white down pillow, surrounded by diamonds and rubies, was a large close-up of Susan's vagina. A man's hand with his three middle fingers were inserted into Susan's vagina. The hand had to be Marvin's. The wedding ring on his ring finger was plainly visible. It was not an ordinary wedding ring. It had been given to him by Eloweiss. She had it specially hand crafted. It was made of white gold with two Blue Nile ring bands that bordered its edges. Within the blue border bands were hexagon lapis inlays representing the Star of David. The ring symbolized that, not only was Marvin married to Eloweiss; the two of them were also married to Israel. Marvin's wedding ring was a replica of the flag of Israel.

Barbara opened the letter. It was from Eloweiss to Marvin. Obviously, he had read it and returned it to her; or Eloweiss had written it, waited until she died for Marvin to find it and the pictures; or she had obtained the pictures and written the letter; and then decided to keep the letter and pictures; and let Marvin find them after she died.

Marvin,

How could you? You know my family loaned you the monies against the jewels so you could bring many thousands out of the holocaust. How many people sold all they had to buy those jewels, at retail prices; then sold them to you at wholesale, to get one family member out? Did you ever stop to think that maybe five or ten people died for every jewel you have? Did you forget your pledge to Meyer? I was there with you at the Flamingo when you promised him that you would return every jewel so he could trade them for arms for Israel. I was so proud of you then, Marvin. Did you forget that, Marvin? You held back, didn't you, Marvin? You turned your back on our people to seek the favors of your gentile whore's cunt, didn't you, Marvin?

How could you keep these pictures of your whore in our home, Marvin? In my bedroom! Shame on you! Did you expect me to not find them; or did you want to torment me;

punish me? Why do you hurt me so? This is very harmful to me, Marvin. You know I do not sleep well. You work with her. You work late with her. You go away on trips with her. You come home to me and you smell of her.

I agonize over your thoughtlessness, Marvin. I have visions of your whore's cunt when my eyes are closed. My mental clarity is obscured. Your affair and these photo reminders have weakened me. Your affair hastens my disease. Is this what you wanted, Marvin? Did you intend to hurt me? You have hurt me, Marvin. You should feel guilty, Marvin. I hurt.

Do I deserve to see your gentile whore flaunting her insatiable lust over the deaths of so many of our people? Did she tell you that she found perverse joy in fornicating over their deaths, Marvin? Did she? What were the two of you thinking? How could you do what you did? Don't you see how shameful you are, Marvin? Do you really believe she is worth so much more than so many of us?

Marvin, in the name of God, please hear me. I can see she is beautiful; her breasts are spectacular; her nipples are like red blossoms floating on white cream. They are not faded brown on graying flesh, like mine. You know I am dying from my disease, Marvin. We both know your Susan is full of life. I see your attraction to her.

But, Marvin. I am your wife! Your wife, Marvin! Your wife! These pictures have hurt me. This is not assimilation, Marvin. This is you running away from your religion and your heritage. Why do you do this, Marvin? I and my family, and your own family, have been very generous with you. It seems that, psychologically, you have some need to mock me. But you only mock yourself and who we are, Marvin. I do not deserve your mock.

Yes, fuck your whore if you must; but please, not in such a sacrilegious way. She is precious to you. I see that. But how can she be more precious than all the lives of so many of our people, represented by those jewels? Is she worth one hundred billion dollars Marvin? Think! Is she? Tell me that is not true! She is a common gentile whore, Marvin. That is all she is. Nothing more. Surely you cannot love her more than you love yourself for who you are! Think about what you're doing!

I have tried to understand the workings of your mind, Marvin. You have her cock thirsting cunt propped up high upon white pillows. It rises like it is upon an altar on a mountaintop, yearning to receive you, yearning for you to sacrifice your life for it. Has her cunt become your god? Is that why you exalt it upon a holy mountain; rise it up high, out of a deep ocean of jewels? Does it demand that your cock enter it and commune with her soul?

Were you thinking that her cunt represents triumphant life arising from the sorrows of death? Do the jewels represent death to you? You have everything backwards, Marvin. Those jewels represent the triumph of life! Were you thinking that her cunt is more sacred than the lives represented by the jewels? Are the pillows your altar, upon which you placed her whoring cunt, so you could worship it?

Marvin, I hear things. I heard how her husband, Joseph, died. Did he find out about the two of you? Did her whoring drive him to suicide? How do you feel, knowing that her whoring caused a man to take his life? His life, Marvin! Shame on both of you! And, I saw the nub on her daughter's finger, Marvin. I know you have fathered the daughter of the whore who was once my servant girl; my handmaiden. I know the Marty child is yours. More shame on you, Marvin.

The child, Marty, is not of her mother's marriage. Do you think the two of you are playing a joke on the world? What kind of mother can your Susan be to that child, under these circumstances? Shame on both of you! What have you done to an innocent child, Marvin? What do you think will become of her life, Marvin? Will she grow up to become a whore? Will she try to emulate her mother? Shame and disgust on her whore mother and on you! You have violated the commandment against adultery! You disappoint me.

I also hear that your Susan puts it around, Marvin. How does it make you feel knowing that other men hold their hands on her tushy and pull her cunt over their cocks while they fuck her? Is that acceptable behavior from your mistress? Perhaps you watch her fuck others, Marvin? Do You? Do you watch them perform oral sex on her, too? Do You? Do you enjoy watching her whore? I don't understand you, Marvin. What do you love about such a vile, despicable, shameless harlot?

What loyalty does she have, except to her own wealth and pleasures? Is she that wonderful, Marvin? Does she strike something inside you by the way she laughs; by how she sucks you; fucks you? What is your attraction to her? What fascinates you about this unprincipled woman? Why do you love her? Have you no pride, Marvin? What does she give you that another woman can not give you? I don't understand you; or her; or any of this.

Why the picture where your whore holds herself open and displays your semen pool? Were the two of you proud of your disgusting lust; your shamelessness, your iniquities? Were you both mocking the world? Were you thinking that your whore lust is all that matters, Marvin? Why would she hold herself open after sex, Marvin? Was she inviting you to lose your face in her cunt to drink your own lust? Did you do that, Marvin? Did you throw away all your dignity and debase yourself in her cunt, Marvin? Did you use your tongue after sex, so you could give your whore even more pleasure? Sure, you did. You are never man enough to deny her her pleasures, are you Marvin? What do you think she was thinking of you while you licked her cunt, Marvin?

Perhaps she was thinking that her victory over our marriage was complete? Is that what that photo was about? And, why the picture of her smiling so triumphantly with your semen spurts all over her breasts? She was thinking that you were surrendering your life to her, wasn't she? Did she say as much? Did she tell you that she expected you to join her life in marriage? What was your mind thinking then, Marvin? Were you pleased seeing her reveling in her whoring? Did you take these pictures to glorify her whoring, Marvin; her conquest of you? How could you honor and glorify such a base woman? How did you reward her for her wickedness?

Surely, you gave her some portion of the sacred jewels to reward her for her whoring. Or, did you give her all of them? The diamond neckless with the ruby pendant she wore was surely your gift to her for her whoring. And the white enameled Faberge Egg with its glittering rubies and emeralds! Lying there beneath her cunt! What did she do to earn that, Marvin? Do you imagine some message when you look at that picture? Is her cunt the gateway to your wealth? Is her cunt more valuable than creation, represented by the egg? It that why her cunt is positioned above the egg? Is there nothing that you held back from her; nothing for me or for David? Did you have to give her everything? How could you do this, Marvin? Wasn't debasing yourself and trusting your debasing secrets to your whore reward enough for her?

I am not happy with you, Marvin. I am your wife! And, words cannot express how disgusted I was when I saw this picture of your hand fingering her cunt. It is your hand. I know it by the wedding ring I gave you. Who took that picture, Marvin? Who else knows of our secret of the jewels? Were you sharing your whore? With whom, Marvin? Who else knows of your debauchery? What has become of you? What were you thinking, Marvin? Were you believing that her widespread legs and whoring cunt are worth more than Israel? Were you psychologically offering up our families and Israel to her shameless, insatiable cunt? What was going through your mind, Marvin? Were you wishing you were a Pagan and not a Jew?

Who are you, Marvin? You go to meetings and give speeches. You go to shul all dressed like a fine businessman. But is that all a façade, Marvin? I think it is. I think, in your heart of hearts, Marvin, that you do not really want to be who you pretend you are. You do not want to dress as a businessman. You do not want to help the tribe. You care nothing for the People of the Book, do you? Our faith is all a big joke to you, isn't it? It's just a way for you to bring riches and glory to your whore, isn't it? You don't honestly wish to pray to the word of God, do you, Marvin? You don't want to carry the burdens of being one of God's chosen people, do you? You really want something much more base and tangible, don't you?

You want to be a Pagan, don't you, Marvin? You want to worship your pagan whore's cunt, don't you? That's what you idolize. Isn't that true, Marvin? You love to plant your face in her whoring cunt and sanctify all the whoring she does; honoring her whoring; worshiping her whoring; adoring her and her cunt for her whoring, don't you, Marvin? You are a pagan worshipper, aren't you, Marvin? Her cunt has become your true god, hasn't it, Marvin? Do you honestly believe that Susan's whoring cunt is worth more than our families; all the friends who care about you; all of Israel and all the Jews who live there; the words of God? You cannot love her that much, Marvin. You cannot lose your soul this way, Marvin. You simply cannot.

Why not Goldie Blinkly, Marvin? Why not pictures of that disgusting whore? That tart cannot keep her mouth shut. When her mouth isn't openly bragging about fornicating, it's open while sucking a cock. That whore! I heard how you fucked her for hours every day, for months; and how your tongue teased her flesh pot, giving her orgasm after orgasm to help her grieve past the death of her husband.

Yes, Marvin, I know! She openly brags about how your tongue pleasured her cunt while she sat shiva. How thoughtful and caring of you, Marvin! But why no pictures of Goldie Blinkly's cunt and her widespread legs? She is also a beautiful woman. And she puts it around. She is notoriously and proudly immoral. Even while she was married, she openly whored without consideration for the agonizing heartache she caused poor Jacob, her husband. She is thoroughly selfishly immoral like your Susan, that way. So, why are there no pictures of your hand shoving our families and Israel into Goldie Blinkly's cunt?

These are profound questions, Marvin. It can not be because Goldie wasn't whore enough for you. She has that tight ass and sculptured body. She is beautiful, witty, charming, carefree, gleefully given to whoring. Surely, she is indecent, shameless, profligate, and immoral trash enough for you. Surely, her cunt is always hot and slippery for your wayward cock. Surely, she would never tire of fucking you. Surely, she knows how to please you. So why are there no pictures of her, Marvin?

I will tell you why, Marvin. It is because Goldie Blinkly is one of us. She is common to you. She is what you can have, if that's what you want. I can forgive your affair with Goldie Blinkly, Marvin. She is of our tribe. Your family and the rabbis would swallow hard, but they would accept her.

But Goldie is not what you want because you, deep inside yourself, do not want to be who you are, Marvin. You want to pretend you are not part of our heritage of suffering and guilt, don't you? You want to pretend you are not one of God's chosen people, don't you? You do not want to carry that burden, do you Marvin? These pictures tell me that you do much more than fuck your whore, Marvin. Obviously, you also worship her! Can you not understand that by worshipping her cunt you are forgetting that only God can be worshipped? Only God can be the sovereign of all humanity. Your whore's cunt cannot be the object of worship for the entire human race, Marvin. Only God can be that. So, why do you wish to forsake God, Marvin? Why do you turn away from God to worship this whore's cunt? Stop thinking with your prick and start thinking with your mind Marvin.

I know what you want, Marvin. You want Susan, your goyim whore. You want to turn your back on your family; my family; your son; and your religion and all your friends. You want to turn away from all of us for your Pagan Susan whore. That's really it, isn't it, Marvin? You, yourself, do not even want to be a Jew! But you are a Jew, Marvin; and you are married to me.

Shema! Marvin! Hear me clearly now. I have tolerated your misguided sense of yourself for too long. I have tolerated because you are a man and I am your wife. I have tolerated the smells of her genitals on your penis and on your face, Marvin. I have tolerated that you fall asleep next to me dreaming of her genitals, Marvin. Yes, I know. I know your dreams, Marvin. But my tolerance ends there, Marvin. You may believe that by placing your penis and your face and your dreams in her genitals that you can escape who you are. But you can't, Marvin.

Let me remind you who you really are, Marvin. You are Mandel Shocketski. That's who you really are. That is your name that your father declared for you at your bris. You are the descendant of a three-thousand-year lineage of kosher butchers. Your Marvin name is your Americanized assimilated name. Remember that, Mandel. You may believe that by creating your artificial corporate world with your Susan whore that the two of you could escape the real world. But you can't escape the real world, Mandel.

You will always be a Jew and Susan will always be a Goyim, Gentile Christian. You cannot mix oil and water, Mandel; nor can you mix Judaism and Christianity. Oh, I know you believed you could. I know the two of you created a child. I saw Marty's little finger before she had her nub removed. I know she is your child, Mandel. And what happened to her? The two of you abandoned her. How cruel and selfish you were. And look at her life now, Mandel. She is fast becoming a notorious, porn star; a profligate whore! Is that what you wanted for your daughter, Mandel? Did you give her life so she could fuck every pair of pants she meets?

Shame on you; and shame on your Susan whore, Mandel. And what do you think will happen to her if David ever learns her secret? You know David is not stupid, Mandel. He may be diabolical and devious. He may be covetous and vengeful. But he will fight viciously to protect what is rightfully his. If he should ever learn that Marty is your legal daughter, by her bloodline, realize that he would likely kill her. He would never allow a tainted bloodline to inherit half of what is rightfully his, by the laws of our tribe, Mandel. So, can you see what you have set into motion here? I have no doubt that David would slaughter her like he would a sheep or a heifer. And that will be the tragedy for both of them, Mandel. You have cast the die that may lead to your daughter's death and your son's tainting as an ungodly Rashbamer, a common murderer. Well, what you have done is done, Marvin. But your madness ends here.

Your life and your soul are chained to my life and to my soul, Marvin. Remember your promises to me and to our families, Marvin. I will hold you to those promises. I will never set you free. I and my family's money made you what you are, Marvin. That is the deal you made. I will not let you break it. You will never take the benefits of our deal and not keep your part of our bargain. I will never grant you a divorce. Never! I would rather ruin you and your business and your reputation. And I would take back the wealth of my family.

Live with it, Marvin. You just learn to live with it. Your whore may have your heart and mind and body, Marvin. But she will never have your soul. When you and I die, our bodies and our souls will lie together in eternal repose in the Mount of Olives, Jerusalem cemetery. Your soul will be chained for-ever to my soul, Marvin. And I will keep you chained to my soul when her soul comes for your soul. And she will never pry your soul away from mine. In death, she will finally learn that her soul is Goyim Christian; and your soul is Jew. And, in death, I will keep your two souls separate. You will not have her in eternity, Marvin. You will only have me.

Oh, Marvin, my darling, do not feel so crestfallen. Remem-ber when we were young? I was a rather saucy piece of meat for you, wasn't I? You loved the pleasures of my bed then, before my disease took its toll on me, didn't you? You pleasured me so beautifully then. Remember how sweet I tasted when you placed your tongue in my cunt? Sure, you do. I know you do. Well, you can remember me that way in death, then. We'll go back to those sweet times. You'll see. In eternity, we will fall in love again. I know we will, Marvin. I know.

Marvin, now listen to me. I speak with reason as your friend. You cannot be well in your mind. This Susan woman has taken over your mind. She has no morality, Marvin. But she will never take over my mind. I never want to see her again. I never want her in my house again. Keep her away from me. You must think about what you are doing. You must step back. Please see our rabbi and talk with him about your obsession with this whore, Marvin. I beg you. Can you honestly tell him that you want to dedicate your life and all your great talents to enriching a greedy, immoral gentile whore? Wake up, Marvin! Your whore doesn't even give you exclusive rights! She fucks several others! She knows no shame! She has no faith in God!

What is it about her, Marvin? Why did you take her with you to Buenos Aires? Yes, I know your secret. I entered your study house one weekend while the two of you were at some investment seminar. I saw the papers in your desk. The cables and the telegrams. You wanted her to meet Colonel Juan Peron. Why Marvin? Was it her Catholic Church connection? Did the Vatican okay your Nazi rat lines? Did Susan fuck Juan Peron, too? Did you fuck Evita? I believe you did, didn't you? Was she any good? As good as Susan? Did the four of you do a foursome? I believe you did, didn't you? Susan would have liked that, wouldn't she? That slut! Did you and Juan compare notes about your women?

What is wrong with your head, Marvin? I read your copies of the cables from State to the GOU Nazi sympathizer Colonels in Buenos Aires. I see your secret, Marvin. I see how you set the payments up with the Swiss Banks and how you managed your network of German collaborators and how you orchestrated your bribery scheme. Brilliant, Marvin. I always knew you were brilliant. But now I understand how you made a second, even larger, fortune on your percentage of money stolen from Europe's Jews. Why would you do that? First you pilfer money from desperate Jews. Then you pilfer another piece of the stolen Jewish wealth from the escaping Nazi war criminals. I see how you kept your rat lines going near the end of the war, and after. I see how you got tens of thousands of Nazi war criminals into the Americas. Why Marvin? How much money is enough? Do you even understand what you have done?

Why, Marvin? In the name of God, why? Why did you help those murderous rats? Is money that important to you? Where was your morality in this? How could you blind yourself to what these criminals did; to the millions they murdered? How could you help them escape, Marvin? Oh, I know. So, your whore, Susan, could have more. Of course! Is her cunt that sweet and wonderful, Marvin? Do you realize what you have done? You have sowed the ugly seeds of Nazism all over the world! They are here, Marvin. They are here through their disgusting Broderbund clubs and their vile Oktoberfest's and their hideous polka music. They dance like drunken morons on the graves of our beautiful, God loving people, Marvin.

And now they have their nutty horse face pretty boy flying around the world, screaming about global warming. They have their insane World Economic Forum. Think, Marvin.

See what is in front of you? Look! You are seeing the world's new Nazis. These nuts have reared their ugly heads again! They want world socialism, just like Hitler did. And when they fail spectacularly, as they surely will, what will they do, Marvin? Yes, of course, these simpleton maniacs will blame the Jews. Well, they are here now. See them. They try to cloak themselves in sweet words like democracy; but they are all wannabe tyrants. They live among us now. They have risen with their evil agendas again.

Hate cannot be contained inside a ketchup bottle, Marvin. It's out. See it. It has found its voice. Oh, yes, it disguises its voice very well; very sanctimoniously; persuasive; smooth talking; coifed hair; worthy cause and all that bullshit based on its fake, unverifiable science. These new globalists are no different than Hitler, who based his bullshit on phrenology idiocy and quackery like Nordic mysticism and similar horseshit that appeals to the feeble-minded numbskulls in America's Democrat Party. They are so pathetically stupid they cannot even invent new, credible bullshit.

But they will blame us when these idiots cause another war; and when they fail, they will take the whole world down with them; then they will blame us Jews. Why? Because these irresponsible nuts only know how to spew their trash talk, like Hitler spewed his trash talk. They can't create anything. They can't build anything. They have no ability; no acumen; no discernment; no common sense; no foresight of consequences; and no desire to better mankind; only to better themselves, here and now, at others' expense. They are pigs!

They are not like we Jews, who do seek to better mankind. They just tear down what works; only thinking of themselves. They are exactly like yesterday's Nazi thugs; but they act smoothly and smile nicely, for now. They appeal to illogical emotion, that's all they do. In their end game, when they fall on their idiotic faces, they will come for all the Jews on Earth. They will blame and seek to murder every Jew on this planet. Mark my words, Marvin. That is their base character. Their creed is destruction and hatred. They are irresponsible losers. They are led by that phony gad fly moron who threw his military medals over the White House wall. So, what sort of leadership is that? It's political stunt gimmickry; gaslighting, not leadership. Did he ever build anything? Did he build a car company? No? A technology company? Any company? No. Did he ever meet a payroll? No, of course not. He is incapable of building anything. He's a pretty boy gladhander who back stabs his own country, Marvin. That's all he is. He's one of those dimwits who think authoritarian China is a good role model for other countries. Can you trust a fool who thinks that way, Marvin? He only knows how to blame others, Marvin.

What did he ever do, Marvin? I'll tell you what he did, Mavin. He figured out how to fuck a ketchup bottle! That's all he ever did, Marvin. And you, Marvin. You would throw in with filth like this? You would let this piece of filth use your great mind? Why would you trouble yourself to set up that empty suit loser filth to succeed? Do you ever think of the long-term consequences of what you do, Marvin? No, of course you don't. All you think about is Susan's slippery cunt, Marvin. And why? Is it really that wonderful in there? What's in there, anyway, Marvin? I know you keep your prick in there. But must you keep your mind in there, too? Look at her morals, Marvin. What sort of mind does she have, Marvin? Look!

She spits on her own religion and her own mother! She believes in nothing except her own pleasures and her wealth.

Her indecency is widely known. Your Susan has no soul. In her bones, beneath her beauty and her sexuality, she is simply a common, conniving whore. Listen to me, Marvin. I am your wife. The two of you are hurting me. Please stop. Please break it off.

But if I must, if you make me, if that is my fate, I will accept what you are doing with her. I understand I have no choice but to live with your disgusting conduct. I understand that I must tolerate her whoring cunt's vile smells on you; but I will never tolerate her control of your soul, Marvin. I will never let her change you from who you are. And I will never forgive you for this, Marvin. I will enter my grave with disgust for you; for what you have done to our families; and me. But I will keep my hold on you as my husband! I know you are sick in your mind, Marvin. I am doing my best to understand why you have become the way you are.

You know that I can no longer be a woman in all the ways you need a woman. I cannot help that. You know I am not well. But, for the sake of who you once were and for who you are; for Israel; for our son, David, please rethink what you are doing. Please see our rabbi and tell him how much pain you are causing me. Ask him why you value this whore's cunt more than our families and Israel. Ask him why you love this woman so much. Be honest with yourself. Ask him, Marvin.

Obviously, I did go through your things. That is how I found your correspondence and your disgusting pictures. Yes, I am a bitch! But I am also your wife. We are both cursed! And we should not keep these secrets from each other. Live with it!

Eloweiss

Suddenly, the significance of Mrs. Rodriguez's diary entries about Marty made sense to Barbara. The final, connecting reason for the mystery that was Marty fell into place. Grandmother Mallory wasn't crazy! Not at all! Well, not in the ways most people think of others as crazy. No, the old woman was not crazy in that way. But she was crazy in another, different sort of way. Grandmother Mallory was a virulent antisemite! That explained her Satan comments to Marty. That explained her scream fest in Susan's office. Grandmother Mallory believed Marvin was the Devil. She knew he was sleeping with Susan. She had probably figured out that Marty was Marvin's child; making Marty the child of the Devil. The psychic burden of what her daughter had done and was doing was torturing the poor woman. She was the personification of bigotry; trapped and steeped in it; going crazy because of it.

'How did Grandmother Mallory come to believe that Marvin was Satan? How could she believe that her daughter, Susan, conceived a child with Satan? And how could she believe that her innocent five-year-old granddaughter, Marty, was a creation of Satan? And what would her beliefs imply about David?

Barbara shuddered at her thoughts. What made Grandmother Mallory so certain in her convictions that she would try to pit her granddaughter against her own daughter? What had happened to get the woman so riled up that she would come downtown to confront her daughter in her office and hold a scream fest that was heard as far away as the front office? What had Susan done, or what had Susan, with Marvin, done, to cause her to be so upset? There were no additional entries in Mrs. Rodriguez's office diary. The drug and prostitution businesses were David's creations. Whatever had upset Grandmother Mallory had happened before David got control of the Firm.

'What could that have been? What causes people to go off the deep end with their beliefs this way?' wondered Barbara. *'Maybe*

this will remain a mystery? Was the old woman being rational? Was it just her prejudice? 'There's no contemporary record from the time of Christ's crucifixion. Everything is hearsay; yet people believe the stories, not as metaphors; and not as homilies, but as truth. The first gospels used in Christian bibles were written centuries after the crucifixion event, if the event actually happened at all. Has humanity been believing in a fairy tale myth all these centuries? Is an ancient fairy tale justification to fight wars over? Really? By what logic? Only if the inner nature of man is to fight and kill! And only if that nature feels a need to justify itself. But are not sports supposed to bleed off some of those hostilities? Isn't that why we invented the NFL?

Barbara reflected. Yes, the Mallory grandmother was a bigot, hidebound in her beliefs. But wasn't David just as much a bigot? How often had David made disparaging remarks about gentiles? What caused him to believe he had the right to torture and murder; or run his office like it was a joke on human values? And what gave him the moral authority to abuse Rublina and her son so cruelly, like he did? And why wasn't Bob good enough as he was?

Why did David feel he needed to mold Bob into a Jew? How did it all begin? She went to the company store room looking for clues. It was a small room next to bookkeeping, almost always locked. Company mementoes were stored there. Copies of prospectuses of the Firm's early underwritings; stacks of miniature plastic cubes commemorating deals done and money raised; the Firm's original typewriters. And there they were! Framed pictures of Marvin and Susan. So much younger with the years peeled away. So vibrant! So clear eyed and engaging. Both remarkably handsome. Their optimism and intelligence beaming from their smiling faces. They had their world by the tail. And they knew it. They were a special happening. And they knew that, too.

How did they come together from such different backgrounds? Barbara wondered. It was almost like they were two particles that would ordinarily repel each other, but placed into extraordinary circumstances. Like two highly charged particles accelerated in a high velocity particle collider, both were racing away from their cultures and their pasts. They were angry to leave what was, and what had been, when they met. Their love was born of their separate angers. And when they collided, those loves were released in an explosion of passion lust. It was unstoppable, irreversible; destructive and creative love; passionate love; love at once and forever thereafter. Lives and businesses were uprooted and rearranged: destruction! And Marty was born: creation!

Barbara wondered what it was like for those two? The kisses. The touches. The intimacy of bodies joining those first times. Was it haphazard? Awkward? Sudden? Passionate? Planned? Savored? Her thoughts went to the characters of the two founders. Marvin was precise; detailed. He focused on what he wanted. He wanted Susan. More than all his world without her, he wanted her; Susan.

And Susan. What about her? She had a will forged from steel. She focused. Barbara knew that from the time she had worked for Susan. And Susan had immense resolve. She set her mind to the way she wanted things. And she got her way. A very Catholic mindset; a Queen Isabella, perhaps reincarnated. Had she targeted Marvin? Perhaps. But Marvin wanted to be slain by her love arrows. He welcomed her arrows. And Susan's willpower fused the two of them together, for life. She went into Marvin's life and decided to stay there. And she pushed everyone else away, especially Eloweiss and David; and hurtfully cruel, she even pushed away her own child, poor little Marty. And once Susan had all the others pushed away, she kept them away; outside Her's and Marvin's private world.

Suddenly, Barbara imagined herself back in time, in the positions of Marvin and Susan:

'Susan became Marvin's escape from his family's and his wife's religious madness; escape from religion's endless neurotic rituals; escape from the rigid mitzvahs of dos and don'ts. His mind questioned, more and more, all the beliefs he was taught to believe, until he felt driven away from them. The drive to leave his religion was powerful. It was an inner force that told him he needed to flee from religion to maintain his sanity. He escaped all of it when he dove into his love for Susan; their uninhibited, shameless, physical obsessive love that crossed all religious and social boundaries. When Susan held Marvin in her arms, Susan became Marvin's true religion. He idolized her. She became his God.

'And Susan, likewise, felt driven to escape her mother's insane bigotry and fairy tale religious beliefs. What drove her to forsake the dialectic of her Catholic upbringing? When she was a mere child, her mother had volunteered her into servitude to Marvin's wife. What happened to Susan during her years as servant girl for Eloweiss and baby sitter for David? Did she see a different lifestyle? Perhaps? How could she not see? But she never converted; never became a Jewess. Obviously, neither Catholicism nor Judaism appealed to Susan. She charted her own course through life and escaped from all religious dogmas and raced into her love for Marvin; uninhibited, physical, romantic, passionate; even perverse and kinky love; but always at its constant core: true, abiding love. From the evening Marvin decided to lay with her, she adored the man and idolized him. She would do and did do anything and everything for him and with him. When she opened herself to his intimacy, she knew what the two of them had; how special it was. Others ridiculed, derided, and scorned her for her steadfast love; but those jealousies and bigotries never dissuaded her. She was always proud to be Marvin's woman.

'Through thick and thin, their ups and downs, the two of them believed only in their love. They always knew and trusted that they could count on that love, no matter what. The two of them went on to make something special. They created their extraordinary Firm. That was very special to them. They also created Marty.

'No doubt, Susan's daughter studied her mother's ways. No doubt, Susan's disdain for organized religion was inculcated in Marty. Likely, Susan's penchant for whoring also influenced Marty. The daughter strived diligently to outdo the mother's licentiousness. Marty unhesitatingly smashed her moral compass with a sledgehammer and willed herself to shed all vestiges of morality. She became a prostitute and porn star, par excellence.

'But unfortunately for Marty, she was never special to Marvin and Susan. She was always the mere byproduct of Susan's effort to legitimize herself as a married woman. Once Susan had that legitimacy, she badgered her husband, Joseph, into suicide and sent Marty to boarding school, essentially abandoning her daughter. Susan was relentless in her driven quest for recognition, wealth, and power. She abhorred the poverty of her parents and vowed to escape that poverty and never succumb to it.

'In accepting Marvin's love, and surrendering her life to that love, Susan found her pathway to her goal. She only experienced motherly affection for Marty, briefly, when Marty became engaged to Bob. When Susan killed David, she wasn't acting out of some sense of motherly love for Marty. Rather, she was enraged at David, not for taking Marty's life, but for having the temerity to take Marty from her. David's audacity sparked Susan's motherly instincts, much like momma Grizzlies fly into rage states when intruders get near their cubs.

'But Susan's decision to commit her acts of torturing and murdering David was only partly born of motherly love. More than any sense of love for Marty, her heinous deed was the culmination of her years of pent-up frustrations with and her hatred of David. His murder of Marty incensed Susan. Marty was her child. David had no right to take her life. As David's lifetime baby sitter, Susan needed to punish him for his capital offense. And, David's punishment was death.

'Who was Marty?' Barbara wondered. 'Was she a modern-day version of Erato, the ancient Greek muse of erotic poetry and love? Were her seduction techniques modern-day refinements of Erato's harp and arrows? Could no mortal man resist her allure? Was she the ultimate, perfectly refined personification of pornography's call to our modern-day libidos? Was Marty offered to ordinary mortals as an attempt by the ancient gods to make us reconsider our dedications to our religions? Were her confrontational ways of flaunting her immorality her method of messaging us that our beliefs are wrongly held; without logical foundations?

'Marvin slept around. Zeus slept around. Both understood women as objects for their love making pleasures. Did Marvin's affair with Susan mirror Zeus's affair with Mnemosyne, resulting in Marty as our modern-day Erato? Perhaps the ancient writers were too modest to extol the antics and romps of Zeus's love child, Erato? Surely Ovid had oral sex in mind when he wrote of Erato's understanding of the tender love that came from the mouth of Venus.

'And surely, as well, Marty appreciated the joys of oral sex. In her hundreds of films Marty was always seen as blissfully mirthful, contented, and aroused to the highest heights of her passions while sucking a penis or while having a tongue lavishing its adoration upon her clitoris. Never did she shy from oral sex or hurry it; or in any way, ever express distaste for it. She loved nothing more than feeling a penis's hot ejaculation of cum streaming onto her godless tongue. She always, predictably, embraced the giving and the partaking of oral love making as if it was a heavenly blessing which the ancient pagan gods had bestowed upon mortal humans. Marty loved oral sex. She adored the intimacy feeling of a lover's, male or female, orgasm spurting or flowing into her mouth; and her own releases flowing into the mouths of her lovers.

'In her brief lifetime, Marty changed the world's perception of pornography. She returned it to its rightful place as human intimacy art, the very highest form of art, vividly expressed as living art. She returned it to the high status that it held in the cultures of ancient Greece and ancient Rome. I know, searching inside myself, that Marty's porn art has changed me. I am now more accepting of the human condition and the human need for love. As I watched her film art, I felt the change taking place within me. I could enter her mind, know her thoughts and empathize with her feelings while she performed with her partners. She was giving of herself in her ultimate, most intimate ways. Her lovemaking was effusive and contagious. And I found myself asking: How could any man make love with her and not fall in love with her?

'Marty was an evangelist for pornography. She made the world see it as a medium where humans could empathize about intimacy, passion, and love. She, along with the other women who create pornography, are modern day trail blazers who propagate love to mankind. They shatter inhibition. They open our eyes to the joys of making love. They encourage our young people to be confident in their sexuality and unafraid to talk about and share their desires for intimacy with others. America still has a morality hangover from Victorian times. But thanks to Marty and many like minded porn stars, the iron curtain of forbidden immorality is being lifted and replaced by freedom and love. More and more, these remarkably expressive, loving women and their beautiful pornographic art films are becoming accepted as mainstream culture. They inspire and lead the rest of us into our new worlds, filled with open, uninhibited love.

'I have my Bob now. At first, I was terribly jealous of Marty; but no more. Not because my nympho nemesis has died; but because through appreciation of her spectacularly beautiful porn art, I have been reborn and made alive. I will never find fault in Bob for falling into love with Marty. There is not a man alive who *could not fall in love with a porn star as loving as she, after having made love with her. Their lovemaking year was a transformative experience for Bob. I suppose it's only natural that men fall in love with their prostitute friends. I accept that now, in Bob and in all men. It is the human condition. It is powerful and true. I honor it.*

'Surely, Marty was the reincarnated personification of Erato's divine obsession with erotica. Perhaps humankind needed to wait these millenniums to have a real understanding of blissful erotica in the persona of Marty? Perhaps prostitution, whore-craft and explicit pornography are as old as "civilized" humanity itself? Perhaps only now are most humans beginning to appreciate pornography's addictive tension-releasing powers and accepting its transformative, deliciously compelling beauty?'

Barbara pondered these mystery thoughts about her former arch rival and the misunderstood sister-like soul that she belatedly came to love; now beyond her reach and reposed forever in Marty's death:

'Perhaps only the butterflies understand such eternal mysteries? Perhaps those lovely flutterers know why different people turn out the different ways that they do? Perhaps their message is that we humans must learn to be more tolerant and accepting; and, yes, loving, of others, especially the maligned who live among us; especially our wonderfully inspirational porn stars? Perhaps butterflies' reasonings are beyond the reach of human understanding? But that illusive truth should not prevent us from accepting and embracing the mysteries of life and human intimacy.

'True love is often born in intimacy. Many men loved Marty as their only true love. They adored her promiscuity and her whoring, and they accepted all of it in her persona. They forsake all others for her, as my Bob forsake me. I have my Bob back now. But do I really have him back? I still watch her films. They haunt me in a most compelling way. I see not a mortal woman, but a goddess muse; a

pleasure-seeking nymph. I watch her making love; putting her whole heart and sentient being into the act and art of it. It is her demeanor that haunts me. It occupies my mind. I know it will never leave me. Regardless of how hard I try; my mind will never forget the images that became indelibly etched in my memory.

'I will always hear her mirthful laughter and her toying giggles as she held a long-stemmed rose in her hand; studied it carefully, lovingly; her eyes smiling at it from her long eyelashes while she kissed it, as if to let it know it was about to experience a wonderful sexual treat; then she rubbed it between her breasts, caressing it before lowering it until it rested upon her vagina; smiling playfully into the camera the entire time.

'Then, while all her fans' eyes were wildly aroused, she left the rose resting upon her vagina and took a huge, erect penis in her hands. She then slathered the penis with her tube of lubricant; all the while beaming her smile and seductively inviting eyes into her lover's eyes, while sinfully rolling her tongue on the inside of her upper lip, exposing its underside to the camera. Simultaneously she fingered and pinched her nipples and thrust her vagina upwards and invitingly spread her legs widely open. She then moaned while wantonly stimulating herself upon the crown of her butterfly just above the positioned rose. She shamelessly stroked herself, inserting and withdrawing her finger from her vagina, while indecently canting her hips from side to side; and saying softly:

"Come into me, Marshawn. I want you to make love with me. Show the world you love me, Marshawn. I want your beautiful, big penis inside me. Come inside me and make love with me. It's time for us."

'She then opened her legs widely to reveal the outer lips of her honey well. The symbolism was wildly erotic and powerful. It was as if her butterfly had freshly alighted upon her rose and was about to suck the nectar from it.

'As I came to know her work, I realized that was one of the first porn films where Marshawn played her partner. I was certain I was watching a man and woman expressing true and heartfelt love while making that film. I am also certain that was the film session that convinced Marshawn that Marty was the love of his life; and that his erotic romantic experience on that set that day was the reason he decided to leave Aaliyah to have more time with Marty.

'There was also no doubt in my mind that millions of men who watched her evocative, smiling face and her fingers touching and holding open her vagina were smitten. It was the perfect beginning of an intensely erotic porn film. I was immediately certain that these same millions of men dreamed of becoming Marty's lover or that many of them called her Premium Service and offered her outrageous monies and gifts to spend intimate time with her; and that she accepted many of their offers. I could see in her smile how much she loved being a notoriously profligate, shameless whore. As I watched Marshawn's enormous penis penetrate her outer vaginal lips, the earlier symbolism with the rose struck home. Her butterfly was also about to drain all the semen nectar from Marshawn's penis, just as it had symbolically drained the nectar from the rose.

'And then, once the penis had entered her, I heard Marty say:

"Oh, I love how that feels. That feels so wonderful. I love feeling your beautiful penis inside me this way. Yes, Baby. Make love to me, Baby. Oh yes Baby, love me. When your penis isn't inside my vagina, I want you to put it inside my mouth, okay, Baby? Which do like better, my vagina or my mouth? You don't know, do you? Well, we'll have to continue doing it both ways until you make up your mind; okay Baby? I want you to let me know by deciding whether you'd like to come into my vagina or into my mouth, okay Baby? I'll love taking your cum either way, okay? I love it both ways. Let's not think about it too much, okay, Baby? Let's make love all night, okay

Baby? We'll do it in lots of different positions until you decide to come inside me, okay, baby?"

'And then, I watched her making love with that man, changing into new, different erotic positions every five minutes or so. I saw the glee in her eyes while she rolled her head from side to side and moved her hands deftly, twisting and stroking his penis while she sucked it. Clearly, she was enamored with Marshawn's penis. She loved touching and sucking it; loved the intimacy of having it inside her mouth. I could see she was giving her whole soul over to her love of his penis; and it was all so natural, unassuming, not forced; enjoyed. Romancing Marshawn's penis consumed her whole mind and all her attentions. There was no room in her thoughts for anything else. She had a unique ability to focus and concentrate. I do not know how any man with a pulse could ever resist her charms or feel his enthusiasm for pleasing her diminish one iota. None of her seductive movements bore any trace of vulgarity. No, everything she did was natural, open, honest, and enticingly beautiful.

'At the same time, I could not help but wonder how Marshawn's wife, Aaliyah, felt while seeing that film. When Marty sat with Marshawn on the sofa, and Marshawn cradled Marty in his arm and began kissing her mouth while he fingered her vagina, did Aaliyah feel her marriage was doomed from that very moment? I think she must have. When Marty showed no restraint, but instead took her panties completely off and gave him deeper French kisses, did Aaliyah begin feeling anger? I think she must have. When Marshawn buried his face in Marty's vagina and lavished her with such an intensity of oral sex that it appeared as if he was a lost, thirsty soul, finally supping from his holy grail, I wondered if that sequence demoralized Aaliyah? It must have.

'She had to have felt her heart was being crushed. And when Marty mounted Marshawn's penis while on top of him, facing his feet; and then bounced her vagina wildly upon his penis, as if it was her newest play toy, would that have caused Aaliyah pain, or disgust? Certainly, both; but by the time she saw those sequences, she had to already know that she had lost Marshawn to Marty. Then, when Marty slavishly sucked his penis and caressed his testicles and spoke, telling Marshawn that she couldn't wait to have his penis inside her vagina again; that she wanted to try some new positions with him; and then, he soul kissed her; did that sequence cause Aaliyah more pain? Absolutely! She must have felt as if arrows were being shot into her heart. And I think Marty enjoyed shooting those arrows. Each spoken idea about how many ways she wanted to experience Marshawn's penis had to sting like a fatal arrow in Aaliyah's broken heart.

'And when Marty lied down on the divan and Marshawn entered her Missionary style; and Marty bumped her vagina to the beat of the accompanying music, while rolling her eyes up to show only their whites, I realized I was watching an erotic masterpiece, complete with fireworks. It was breathtaking. But, what did Aaliyah feel? Did she know she'd never get him back? I think she must have known that. And when Marshawn entered Marty doggie style and she twerked and laughed and giggled the entire time while he hugged her and kissed her back and neck, did the Mrs. think, perhaps, that it might only be sex; and that Marshawn would get over it? Perhaps she did.

'But then, after Marshawn came into Marty's mouth and she finished sucking all his remaining semen from him, they did not stop filming. The director knew what he had. It was too good to stop. The film showed Marshawn taking Marty, the worlds most profligate whore, into his arms and kissing her soulfully in her mouth; the two of them holding their embrace and kisses for the longest time; and then hearing Marshawn telling Marty that he loved her; that he adored her; that she meant everything to him; even more than life itself. If Aaliyah had held out any hopes for her husband and *her marriage, that final scene would have crushed it. It ended with Marty displaying her open mouth, blowing a kiss to the camera, and saying to Marshawn:*

"Call me."

'There, in front of the entire world, Marty invited Marshawn to have an off-set relationship with her. She brazenly took Marshawn from Aaliyah and her family.

'Did Aaliyah see Marty as a white woman taking her black husband from her; turning him into her love slave? Did she feel resentment? Hatred perhaps? If she was anything like most normal women, I think she must have felt bitterness by then. Bob knew about Marty's involvement with Marshawn. He related to me that Aaliyah was very ordinary looking; a plain dresser; very meek and modest and committed to her family, her mosque, and her religion. She saw her place in life as a homemaker, child bearer, and nurturing mother. I can only imagine her distress. Once Marty had engaged Marshawn's limbic zone, the poor woman had no chance of holding on to him.

'And what thoughts must Marty have had while indulging her carnal pleasures? Did she understand that she was destroying a woman's marriage while she was joyfully fornicating with her husband? I think she did. She must have. How could she not have known? Did she even care about the hurt she caused, assuming she knew? I doubt whether she did. Because she didn't just destroy that marriage. She shattered it. I counted no fewer than seven orgasms that Marty experienced while making that film; each expressively, convulsively more emotive, and more breathtaking than the one before it. Those joyous vocal outbursts, each one pulverizing and crushing Aaliyah's marriage into ever finer dust, were where Marty's thoughts were focused. She could not, for one second, have reflected about the pain she was causing another woman. Her singular focus on pleasure was captured by the cameras. And that's what makes

Marty's pornography so spectacular. That's what causes her fans to demand ever more of her.

'And what about Marshawn? Was his romantic involvement with Marty his intention from the outset? I think it was. Knowing that she was a profligate whore did not deter him in the slightest. He had previously been one of six men who made an orgy film with her. Surely, he knew she had fornicated with hundreds of men before she made that film with him. That did not, in any way, give him pause or repulse him. Quite the opposite effect took hold of him. Maybe, by being one of many, he felt himself the equal of all others? Perhaps he was overcoming an inferiority complex? I do not know.

'I only know that Marty's vagina became Marshawn's obsession, his all-consuming religion. The fact that she was an incorrigible whore gave him the cause he needed to worship her even more. I guess that's the mystery of faith and obsessive love. By surrendering his soul to Marty's vagina, he lived the opposite of his religion's teachings. He was not looking for faith and prayer to take away his sins. He was looking to embrace sin by marrying his soul to the most profligately sinful woman in the world. He obsessively sought her sexual liaison. He wanted Marty to take away his religious faith and absolve him of all its effects on him. He wanted to flee from goodness and righteousness.

'He loved Marty because she accommodated his quest for freedom. Thus, Marshawn gave Marty all the worldly possessions that he had, little though they were. He left Aaliyah nothing. He abandoned her and his children for Marty; surrendering his very soul for her; all the while knowing full well that he could never have her exclusively. I wondered whether Marshawn's full measure of devotion to her pleased Marty? I think it must have.

'I think, with every thrust of her vagina over Marshawn's erect penis, Marty knew she was grinding another woman down into dissembled pieces of her former self; pushing Aaliyah's spirit deeper *into helplessness. And I believe making Aaliyah's life irrelevant gave Marty as much or more pleasure as her explicit lovemaking. She could be merciless that way. While she bounced her body and thrusted her vagina over Marshawn's penis, she had a certain way of laughing; of moistening her lips; of chortling and giggling, while she rolled her head casually from side to side. She made similar facial gestures and mirthful sounds while making love in the maiden and doggie positions.*

'Watching her extravaganza of joyous lust expressions, I could not help but wonder if they were coming from the sensations of Marshawn's penis gliding over her clitoris, wildly stimulating her; or if it was her smug feelings escaping; knowing that she was being wildly successful in taking Marshawn from Aaliyah? Perhaps her innermost immoral soul was releasing its confidence, knowing that the other woman's medieval cultural norms left her unprepared and unable to compete in the arena of explicit erotica? Marty was incredibly quick-witted and insightful. If I had not known her background, I would have guessed she had an advanced degree in psychology. One exchange occurred while they were on set. It wasn't cut from the scene. Perhaps the director knew it would enhance the ribald flavoring of the film.

'Marshawn blurted out:

"Aaliyah is not at all like you. Making love with her is like making love to a stiff board. She doesn't smile and laugh during sex like you do; and she doesn't orgasm and giggle and scream out 'yesses' and cries for me to fuck her harder, like you do; and she doesn't suck my cock, like you do; the ways you lick it and touch your teeth over the top of it. I love it when you do those things. And she doesn't like me doing her doggie style like you do. You like me going in you that way and getting in deep and moving slowly. She thinks there's something wrong with that. She doesn't squeeze down on my cock with her vagina muscles, like you do. And she doesn't gyrate and thrust

and pitch and yaw her vagina, like it's thrilled to have my cock inside it, like you know how to make your vagina do. And she never French kisses me while we make love, like you do. She thinks that's dirty; but I think it's wild and beautiful and wonderfully, romantically erotic. I just wish I could get her to see things the way you see them."

'Marty intuited that Marshawn had fantasies about changing Aaliyah into a woman more like her. Her response to Marshawn was brilliant:

"You'll never change her into a woman like me, Marshawn. She does not want to be anything like me. She wants to be the opposite of me. If you want a woman like me, you can't let her stop you from having what you want. Don't let her put down your needs. You don't need to let her mind game interfere with the special love we have. You can have a woman like me, and you should have. It's simple. Just leave her. Come stay with me. I already am a woman like me. And I'm here for you. Tell Aaliyah you are leaving her, tonight. Come stay with me. I want us to make love all night, until morning. You don't need to live with a board. You're my sweet love, Baby. I need you. I need you to make love with me, all the ways you like to make love. Come stay with me."

'Marshawn paused. He knew Marty lived with Bob:

"But doesn't your steady man live with you?"

'Marty had her response ready:

"Mostly, yes. But he has his own place. I'll tell him he needs to stay at his place while I'm entertaining a special friend. He'll understand. He knows I'm an immoral whore. And he loves me and respects me for that; for being truthful about myself. He accepts that, because of my work as a porn star, I naturally develop other love interests. He tells me that aspect of my work fascinates him; that he's totally okay with it; and that he adores me for it. We even laugh about it. We say it helps me keep my skill sets performing at my optimum level in my porn films. In my bedroom and in his bedroom at his place he has

mounted twenty glossy eight-by-eleven photos of me having explicit sex while making porn. I'm having my vagina licked by different male partners in about ten of them. In the others I'm fucking and sucking penises, and their semen is flowing onto my face and titties, or out of my vagina. He loves those photos."

"He does? Isn't he upset about you having so many lovers?"

"No, he isn't. Not at all. He used to be hot for this Indian girl. She didn't let him have sex with her. She was one of those who wanted to save herself for her wedding night. I taught him there's a whole different way of thinking about love. I made love with him. I showed him that a woman can have many lovers and how that contributes to making her love making even more wonderful. He came around to understanding love the same way I do. Now, he wouldn't have a woman who has inhibitions about love making. I took him away from that prude. He loves me now. He's crazy about me. Seeing me fucking other guys makes him wildly passionate about me. He totally loves me. And he adores my photos. Now, he loves me more than he could ever love her, because he knows I'm an uninhibited whore.

"Remember our orgy film? He has a still captioned photo of our scene near the end of that film. Remember? It's the moment when I broke out in my giggles. I was lying on my back, smiling. Two of your friends were ejaculating their huge black penises over my smiling porcelain white face. Semen was on my lips, cheeks, and forehead. Two of your other friends were ejaculating their beautiful black penises onto my lily-white tummy while they were rolling my nipples in their fingers. Semen from their gorgeous penises was dribbling onto my tummy and rolling down my sides. Remember? Your tongue had given me those fantastic orgasms. I had gushed so beautifully into your mouth. And then, you, my love, had just finished ejaculating inside my vagina. I held my hand against your heart. It was beating so wildly fast! You were excited! Surely you remember, don't you? Your penis's semen was gushing from my vagina. Your fantastically wonderful, glorious, victorious enormous black penis was there, only an inch from my white semen pool.

"In that moment, Marshawn, your adorable black penis became my god. That photo captured my ultimate happiness, Marshawn. It's me. It's nirvana! It's me accepting dominance by you and your black porn partners. I was loving it. All my inhibitions were shattered and gone. I was feeling, and my body was speaking, the desires of millions of white women. My acceptance of your dominance shows in the joy in my face. I'm an unapologetic, uninhibited nympho. Yes, I proudly am. I love the feelings I experience while I'm making love. That's why I love lovemaking so much."

"The photos continuously remind Bob of that. They turn him on and keep him hot for me. He's always eager to make love with me. I appreciate that. I truly do love him. He understands my sex drive and he's fine with it. He knows I need to have other love affairs, especially with black men. It's a natural, essential nymphomania need I have. I must express it. I can't help myself. I must have other men. I can't resist my urges and I don't want to resist them. When I express them, I become beautiful, inside myself. I feel love. I must be progressive, Marshawn. I can't allow outdated notions about morality to stop me. I've advanced beyond that. I must make love with you, Marshawn; not because you are black and I am white, but because I cannot see that we are of two different races. I only see us as part of one human race. I must confirm that our love is stronger than thoughts about race. I love you and I must express my love. I need you to become my lover, Marshawn. I must make love with you. I must. That's who I am and I don't want to change.

"Bob understands this about me. He accepts me as I am. He always respects my needs, especially when I develop a new love interest. Do you remember the film we made when I tried on six different bikinis for you?"

"Yes, I remember."

"And do you remember how you felt when I asked you about each one; how I asked you if different ones showed off my breasts, and made men want to hold me and feel me? And how others showed off my curves and made men want to grab my ass; and how others accented my mons pubis and made men want to tear off my bottom and fuck me?"

"Yes, Marty, I remember."

"Well, did thinking about me with other men while they explored my bikinis turn you off or did that turn you on? Tell me. Be honest."

"On. It turned me on. It made me want to feel you and fuck you myself."

"Okay, well there's your answer, Marshawn. You see, when I get it on with other men, that stimulates your limbic zone. It makes you desire me more. You lose all thoughts of possessing me, don't you? You only want to hold me in your arms and kiss me, and fondle me, and fuck me, isn't that true?"

"Yes Marty. Oh my God, yes. I get so turned on and so hard when you talk and act that way, I can't restrain myself. I have to have you. You know that, don't you? I mean, you know what you do to a man when you tease him like that, don't you?"

"Yes, Marshawn. I do. It's called tradecraft. Some would call me a tease. I don't care. It's only a tease when I don't want to give my man what I've made him excited about. So, I don't really tease. I'd rather say I'm a 'turn on.' And just like I turned you on when I tried on those different bikinis and teased you about which ones would make other men desire me, I also tease Bob about the wonderful times I've had while fucking other men.

"Bob has told me that he loves that I love doing other men. The thought of me doing that excites him and makes him want me. He loves that promiscuity gene that lives inside of me. I am exactly the kind of woman Bob wants. My shameless promiscuity makes him love me and appreciate me more. He accepts that about me.

He adores that naughtiness about me. You need to understand that Bob would never be happy with a woman like Aaliyah. He'd much rather love a whore and a porn star. And he knows that a woman cannot be both a meek housewife and a successful porn star; so, Bob accepts me as I am. He embraces me and all that I do. He loves me. So, don't worry about Bob. He won't bother us. I promise. He'll be happy for me, knowing that I'm finding love and pleasure by making love with you; honest, he will. He doesn't want a dull stiff board for his woman.

"And neither should you, Marshawn. He wants a woman like me; and, so should you, Marshawn. You should be happy to have a woman who loves to make love and who loves making you happy. Please, don't overthink this. Just come to my place tonight. You'll see. You will have a woman like me. She is me. I am she. That woman you need and want is me. You deserve to have me and you will have me, from tonight on. My vagina will be waiting for you. She loves pleasing you. She needs you to be inside her. We will make love all night long. We will have a night you'll always remember; I promise."

'Hearing Marty's confident banter brought my thoughts to my wonderful Bob. When Marty was sleeping with another man and Bob was alone in his bedroom with her photos, what thoughts, what inspirations held him in her powers? Did he believe the photos were proof that she was a modern-day muse; Erato perhaps? Did her widespread legs and butterfly reveals prove to Bob that, if he would only continue to honor her and forsake all others, me included, that she would also bestow her divine favors on him? How many of her films did he see? All of them? How many of her live, on-stage porn shows did he attend? Did he participate on stage? I suppose I'll never know the answers to my questions. I can only allow my imagination to guide me, knowing that Marty was proudly and unashamedly immoral.

'I still can not fathom how my manly Bob was able to cope with Marty's conduct. Did he feel he was in some sort of love slave bondage to her? I cannot imagine the two of them at a social event where Marty meets another desirable male. Did she ask Bob to wait patiently at the bar while taking her latest fascination to a hotel room and fucking him? When she decided to do an all-nighter with one or more of her Premium Members, did she call Bob and tell him not to wait up for her? Or did she tell him to go home because she chose to have another dude in her bed that night? How did the two of them handle the evenings when she stayed late at David's to murder someone and have her threesome with her assistants afterwards?

'Dear Lord, Bob, didn't you ever suspect anything? Didn't you ever say anything? Did you wait outside her bedroom while she did another man? Were you okay with that? I understand that you accepted her nymphomania. I get it that she could not keep her panties on. I know she was male eye candy. I know she was seductive; hard to resist; impossible to say no to.

'But Bob, what about your pride? You were such a strong man, unafraid of anything or anyone; yet you allowed Marty to treat you like you were her Sampson and she was your Delila. She was your weakness, wasn't she, Horse? Anyway, Big Horse, I have always loved you and I love your spirit and my thoughts of you. Know my thoughts, Horse. I have never thought of you as damaged goods. No, honestly, I have not. I have always believed that the Great Spirit willed you to have your year with Marty. I accepted that and I believe it has made both of us better and stronger people.

'I ask myself, what, in my Big Horse's mind and thought processes, made Marty's immoral cavorting acceptable; even desirable? Did he feel himself special, among those few spiritually worthy and chosen by her to receive her sexual favors? There had to be something other-worldly going on in my Bob's mind during that year. Some transformative experience directed Bob to place profligate porn star Marty upon his mental pedestal where he felt free to worship her as his goddess. She had that similar effect on many men. I have grappled with it, tried explaining it to myself, but my most burning question remains unanswered: What is it about an immoral whore that seduces a man's mind and compels him to love her more than he would a chaste woman?

'He doesn't object to her promiscuity. Instead, he adores it; seeks it out and embraces her for it. He does this not to rescue a fallen woman, but to fall down with her; embrace her for her immoral revelries; and love her. Does he think he will become her protector? Her change agent, perhaps? Or does he feel that, by embracing her behaviors, he will become more acceptable to her as a partner-lover himself? I simply have no explanation for it. I know that I will, perhaps, never understand men's minds.

'I watched a proud, religious man, Marshawn, bite hard upon Marty's lure. Like a frenzied bass attacking the fisherman's hooked plugs, Marshawn had to know he was doomed to fall into Marty's net. He had to know she would consume his life; yet he continued his wild death rush to possess her, if only for the brief time his imagination could believe he had her for his own. He never had a chance of possessing her. Yet, once he could see he was sliding into her net, he gave no further resistance. He knew she had him. He wanted to be in her net. And he allowed her to eat his soul. It must be the Spirit's way with men. I always believed that religion strengthened a man. Now I am not so sure. Perhaps religion weakens a man, makes him ripe for the lure of a prostitute or porn star? Perhaps the man who embraces prostitution and pornography becomes the stronger man? My convictions are shaken.

'After he performed in that film with her, Marshawn accepted Marty's offer of continuing intimacy. He left Aaliyah that night, choosing Marty's butterfly love over monogamous marriage. He *stayed with Marty for an entire month before he got his own place and Bob returned to live with Marty. I think Marty knew that, once she had Marshawn's limbic brain sexually engaged with her, that rigid, frightened Aaliyah would have no chance whatsoever to regain his affections. Marty was calculating that way; she was an exemplary sexual predator.*

'Towards the end of Marshawn's life reordering film, he ejaculated into Marty's mouth. She smiled her cherubic, joyful, schoolgirl smile and laughed and giggled and teased him while continuing to suck his penis, long after it ejaculated. I wondered; did she know then that she would be victorious in her conquest? I think, surely, she did. She always had supreme confidence in herself and her seductive powers. It was an unforgettably spellbinding scene. I felt the love flowing between her and Marshawn. Did she intuit during that profoundly intimate moment that Marshawn would soon thereafter call her and confess his love for her? I'm sure she did. She is, after all, the consummately confident vixen sexpot; and poor Aaliyah is sexually crippled.

'I felt happiness for Marty and her all-conquering libido. Something within me wanted to see her succeed in destroying Marshawn's marriage, because I understood how badly she needed to do that. I found myself wishing I could embrace her and hug her tightly to me. I wanted to tell her that I wanted to see her succeed spectacularly in converting Marshawn into one of her lovers. I suppose that's when I began seeing her as a liberator. I began wishing her success with her love interests. That's the effect of her breathtaking pornography. It transferred her feelings and desires to me. I couldn't help myself. I became one of her fans. Yes, I am certain she anticipated Marshawn's call. And when it came, I am equally certain that she gave Marshawn an evening of the most fantastic, most memorable love making the man ever knew. I think Marty knew exactly what she was doing from the moment Marshawn walked onto that set with her.

'What was it about Marty that made men go crazy over her? Of course, she was exceptionally beautiful; perhaps the most beautiful of all the porn stars, and much more beautiful than many actresses or winners of beauty pageants. But there are many porn stars who are exceptionally beautiful, so I do not believe beauty alone was the main reason for Marty's fame. Nor do I believe that her fame can be attributed solely to the many films she made or to the many explicit and depraved scenes she causally performed. I suppose her fame is the result of a combination of her beauty and her enthusiasm for explicit debauchery, especially her orgy scenes. But that still doesn't hit the proverbial nail on the head. Other beautiful porn stars also perform debauched explicit sex scenes. So, what accounted for Marty's huge separation from the pack? Her film downloads, memberships to her Premium Members' Service, advertising buys where prostitution services pay to link their offerings to her porn films, her income from her product indorsements, and her overall income dwarf the performance metrics of all other porn stars; even exceeding the next five below her in porn rankings, combined! She was a phenomenon.

'But why was she so adored? I wondered until I found the only answer that sits well with me. Marty was famous because she stood for something. She was openly anti- morality; against religion; against marriage; against male controlled institutions of all stripes. The scrappy young girl who defied the mighty authoritarian bully, Mrs. Raybenald, grew up and fluttered her wings. Marty became symbolic of everything structured and moral. She became the anti-God of our time. The only idea she ever bought into was herself. If Christ had come to Earth a second time and met Marty, she would not have bowed down before him. She would have seduced him and fucked his brains out, just like she seduced hundreds of other men in her porn films. There was no duality or equivocation about Marty, whatsoever. She was iconic; polarizing. You were either for her and with her or you were against her. She left no room for middle ground or nuanced interpretations of what she stood for. She stood for adultery and sin. Where others saw immorality, Marty saw moral freedom. Many more are persuaded by her message every single day. Even after her death, her sales continue rising. Like followers of the departed Christ, Marty's legion of followers continues growing.

'I cannot think of porn star Marty in pejorative terms. No, I can't. I have to believe that God created her and placed her, and others like her, among us for a reason. I have to ask myself: Why do so many men, and many women, flock to her? Is it that they love her? I think, in a large part, that they do love her. But is there more than love going on in their feelings? Perhaps they are rejecting something; God, perhaps. Yes, that must explain the phenomena of pornography. People are rejecting. Rejecting God; rejecting their life's condition; their marriages; their families; their employer; their social circle and friends; their life's decisions. So, when they walk away from their beliefs and their lives as they know them and live them, where can they turn? What structure is there that supports their decision? What refuge is there that understands their need? It is not a different church; a new preacher or bible thumper. It's not that these people want to hear the same messaging pounded into their skulls more forcefully than before. No, it's not.

'They seek acceptance and understanding. They seek to go where they feel loved, despite their moral weaknesses; despite their failings. They seek to be loved for who they are: weak mortal beings of flesh and blood. They seek Marty. They are accepted when they are with her; even if it's only vicariously. They feel warmed by seeing her touching and being touched; kissing and being kissed; and making love. Her vagina becomes their new holy place. It welcomes them. It accepts them. It feels no guilt and demands no rules of conduct. It just loves and understands that they need love. She becomes their new God; and, in their minds at least, their new God loves them back.

'Marty is a natural phenomenon, a product of our societal decay. She is a natural force of nature, a woman who needed, for her own reasons, to conquer and destroy the relationships that other women had with their male interests. Like a fungus in a fruit basket, she invaded all male minds that her suggestive seduction spores touched. She invaded my Bob's mind like a fungus finds a way to probe and enter a ripe fruit. Perhaps she intuited a weak moment when she first offered Bob her intimacy. Her fateful spore must have intuited a moral weakness; perhaps his hunger from his abstinence; and, through it, invaded his receptive mind.

'Perhaps I should have ignored the counsel of my father, Chief? Perhaps I should have given my body to Bob when he first wanted me? Then, might Bob's will have been hardened to resist Marty? I like to think so. But perhaps it is far better that things happened the way they did; a blessing that he whored with her. Marty, despite what anyone may have thought of her, opened my eyes to human needs. I learned to appreciate the need to be more sexually aggressive with my man. Uninhibited aggressiveness became natural for me. And Bob loved it. And our love was sweet and bore us children. For that I am grateful.

'But now I am without my wonderful Big Horse. His body died a month ago. I am alone these many nights with my thoughts. I wonder, my sweet Big Horse, where has your spirit gone? Has it found Marty's spirit? Does your spirit hold hers in your lap? Do you wrap her in your big strong arms while she kisses you and places her hand on your penis? Do you and she enjoy oral sex as you did in life; and do you bed her with your erection securely inside her each night? Are things the same for you and she as they were in life?

'My doctors tell me I may live another fifteen to twenty years, Big Horse. Am I once again placed in the position where I must wait to be with you, as I was in life? Can you understand why I cry myself to sleep at night? Does your spirit know how badly I long to be with you? I am driven to continue the work we have started, Big Horse. Please understand that I must do all I can to help our people while I still have a breath of life inside me. But know that I also long for my spirit life to come. Know that I want my spirit life to be shared with yours. Will you come for me when it is my time, Big Horse? Perhaps you would rather be with Marty's spirit? I have asked the Great Spirit for a sign of what is to come but I am given no answer. Perhaps your spirit will be with both Marty's spirit and my own? I do not know the ways of the spirits; but whatever comes, I will accept, as I have in life. Only know that I love you, Big Horse. I will always profoundly love you; and my spirit will always love your spirit. I will it to be so. I must leave these thoughts now, Big Horse, and return my thoughts to understanding others and the work I must do. Goodbye, my sweet Big Horse, until tomorrow night.

'I see rot everywhere. Society is now enveloped in decay; drowning in corruption; awash in spores of adulteries. These omnipresent immoral spores have pithed and rotted the People. They have sapped away the strength of our families. Yet, touched by the breath of an evening's mold, our mold blushed fruit is often our sweetest, most delicious tasting fruit. One acquires an addiction to its full, fermented, tarty tastes, much as we have come to savor the antics of our deliciously delectable porn stars. We, men, and women alike, yearn to allow our minds to imbibe their sapor and cavort with them. We shun or suspend family life while we adore them and idolize their anti-religious messaging.

'We adore them and imagine ourselves as them or as their partners. They are the modern-day prophets of our new progressive order. Marty's new morality and Mrs. O'Dell's Modern Morality Standard have arrived. We see it unfolding before our eyes. We willfully follow the new immoral standards of our porn stars as they lead us further into anarchy and disorder. And, yes, we love them and cling more tightly to their immorality with every passing day.

'Porn stars are not ephemeral creatures. They are not about to fade from our presence. No. They are personifications of the modern progressive us; here to stay; their influence only to increase. They are onto something; boldly leading us away from our religious heritages; uprooting those old diktats; holding them up to challenge by their messaging and their reality logic. The porn star offers humankind clarity of moral choice.

'What is morality? They ask us. Can we honestly answer? Is it confining a woman to an ignorance-based male ordered world? Is marriage itself moral or is it merely an institutionalized form of enslavement? Are we mindlessly praying to idols of female enslavement? I think. I wonder. Is it logical that a male, whose emotions live and die on the successes of his favorite sports teams, should be the best choice to lead a family or make sound decisions about anything? Really? Why? The porn stars are leading us into an entirely different vision of our future order.

'We should ask ourselves: Why does the whore endure, while civilizations and institutions rise; then wane and pass away? The whore has been part of us since prehistoric time, when we worshipped her fornications and sacrificed our children to her glory. She is here with us now, in the form of the dazzling, libido lifting porn star; and we again have chosen to worship her.

'We again sacrifice our children to her. Now it is the not yet born children, given up and devoured by abortion clinics, lost to the overpowering need for the female vagina to experience natural, earthly, human pleasure. Why? We worship the female vagina because it is natural and it is real; as are its needs. It is the Great Spirit's most wondrous gift to mankind. Acceptance of some mystery of faith homily is not required to love it or to surrender our souls to it. We worship the female vagina because we know it offers the blessings of human life and assures us the survival of our species. It represents the mystery of life. Pornography is not a religious cult of *death worshipers. Pornography is the cult of life worshippers. People are flocking to pornography because it represents their love of life and their abhorrence of death.*

'Perhaps whoredom stays with us because it allows us to look into the mirror and see our yearning souls. We see our most fervent desires in the female vagina. It permits us to enter its holy tabernacle, express our desires and be human; and meet our most sacred human need; the need to copulate; make love. It is the opposite of unnaturally repressing that human need, as dictated by an imaginary persona with a long white beard who sits upon a chair up above us in the sky somewhere, presuming to judge us. In this way whoredom is the truth. It is honest, reliable; a free of fairy tales' institution. It predates religion.

'Perhaps Bob understood these truths, or at least felt them, when he framed Marty's most explicit porn scenes and mounted them on his bedroom walls. Seeing her cradled in the arms of another man; kissing him; her legs widespread, revealing her eagerly thrusting butterfly with her lovers' fingers pleasuring her, must have reinforced Bob's love for her. Must have affirmed that his Marty was a living goddess; must have affirmed that he need look no further to discover his sanctuary; must have assured him that she would not deny him his most fundamental human need; to experience real human, tangible love; must have placed her on his mental pedestal as his idol to be worshiped and loved; must have made him willing to sacrifice me and our love to her passion quest.

'I can now think back on the experiences I have had. The manipulations, the turmoil, the insanity and greed-possessed antics of Marty and her true parents, Marvin, and Susan; the Firm, with its evil, dark secrets; a corporate organism for greed, murder, lust; an ex-officio insane asylum for David and Marty. I wonder, sometimes, whether they really were the children of Satan? Perhaps they were? They dutifully served Satan's goals. They disrupted and destroyed

the lives of others. Why? I don't know. Perhaps the Devil had a hand in all of it? Their motives were power and money, mainly for themselves; although Marvin was generous to charity. He was somewhat different that way, until I consider his intensely loving feelings for Susan. Perhaps Susan was Marvin's favorite charity; one that gave generously in return? I still have questions. I am still learning the white man's ways.

'But I try to know myself. My motive is my family and my people. I try to be a humble and truthful woman. I know I will always love and honor my husband, Bob, and my memories of him. After we married, I healed Bob of his obsession with Marty. Of course, I gave him all the sex and erotic love making that he desired. But I also showed him the beauty of a greater love. He learned the love of nature and the spirit souls of the animals. He learned the love of the People and their ways of grace and humility. And he learned to love the horse and the buffalo and their wonderful relationship with mankind. He learned the respect of the needs and feelings of others. And Bob became an even more wonderful man that he was when I first saw him. He became my man, my wonderful Big Horse.

'Remarkably, despite all the machinations of David, Marty, Susan, Marvin, and many ethically compromised employees, I was the one who ended up with all the money, the companies, all the properties, and all the jewels. Go figure! Such irony! Perhaps goodness and grace do prevail over evil in the end, after all? I hope so. I only know that I have been blessed with the love of my husband and our beautiful children. Money or no money, love is the true tie that binds.

'I love watching Marty's films now. She fascinates me like no other person ever has. I learned so much by accepting her into my mind as a beautiful, loving woman. She had a special way about her immoral shamelessness that personified a woman's pleasure while love making. She was unhurried, undeterred, and unconcerned *about the immorality of her pleasure takings. She flaunted her licentiousness; unwilling to retreat one iota from her right to openly enjoy her pleasures; as if announcing to all mortals who watched her that it is a woman's normal, deserved, expected human right to live for her experiences of receiving explicit erotic pleasures; and for no other purpose than pleasure itself, if she so chooses. Marty let no one dare to criticize her for exercising that profoundly human right or for the way she resisted the placement of the marriage yoke upon her life.*

'I know, while I watch Marty's exquisite fornications, that I am watching uninhibited freedom expressing itself, expressed before me as a goddess, creating her masterful living human art; showing me humanity's inhibition-free path forward. When Marshawn finally came into Marty's mouth, I never saw a more joyful expression on any woman's face than hers, while her eager tongue was receiving Marshawn's ejaculation. She then burbled his semen, laughing gleefully while stroking his penis and while his semen continued flowing. Then she swallowed his semen and continued sucking his penis, alternatively licking her lips between her sucking. Clearly, she knew she had made an exceptional, romantically erotic porn film; and just as clearly, she knew she had her man.

'Aaliyah had no chance in the face of such a captivating, overwhelmingly explicit onslaught. Marty simply stole Marshawn's love away from her; deliberately and casually, unconcerned about Aaliyah's feelings; as if she was declaring for all to know that her pleasures were more important to her and the world of her fans than another woman's insignificant marriage. Marshawn became hers from that film onward. He made several more films with her, becoming her devoted love slave both on film and off film. I wonder if Aaliyah had the strength to watch any of them?

'Marty and Marshawn made one film that was the highest rated one on one porn film ever made. I hope Aaliyah didn't see it. It would have been unbearably painful for her to watch. Like in many of her

films, Marty wore the color combination of red and black, symbolizing her commitment to anarchy. Were her red spiked heels, black laced stockings, red panties, red bra, and black skirt with a designer red and black top worn intentionally to symbolize Marty's triumph over her rival's religion? I think so.

'Almost every nuanced thing Marty did was intentional. After several different positions, Marty went Missionary; legs widely spread butterfly for the final minutes of the film. Marshawn and she kissed frequently. I could feel their passions. Their love was indelibly real and hot. In that film's final three minutes, Marty announced that she was about to come again and that she wanted Marshawn to come with her, inside her. She told him several times that she wanted him to come together with her, inside of her.

'When they finally came together, it was explosive and beautiful. Marshawn collapsed onto Marty, kissing her in a way that was certain to bind their souls together. She rubbed her hands over his head and cradled his body between her legs, while rubbing his legs with her feet. They did this while emitting groans of pure pleasure for what seemed like an eternity. When Marshawn finally pulled his penis out of Marty's vagina, an enormous volume of his creamy white semen gushed from her honey pot.

'She smiled to him and her cameras while cooing that she loved him. I'm certain that she did love him. As the film fades into blackness there is one final caption. Marty held Marshawn's huge black penis in her hand, close to her smiling, joyous lips as if she's about to suck it again. She faced the penis and held its head only a half inch from her moistened, glossy lips. Then she rolled her tongue several times across her upper lip, revealing her inviting open mouth. She kissed the penis with an intimate, loving kiss and spoke sincerely to it:

"You love being inside me, don't you? You want to come inside me again, don't you? Being inside me is the most wonderful place you've ever been, isn't it?"

'When she said those words to the penis, I watched it respond to her as if it had a mind of its own. Even though it had just ejaculated inside her, it visibly strengthened; becoming harder, resuming its erection. It seemed to understand that, by fornicating with Marty and ejaculating inside her it was releasing itself from guilt and inhibition. It knew it belonged safely inside her, where it could live in freedom. Clearly it was eager to abandon Aaliyah, reenter Marty and make love again.

'It was an amazing, telling moment. I appreciated that Marty had unique empathy with the male penis. She related to it as if it was her truest, most honest romantic love; and the penis responded as if it knew that was the truth; and that it had an honor-bound, chivalrous duty to truly love Marty in return, even to the point of its physical exhaustion; possibly causing a heart attack or stroke.

'I knew I was seeing a penis honorably pledge that it would, even upon risk of mortal death, perform at its utmost sexually pleasing best to satisfy a woman's sexual desires. My mind wondered: had the biblical homily of Aron's sons deaths, unexplained outside the holy of holies, originated as a parallel to the reality of death from fornication pleasures that some ancient Hebrews experienced? It makes plausible sense if Moses and Aaron were trying to sell their religion to a tribe of skeptics.

'I recognized another unmistakable message in Marty's pointed questions to Marshawn's cock. Marty was letting the entire male world know that if a man sought the most exceptional, finest romantic intimacy for his penis, he needed to call her. She had to intuitively know that Marshawn's penis would harden again before she even asked her questions. The fact that it hardened so impressively confirmed to the entire world that Marty possessed, beyond any man's doubt, the world's most desirable and recognizable fornication loving vagina; that she was the most uninhibited, shamelessly wonderful woman that any man could ever make love with; and that she was deservedly ranked as the world's most fabulous porn star.

'In her final remaining seconds of that film, she smiled her childlike, innocent, devilish, coquettish smile to the camera; then puckered her lips and mouthed a sensuous kiss to her fans. Her signaling was abundantly clear. Marshawn's penis was no longer Aaliyah's. It was now hers; hers to fondle, suck, and copulate with, whenever she pleased to do so. And Marshawn's mind and soul were also no longer Aaliyah's; but now Marty's. He had capitulated his body and soul to Marty; surrendered his life and future to her desires for erotic love making. He became Marty's devoted and willing victim, absorbed in her debaucheries and loving every moment of it. I am certain that, if Aaliyah saw those final scenes, she likely felt like slitting her wrists; or leaving Marshawn to move to another city.

'It was in a later tabloid publicity piece where I read how Marty chortled about taking Marshawn away from Aaliyah. She described her seduction and capture as a controlled, seamless process. It started with their films; then moved to their off-set dalliances; then progressed to where Marty would brazenly call Marshawn at his home. With Aaliyah listening on the extension line, Marty often urged Marshawn to come to her place right away, telling him that she needed to feel his penis inside her.

'She would tell him that she had to make love; right then, that night; that she could not bear herself to wait another minute to have him in her arms. She often elaborated, whispering to him how badly she needed to feel his tongue inside her vagina, lavishing its loving strokes over her clitoris; and how much she adored his penis; and how she was having this overwhelming urge to suck his penis; and that her mind could know no peace until she had her hands stroking it and her lips placed upon it.

'Brazen and relentless, Marty wanted Marshawn all to herself, and she took him. Aaliyah was powerless to stop Marty's determined assault on her marriage. To Aaliyah, marriage and children were her entire life. I can't imagine how any woman could bear up as a worthwhile human being after witnessing the liberties that Marty took with her husband. Clearly, Marty's seduction succeeded. Marshawn fell hard for Marty. He loved Marty with a love that was, for him, intensely real. Marty became his world. He sacrificed every possession he owned to give Marty his full honest expression of love for her.

'But from Marty's perspective, Marshawn was only another lover; a toy, actually; someone to indulge her pleasures until she found another, newer love interest, like Dominick. Marty regarded marriages as merely meaningless, senseless idiocies. She destroyed other women's marriages as casually and thoughtlessly as if she were eating potato chips.

'Marty's lovemaking was visually breathtaking, inspiring, always passion charged; beautifully explicitly erotic, beyond what words can express. Her pornography was mind altering and inhibition freeing; expressively, memorably so. It was attitude changing and morality changing. It returned us to nature; to the same understandings and appreciations held sacred by our ancient ancestors. It destroyed nonsensical myths and illusionary fantasies. It lifted libidos. It was spectacular, riveting and adoring. I finally understand her. I cannot fault her for having different moral views. I am at peace with her and her message to the rest of us. I can now embrace her soul and love her. I will always love her.

'I appreciate that, even though Marty has since died, her soul will live on forever. I know that my Bob loved Marty's soul as well as mine. How could he not love her? Love is all encompassing. It's not exclusive that way. I've learned that truth about love. Once one soul loves another, that love attaches and stays with both lovers, forever; regardless of what the future holds for them. Love is inclusive that way. It stays; resonates within the soul; endures forever; accepts;

understands; forgives; cherishes how special their love was and will always be. My new understanding tells me that love, that intimate and ultimate human connection, however arrived at, is precious. I must always respect it. It is such a powerful, indestructibly special, perhaps uniquely human bond.

'And, yes, a man can fall into genuine, honest love with a profligate, immoral porn star; and she can become his true heartfelt love. That happened with Marshawn and with Bob; and no doubt there have been many others who loved Marty in such an intensely personal way. Now, whenever I observe a butterfly visiting flower after flower, I see the free spirit of Marty Mallory; I see love fluttering in the air.

'I know that the butterfly is the messenger of truths. It tells me that it is normal and permissible to be honest with myself; that when I see a man I desire, it's all right to admit to myself that I want to make love with him; that I want to fuck my brains out with him; that I want to fuck him with such an intense physicality that he nearly has a heart attack or stroke; and that, like I wanted my Big Horse, I want no other woman to have him; that I want to completely possess his mind and soul; and that I want to fall asleep with him holding me, with his erection deeply inside me; and I want to awaken often during the night so we can make sweet, tender love again.

'Like the Monarch has a four-stage cycle of life, so has womanhood. We have come from being deified in Pagan times as goddesses of fertility. Promiscuity was our natural right then and we were glorified for it. Then we used herbal concoctions to avoid conception. When our efforts failed, we gave birth. Our unwanted children were sacrificed, tossed into fires and volcanos to appease our deities.

'Then religion came. For thousands of years, we women were vilified and subjugated to male-ordered decrees. Fornication and adultery were admonished and became labeled as sins. Abortion was our most unforgivable sin. We were ordered to go forth and multiply. We did. We filled the earth with our offspring. We lived our lives as dutiful, prayerful mothers and kept our mouths shut about our adulteries, less we be stoned.

'Then, gradually, through the eighteenth, nineteenth, twentieth and twenty first centuries, thanks to science, we gained a toehold on our reproductive rights and our freedom. We got the pill. We took the pill and the pill took the scales from our eyes. Many of us realized we could have the same sexual freedoms that men had. The male world opened a small concession door to us. Promiscuity was quietly tolerated, but with its secretly understood shadow existence and institutional admonitions forbidding us from becoming naughty women. Abortions became possible, as long as we were not vocal about it.

'The male-ordered religious world was yielding ground, if grudgingly. And now we have come to our present day; our new, fourth phase of our female cycle. It is emerging from its cocoon and it is profoundly magnificent. Marty's life personified it. It is beautiful sexual freedom and it is again being recognized and accepted as our divinely human right. We are emerging as free butterflies! Finally! After our millenniums in darkness, finally! Not only is our promiscuity being grudgingly accepted. Like in our more natural pagan times, promiscuity and whoring are being applauded and glorified; actually, being deified again, as it is in Marty's spectacular, mesmerizing porn films.

'Porn stars are in the process of becoming adored, applauded, and yes, loved. And compensation of top porn stars is beginning to skyrocket, competing now with incomes of professional athletes and corporate executives. Whoring is no longer stigmatized. In circles of the cognoscenti, porn stars are appreciated, venerated, even idolized. A porn star wife or dating partner is a symbol of social status now. In our godless, immoral satanic society, this extolling of debauchery seems righteously, rightfully so.

'I honestly believe that, for every man who seeks to marry a chaste virginal woman, there are now at least a hundred men who would greatly prefer being married to a profligate, thoroughly immoral, porn star; especially one who is a notoriously famous celebrity with more than three hundred porn films and over four hundred explicit erotica scenes to her credit. Yes, I tell myself. I am serious. Americans love to immerse themselves in their debaucheries. Americans adore their whores and they idolize their porn stars.

'I believe we are seeing the birth of a resistance movement. People are questioning religious dogma. When they pay their tithes or put their cash in the collection plates, they are asking themselves: "What am I getting in return?" The religions claim the spiritual high ground; but how does that reconcile with their foundations built upon the bones of their genocides? Twenty million Native Americans and millions of Jews and Moslem Semites were marginalized and exterminated by Isabella; and all of it blessed by Pope Borgia. Hebrews took Canaan in a series of brutal fights that drove out nomadic Bedouin tribes. Islamists are no strangers to religious violence, either.

'Perhaps humanity has had enough of the mayhem? I can only hope and observe. Perhaps there is a new awareness and a new type of religious sovereignty arising? Perhaps people are saying to themselves that, when they give money to a prostitute or porn star, they are getting something of value in return? They are not getting a lecture about their shortcomings; or a sermon about what they must believe; or a guilt trip about what they did wrong; or a thinly veiled shove to vote a certain way.

'They are getting the feeling that they are worthwhile; that someone is listening to their needs and feelings; that they are loved and appreciated; and that they are not guilty of being imperfect persons. They can feel like they are with someone who is like them;

an immoral sinner; and that they are loved and accepted for that; that they need not repent for being sinners; rather, that they are welcomed as they are; and that there is no shame in their sinning.

'Religions are organized. They control the high ground, politically. Control is power. Religions have tax exempt status; porn stars and prostitutes do not. But perhaps this new, individual religious sovereignty, will morph from its nascent incubation stage and coalesce into a movement that results in legitimizing Paganism, practiced as pornography worship services.

'Perhaps there will be big tents and worship temples where porn stars are deified; where pagan prostitution worship practices return? Perhaps natural human proclivities will reassert themselves and claim their share of power in the body politic? Perhaps these Pagan temples will also have tax exempt status, as legitimate religions? I cannot know the answers to my questions. I am old now. I have few years left to see all that I foresee come to fruition. But I know something profound is happening to the human orientation towards pornography.

'On one of our Foundation weeks, I had the pleasure of meeting with about twenty young girls from a major city. They were all fourteen and fifteen years old. After I explained the Foundation and its goals, I asked them what they wanted to be when they graduated. Most of them answered as I expected they would. They were telling me that they wanted to become teachers, nurses, doctors, and scientists. About halfway through the group, one particularly attractive, long legged, red-headed girl stated, matter of factly, that she was going to become a porn star. I was stunned. She was beautiful; but so young!

'I asked her: "What makes you think you'd like to be a porn star?"

"Well, actually, I already am," she answered.

"But, aren't you underaged?" I asked.

"Yeah," she answered. "You're supposed to be eighteen. But my director sent me to this guy named Celt; and he made me a fake driver's license and a fake birth certificate to give to my producer. It wasn't a big deal. I didn't pay for the fake papers, he did."

"I see. But why do you want to be making porn?"

'Without batting an eye, she smiled and answered me. "Because, I love to fuck and suck penises; and I love having my vagina licked and I love having orgasms; and, the money is terrific. I get a thousand dollars for one scene that only takes me about an hour to prepare, an hour to shoot, and twenty minutes to clean up and shower afterwards. I can easily do four scenes in a week. So, I think that's better than going to college and spending money for a degree where I'll make less money."

"But aren't you afraid you'll get a disease; or get pregnant; or have a bad experience with one of your partners?"

"No. My director has everyone tested weekly for diseases. My partners are all clean and healthy. Sex with them is safer than sex with the boys in my high school. And I won't get pregnant. I'm on the pill. And if I screw up, the studio will pay for my abortion. And my partners are all very good-looking men. They know how to fuck a girl so it's a real pleasure for the girl. I've been making porn films for two months now; and I've gotten so that I love fucking now; more than I ever did."

"Do any of the rest of you feel this way?" I asked.

'A very petite young blond girl raised her hand. "I do," she said. I've been making porn films as long as Kay, here. We started the same day."

"And, you like making porn, too?" 'I was stunned that ten percent of these underaged girls were making porn films and thinking nothing consequential would come of it.'

"Yeah, I do. I love it. I love having those men's penises inside me; and having my clitoris licked; and having orgasms. I love sucking men's penises and having them come on me and inside me. My porn partners are all adult men, and they stay hard longer before they come; not than the boys I fuck in my high school. They know how to use their penises to make me come. It's a much better sexual experience It's a beautiful thing and I feel good about doing it; like I'm already a grown woman. It's a lot of fun. We all laugh while we make the films and we have fun making the films. Nobody gets embarrassed or anything. We talk about sex and how we feel and what positions we want to do and what feels better. You know, we just have honest fun while we're having beautiful sex."

'I invited Kay to my office for a discussion about young women's career goals. I offered her an internship at my Foundation. I could tell she had a high emotive intelligence. She did not want to offend me by declining my offer outright. Instead, she told me that she'd like to think about it for a month or so and then get back to me. I then asked her whether her budding porn career prevented her from dating boys. That's when she began confiding in me. She told me that, while she had promised her producer and director that she would limit herself to dating her weekly tested porn partners, her cravings for sex were making her break those promises. She and the blond girl, Trudy, had formed an exclusive sex club at their school. Kay, Trudy, and ten boys were the club's only members.

'This so-called club was an informal liaison of sex partners. Kay and Trudy were going to boys' houses when parents were away. The host boy often invited other boys in the club to come, too. Kay and Trudy were fucking these boys in their bedrooms and their parents' bedrooms; and in their living rooms and kitchens. The girls also fucked their club members in closets of vacant rooms in their school. They sneaked away from their study halls. And by prearranged coded text messages, they spent an hour of more, every school day, fucking boys in their school building. They also fucked their club members in the back seats of cars. The club had a voyeuristic nature to it. Kay wasn't concerned about getting found out by her producer or director because, she said, all the boys had sworn to her and Trudy that they would keep the club and its escapades a secret from everyone. Oddly, Kay never mentioned that she was concerned about her parents finding out about her porn career or her sex club.

'When I asked Kay how she envisioned her porn career future, she became effusive. She revealed that she studied many porn films; that she had downloaded about one hundred of her favorite ones, at a cost to her parents' of about a thousand dollars. She told me that her director was very impressed with her. She told him she had become fascinated with the sizes of black penises and asked whether he could arrange a scene with a black man who had a very large penis.

'He was eager to oblige her. He already gave her the script outline for the scene. He wanted her to perform a scene where she would wear only a string bikini. She would sit by a swimming pool, her legs and painted toenails dangling in the water. Her porn partner, an exceptionally handsome, muscular young black man, would then appear and call to her. She would rise and go to him. He would embrace her from behind and kiss her neck and her ear. He would then pull down her bikini top and fondle her breasts, spending a lengthy time pinching and massaging her nipples while kissing her neck. She would then turn around, drape her arm around his neck and French kiss this complete stranger for several minutes while the camera captured their tongue play; while her other hand searched his pants front, probing for his penis. I thought, hearing this, that the director knew his craft. After all, sexual intercourse occurs in the mind. And the tongue, with its taste for sex, is the closest organ to the brain.

'Her partner would undo her string top and fondle her breasts; then pinch and kiss and suckle her pink nipples for several minutes, while his hands touched all over her body, pausing to squeeze her behind. He would then lift her up and she would wrap her legs around him. He would push her against a wall while they continued French kissing. And while she touched his neck and his arms and his huge, muscular back, with her hands. The two of them would then proceed to a bedroom, where her partner would next sit on the bed. She would unzip his pants; pull down his pants and underpants, revealing his huge penis. She would then hold the penis, and stroke it, for an extended period of time; and, all the while, she would marvel at how impressive it was. She would tell her partner how much she loved to suck and fuck penises; and she would rave about how beautiful his penis was; how it was the most magnificent penis she had ever seen; and how she couldn't wait to begin sucking it.

'But first, her partner would remove her bikini bottom and perform cunnilingus with her. She would lie back upon the bed while his tongue worked its magic; lovingly stroking her clitoris. She would smile a heavenly smile and moan sweet, loving moans, until she had her first orgasm. Then, she would return her mouth to the penis. She would spend considerable time kissing the head of the penis, and licking its head, while stroking it. She would coo to the penis and profess her adoration of its beauty and remarkable size. Then, she would commence licking and sucking it. Her hands would be slathered with lubrication oils while she stroked the penis with both hands as she sucked it. The penis would come very close to ejaculation; but that would come later.

'After the penis was fully aroused and very hard, she would then straddle it and have sex with her partner in at least three different positions, to get the full satisfaction of a thorough sexual pleasuring. She would moan and smile and coo and comment freely and frequently about how much she was loving her intimate experience; and about how much she wanted to do this again, and often. Her director told her that it was impossible to overemphasize the importance of smiling while creating a top porn film; particularly *the importance of smiling and giggling while fornicating. He was a good director. He educated her. He helped her understand that the viewing fan likes to believe that the porn star loves what she's doing; especially that she loves intimacy. So, no matter any discomfort or pain from initial penetration, she needed to smile and find a way to convince herself and her fans that she loved every minute of sexual intercourse. Her director assured her that they would lube the penis and her vagina prior to every penetration scene; and that discomfort would likely be non-existent or negligible.*

'Kay explained further. When her partner indicated that he was ready to ejaculate, she would again change positions with him. She would kneel before his penis, facing the cameras; and nod her head in an assuring, affirming way, smiling while he ejaculated its semen into her mouth. Then, lick her lips, scoop up and semen on her chin or cheeks and place that semen into her mouth; and then open her mouth widely to display her semen reward, which the director told her was her triumph over the penis's resistance to her.

'She should feel glorious in her triumph. She was to smile and wink to the camera. Then she was to burble the semen and smile, while she swallowed it. After her swallowing of semen, she was to turn to the camera and give the lens a coquettish, naughty girl smile, followed by a broad joyful, playful smile; one during which her face was to positively beam with joy. She would then continue, alternately sucking the penis and turning her head and smiling to the cameras, for another minute or two, until just before the filming ended; at which point she was to mouth and blow a kiss to the camera. Then, the director would wrap her film.

'Kay's director assured her that, if her first film with a black partner was well received, he would have her make more of them. He wanted her to do one with two black partners. In that film he wanted her to change positions several times while simultaneously sucking one huge penis while her vagina was being ravaged by the

other. The partners, of course, would both have exceptionally large penises; and they would alternate their positions while having sex with her. At the end of that film, the director wanted to see semen flowing from her vagina as well as having her displaying semen in her mouth.

'Assuming that both her first black on white and her second black on white films were well received, her director intended for her to perform and orgy scene with, probably six black porn partners, all with enormous penises. He explained that she would spend considerable time performing extensive foreplay. She would laugh and giggle and smile; and she would lavish effusive praise upon her partners while they fondled her and touched her everywhere.

'She would French kiss them, one by one, while the camera captured close up scenes of her tongue play and her lips pressing against her partners' lips. They would take turns pinching, kissing, and suckling her nipples. They would massage her mons pubis; and lovingly finger her, stimulating her, while they kissed her mouth, face, neck, and torso; and lovingly squeezed and massaged her ass. The cameras would do close up shots of these intimate moments. She was not to hurry them; but rather, prolong each of them until she experienced the full eroticism of every moment of foreplay.

'She would frequently squeal and proclaim how much she loved the many ways they were touching her, all over her breasts and belly, and ass, and arms and legs. She would tell them she could not believe how excited and thrilled she was; and how eager she was to begin sucking and fucking all six of them. She would change positions many times during this marathon fuck fest. Every partner would experience sex with her in many different positions; and at least three of the partners would perform cunnilingus with her and bring her to repeated orgasms.

'For this film, the director wanted her to experience sexual stimulation in every orifice. Thus, she would need to do a colon cleanse *the day before and a double enema, and a lubrication treatment, during the half hour before filming. At the film's conclusion, the director wanted to show semen on her lips and tongue and in her mouth; and flowing freely from her other orifices. And he wanted her to smile effusively to the cameras the entire time. She told me how important it was, while performing porn, to not only concentrate on her own pleasures; but to also continually remind herself to compliment her partners and tell them and the cameras how much she was loving the experience she was having.*

'As I listened to Kay describing her upcoming performances, I visualized her future. She would soon outgrow her high school sex club. She would go on to creating, easily, three hundred to five hundred porn films with dozens, perhaps hundreds of partners in many different scenes and locations. Undoubtedly, she would travel the world. Undoubtedly, she would love her work. She would eventually develop a clientele and other revenue streams, as Marty had done.

'And, I imagined that she would perform many scenes with her Premium Members as partners. If there were forty hours in a day and if she were able to have intercourse every hour, she would not, even then, be able to fulfill one tenth of the demand for sex with her. She would be chased by paparazzi and autograph seekers and her peccadillos would be the subject of many tabloid articles and gossip columns. She would go far, in part because she was starting her career early, as an underaged teen. As a teen, she would likely make at least two hundred porn films. I knew I was seeing the loss of innocence.

'Marty rose to the stratosphere of porn even though she waited until she was twenty-one before she made her first film. I saw many similarities when I compared Kay and Marty. Kay, like Marty, would undoubtedly become a trophy girl, invited to major social events all over the world. And she would develop serious liaisons *and love interests; and, yes, some man would win her heart, much as Bob won Marty's heart. And she would likely discover true love outside of her sex work.*

'I saw in Kay a face I had seen before, in Marty. Kay was beautiful in every way. Her skin was unblemished, porcelain white; her eyes were a stunning, dazzling blue; she had high cheekbones and perfect teeth. Her face and red hair would drive millions of men crazy into lust over her. But the key to her success would be the same key that Marty possessed: her innocence.

'In Kay, as in Marty, I saw a budding young woman who saw nothing wrong in her immoral conduct. She never gave a thought to the fact that she was sucking all the oxygen out of other girls' chances for dates with boys, especially boys in Kay and Trudy's sex club. She would, undoubtedly, go on to seduce men; many of them married men. She wouldn't hesitate for a moment to destroy a marriage or a family. She would entertain her intended male lovers with her exquisite pornography. They would clamor to become her Premium Members; shower her with gifts, money, and invitations.

'She would master time management; become proficient in juggling her times between lovers and carrying on several affairs at a time; never seeing a contradiction in her divisions of her time among them. I saw in Kay another Marty. Neither woman did porn for money; not really. Oh, the money would come to Kay; no doubt. But the real reason both women did porn was, as Kay blurted out when I first asked her, that they loved to suck and fuck penises. I saw that quality in both Kay and Marty. Both of these gorgeous porn stars absolutely loved to suck and fuck penises; and both made no apologies for their passion; nor did they ever pretend otherwise. Sex was a form of addiction for them; an addiction they only sought to satiate and fuel; never control or contain. I realized that Mrs. O'Dell's prophesy was coming true. More and more, young women were turning to porn, or prostitution, as a way of life; and more and

more, society was accepting this new trend; even turning toward it, loving it, and embracing it.

'I do not know, from that small sample of young girls, how pervasive porn has become in our society. I could not help but wonder; with more and younger girls flooding the marketplace for pornography films and prostitution, would not the prices of their services drop? Perhaps drastically? How should a young girl assess her career potential in porn? Should she think like a professional athlete; try to make as much as possible, as soon as possible; and then retire. And do what? How many endorsements deals and advertising and general film roles can there be?

'A butterfly's life is filled with risks. There are the swifts and finches and swallows; and all manner of insect eating fowl who love to dine on butterflies. There are also the risks of spiders' webs; and sticky tree sap that fastens them to trees; and the treacherous praying mantis; and then there is the unpredictable weather which could prematurely freeze them or send rains and hail to knock them to the ground where all manner of fauna, especially mice and cats, love to make a snack out of them.

'Porn stars, like their butterfly cousins, also face daunting risks. Their profession may bring them into contact with a bad manager; a bad customer; a jealous wife or girlfriend; or someone who becomes insanely obsessed over them. Then, like sticky tree sap is to a butterfly, there are bad pimps, drugs and alcohol for prostitutes and porn stars. So, like their winged cousins, a porn star prostitute must always be alert and wary; always have an escape plan B; and never assume her environment is free of risks. She lives a dangerous life.

'And what does an aging porn star do, anyway? Would she write books about her experiences? Would she go into some sort of community outreach or community service work? I have no idea. I don't know whether Kay and Trudy contemplated the economics of their budding porn careers? I don't know whether they thought through a comparison between a career in porn and an education for a more mainstream career? And, after giving the question some thought, I realized that I don't even know what mainstream society is anymore. It has become unrecognizable to me. I am a creature of years past. I am a dinosaur.

'But this much I do know. Our modern-day porn stars have shredded their confining cocoons. They have shaken free of their Victorian-era moralist restraints, and they have ascended. They are not at all embarrassed or shy about their profession. They are shamelessly uninhibited about their craft, and openly discussing it. In this way they are no different from sports stars or stars of general films.

'But we notice them more. We marvel at them and their films; much like we feel butterfly love whenever we see one of those lovely winged heaven-sent creatures fluttering past us or near us. We cannot help but love them. Many of our porn star butterflies invest their earnings. Some even sit on corporate boards. Some become mainstream personas. And on their life's journeys, they flutter freely over us mere mortals, dispensing their licentious, pornographic wantonness; inspiring us to join their memberships; partake of their spectacular immorality and imbibe in their unbridled shamelessness.

'And we eagerly accept their invitations. We sought them out, timidly, at first; and went to them slowly, at first; but now, suddenly. Millions of us flock to them. And millions upon millions more of us await to partake of their acclaimed, illustrious, magnificent promiscuity. Our children learn of their exalted exploits and performances early in life. Pornography is now taught in some of our schools. Like learning about butterflies, learning about pornography fascinates the young impressionable mind.

'And, predictably, many of our daughters await the day when they, too, can become porn stars; society's humanized butterflies. Our ravishing porn stars are our goddesses now. We love them. We adore them. We cannot get enough of them, or their fluttering copulations; or the films they produce, like so many butterfly eggs. We turn to them for our salvation in an uncertain world that we no longer comprehend. We hang on their words and deeds, seeking wisdom in a troubled world. We salivate while watching their films and we pine for more of what they do; always more.

'They have addicted us to their smiles, their flashing eyes, and their welcoming, insatiable vaginas. Men desire to hold them and kiss them and fuck them in every conceivable position. And men adore them even more, while they are kissed and held and casually fucked by other men in their presence. Their devoted supplicants love nothing more than observing their male partners ejaculating semen into their vaginas; or onto their mons pubis's and breasts; or into their mouths. Their admirers cannot get enough of those scenes. They are our human butterflies; the most dazzling, spellbinding creatures who live amongst us. And, like their insect butterfly cousins are highly vulnerable members of their species, our delightful porn stars are among the most vulnerable people of our human species. And, subconsciously at least, we know that and we appreciate the enchanted, yet highly vulnerable lives they lead.

'And we love them. Butterfly love. Butterfly love explains why their admirers send them gifts and money; and why they subscribe to their services; and why they pay out their savings, their investment portfolios and pensions, their home equity, and their maximum credit limits to have sexual intercourse with their beloved porn stars. All this butterfly love we shower upon them, because deep down inside ourselves, we understand that their butterfly lives are fleeting. Their career peaks are generally short lived. They flash and dazzle us; and then they fade away from our sight somehow. That's why many of us try to capture their beaty and their essence while they are here with us. It's Butterfly Love. We try to unite with them, if only briefly. Copulating with them, for many men, is life's greatest, most treasured, fondest memory, trophy prize.

'These women's immoral, sinful revelries do not offend or discourage their admiring devotees in the slightest. Fans adore their porn stars' immoral debaucheries; praise their adored goddesses for performing them and worship every scintillating erotic scene they perform. Our porn stars are our Goddesses now. They captivate our hearts. They own our prurient desires and our souls. We empathize with their need for sexual stimulation; and applaud their expressive orgasms. We love them more than we love ourselves; and far more than we love our misogynists' rules-based God. Our porn stars, chased by fascinated autograph hunters and paparazzi, now circulate freely, openly in our liberated progressive society which honors and pays deference to their glorious immorality. We worship the female vagina!

'Our femme fatales have brought humankind full cycle circle, almost. There is still much to do to complete us. I appreciate them for what they represent and for what they do. I glorify them for the redeemers that they are. They are boldly liberating all of us, these gutsy modern-day trailblazers; freeing us from religions' morality yokes; freeing us to make our own choices. But what, I wonder, do the porn goddesses worship? It must be the penises they fuck and suck; and the tongues that probe their mouths and vaginas; and lavish loving strokes on their clitorises.

'As for me, I chose to be a mother with a husband and a nurturer of my babies. I see others following Marty's path. And I see still other women who choose to have both paths available to them. Those seek to be mothers and to feel free to indulge their pleasures in affairs; even producing porn films, should those opportunities present themselves. I see nothing wrong with their choices if their children are given love and nurturing. I am not qualified to judge any woman for her choices. I don't believe anyone is.

'What was important, for me was a happy home with a loving husband and wonderful children. I know that those little butterfly *flutterers are the Spirits' way of reminding all of us that it is normal and healthy to seek love; to be loved; and to make love; and always to love. My husband knew true love. He didn't have time or interest in ladies of the night.*

'And now my mind leaves its thoughts of Marty and remembers David. David makes my thoughts explode. I must never forget the enigma that was David. There must be a moral lesson in his complicated persona. Why did he exist? For what purpose did God create such a distorted psychic monster?

'I remember when Chief explained the lesson of the leech. He told me the leech camouflages itself well. It blends its color with the muds on stream bottoms and ponds; appears benign and harmless. But it will weaken you and possibly infect your blood and leave you paralyzed or dead. It's purpose is to cull the careless and make the surviving population stronger, Chief said.

'Then he cautioned me to beware of the human who adopts the persona of the leech. He said they are skilled predators, wolves in sheep's clothing. They often disguise themselves as do-gooders. Some become priests; others scout leaders; others serve communities in political or benevolent capacities of one sort or another. Those cloaks of uprightness are their wrappings. But I must, father said, look beyond the wrappings and note what I see. I cannot let the wrapping blind me.

'Father's lesson of the leech helped me see David. Bob believed David was like a father-figure to him. Bob was blinded by David's disguise. Marty believed David was a true partner and potential lover. She, too, was blinded by his disguise. I thank you, father, for helping me see David for what he really was.

'He wrapped himself in his Judaism. It was a good disguise for him. Anytime anyone reproached David, he would scream that his challenger was an antisemite. His disguise worked against most people. It cloaked his vile, despicable evil; his predatory approach to

life; his assault on all things descent and honorable. It enabled him to freely mock many good, somewhat flawed, and imperfect people, who tried to live respectable lives; and insidiously corrupt and destroy them. I thank you, Father and Great Chief for your insights and wisdom. You taught me to see each human individual as they are; and not to associate their nature with others of their kind, whether they be Flathead, Crow, Cheyenne, Blackfeet, or even the hated Pawnee; for there are more good Pawnee than bad Pawnee.

'You helped me see that David is not a Jew. He is not even an honorable Kasarian, forced into his faith and to live it; but hating it and hating himself. No, David uses the Hebrew faith as his disguise. And he uses his Kasarian blood roots to justify his conduct, at least in his own irrational mind. But in his heart of hearts and in his soul, David is evil; and evildoer who loves his evildoings.

'I figured out that he butchered Marty like she was a common heifer. And that taking of her unfortunate life was David's greatest evil of all. And that is also why I chose not to kill David. Susan was Marty's mother. She deserved to know the truth of what David did to her daughter; and she deserved to have that closure of the kill. She deserved David's kill. It had to be her honor to kill him. I am sad for her great loss; and I am happy for her closure. I hope her kill took away some of the bitter sting that she carried in her heart.

'I sometimes wonder: did Marty's Grandmother Mallory get it right? Did she figure Marvin out? Was Marvin really Satan? Was David then, the Son of Satan? Did the Spirits place him among us as the example of what we must never become? Was David the antithesis of love; or did he also find love, somehow? What might the butterflies be telling me about him?

'David's life was tortured; but much of his torment was self-inflicted. He refused to open his eyes to love. Instead, he willfully nurtured his prejudices and his hatreds. He liked to feel resentment, bitterness, and anger. Why? No one knows. Did he have Satan's

DNA? But Marty was Susan's child too; yet her quest was unlike David's. Marty focused on love and love making. What, then, explains David?

'His childhood hurts were amplified by the love he saw his father vest in Susan. Love, to David, was like a spark that fell on cold ice. The love that his parents tried to kindle inside him never ignited. Instead, it burrowed deeper into the coldness of his hatreds. His heart became embittered. But he embraced that bitterness. He hated himself; and thought of himself as an insect, devoid of any human emotions. He reveled in the destruction of others, and in his own debaucheries.

'Torture and murder were David's way of exerting his power over weaker humans. He became a merciless loan shark; a spiteful, vindictive employer; and a sadist. Watching other humans suffer while he bled them of their monies was David's greatest joy. I shudder when I recall how he destroyed Rublina and her son. Hearing his victims plead for mercy thrilled him beyond measure. Of course, he never showed mercy to anyone. To David, a tortured human; an arachnid with dismembered legs; a fly without wings; and an ant writhing from its burn wounds were all one and the same; sources of his sadistic pleasures. His feelings meter didn't differentiate between a crippled insect and a damaged human being. Both creatures had null value, other than the sadistic amusement pleasure that their pathetic conditions aroused within him.

'Murder especially fascinated David. Through murder's emotional release, David best expressed his hatred for all other humans. His reconfigured Firm specialized in drug sales, prostitution, and child trafficking. All the Firm's nefarious activities were like a flow chart in David's mind. They all led to sadism, death, and murder. His lieutenant purveyors of drugs and young children were not selected because they were savory people. David knew human nature very well. The human dregs he employed were morally weak men; highly susceptible to larceny.

'David understood that dark side of human nature. Like a leech, he sidled up to these men. But David knew many of them would skim profits from his operation. His arrangement with the drug cartel took care of those who cheated his criminal enterprise. The cartel policed the houses. Cheaters were identified and brought to David's house for execution. After these men sucked the lives and monies out of many in their communities, David, with Marty's help, sucked their lives from them. And David kept all the money.

'Crime and murder were David's psychic way of repaying his parents, Susan, and any others who found love in their lives. The Firm became David's revenge machine. He used it to vent his hatred against humanity. He hated his parents. He especially hated Susan. He hated his half-sister, Marty, to the deepest depths of his soul, although he was masterful at pretending otherwise. She was carefree and loving; easily given to her romantic passions; profligate with her intimacy and the joys of her immorality. Ultimately, consumed by his hatred, jealousy, and tortured sense of revenge, David murdered her.'

'But David did not get away clean. No, he didn't. My patience and tracking skills undid him. He thought Susan would eventually forget her daughter. But I knew Susan too well to believe that. I directed Susan to the clue in Bob's fox picture. Then, like the patient Lakota Sioux game tracker that I am, I watched and waited. Susan seemed at peace after David went missing, I knew what that meant. My tracker eyes told me that Susan had made her kill. No police, no explanations. Just missing person reports, regulatory reports. I helped Susan prepare those. We both knew what we knew and we knew not to speak of it. That made Susan's kill more special. We became like Mother and Daughter.'

After that time of Barbara's reflections, Susan and Barbara smiled at each other a lot. They shared warm, understanding smiles; silent, loving smiles; knowing heartfelt smiles that spoke unspoken words. Perhaps Barbara's understandings still fell short of the inescapable truth of human nature. Marty, daughter of Satan Marvin, had to have elements of Satan within her. As Satan's son, David surely did. But Marty's soul sought the goodness of love, unlike David's soul which sought the evils of manipulation, retribution, and hatred. Perhaps all human souls have elements of good and evil within them. After all, we are all descendants of Adam and Eve. We all have that taste from the apple's knowledge tree within us.

Barbara finally had Bob. Their love at first sight love became their permanent love. And they lived it and bore children. Susan and Marvin had also lived their love. And Marty had lived her many loves. Only David never experienced love; or did he?

When David rendered Marty's body, he searched diligently for that secret weapon that all women possess. He searched her entrails, seeking to find that mysterious horrible thing she possessed; that same terrifying weapon that his mother had; that death weapon that had sent his father, Marvin, running to the bathroom to cleanse his mouth of his mother's dreadful poison.

David's deranged, demented, mind mistakenly confused a woman's capacity to create life with some sort of horrible secret death weapon. And, while hacking Marty's body apart, he finally found it! When he first saw Marty's fetus, David believed that the fetus was the female's dreaded secret death weapon. He thought human life itself was the woman's super-classified, top-secret death ray; mysteriously contained, somehow, in the body of Marty's fetus; and that the dreaded death ray could lash out and suddenly destroy a man. His unformed childhood mind haunted David's feeble thought processes through his adulthood. He never outgrew it. Did he experience the same mental influences that prompted our ancestral men to invent their religious homilies and accompanying tales? Who knows?

After David possessed Marty's fetus, he placed it in a form-aldehyde jar where he could control it and where it couldn't hurt him. He felt safe when he understood he could dominate the fetus. He noted that the fetus had all the features of a living human form; and that it was helpless outside the female womb. Finally, for the first time in his life, David felt empathy for another human being. He obsessed over Marty's helpless, preformed human. He experienced the human instinct to nurture; and he redirected his obsession with hatred to nurturing love. He invested his mentoring inclinations in the humble, helpless, dependent human; his would be protégé; the love child of Bob and Marty. With the fetus safely contained in its jar, David rediscovered the comradery he once had with his good friend, Hirsh. He shared his life experiences with the fetus. He bared his innermost soul to it. Yes, sadly, David became certifiably insane; full woo-woo; la-la land.

Barbara never learned about the murders of Bertie and George. Marty never mentioned a word of their demise and Barbara never saw their bodies. But the insects knew. David fed them both bodies simultaneously. Ingesting so much flesh in such a short period of time made David's roaches, crickets, centipedes, lice, silverfish, and ants wax fat and multiply.

During evenings in his green room with Marty's fetus, David was finally able to share his joys with another human being. Together, David and his fetus protégé watched David's insects cannibalize each other. That same rush of trusting male friendship that David knew while Hirsh bit his moles off his back, finally returned to David. The feeling of safe, loving male friendship was restored to David's incomprehensibly twisted world. With his trusted fetus, watching insects fight to their deaths, David escaped from the terrifying world of females. In this twisted, perverse way, David discovered love.

Barbara's reflection brought her another understanding. Humans are, by nature, fearful creatures. They need the comfort of being part of something bigger than themselves. It's even better if that group, which they join and become part of, is somehow superior to other groups. That's why Cain murdered Able. Cain insisted that he, the hunter-gatherer, was superior to Able, progressive tiller of fields. It's why America dropped atomic bombs on the Japanese. American showed the Soviets that progressive America would be the dominant hegemonic world power with its Dollar as the dominant currency in the world; not the Neanderthal Soviets with their ridiculous Orthodox Christianity and their silly Ruble currency.

It's why every fight, war, and dust-up that has occurred between those two historic events was the product of our horrible, but normal, human behavior; for the human animal is not like the other animals. No, it is not. Not at all. It does not murder to eat. It murders to dominate and subjugate. And it will continue murdering, dominating, and subjugating other humans with ever bigger and deadlier weapons; murdering ever larger numbers of fellow humans; and forever rationalizing its reasons for murdering them. Why? Because it's what the human animal does. That this is our natural nature is the only answerable why. Barbara realized the profoundness of her father's wisdom. Chief had repeatedly asserted to her this inviolate universal truth since she was a young child:

"All animals behave true to their natures. They are, every one of them, and every species of them, as the Great Spirit made them. They cannot help but being what they are. And they cannot ever change what they are. Only the Great Spirit has that power to change us; and the Great Spirit chooses not to."

Susan suffered a slow, agonizing emphysema death, gasping her last breaths for oxygen that her lungs could no longer absorb. When she passed away, she was given a Catholic funeral mass and buried next to her parents at Mount Holy Ghost of Saint Mary's Sacred Blood of the Immaculate Conception Catholic Cemetery in Plaintown. She was later joined there by her younger brothers and sisters.

Mrs. Rodriguez resigned her post as the Firm's chief guard dog when the new generation of owners took over. She took a new position as the assistant warden for prisoner monitoring at the U.S. Federal Penitentiary in Canyon City, Colorado. After her retirement there, she left the United States forever to live out her days with her brothers and sisters. She eventually died in Torreon, Durango State, Mexico.

Bob and Barbara built an investment advisory practice in Plaintown. Barbara bore two children, a boy, and a girl. They named their son Ehud, or Hud, for the Benjaminite of the Book of Judges, who slew the evil King Eglon of Moab. They named their daughter Deborah, for the judge who, with Barak, drove the Canaanites and their evil leader, Sisera, from the land of Israel. Deborah married an Israeli Jew and gave Bob and Barbara six grandchildren. The new bloodlines from Bob and Barbara's grandchildren strengthened the bloodlines of the Tribes of Israel and helped to ensure its strength and survival for the next five thousand years. Bob freed himself from David's emotional bondage and personal betrayal. Barbara's love helped that happen.

Barbara, or Little Sparrow, as she preferred to be called, realized her childhood dream and the dreams of Big Chief, her father. She established the "Following the Path of the Buffalo Foundation" and dedicated it to restoring America. As the foundation raised monies, it acquired land, acre by acre, section by section, farmhouse by farmhouse, town by town, and road by road. The foundation returned the vast American prairie to its natural state and returned the Buffalo, the Elk, the Deer, the Antelope; all manner of birds that spread seeds; and all manner of birds of prey; and the great majestic Sand Hill Cranes; the Wolf; the Black Bears and Grizzly Bears; the Lynx; the Cougar; the Coyote; the Badger; the Prairie Dog; the Wolverine; and all the other native animals to the hills and lands, which had been their rightful home.

Native peoples were permitted to roam free upon the lands with their horses, but no wheeled vehicles of any kind were allowed. White, black, brown, and yellow Americans who wished to live the ways of the true Americans were invited to live upon the lands, along with the native peoples. They were permitted to come and go as they pleased, but they were not allowed to build permanent structures upon the land or own any part of it. The foundation took in castoffs and demented refugees from America's urban blight and its prisons; and with nature's assistance, helped them rediscover their humanity.

Sparrow always believed the Great Spirit and Spirit's natural blessings would heal all manners of mental conflicts created by the white man's ways. Only hunting and fishing with naturally made materials was allowed on foundation lands. No guns or fishing poles, no steel traps or artificial metal lures of any kind were permitted. As the foundation grew. it swallowed up the white man's world from the Canadian prairies to the Rio Grande. The vast Great Plains of fifty thousand years ago returned to its natural rhythm of life.

Big Chief lived to see the beginnings of the Foundation's progress. His wise old eyes saw little Indian girls laughing and running through the prairie grasses. He saw braves riding bareback on horses with their bows and arrows, resuming their traditional buffalo hunts; and he saw squaws tanning hides, gathering wood, making fish hooks, arrowheads, pottery, jewelry, tapestries and weavings, music, babies, and family happiness. The products of the Foundation were highly sought after. Only the honest monies of gold or silver were accepted in exchange for Foundation goods. The tribal council wisely invested in start-up enterprises and all tribal members became interested shareowners. The foundation prospered because the people were able to integrate their ways of life with the land with ways of modernity. Chief saw Sparrow's work and proclaimed it was good. His cried with joy on his final day when he left his people to join the Great Spirit.

Bob and Barbara's son, Hud, became interested in geology while searching for arrowheads as a young boy. Later he went to the Colorado School of Mines and earned his degree in geology. He entered corporate life for the family when he formed a company for mineral exploration. In the course of his prospecting in northern British Columbia, he discovered some highly irregular rocks and staked and filed claims for his discovery. He earned a degree in business administration and learned corporate management at his mother's hand.

Deb married Richard Stone, or Dick, a stockbroker with a wealthy clientele. As fate would have it, conditions at the Firm deteriorated after Bob and Barbara left and after David and Susan died. The Firm was charged by federal prosecutors for violations of the Racketeer Influenced and Corrupt Organization Act (RICO). David's co-conspirators in bribery and extortion were imprisoned. The firm was placed in trusteeship of a federal judge until injured parties were compensated and fines were paid. The only surviving heirs to the firm were David's distant cousins. They were eager to sell the beleaguered asset. Dick, Deb, Hud, Barbara, and Bob put their heads and pocketbooks together and acquired the old

Firm. Because of tax considerations, Hud's exploration company was folded into the complex as a subsidiary company of the new Firm's holding company. Thus, the new Firm held claim to Ehud's irregular rocks claim group.

In an unexpected development, the Firm's new legal counsel received a call from the British Columbia Department of Mineral Surveys asking permission, in cooperation with the United States Department of Defense, to run secret tests upon Hud's strange rocks. Testing revealed the rocks had unique properties related to electromagnetism; and, with the proper molecular combinatorial bindings, the rocks could be invaluable to NATO's defense needs. But, of course, much work needed to be done before this could be confirmed.

Shortly after the call from B.C. Minerals, the Firm's new corporate counsel received another call from a lawyer in New York who said he had an undisclosed client, who wished to make a friendly tender offer for the Firm. After a Seder dinner, the family discussed the matter of the potential takeover offer. It was decided that they would heed the wisdom of Bob and Barbara, their elders. Bob and Barbara recounted the wisdom of Chief in such matters and advised the family to be patient. In all likelihood more information would be forthcoming with the passage of time.

The matter of the takeover offer went silent until ten years after Bob died. Hud, Dick, and Deborah were then informed that the New York client had renewed its interest in the acquisition of the Firm. Hud opined that enough time had passed for the chemical tests and molecular studies to bear out the potential of the rocks. Out of respect for Barbara, who was in failing health, the next generation decided to rule out any discussion of merger or acquisition talks until a year after their mother's death. The spirit of Chief, the wise one, observed the patience of this new generation and opined to the other spirits that it was good.

When Bob died, he was buried next to Nevin, his assumed father, in Milltown. Estella never told Bob about Paul, his true paternal father. Before Estella's death, she made futile inquires to the German government about her true love, Paul, but she received no answers. She assumed he had died in a Soviet concentration camp, and every evening until her death she prayed to God for mercy on his soul. Estella was buried by Nevin's side, opposite Bob. Her headstone bore a Christian cross; Bob's had the Star of David with the inscription *'Here Big Horse rests in eternal peace.'*

Barbara continued her work on her Foundation for fifteen years after Big Horse died. Many who knew her remarked that she worked at a fevered pitch, constantly flitting about the world like a hurried sparrow, raising money, and giving presentations about the foundation's work and the beauty of wilderness and native grasslands. She made Chief's former ranch the Foundation's headquarters. There she regularly invited children from participating schools to come visit for a week on the prairie.

One late summer's afternoon, Barbara was sitting in her rocking chair on the ranch's massive porch. Her legs were covered with a shawl to shelter them from the cool mountain air. Her hair was gray now. Her face showed the wrinkles of age and her tireless dedication to her work; but her eyes still glowed with the fire of a woman determined to make the world a better place for her family and her people.

Off in the distance, children were playing a game of 'Capture the Flag' in the high prairie grass. She watched them running and laughing. While she smiled a happy smile, a soft breeze from the mountains to the west danced across the prairie. She observed the wind toying with the heads of cheat grass. Her gaze turned to the corral near the ranch house which held several wild Mustangs. Barbara adopted wild horses. She loved them and believed they had every right to live. They represented freedom. She was pleased with herself. She had saved this group from slaughter. Some would be tamed and ridden by children, or given away to outfitters whom she trusted to be good to them. Others, she would turn loose to roam and run free over the prairie.

One particular, proudly tall, well-muscled mustang caught her eye. He held her gaze as if his spirit knew hers. He was a very fine, very strong big horse, a chestnut-colored sorrel stallion. His ears turned forward toward her as if telling her he trusted her friendship. Then, he moved closer to her and lifted his head high. The big horse eyed her steadily from the nearest edge of the corral. It seemed as if this strong, proud big horse was inviting her to come mount him and ride him.

Just then a little sparrow wren alighted upon the log porch rail in front of Barbara. It chirped and flicked its tail twice; and then it flew over to the corral. It alighted a second time upon the rail of the corral, beside the big stallion horse. There it chirped a long, melodious warble call. It seemed to Barbara that the little sparrow was calling to her.

Barbara smiled a knowing smile at the little sparrow wren at the same time the tightness in her chest seized hold of her heart. Her last vision was the little sparrow chirping a few final notes as it hopped onto the back haunches of the big horse. She knew then that the little sparrow's spirit belonged with the spirit of the big horse. The sparrow faced Barbara; it knew she understood its call. It chirped again, and then it flew away over the grasslands.

Little Deer, Barbara's granddaughter, was laughing and running through the prairie grasses. She was a natural leader. Many said she was much like Little Sparrow. Her beautiful soft hair lifted on the breeze as the little sparrow flitted over her head and flew towards the afternoon twilight. Barbara smiled at Little Deer. She knew the child would grow up learning both the white man's ways and the native ways. She would speak English and Lakota, and Navaho. She would do well in a white man's college; and she would also know her heritage; the wonders of her people; their traditions; their respect for nature and their oneness with it; and she would know all the animals and their ways; and she would know how to love life and how to love a man with her whole heart. The little sparrow disappeared from sight into the twilight. Barbara knew the Great Spirit had given her a sign. Spirit was calling her home. It was her time.

Little Sparrow's body departed from life that day. Her spirit went to join with the spirit of her beloved Big Horse. Over her last eleven years, Sparrow missed him terribly. Many nights she had cried in her loneliness. Nothing could ever replace a love like theirs. She held fast to her wonderful memories with Big Horse until the end. They gave her strength to go on with her work. As she surrendered to death's grasp, she knew her spirit would reunite with his in another place and time. Chief had told her that that was the way of the spirits. She knew his wisdom could never fail her.

A Foundation worker found Barbara sitting in her favorite rocking chair. Her eyes were closed and a there was a faint smile on her face. She had lived the life chosen for her by the Great Spirit and she had lived it well.

Hud and Deb arranged to give their extraordinary mother an extraordinary remembrance. A bronze statue of Little Sparrow standing beside Big Horse was erected on the ranch, now her Foundation's headquarters, where the work Sparrow began continues to this day. A memorial service was held two weeks after Sparrow died. For the service, Hud and Deb arranged to have the entire Plaintown Philharmonic Orchestra flown to Montana to perform on the lawn of the Foundation's headquarters.

The music selected was Symphony Number Nine in E minor, opus ninety-five, *From the New World* by Dvorak. The first movement recalled the forest funeral of the Indian princess, Minnehaha, or *'Laughing Water.'* Deb loved that piece because it so personified Sparrow, her mother; who, like moving water tumbling down a mountain stream, was high-spirited and life-giving. The *'Going Home'* theme of the second movement helped everyone reflect that it was finally Little Sparrow's time to rest. The finale represented the frenzied energy and boundless spirit of Little Sparrow, which her foundation pledged to carry forward.

When they heard the final movement, the animals and birds that lived on the surrounding prairie all stopped whatever they were doing. They raised their heads in honor of Little Sparrow. And all the animals listened with rapt attention. They sensed something special and wonderful had changed their fortunes for the better. And all the animals were happy. More than a thousand people from all over the world attended the service to honor the remarkable life of Little Sparrow.

Barbara's body was flown to Milltown and buried beside Bob's. Her headstone bore a Star of David, like Bob's headstone, and an eagle's feather befitting an Indian Princess, along with an inscription. *'Here, together with her beloved Big Horse, our beloved Little Sparrow reposes with the Great Spirit.'*

RESTING PLACE

The Milltown Cemetery is a quiet peaceful place on a small plateau above Cedar Creek with views to Cedar Mountain and Broad Mountain. The rains somehow fall more softly here than they do on other parts of the surrounding valley; and the raindrops linger longer on the leaves of the occasional maple trees than they do in other places before they drop quietly to the ground. Pleasant breezes gently caress the gravestones in the spring and fall. The winds are never harsh here. Their force is blunted by the sheer face of the bluff as their currents rise from the valley floor below. Birds sing their tweets and warbles here. Honeybees drone about the perennial flowers, which seem brighter and more cheerful here than the flora in the valley below. Rabbits hop about. They mate freely, unconcerned about the world's unimportant happenings. Squirrels scamper about. They gather up their nuts from the assorted pine and acorn trees that populate the grounds. They seem less hurried here than other squirrels from other places, as if they know the Great Spirit will always provide plenty for all.

The spirits of the original German settlers and the Hackatopas Indians, who died together in the bloody horrors of the Great Segan Treffpunkt Massacre, knew that Bob and Barbara had come home and joined them in eternal peace. The bodies of the two true and faithful lovers and their good souls were warmly welcomed by the now peaceful ancients. And all the bones were pleased.

CHAPTER THIRTEEN

It is an honest ghost that let me tell you (Shakespeare: Hamlet)

SPIRITS

It was a still, half-moon night with passing clouds. The barn owl flew up to the Milltown Cemetery from the forest beyond. He perched high above the grounds on the outstretched limb of a maple. It was a good spot to hunt mice and small squirrels. By the ringed mass grave of the settlers and Indians sat two, fifteen-year-old, high school boys. They were sharing a quart of stolen beer when a strange wind came up. It came at the boys from all directions. Some say the cemetery bluffs cause that freakish wind pattern sometimes. They only happen here; never anywhere else.

The boys crouched behind a headstone and peered over it. They heard the eerie sound of people talking. The owl saw something rise up from the ground. He hooted. He saw two, white, misty figures. They walked together; then floated and wavered in the air. There was a naked man, and a naked woman. Their spirits shimmered magically in the light breezes. The woman took the man by his hand and made a whooping sound, like an Indian woman calling her children. The spirits spiraled around each other; then, together, they rose upward into the sky for a bit. They then flew away in beautiful graceful flight, toward the northwest.

The boys were terrified. They ran from the graveyard that night. What they saw shook them to their core. No one believed them when they spoke of what they had seen. The owl lifted off his branch. He followed the spirits for a bit before he wisely returned to his limb; but he knew what only owls of the night could know. The spirit of the Indian woman took the spirit of her man with her to their happy hunting grounds that night. The owl understood that can only happened when two people know true love. He knew those two spirits would live happily together; forever.

A few days later, Buzzy and Wayne, two grave diggers, were sitting with their backs against the cemetery's equipment building. They had spent the entire day digging three graves for a family that had died in an auto accident. Wayne pulled out a bottle of whiskey. Buzzy took his shoes off to air his feet. They faced the setting sun. The warmth of the cement wall heated their backs. It made them feel good to rest against the warm wall. As Wayne took a sip, he observed a Monarch butterfly come up from the creek below. It fluttered toward the northwest section of the cemetery.

"See dat butterfly?" Wayne said.

"Where?" asked Buzzy.

"Dere," Wayne pointed to the northwest section.

"What of it?" Buzzy was rubbing his feet.

"I seed it befur," said Wayne. *"It comes up from the crik late afternoons. I knows it's da same butterfly. It's one of dem Monarch butterflies; but bigger and purtier den da rest of 'em. It comes up with da oder butterflies like its ones of 'em; den it seprates from da oders and it goes to da same place about dis time. Den all oder butterflies is gone for da night, but dat one stays a while. I watched it real close after I seed it come up about four times befur."*

"You're nuts. Dere's lots of butterflies." said Buzzy.

"No, I's ain't nuts, Buzzy! Dere's somepin goin' on about dat butterfly. Watch. It will go to dat one headstone, the one of dat guy dat had the Injun wife. Watch it."

"Oh, yeah, I sees it," remarked Wayne. "You're right. Dere, it sits on dat headstone, like you sez. It's like putting on a show for all to see. How'd you know it'd do dat?"

"It always does dat," declared Buzzy. "Fans its wings open and closed like a whore opens 'er legs. I went there once and it leaves behind a drop of moisture, a tiny drop on that headstone. Then, just as the sun sets, it flutters off west and goes back down to the crik. I think it's got somepin goin' on with that headstone or the body dat's in dat grave, maybe."

"All dem headstones in dat plot is fucked up," opined Wayne. "Mudder and Fadder got crosses; son, and Injun wife got Chew stars. How'd dat happen?"

"Maybe mum went into da hospital an' dey got a Christun baby mixed up wid a Chew baby. Maybe it's da Suckulists." Buzzy guessed.

"Whatcha mean Suc-ul-tits?" asked Wayne.

"Not Suc-ul-tits, Suckulists!" corrected Buzzy. "Pay 'tention 'for I smack you upside da head! Suckulists is dem dat don't give a shit 'bout religion. Dem's da ones dat want all us dumb shits mixed together, like fish in a big fuckin' food blender machine. Ya goes in Christun, ya comes out a Chew. You's a Christun or a Chew, you marries an Injun. You's an Injun and you switch to Chew. You can even goes into da U.S. Senate as Christun and you flips a switch in der, in da Senate, and presto, you's becomes an Injun!"

"No shit! Dey can do dat? In U.S. Senate, dey cans do dat?" asked Wayne.

"I tink so. I heered it on da raddio. Some Lizzy Warren gal gots herself 'lected into U.S. Senate, an' when she gots dere, she flipped a switch an automatically became an Injun!" affirmed Buzzy.

"What? She change her name too? Is she Pocahontas or Sacawag-eesus?" Wayne was confused.

"Nah, dat gal is jest totally fucked up. She insults real Injuns. She's just nuts is all." Buzzy set Wayne straight.

"No shit. Cans we go dere to dis Senate place too an becomes sompin oder dan whats we is?" asked Wayne.

"Maybe. I heerd it on da raddio bout dat switch in da U.S. Senate all dem Senators do. Dey goes in poor and comes out rich. We's could flip dat same switch an becomes rich!" asserted Buzzy.

"Yah, why'd she flip the Injun switch instead of da rich switch? Why da fuck she wanna be an Injun anyway?" Wayne couldn't make sense of behaviors that didn't make sense.

"How da fuck do I know?" shrugged Buzzy. "Maybe she likes to fuck Injuns. Like I told ye, she's fucked up. Some people jest don't know der own minds is all."

"You's drinkin' too much whiskey. Gimme some." said Wayne.

Wayne handed the bottle to Buzzy, who took a swig.

"You think dem butterflies got brains, Wayne?" Buzzy asked.

"Sure, more'n you got, dumb fuck," laughed Wayne. "Hell, you's so dumb your wife bought you dat motion movie pitcher kamer and you put it on da tree wheres you was huntin, and you fell ta sleep dere whiles deers walk by right in front of ya. Dey even hump-fucked and made house right in front of ya an ya dumb shit slept through it all. Then ya dropped a lit c-gar in da woods and torched evra thing up. Lucky ya wasn't jailed. Ain't no butterfly dumb as you, Buzzy."

"Yeah, well, yer kid bought ya a compooter an' all ya use it fer is to sit your ammo reload 'quipment on it. You ain't so smart, neither, Wayne. "What makes ya think dat butterfly's smart?"

"I tink dat one's got a brain and it's got somepin in its head dat it can't lay off and go aways from. Maybe it's had a life frem befur and it's come back to somepin it didn't git right in its oder life. Here, gimme dat whiskey back. I needs a swig." said Wayne.

"You tink so?" Buzzy was agog in wonderment.

"Could be," said Wayne. "Dere's a story about dat guy buried dere, under dat headstone. Before he married the Injun gal, he was *hot and heavy with some high-class hooker, way out west some-wheres. Maybe dat butterfly is her. Gimme back dat whiskey."*

"Why ya tink, it leaves a water drop on da headstone?" wondered Buzzy.

"It ain't water, you asshole, asserted Wayne. "I smeared my finger in it once't. It's sticky, has a spicy sweet smell, like dem gardeenya flowers. It tastes like pussy, too. I tinks it's butterfly pussy juice. I tink dat butterfly is somehow dat hooker's pussy come back to life, an' it still wants to fuck 'im."

"You knows a lot about da bodies in here, don't cha?" asked Buzzy.

"Yep, I doos," boasted Wayne. *"They's all got stories. Dat's why I tinks like I do. Dere's stuff goes on in here dat makes me knows dere's other lifes dan da ones we's got now."*

"Dat so, Wayne?"

"Damn right dat's so, Buzzy. Dat butterfly proves it to ya right now. Know how I'm sure it's 'is long-lost lover?"

"No. How can ya know?" Buzzy wanted proof.

"Dat butterfly does other things dat dem other butterflies don't do. It opens an' spreads its wings real wide like, holds 'em opin fer da longest time, like she's a whore spreadin her legs wide, 'cause she's itchin to fuck. Den when it leaves dat headstone, it always flies away to da west." Wayne sounded like the authority on butterflies.

"I never seed butterflies dat way. Why ya tink it goes west?" Buzzy asked.

"It keeps comin back to 'im 'cause it wants 'im to go wit her. Wants to take 'im back west." answered Wayne.

"Well, how'd ya know he ain't gone with it just now?" asked Buzzy.

"I don't know." said Wayne. *"I just figure he wants to be with da Injun girl. I heered she was out-of-dis-world beautiful, even more beautiful den 'is whore."*

"'Cause they's buried together?" wondered Buzzy.

"Yeah, I tink so," opined Wayne. *"He loved her. He loved the Injun."*

"But da Injun girl got buried next to 'im, years later'n 'im." Buzzy pointed out.

"Well, maybe spirits can love two womens, be in two places at once't," guessed Wayne. *"Maybe his spirit waited for the Injun and finally she came to 'im. But anyways, I knows dat butterfly proves one thing fer sure."*

"What's dat?" asked Buzzy.

"A great pussy never quits! Ha!" Wayne sought to end their speculations.

"Yeah, you're right! Pass me back the whiskey." Demanded Buzzy.

CHAPTER FOURTEEN

Absence from whom we love is worse than death, and frustrate hope severer than despair. (William Cowper: Hope, Like the Short-Lived Ray)

MIDNIGHT

Susan's soul yearned for Marvin after they died. Every Shabbat evening, and every evening during High Holy Days, her soul's spirit wisped across the hemispheres to the Mount of Olives Cemetery in Jerusalem. There it hovered over Marvin's grave and beckoned his soul to arise and fly away with hers.

"Be happy. Know my eternal love. Hold me in your arms and kiss my sweetness," it whispered to its dead spirit companion.

Occasionally, a bird heard the haunting disturbance; and it startled from the sounds of the whispering spirit. But the bird could not see the maker of the sounds. Then the bird would jump up and look around, for the spirit's urgings were answered by the faint voice of a second spirit. It was Marvin's spirit, calling to Susan's to wait for him. It promised it would try again to arise that very night, as it had tried so many nights before.

The faintest, almost indiscernible rattle of a chain alerted the bird again. It was Marvin's chain. Its soul was tangled up in chains to Eloweiss's soul as they lied there waiting to be called away together at the end of days. Marvin's soul tried mightily to follow its yearning heart to Susan's soul. But despite its exertions, it could not untangle itself from its chains; not this night.

"I will have to try again next time," Marvin's soul said to Susan's soul. *"When will you be back for me?"*

"Soon," said Susan's soul to Marvin's soul. *"You must try very hard, Marvin. Untangle yourself and be ready to come away with me."*

"I will. Soon then, Come again, soon," replied Marvin's soul. Then it fell back into its grave to suffer in torment next to Eloweiss.

The bird cocked its head. It heard a moan of exhaustion, an anguished whimpering cry from a soul that was condemned to be forever joined to its betrothed, wedded both in life and forever in death after life, in their paired suffering. When the ghostly Shabbat visitor from the other side of the world flew away, the bird also left.

CHAPTER FIFTEEN

Either a beast or a God (Aristotle: Politics)

The coward wretch whose hand and heart can bear to torture aught below, is ever first to quail and start from slightest pain or equal foe. (Bertrand Russell)

LOBO

Some hunters were in their bunkhouse playing poker this full moon night. The air was cool with Rocky Mountain stillness. Light breezes came from the west, teasing the fall aspens on the mountainsides above the valley floor.

Coyote howls sounded: *"A Whooo; Yip; Yip, Whooo Ahhh Wooooa!"*

"Listen to them coyotes going nuts," remarked Big Jim, looking up from his cards. *"Must be they's hot onto a bitch in heat."*

"They's gonna have fun. Funny ain't it? Coyotes smarter than us. They's having fun and us playing cards?" John, the second hunter, gave out a chuckle. *"We should have brought a woman with us."*

"No women in elk camp. Forget it." Jake, the fourth hunter and camp boss, laid down the law. *"Women fuck up a good hunt. They don't belong."*

Jack, the third hunter, chimed in: *"I don't know about that. What could it hurt?"*

"They distract you. You forget about getting up before sunrise. Your mind ain't on killin elk. It's on pussy. Pussies are distractions.

We ain't going to town for no women. That's not happenin." Jake sounded authoritative. The trucks that brought them to camp were his and he kept the keys on his person. His pronouncement carried his control with it.

"No need to get distracted," spoke up Big Jim. "We could just dash into town and pick up a whore; bring her out here and take turns fucking her. Nobody needs to fall in love with her. What could it hurt?"

"Pussy don't mix with hunting." Jake's voice was lower now, threatening.

"I knew this Navy gunner's mate," said John. "Terrific guy. Killed thousands of Dinks in the Nam war. He had the right perspective on pussy. He said nothing got his mind off of war like pussy; no better way to de stress. Said you need to be realistic about women. They serve an important purpose. Said all women are basically the same. When you stand 'em on their heads, they all look alike 'cause they's all got pussies. You just fuck their pussy or eat it; then you let go of them. Said they liked getting eaten and fucked. He was totally into whores; liked them; felt a place in his heart for them."

"Navy, huh. He ate pussy, too?" sneered Jake.

"He said he did; matter of fact."

"How'd he get past the smells?"

"Oh, that part never bothered him. He said it was like a combination of salty dog and spoiled fish with olive oils. Said it was a matter of getting an acquired taste. He likened it to savoring caviar, only with more of a buttery slipperiness about it. Then, when he got more into it, he said it was like slurping a dirty martini, one with texture, and lots of vermouth and olive salts. He loved eating puss; was totally into it. Said, once he got immersed in it, it was like slurping one of them big Chesapeake blue oysters; pleasant aftertaste. Said it becomes addictive; once you get into doing it, you want more of it. He said he uses his tongue on the woman's clit to connect him and *the woman together. That puts him in sync with her mind. And then she pops and flows. Then they can relate to each other. Special like feelings come over him. Put him in a different world, relaxing him, like his mind goes someplace special. That pop juices her up, and the sex gets terrific wild after that. He likes whores, all right. Thinks of 'em as real people. Says they're regular women, once you know 'em."*

"Connected with a whore? Real women? Your friend is plum crazy. Anyway, you guys ain't changing my mind. We're here to kill elk. And I ain't having no whore in my elk camp, and that's that." Jake's final pronouncement was interrupted by a monstrous bellowing howl. It came from an animal with a deeper roar and a more voluminous chest than the yipping coyotes that were sounding earlier.

"Listen to that fella. He's a bigun. He howls deep and mournful. Didn't hear 'im last night," said Big Jim, the first hunter. He laid his cards down and looked at the other three hands through the dim cloud of their cigars' smoke. *"I heered he's the same one, really huge, big fella, comes ever night when dere's a full moon. He yelps up on da ridge top. Rancher Birch says he's seen da animal early in da mornin up dere sometimes. Birch says it's a huge Lobo. He's staying up on the ridge, feeding on something. He's half wolf and half coyote. He wasn't around these parts before dey found those bones up there."*

"What's a Lobo," asked John, the second hunter.

"He's part wolf; but much bigger than a wolf. And he's part coyote; but much smarter than a coyote," said Jim.

"Well then, which is he? Wolf or coyote?" asked John.

"He ain't neither," said Jack, the third hunter.

"Then, if he ain't neither, what is he?" asked John, again.

"He's hatred," said Jack. *"He's meanness. He's all the evil around you for a hundred miles, all packaged up into a canine animal that's bigger than an English Mastiff; maybe almost twice as big as one of those. He weighs a good two hundred fifty pounds. His bite force is*

twice as strong as a wolf's. He can bite through a buffalo's leg like it's a toothpick.

"And, the special thing about Lobos is they are angry. Always angry. And it's an anger that carries hate inside it. Not ordinarily angry like a dog gets when it snarls at you. No, not like that kind of angry. A Lobo's anger is different. It's an anger that wants to tear your body apart and rip your guts out of you and snap all your bones in half, because it wants to make sure, you'll never walk again, even after it has killed you. It's a demon's anger, packed up tightly inside a canine body. It hates what it is and it hates every living thing that it isn't even more that it hates itself.

"And it's a demon so God-awful fierce that it can't help itself for being so hateful mean. And it's got canine teeth that are like needle pointed daggers; only much longer than a dagger and much sharper than any needle. Those teeth are twice as long as a Timberwolf's canines. Those teeth are for biting into you and ripping chunks of your flesh out of you. It's got paws with claws that are longer and sharper than a cougar's claws, for ripping and shredding your guts out. And it loves shredding your flesh while it eats on your body because it knows that shredding you like it does, causes you the most pain. It loves to cause pain. So, you asked me what a Lobo is. I tell you. A Lobo is living horrible pain. He's God-awful, horrible, never ending miserable pain. It's all the pain that comes from hell for you. And the Devil himself packaged all that vicious, unforgiving pain into one hateful animal. And it's got those yellow green Satan eyes that glow in the faintest light. It sees better than a lynx in the dark. It hears better than an owl. And it likes to kill because killing is what it lives for. Killing gives it pleasure."

"Jesus Christ, God help us," said John.

"A ranger saw it too, said it was a monster Lobo from up Wyoming way; a killer, come down from Canada or Yellowstone through the Wind River Basin an' down here to Colrada. Ranger said the

Lobo must have smelled da poor devil's body all the way from Wyo and come here to feed on it. Sometimes dey's three or four of dem coyotes in dat same spot wid da Lobo. They run 'round in circles and yelps like dey's insane, and their eyes flashes red and green and yella in da moonlight, like they got devil's inside 'em. Birch says dey do dat 'til mornin' twilight gits bright. Dey runs in circles round in dat aspen grove up on top, dat spot where they found da bones of dat poor bastard dat got killt up dere," said Big Jim.

"You don't say. I never heard this. What poor bastard guy?" asked John as he popped open another can of beer.

"Well, da rangers found bones scattered all ober da place. The man'd been dead a while. Lobo cracked da bones, ate out 'is marrow. Bones was chewed by da rodents, not much left of 'im. Dey was stakes in da ground, some leather straps an' ropes. He was tied down to die, looks like. From da teeth they found, they figgered it was some big investment guy," said Jim.

"Oh yeah, I think I read sompin bout that in the paper once't," John said. *"It said he left some money to some homosexual foundation or sompin. He was one of them gay guys."*

"Somebody musta had it in for dis one, but they ain't never found out who done it. He was into all kinds of bad shit; had enmies. My theory is dat big Lobo was into eatin' off 'im and he comes back 'ere and howls to da coyote gods to send 'im another helpin. Rancher Birch says he's seen them coyotes up dere in the mornin' pissin' all over da place; pissin' on the ground where dat poor bastard was staked down and pissin' on da trees all bout dat place," said John.

"Well, sometimes the animals knows what's what. They knows; I tells ya, When coyotes piss like that, that's their way of prayin to their devil gods for another helpin of the same." said the fourth hand, Jake, as he took a swig of whiskey from the open bottle on the table.

"Whatcha mean?" asked Jack.

"I mean they knows, damn it. I means what I says, that's all. They's smart. Maybe those coyotes knows that this big shot was some no-good son of a bitch and he got what was coming to 'im; so, they ate on 'im while he was still alive, chewed off his ass, chewed off his legs and arms and face. And now they go back during full moons to celebrate what they done to 'im, and they celebrate by howling and pissing all over the place, pissing on his remains, pissing on where he died."

"Ya think so, Jake?" asked Jim.

"Damn right I think so." The other hunters stared at Jake, amazed by his wisdom. *"Dem coyotes are smart as hell. They's smarter'n we is. I always avoid 'em; never fuck with 'em. No sir. I never even shoot at 'em. No sir. I jest avoid them sons-a-bitches. You don't want to go fucking with no coyotes, 'specially when a Lobo's around. Noooo sir. No way! They will get the best of you; take a good bite outta you, when you least expect it; 'specially a Lobo. They's got those watchin', cunnin' yeller eyes. They's always measuring; figgerin' when you's weak. I saw this guy, once't. He was a poor homeless bastard; and he slept out on his bedroll. One night a coyote got 'im while he slept, bit a cheek right off dis poor bastard's face. A lone coyote did it. Blood everywhere; screamin' crazy like a mad man, he was. Poor son-a-bitch he was. Coyotes kill; I tell ya. Dey kills anythin'."*

"Sometimes," said Jake, *"I got to thinking, which ain't too often. But one day I had this thinking spell about coyotes. I thinked they was God's voice for all the animals of the world; that their yips, and howls are for all the sufferings of all the animals of the world and for all the bad shit people do to all the other animals. They got hearts, them coyotes. And they's there waitin' to get even with us humans for all the animals we hurt. They's killers! John's right, I tell ya. They's out there now; watchin' us; measurin' us.*

"Specially that big Lobo. He's watchin' us, all right, with dem big red and yellow eyes. He's lollin' his tongue and flickin' his

tongue over those huge canine teeth. He's droolin' and tastin' the air for us. Don't go out the cabin alone with the big Lobo out there. No sir. Once he's et human flesh, he's got a taste for us. Ranger says he's gonna want more."

"Jesus H. Christ," yelled big Jim. *"I don't want to hear no god- damn more shit 'bout no fucking goddamn coyotes or no goddamned Lobo, or I ain't gonna be able to sleep! I'm gittin' shivers up my back- side an' chills all over. All you, jest shat ap! It's my turn. Over to you, Jack. I'm raising you three bucks. Pass me the whiskey."*

CHAPTER SIXTEEN

The wisdom of our ancestors (Edmund Burke: Thoughts on the Cause of our Present Discontents)

SPIRIT VISIT

Hud was camped near the base of two glaciers in northwest British Columbia. He and his exploration crew had been taking stream sediment samples, chipping rocks, and searching for gold for the past four months. Fall was in the air. Geese were flying south; leaves were falling; bears were fattening themselves for winter. Before the snows came, Hud would break camp in another week and go to the lower forty-eight. He slept alone in the giant wall tent that held his boxes of chip and sediment samples. The rest of the crew had a tent nearby. It was nearly three in the morning. He'd worked hard the day before. He was in a deep restful sleep. Then, they came.

A pair of huge hands took hold of his shoulders. They gently shook him until he awoke. He propped himself up on an elbow and rubbed sleepers from his eyes. When his vision cleared, he sat bolt upright. His grandfather, Big Chief Eagle Feather stood imposingly before him. Chief wore his majestic ceremonial finery; a white buckskin fringed coat and riding chaps. His head was adorned with his signature headdress of eagle feathers, which trailed down his back. Standing next to Chief was Hud's mother, Little Sparrow, and his father, Big Horse. All three spirits appeared to be in their early thirties. Standing next to Chief was an intense, wiry, man with bony hands and thick black hair. The man wore wire-rimmed glasses. Hud had never seen him before.

"Hud, my grandson," spoke Chief, *"we spirits were sent by the Great Spirit of All Living Things to come and visit with you. I bring with me your father, Big Horse, and your mother, Little Sparrow. I also bring the spirit of Mr. Nicola Tesla, a man whom I met in the realm of spirits. He and I have had many talks and we are good friends now. I wanted you to meet him."*

The spirit of Nicola Tesla stepped forward and shook Hud's hand. Hud felt a sudden warmth flowing throughout his entire body. He felt a slight burning on his right arm. He looked down at the source of the burning sensation. There were three brown dots the size of paper punch holes arranged in a triangle slightly above his elbow. The spirits of Big Horse and Little Sparrow moved nearer to Hud. They hugged him closely. Then the spirits stood back. Chief stood alone before him.

"Hud, we have been sent to guide you in a new direction. The Great Spirit of All Living Things is unhappy with the path you are on. You have a gift of intelligence; but you spend all your waking hours in your quest for gold. You work hard but you live like an animal for months at a time. Every two or three weeks you go to the town of Stewart. You drink alcohol; clean yourself up; then you bed down with whores, before you return to camp. There is a better path for you, Hud.

"You have a claim group further to the north with some unusual rocks on them. The rocks have properties that open the universe and allow mankind to travel into and out of life among the spirits. Mr. Tesla's spirit can tell you more about their properties."

The spirit of Tesla stepped forward: *"The rocks on your claim group were placed there by universal electrical energy transition mechanisms,"* Tesla's spirit spoke. *"In my papers, I explained the* methods whereby large quantities of energy can be transmitted wirelessly. This mechanism is universal. The rocks on your claim group can take the normal eight hertz resonance of the Earth and focus Earth's energy into an amplified magnetic force field. The sun resonates at four hundred-forty hertz.

"That force field can be amplified as well. The amplified Earth's field lies within an electrical plasma field. Its electromagnetic force can flow within the Sun's amplified electrical field and those fields can be directed to other stars and galaxies and universes as amplified fields folded into ever stronger and stronger fields. Selected pairs of living persons can use these fields to move freely among the galaxies and universes. They can visit all the planets in the universes as if they were swimming from one spot in a swimming pool to another. The rocks enable you to be in endless universes in endless galaxies with endless swimming pools of stars and planets. Each drop of water is a planet that you can enter and live on; and you can assume a human form if you choose. The rocks hold the key to end all wars, strife, hunger, and unhappiness. Every human person pair can own millions of planets to do with as they choose. There are endless habitable planets available for endless human pairs. There is no need for friction among the peoples of Earth."

Hud was dumbfounded by what he heard. He looked at Chief, who moved closer to him and spoke again. "Hud, I bring you this message from the Great Spirit of All Living Things. You are to leave this place and go to Plaintown. You are to study the Tesla papers and the principals Mr. Tesla explained in them, and you are to give up whoring and marry a good woman and have children. You are the uncle of Sparrow's grandchild, Little Deer, and you must set a good example for her. The Spirit demands it for he has great plans for her. You will take Deborah, Rick, Little Deer, and your woman with you and go on a journey. The Spirit commands that you live a righteous life, Hud. It is necessary to prepare you for your journey."

"But how will I find the Tesla papers? And where will I find a good woman?" Hud was in a quandary. The Spirit wanted him to change his whole life.

"You will begin your search for knowledge of energy fields in Plaintown. There is a bookstore called The Ragged Cover. In the basement of the bookstore, there is a science section where you will find books about Mr. Tesla's papers. Get the books, read them, and understand them. You must follow wherever they lead you. They will take you on a journey where you will travel freely in the company of your woman, your sister and her husband and children; and the spirits of your mother, and your father. Your life and the life of your partner will never die."

"And how will I find a good woman to marry, Big Chief? The only women I know are whores."

"You are not to concern yourself with that. We have met the spirit of your future woman. The Great Spirit of All Living Things brought all of us together for a meeting. The Spirit is in her now. Her spirit is that of a very fine and good woman. Make yourself ready for her. When you are ready, she will know. You need not search for her. She will find you. That is the way with women. Now waste no time. Go to the bookstore as the Spirit commands you, get the Tesla papers; read and understand them."

With that last message, the spirits disappeared. Hud went to the entrance flap of his tent, searching all around and up into the sky. There was no sign of his visitors, and they left no footprints. The first rays of morning twilight pierced the black night as a meteor streaked away over the horizon. A shiver shot through his body and the hair on the back of his head bristled as if rubbed by an electrostatic charge. It was the start of a new day.

More to come.

PREVIEWS FROM CRIMSON MARIPOSA

"Very good Sheila; then I'll confirm. Meanwhile, take this. It's from the special project group you'll be working with, Department of Defense Special Operations. It's a sealed package for you about security matters. You have to answer their questions and be interviewed by some FBI types before you're official. You need to take care of all this before you leave Boston. And, there's one other thing, Sheila."

"Yes?" Sheila's voice revealed apprehension.

"You must leave your personal life behind . . . . . . Chapter One.

I understand something much more important than my theorems now. It's not found in books or classrooms. My inner voice is telling me, it's about life:

"The most important thing in life is getting love right."

'Yes, I can see that now. I don't have love right. I'm miserable inside. I'm flunking life.' . . . . Chapter Two.

'What man thinks there's some woman out there without emotional baggage . . . . Chapter Three.

Walter's extension rang. He picked it up without saying a word. The voice on the other end was low and raspy. "They're going up now," it said. Then the voice hung up. . . . . Chapter Four.

"Wait a minute!" Walter broke his own passive response protocol. He sounded frantic. *"Who ever said we went to plan B?"*

"I called and told you we needed to go to plan B three days ago when plan A didn't call in."

"I never got that call," declared an anxiety-stricken Walter.

"Well, somebody did," said the raspy voice Chapter Five.

"I never took their fondling and pinching personally while I worked with the stock traders. That's how they treat every woman who goes in there.. Chapter Six.

The irony was that Gibby didn't realize his map had any value at all. It was just a perplexing oddity he'd acquired. He traded a Tillamook squaw for it when she showed it to him. She told Gibby she got it in Alaska from a Tlingit woman. And she got it from the squaw of a dead prospector . . . . Chapter Seven.

"What do ya know about this guy?" asked the driver. The driver's voice betrayed a trace of trepidation. He was second thinking the deal he'd made with his passenger.

"Don't care to talk about him." said the rider with the rifle

Chapter Eight.

Their God took for his consort a winsome Aztec woman. The new God ran her husband through with a lance. The people watched this and accepted the murder because it obviously pleased their new God. And they accepted his taking of the murdered man's woman and sharing her sexual favors with his God-like friends, because watching her fornicate with his friends seemed to please their new god. . . . . Chapter Nine.

"Look you two assholes, you're the ones who borrowed the money and the bank wants its money back! I don't want to discuss this fucking mess of a loan any further. Our terms are final. Now I need to end this wretched conversation to make another call. And don't

you cry. Grow up, both of you! The next time you hear from me I'm going to be taking your scalps. Sensitivity training was never my hot button. Got it, assholes? Okay! Thanks for the nice language, then FUCK OFF to you, too!" Click. Linda slammed down her phone. *'So much for those bull shit friendly banker commercials,'* she thought………..Chapter Ten.

As the elevator car began to ascend Sheila asked, *"Who goes to the fortieth floor?"*

"I don't know. It's super doper, double top secret; need to know only. I don't believe any of us knows," relied CC, matter of factly.

"Oh," Sheila responded, a touch disappointed. She liked knowing things, even extraneous things. The two women were silent as the car whooshed speedily upward, finally slowed, and stopped at floor thirty-nine. . . . .…Chapter Eleven.

'Take your time with her. Always be a gentleman. Savor her. Savor and enjoy every second of her intimacy. Help her know that you will be her greatest love; her only true and lasting love. Remove her inhibitions slowly and naturally. Release them tenderly, one at a time. And, love her, Carlos. Always love her. And above all else, fall in love with her . . . . Chapter Twelve

"What the hell is so special about him Jo? He's always abused you one way or another. He threw you out. He told you he never wanted to see you again. What more do you need to know, Jo? Gibby is a nasty asshole, no good son-of-a-bitch. He's always been an asshole and he'll always be an asshole. For the life of me, I can't understand what you see in him?" Sam reached over the bar and put a big right hand on her shoulder, as if that might snap her out of her funk.

"Don't do that Sam," she shrugged off his hand, *"I just need time to figure this out,"* she pleaded . . . . Chapter Thirteen.

'*What I've always wanted in a man is sitting right here in front of me! I'm standing right across the room from him. He's perfect. He's just like Daddy!*' . . . . .Chapter Fourteen.

"*What does that mean?*"
"*Well, for a rocket aloft it means the mid-course corrections come every seventeen microseconds instead of every hundred microseconds.*". . . . . Chapter Fifteen.

"*The time for words is quickly passing, sweet Linda. This is the time for making love.*" Carlos stopped talking. He put a finger over Linda's lips to silence her questioning. Then he began to kiss her. And he kissed her everywhere . . . . Chapter Sixteen.

"*Walter, the one thing I hate in my line of work is a fuck up.*" Now the General's voice boomed into Walter's ear. Walter hated hearing the General when he got angry. He sounded like a snarling Doberman, chewing on a bone. Today, his bone was Walter. "*You're a God damned fuck up, Walter. I lost a good man killed on that mountain. I also sent a chopper with five marines up there to look for some God damn fucking map that you say you THINK holds the key to control of our entire government. They were my best men, Walter. They found nothing, Water, N_ O_ T_ H_ I_ N_G!*" The General first spelled out the word and then he screamed: "*NOTHING!*". . . Chapter Seventeen.

The harder everyone tried, the louder the child wailed: "*I want my Mommy! I want to go home! Please Daddy, take me home to Mommy! I don't want to be here! I miss my Mommy!*" Plainly, little Margaret was distraught. She clung to her blanket and her teddy bear, while crying herself hoarse. . . . . .Chapter Eighteen.

But his efforts to push Jo out of his mind weren't working. They were failing terribly. He thought of the many times he held her naked body tightly to his own and all the ways they made love. He remembered every minute detail about her; her smile; how she licked her lips; the way she brushed her hair from her face with her hand; and how she blinked her eyes with her disarming soft blink. He couldn't resist her when she blinked that way

Chapter Nineteen.

All around her lightning cracked like deafening rifle shots. The thunder booms reverberated through her body. They terrified her. "Please God, let this end," she cried out to the heavens. *"Make it go way. I promise to be a good girl. I'll never whore again if you'll just make this storm go way. Please."* . . . . Chapter Twenty.

"No, silly, these were tough men. They were all career criminals. They were, in many cases, murderers themselves. David used an ingenious plan to lure each of them to his farm. He relied on the old Aesop fable. You know the one. It's where the fox looks up to the tree branch and tells the crow how beautiful it is. The crow is holding a piece of meat in its beak. But it can't resist crowing its approval of the fox's praises. It caws; thus, dropping its guard and its meat. The fox gets the meal that the crow loses. It's a technique that David perfected." . . . . Chapter Twenty-one.

She tried to analogize her problem; but the best she could do was to visualize a man with a sledgehammer. That would be the defense department trying to use it to smash a million mosquitoes. The mosquitoes would be the terrorists, flying freely inside a vast indoor convention hall. Sure, the sledgehammer wielder could kill some of them, maybe with a tremendous amount of effort he could even kill most of them; but he could not kill all of them before one of them drew blood from someone in the convention hall. And, the mosquitoes were reproducing themselves!

Chapter Twenty-two.

A message from author Rosemary:

When we continue our journey, we will meet a very special woman and travel with her as she searches for her new life. Will Mr. Tesla's spirit reveal things he didn't tell us while he lived among us?

Am I the only one that wonders: Did the God of Moses screw up? Did She forget a commandment? Wouldn't the Spirit have given Moses eleven instead of ten, another one that says "Parents, love your children with all your hearts, for they need that love to grow and become a glory unto me." And Lord, since we mortals now have birth control and perfectly safe clinical abortion procedures, do we still need that pesky commandment about not committing adultery? Really? I'm just wondering, God, since I was taught to ask questions.

As we flutter on through life, have faith dear readers: A butterfly will NEVER lie to you. A butterfly will ALWAYS love you. When you open your heart to a butterfly, your spirit will be free. And WHEN YOU LOVE A BUTTERFLY, YOU WILL BE BEAUTIFUL.

BUTTERFLY LOVE concludes our fourteenth book in THE SECRET AND THE BUTTERFLY series. In our next adventuresome tale, we'll discover romantic love's reincarnation. Connie, Linda, Pattie, Sandra, JoAnne, Sheila, Cecilia, Hud and Gibby are all searching for love. Sheila, our heroin, blessed with genius and cursed with an indescribable lust that was carried into her body from the spirit of Marty, must thwart the dastardly murder scheme of evil conspirators. As challenging as that task is, Sheila has an even greater personal challenge. She's in her mid-twenties, a well-known, accomplished, brilliant and beautiful mathematician; but she has never discovered love!

That's right. A boy intentionally misled her. Because of his lie, she's still a virgin! This complicates and confuses things for her. Not just any man will do for her first time in this tale of neurotic intimacy, discovery, adventure, and erotic love. I'm Minna Morinette, your narrator. Our next story, CRIMSON MARIPOSA, (Spanish for butterfly), and the fifteenth book in THE SECRET BUTTERFLY SERIES™ is a wildly erotic, romantic, edge of your seat thriller. And it's also the first book in the SERIES' REINCARNATION VOLUME. The morals expressed in the PASSION VOLUME return in modern day adventure settings. Lesbian relationships, office intrigue, power dynamics, limbic lusts, marital romance, and rediscovered long lost will make you flutter! Are you ready for much, much more? Then, come along with me, Minna Morinette! Let's flutter on!